# B-BOY BLUES

# B-BOY BLUES

a seriously sexy, fiercely funny,
Black-on-Black love story
by
## JAMES EARL HARDY

Boston ♦ Alyson Publications, Inc.

Typeset and printed in the United States of America.

This is a trade paperback original from Alyson Publications, Inc.,
40 Plympton Street, Boston, Massachusetts 02118.

First edition: November 1994

5   4

ISBN 1-55583-268-7


**Library of Congress Cataloging-in-Publication data**
Hardy, James Earl.
    B-boy blues : a seriously sexy, fiercely funny, Black-on-Black
love story / by James Earl Hardy.
        p.    cm.
    ISBN 1-55583-268-7 : $10.95
    1. Afro-American gays—New York (N.Y.)—Fiction.   2. Afro-American
men—New York (N.Y.)—Fiction.   3. Gay men—New York (N.Y.)—Fiction.
I. Title.
PS3558.A62375B15   1994
813′.54—dc20                                                94-29727
                                                              CIP

To My Brothers, Here and Abroad:
*This One's 4 Us.*

⊕

# ACKNOWLEDGMENTS

First, I give God the Glory. It is He who has given me the Gift of Life and the Gift of the Written Word. I will continue 2 let Him use me 2 tell those stories that need 2 be told.

To Renie: My #1 Cousin, My Sister, My Friend. Thanks 4 being there. I love you.

To Sheba: My school chum and lifetime confidant. Stay wild and crazy. Thanks 4 the years and the tears. Love you lots.

To Cassandra: My gossip girlfriend. So, like, when's our next date 2 dish the dirt?

To KMJ: The big brother I never had and the best friend I always wanted. It is *your world* – thanks 4 letting me be a part of it.

To *The Golden Guys*: Gordon, Steven, and Bernard. Thanks 4 the times of my life. Friends 4-Ever.

To fabian: Your energy, your spirit, your lust 4 life are all contagious. Keep infecting us, dahling!

To Matthew: Did you ever know that you're my (no, *not* hero) "first love"? Well, you do now. In the immortal words of Whitney Houston (or is it Dolly Parton?), "I Will Always Love You."

To ARJ: Thanks 4 burning the midnight oil with me. Who says long-distance relationships can't work? I luv ya, Yogi!

To Alvin, one BBM (Beautiful Black Man): Thanks 4 the phat photos. Stay sexy, strong, and sweet.

To Wesley Snipes: I'll never 4-get our meeting in January '91. Thanks 4 the encouragement and spiritual upliftment. I *told* you you'd be a BIG star. U-R-THE-MAN, so go, boy!

To Keith Hefner: You've been more than a mentor. Thanks 4 the eye, the ear, and the heart.

To Andrea Estepa: 4 being a good friend and laugh partner.

To New Youth Connections (NYC): The place where I discovered how powerful the pen is. Keep on inspiring.

To Denise Stinson, my agent: Thanks 4 the advice and guidance.

And, 2 Ashford & Simpson, Patti Austin, Regina Belle, Tracy Chapman, the Emotions, the Eurhythmics and Annie Lennox, Miki Howard, Phyllis Hyman, the Isley Brothers, Miles Jaye, Cheryl Lynn, Me'shell NdegeOcello, Nu Colours, Mica Paris, Bonnie Raitt, Dianne Reeves, Rufus & Chaka, Brenda Russell, Dionne Warwick, Cassandra Wilson, Nancy Wilson, and, of course, Aretha, 4 keeping me company as I tip-tap-typed away.

"What's Love Got to Do with It?"

Tina ain't the only one who feels that way.

She has a "soul sister" in my very best friend, Eugene "Gene" Roberts. A native Virginian who bears more than an uncanny resemblance to Arsenio Hall, Gene is what you call a certified cynic – he is skeptical of everything and everyone. He does not believe in anything that he cannot see with his eyes, touch with his hands, smell with his nose, taste with his mouth, or hear with his ears.

Which, of course, rules out God in all three of His manifestations.

This also 86's love – even though he did believe in this once.

Because he has been burnt very badly in the past, he has given up on it. I guess I really can't blame him for feeling the way he does. I would be more than bitter if I had spent four years of my life working days as a bank teller and nights as a waiter to help put my lover through medical school, and he up and leaves me for another man the day after he graduates. Now, if our relationships were recognized by the law, Gene could have sued his ass for all the time and money (not to mention the love, sweat, and tears) he spent on him. But that bastard made off like a bandit – free rent, three meals a day, and a warm bed to sleep in at night. Unfortunately, the doctor was playing doctor in that bed with another while Gene was taking orders for cheeseburger deluxes and strawberry malts.

So, after he stopped being angry, stopped being upset, and stopped being *homo*cidal, Gene started getting even. He never wants to be hurt again and has gone to some very drastic lengths to see that it won't happen. I know better than to even say the word *love* around him – his eyes will retreat to the back of his head and he'll start palpitating. But he especially doesn't like to hear it from any man he dates. He sees them only as his playthings. When he hooks up with a man, it is to do one thing: "Get with it, hit it, and quit it." He will not let love cloud the picture. When he thinks that things are getting a little too serious, he'll end it (four weeks being the cutoff point). More than anything, he wants to be the dumper and not the dumpee. For him, "Lust Is a Many Splendored Thing," there is only "Lust at First Sight," and, when all else fails, "Lust Conquers All."

I've told him that it is unfair to hold what happened to him against every man he meets. Not only is he setting up these unsuspecting souls for inevitable heartbreak, he is depriving himself of something we all need. As they say, it is better to have loved and lost than to not have loved at all − even if that love hurt like a motha-fucka.

But Gene doesn't see it that way. He is convinced that love is for simpleminded, sentimental saps.

Well, call me Mr. Sap.

I love love. It is the most basic human emotion yet the most complex. Any "feeling" you can think of can be linked to it − good, bad, or indifferent. People will fight for it, sell their souls, their lives to keep it. Nations go to war over it (I know, I know, but I'm going for a moment here, OK?). The world thrives − and multiplies − on it (don't ya just love that one?). One can easily argue that without love and the many forms it can take, none of us would be here.

And can folks sing about it, or what?

It just baffles me that there are so many songs about love, but then again it shouldn't. Folks have been trying to figure it out for centuries; it is such a mystery. And you can find that doubt, that uncertainty, that confusion, that despair, that anguish, that pain, that hurt in so many lyrics. But you can also find joy, inspiration, and salvation, too. In fact, songwriters and singers are the best psychiatrists when it comes to love. No others can drop the five and dime better on why something that is supposed to feel so good can hurt so bad. Why waste $150 an hour on a shrink when you can be counseled for the mere price of a $15 compact disc? I've celebrated lustful yearnings, love found, and got through some very tough love-on-the-rocks times thanks to Luther Vandross, Anita Baker, Teena Marie, Roberta Flack, Gladys Knight and the Pips, Niecy Williams, Atlantic Starr, and the late, great Minnie Riperton. Even Sade and Lionel Richie, considered by some to be two of the corniest songwriters and most flaccid singers on earth, supplied me with comfort and confidence when it seemed like the hurt was just too much to bear. I'd fall asleep smilin', laughin', broodin', or cryin' as the music filled my mind, helping my imagination run away with me.

I don't know whether this love for love songs ignited my passion for love itself, but it sure did shape the way I see it. And, needless to say, it is a romanticized view. Sure, there are ups and downs, trials and troubles, but a dance is supposed to turn into a romance; friends can be lovers; you can have an endless love; and, contrary to what Gene says, *love* conquers all. The world will always welcome lovers ... as time goes by. Right?

Wrong. And I've had to learn this lesson the hard way...

Love has a mind of its own, and it don't give two flyin' fucks about Mitchell Crawford (that's me) or anybody else. Yup, in the immortal words of the Spinners, "Love Don't Love Nobody." It is not something that you can make happen; you might wish for it, hope for it, pray for it, but all that wishin' and hopin' and prayin' (and, yes, plannin' and schemin') ain't gonna make it happen.

And you have to be mindful that, if and when it does happen, it does so on a two-way street.

There is probably no feeling worse than being head-over-heels for someone who doesn't feel the same way about you, and this seems to always happen to me. The school crushes, the love affair with my high school coach, the half dozen boyfriends I've had in my first eight years as an "admitted homosexual" – all of these men said they were "in love" with me, that they "loved" me, but their actions (or inactions) told a different story. Imagine being told that what you mistakenly thought was love was only infatuation, only an affair, only an illusion in your own mind, just "one of those things." I've heard it all. They start off with one of the following lines:

*"I said I love you because..."*

or,

*"I said I was in love with you because..."*

and end it with...

*"It seemed like the right thing to say at the time,"*

or,

*"You made me cum like no one ever did,"*

or,

*"You said it first, and I didn't want you to think I didn't feel the same way – even though I didn't,"*

or, my favorite,

*"I thought I felt that way but I don't ... I'm sorry..."*

... as if "sorry" is gonna somehow make it all right and make me feel better.

I know that I did love all those men, but in different ways and to different degrees. In fact, I still "love" a couple of them, but not in *that* way. But the fact that most didn't, couldn't, or wouldn't love me or be in love with me the way they said they did (or maybe I knew they didn't but wanted them to anyway?) made me feel as if the love I did have wasn't enough. I would beat myself up trying to figure out what was wrong with me. How is it that none of these men could appreciate me or the love I wanted to give? While they all could obviously see it, they chose to take advantage of it and me.

I am willing, though, to admit that, in some cases, I gave them a license to use me the way they did. Whoever said that love is blind and that it makes you do stupid things must've known that I was gonna come along one day. I put up with a lot of shit, letting them get over on things they should've been called on — all in the name of love. But does having a trusting, open heart mean that you ask to be stepped on?

After so many emotionally draining, stress-inducing, heartbreaking experiences, you'd think I'd be a gold-card member of Gene's "I'll Never Fall in Love Again" fan club. But I refuse to give up on it.

But, after being burned myself so many times, I did make myself a promise regarding any other man I became involved with: No matter how much I feel I like him, no matter how much I feel I love him, no matter how much I feel I am in love with him, and no matter how much I feel I want to tell him about how and what I feel, I won't let my feelings be known. I will not be the first to say, "I'm in love with you," or, "I love you." These feelings have gotten me into too much trouble before, leaving me feeling like a fool. Everybody does play the fool sometimes, but it seems that I play it more often than I should. And so, if love happens, I told myself, I'm not going to be the one to point it out — even if it's staring me right in the face.

When I put my mind to something I do it, and this pledge was no exception. And, because I stopped wishing so hard for it, hoping so hard for it, praying so hard for it, and planning and scheming so hard for it, it happened — and I didn't even know it.

Yes, I am a witness: the best love happens *when* you least expect it, *where* you least expect it, and with *whom* you least expect it to happen.

And, for me, that "when" was the summer and fall of 1993, that "where" was New York City, and that "whom" was Raheim Rivers.

This is our story.

 It all started on an ordinary Saturday night.

After eating dinner at Gene's co-op in Chelsea, we started our midnight manhunt at Harry's, one of the only bars in "the Vill" (that's Greenwich Village) that the brothers can call their own. And it figures that it would be located at the boondocks end of Christopher Street, where one can find the Pier, the West Side Highway, and the Hudson River. Because it is so far from mass transit, and "walking the runway" (as some folks refer to the Christopher strip) no longer tickles Gene's fancy, we catch a cab. But it is obvious that Gene really likes to pull up in a cab because it makes him look grand. Me? I could care less, as long as he pays for this indulgence.

It was two weeks before summer officially arrived, but Mother Nature didn't care. Temperatures were already in the low eighties with the humidity up. That night it was seventy degrees and the air was thick and hot. And the kids were *feeling* it: there were at least a dozen men standing outside the bar, most of them in tank tops, t's, and shorts, all too happy to show off the bodies they had been working on all winter. Gene surprisingly didn't know any of these fellas, but he did trade some very suggestive looks with one: a tall, slim, cocoa-skinned gent with a head shaped like a pear, a short 'fro, and big pointy ears. A pair of gold horn-rimmed glasses sat on his nose, and he was wearing a cranberry pin-striped suit. Now, *he* was dressed to impress.

The child talking to him, though, was not. He was trying to look cool and comfortable in a pair of black Spandex. You could certainly pinch more than an inch on him, particularly the blubber that was spilling over his waist. Gene, never missing an opportunity to be vicious, saw and sized up this target.

"See that cow over there?" he whispered out of the corner of his mouth. "Looks like we've had one too many Happy Meals."

"You're a mess," I said, trying not to appear so obvious laughing at the guy.

"Puh-leeze, doesn't he know that just because they make those things in your size doesn't mean you should wear them?" he declared, opening the entrance door.

As we stepped in, all eyes fell on us. Anyone who walks in is, for those inside, new meat to greet and seek. Martha Wash's "Carry On" blared from the CD jukebox, which is sandwiched between a pinball machine and a pool table in the middle of the bar's right side. As we made our way to that spot, Gene shook hands, kissed, and hugged folks on the way. I walked behind him. I felt like his bodyguard: nudging him along as he acknowledged his fans, not allowing any one person to have too much time with him, while I nodded and forced a smile.

"What, not signing autographs tonight?" I asked as we reached our cruising corner.

"Very, very funny, Jeeves," he said, taking off his black spring jacket and placing it on top of the CD box. "Keep it up and you'll be on the unemployment line Monday." He clapped his hands. "So, who buys drinks tonight?"

He only asks that when it is his turn.

"You do," I answered.

He placed his hands on his hips and looked toward the ceiling. "Well, hold court while I'm gone. And if anyone should call, tell them I'll be back in a few."

As he glided through the crowd to get our drinks, I surveyed the room. There had to be at least sixty men up in the place in every size, shape, and shade of brown. It was still early, but the types were in the house in full effect: your hip-hop kiddies (they'd be right at home in a rap video); your buppies (Brooks Brothers brothers and the like); your butch boyz (most standing in a corner or off alone, acting as if they are the only "men" in the room); your self-crowned queens (primed, perched, and performing up a storm); your "daddies" and "grand-daddies" (older gentleman trying their best to fit in); your divas (talking loud and saying nothing); your "bum boyz" (hustlers, homeless strag-glers, and "porno stars" who cum cheap and easy); and guys like me who, because they don't fit into any category and choose not to wear a mask, are the odd men out.

And, there was the obligatory Caucasian lurking about, lying in wait for the first Negro to so much as *look* in his direction.

Everyone was dressed *down*. The perfume was overpowering; I'm quite sure that some took their baths in it. The chatter and laughter was high and low, with shouts and screams of "Work!" and "Get outa town!" bouncing from one end of the room to another as if it was all contagious. And, of course, there was some serious shade goin' 'round:

folks with their noses all the way up in the air, just knowing it's all about them, looking down on everyone else in the room but expecting these very same people to give them the attention and adoration they so desired and believed they deserved. "Oh yes, all you tired faggots, you all know that *I* am the one, it is all about *me,* so look at me, look at me, *look at me, dammit!"*

Yes, the scene was happenin'. It is always good to be in a room full of Black men when, during the week, you are the only one (or just one of a handful) at school or work. But it baffles me that folks would put on their best rags, beat their faces, and spray themselves from hair to toe to stand around in a smoke-filled, dimly lit, damp, and cramped hole like Harry's.

But I couldn't talk — *I* was one of them.

And why? The answer is simple: I as well as every other person up in the place had one thing on the mind — sex. Anyone, be they gay, straight, bi, or otherwise, who tells you that they go to a bar or club just to dance, just to have a drink, just to hang out with their friends, just to get out ... is lying. Sex is in the music, in the conversation, in the body language of the crowd. And, that night, I was ready to explode: I had been in dry dock for six months.

Harry's has a bountiful supply of men for the taking. But, as you wait for The One to walk through the door, you have to tolerate the Killaretha Chorus. There are too many "Queen of Song" wannabes in the house (Aretha is not just the Queen of Soul). But no matter the songstress playing on the CD box, rest assured that at least several of the kids will try to turn it out by doing runs, topping high notes, and hitting octaves.

But it's hard to cruise when you have church queens who think they can blow killin' your eardrums.

Which is why I was glad when, after Martha finished carrying on, the Marthettes next to me did also. And, as Sylvester's "You Make Me Feel (Mighty Real)" came on, and Gene returned with our drinks (as well as the news that Carl, the guy he scoped outside the bar, was asking about him), I was able to relax. But then I remembered these children can't play just one Sylvester song; they have to hear at least three in a row, all of them the elongated ten-minute versions. I mean, I love Sylvester, but even those things you love you have to take in doses or you'll overload (these words I would eat later on).

Yeah, just another night at Harry's, I said to myself, as I settled against the right side of the CD box, sipped my rum and Coke, and listened as Gene went on about Carl. The same old songs, the same old stories, the same old faces...

And then, *he* walked in.

There are fine men and then there are *fine* men, but this man was neither. That word couldn't even begin to describe him. He looked like he'd stepped out of a Cross Colours ad. A green cap was on his head. His nipples poked out of his long-sleeve blue-block green-striped shirt, which nicely draped his protruding chest. I couldn't see what color pants he had on, but he was at least six feet tall, maybe two hundred pounds, had pretty Hershey's Kiss chocolate-drop skin, and a big, bright smile.

He was *beautiful.*

As he made his way down the "Soul Train" line, greeting people on both sides, my voice got caught in my throat. I wanted to get Gene's attention, so I started yanking on his prized sky blue silk shirt.

"Damn, take it easy already!" he exclaimed, knocking my hand away. "What the hell..."

"That, that guy, over there ... do you know him?" I was trying not to point, letting my head do the directing.

Gene zeroed in on the object of our observation. "Oh, him."

"What do you mean, 'Oh, him'? Don't you think he's ovah?"

"Uh, yeah ... if you like that type."

I got really testy. "What do you mean, '*that* type'?"

"Will you chill out. Homeboy is a serious player. You can tell just by looking at him—"

"Well, I've got to know who he is ... uh, do you think you can find out for me?"

Gene laughed. "Uh-huh, Mr. I-Wanna-Know-Your-Name can't seem to find it out for himself. Can I find out ... can I find *out?* Are you forgetting who you're talking to here? I am the eyes, ears, nose, *and* throat of this place. There's almost nobody I don't know, and if I don't, you sure as hell can bet I know somebody who *does.* I'll have the vital statistics for you in less than a minute."

And, after squeezing my arm, he went toward the back of the bar and my eyes rested on *him* again. He was now six feet away, talking to someone I absolutely did not like. Thompson Williams is one of those guys who thinks he can get any man or woman he wants. Well, he usually does. So, since I refuse to go out with him, he sees me as a challenge. No matter how dirty a look I give him, no matter how much I ignore him, no matter how many times Gene and I break out into a chorus of En Vogue's "My Lovin' (You're Never Gonna Get It)," he continues to ask me out. He is, some might say, a major catch – imagine Denzel Washington, only lighter, taller, and thicker. And he's got most status – cash, cars, and a condo – thanks to his very lucrative career as

an entertainment lawyer. But he is just too stuck on himself. He knows
he is fine and he never lets you forget it. ("Doesn't this new haircut
make me look even more gorgeous?" "No one can wear these shoes
like I can!") He is the type of guy who probably screams his own name
out during sex. He hasn't seen me yet, but as soon as he does, I know
what he'll say in that Jamaican accent:

"Hi, Mitch, How are you, You're looking good tonight, So, when
are we going to get together, Come on, Give me a chance, You know
you want to, You'll say yes one day, I'll be waiting..."

I would be able to stand that nonsense right now, though, if he did
notice me, if for no other reason than to have him introduce me to *him*.

As I contemplated how I would get rid of Thompson while me and
*him* got to know each other, Gene returned with the all-important info
in record time: forty-nine seconds.

"Name? Raheim..."

*Raheim* ... how manly.

"Age? Twenty-one. Occupation? Homeboy..."

"Oh, please..."

"Well, you got eyes..."

"Oh yeah, I sure do..." I sighed, not letting *him* — oh, *Raheim* — out
of my sight.

Gene rolled his eyes. "Shoe size?"

"Uh, Gene?" I glared at him. Gene believes that shoe size is a "great
indicator." I couldn't believe he asked about it.

"Well, you wanted the résumé...," he argued.

"Yes, but I didn't ask for that!"

He batted his eyelashes. "So, you dun't wunt to know?"

I did. I nodded yes. We both cracked up.

"It's a thirteen — and we know what that means!"

I sucked on my straw. "Could be a big boy."

"Yeah ... and he is very, *very* single."

*"Very* single?"

"He is very poopular, if you haven't noticed," Gene said, joining me
as I gazed at Raheim. He was now three feet away, talking to two fellas
who were probably lovers: both were wearing the same gray-and-white
Nike nylon sweatsuit. I could now see that Raheim's eyes were light
brown, there was a gold hoop in his left ear, he sported a mustache and
"nasty goatee" (a thin line of hair connected the middle of his lower lip
to his chin, where a frazzled patch of hair also sat), and tucked in his
open, loosely laced tan construction boots were baggy khaki pants,
which he was wearing well.

Uh-huh, he had that sexy thang goin'-on.

"Gene, you of all people should talk...," I argued.

"My dahling, I may be poopular, but I'm sure I am for different reasons."

"Oh, he's going to walk by us," I said, ducking into the corner of the CD box.

"Boy, what *is* your problem? You're salivating over the man like he's the last one on earth, I get you the bio, and now you're gonna hide from him? You better make that move before somebody else does — like *him*."

I peeked over Gene's shoulder to see whom he was pointing at — and I cringed. Charlie Sutton, or Chuck the Slut, had his right arm on Raheim's left shoulder, his left hand squeezing his right biceps. Chuck will do it with almost anybody (Tom, Dick, or Harry), and, so I'm told, is one great fuck (I guess practice does make perfect). He has a beer belly, one too many pimples on his face, and a mouth full of tobacco-stained teeth. But he does have some of the roundest, thickest DSLs — that's dick-sucking lips — I've ever seen. And, according to legend, many men have been sucked by them. Many, *many* men. I don't know if Raheim was one of them, but he won't have to again if I have my way.

Of course, he has to know I'm alive, and, at the moment, my feet weren't moving anywhere in his direction.

"God, I can't, I just can't, Gene," I cried, still hiding. "Why would a guy like him want to be with me?"

"Well, you don't know: he may like them compact and cute like you. Anyway, it's not like you have anything else better to do. I am so tired of you falling up in here every weekend watching me work the boys." He grabbed his jacket from off the CD box. "I'll be waiting near the door. That way I can corner Carl and watch the festivities with a view. Good show."

And, with that, he smiled and walked away, leaving me standing there with my mouth open.

He was right about my being a wallflower. I've never been good at approaching people in a bar or club. And for that I know I have lucked out. There have been scores of fine guys who have cruised me over the years, but because I didn't make the first move we didn't connect. Of course, I've always reasoned that, if they were that interested in me, *they* would've made the first move. But Gene says that that is just an excuse I use to stand around, look cute, and get gushed over. And I admit that it certainly is a lot better being the hunted than the hunter. You don't have to worry about what signals to use to let a person know you're interested, when you should introduce yourself, or how to start and keep a conversation going. It is all so intimidating. I fear, like most, that I will be flat out rejected – and that everyone in the place will see it.

All of the guys I've been involved with came after me. But Gene argues that, if I stopped playing the coquette, my network of men would multiply. And the thought of letting a guy like Raheim slip by without even attempting to get him was getting to me – not to mention the fact that B.D. and Babyface, my other best friends, would be arriving any minute so we all could continue on to a party in the Bronx.

So, I told myself, it's now or never.

There were people standing in front of me, so I couldn't even see where Raheim was. But when these folks moved, I looked across to the bar and there he was: his right arm leaning against the wood-finish railing, a beer in his left hand, his head cocked slightly to the floor but his eyes looking up toward the back. It was a fierce pose – and it was turning me the fuck on.

He must have felt me staring, because he quickly turned his head and his eyes met mine.

I was *gagging*. But he was smiling.

I coughed up a laugh, our eyes still locked. He was still smiling. Those pearly whites were doing a job on me.

I finally managed to smile. And he winked.

I blushed and got so nervous that I turned a little to my left, leaning on the side of the CD box, so that I wouldn't have to make direct eye contact. I also did this so that he could get a good gander at my big bubble-butt, which is, according to all of the men I've been with, one of my greatest assets. I'm a small guy, a mere five feet, seven inches, and 135 pounds, but my "two giant melons" (as one admirer called them) have definitely made those who normally wouldn't look twice at a guy my size do just that.

Like Raheim. After I made the change in position and got the courage to look at him again, I found his eyes fixed on my behind. He rubbed his lips together, then licked them. When our eyes met again, he blushed. This was getting good!

I had newfound confidence. I gave him a serious come-hither glare. He laughed. I looked away not really knowing how to interpret what had just happened. Was he laughing because of me or at me?

When I turned back, he was gone. Guess that answered my question. In an instant I went from being elated to being embarrassed. This is just what I wanted to avoid.

And then came The Voice.

"Lookin' fuh me?"

It was bass boomin' and velvety smooth, its deep resonance making me shiver. I twisted my body around and came face-to-face with those dreamy, twinkling eyes and big, scrumptious lips. I was weak.

And so was the CD box. Sylvester finally said his last "mighty real" and on came SWV, Sisters With Voices. Gene hates them; he says they sound like the Chipmunks on crack. But I like them. And their song, "Weak," was certainly the right tune to be playing at that moment. My heart *was* beating triple-time and my knees were about to give out.

I sighed, leaned against the CD box, stirred my drink, and tried to relax.

"Hi," I said, shaking.

"Wha's up?" He rested his left arm and Budweiser on the CD box, getting so close that his lips were inches from my right cheek.

I wanted to say, "You — that's what's up," but smiled, "Nothing really," instead.

"Don' look that way ta me, cuz you wearin' them jeans," he grinned, his eyes going not over me but through me. I swear, I felt the heat of those laser beams as they penetrated my ass. He picked up and took a sip of his beer — and was still all in it. I sneaked a peek at his stance. His right foot was on the back of the pinball machine. His right hand was on his crotch.

Boy, was it getting hot in here...

I placed my left hand over my heart, which was still beating out of control. I felt rather bummy next to him in faded blue jeans, a generic tan blouse, and brown sandals. But if he said I was workin' these 501s, I had to believe him.

I giggled. "Uh, thanks. I don't have anything on you, though. That outfit is fly."

He checked himself out and smiled. That dimple in his left cheek was dangerous. "Thanks."

"You're welcome. What's your name?" Like I didn't know...

"Raheim."

Oh, I *loved* the way he said it. It just rolled off his tongue. I'd love to scream it out during sex. Hell, I'd bet *he'd* sound good screaming it out, too.

Mitch, get a*hold* of yourself...

I put my hand out. "My name is Mitchell."

He shook it and I almost lost it. His hand swallowed mine. His fingers were long and thick, yet smooth and tender. I bet he knows what to do with them...

"Your hand, it, it ... feels nice," I tripped. But he laughed, hearty and heavy. Guess I'm not doing that bad.

"So, Raheim" — oh, how I *loved* that name — "how old are you?" Like I didn't know *that* either...

He gulped down some beer. "Twenty-one. My bir'day was yestaday."

Yeah, right.

My eyebrows raised. "Oh really? Hmmmm..."

"Wha'?"

"Oh, well, not only can you be drafted and vote, but now you can officially drink — not that you haven't before."

He laughed again. "How old are you?"

"I'm twenty-seven."

"Yeah? You look *jood* fuh yo' age."

"Jood?"

"Yeah ... betta than good," he winked.

I blushed.

I then glared at him. "I look jood for my age? Well, just how is a 27-year-old supposed to look?"

"You know..."

I peered up at him. "No, I don't ... tell me."

He chuckled. "You know, you ... you jus' look my age."

I placed my right hand to my mouth. "I see ... well, you look jood for *any* age."

He laughed, *again*. I was on a roll.

I stretched to see the hoop in his left ear. "Uh, how long have you had your ear pierced?"

"Oh..." He brought his head down closer. "I got 'em done on my bir'day three years ago..."

"Three years and a day," I corrected him, playing with his lobe, which was so soft. We both smiled. Lord, those teeth were like sugar cubes.

I reached for his right lobe. Even his ears were cute and delicate. "Do you ever wear both at once?"

"Sometimes. I hafta be feelin' it."

Hmph, *I'd* love to be feelin' it...

"I've always thought about doing it, but I don't think I'd look right," I admitted.

"I ain't think I would..."

"So, you do know that you look, uh, *jood* with it?"

The blush on his face was priceless.

Mitch, you're really working him...

I was about to ask what cologne he was wearing — it was unlike any I had ever smelled before and it was turning me the fuck on — when

Lalah Hathaway's "Smile" came on the CD box. He started moving to its mellow groove.

"You like Lalah?" I asked.

"Yeah. This song is dope."

I then did something I never do in public – I sang. The only place I really sing is the church, and I haven't done that in years. I might sing around Gene and the crew if a favorite song comes on, but that is not the same as singing in front of, singing *to,* a man I don't know. But the song was just right, for I certainly liked his smile.

While I sung, I occasionally glanced at him. He loved it. And so did the people around us.

"You betta sing," said one guy after the song ended.

"That was really fresh," said another.

And another, as the Sylvester parade struck up again with "You Are My Friend," patted me on the shoulder with: "Finally, someone who sings like a man up in here."

I didn't know whether to thank him, so I just nodded.

The only person whose comments I was interested in, though, still hadn't said anything yet. All he could do was (you guessed it) smile.

"Yes?" I queried.

He laughed – *again* – folded his arms, and leaned into me. "You got a nice voice."

"Thanks." I took a sip of my drink; my throat had become dry after that performance.

"You a singa?" he asked.

"No."

"You like my smile?"

Well, well, well, aren't we being a little presumptuous. I didn't care. I played right along.

"What do *you* think?"

He blushed, two times. Spell it V for Victory.

At that moment, Babyface (no, he doesn't favor the singer) walked up to me. He bent his tall, lean frame down, bringing his mouth to my ear. "Hate to interrupt. We're ready. We'll be waiting outside." I whispered an "OK." He nodded at Raheim and walked off.

"Well, looks like I have to be going...," I announced.

"Uh, was that yo' man?"

"My man? Do you think my man would allow me to stand over here and talk to *you?* He'd be stupid."

He chuckled. There goes that dimple again.

"I don't have a man," I added. "That guy was one of my best friends."

He grinned. "Jood."

"Jood?"

"Yeah. I wanna talk ta you. Gimme yo' phone numba."

He wasn't asking for it; he was demanding it. I felt like doing a somersault.

"Sure. Can I have yours?"

"I'll be Black..."

I took that to mean that he would return, and, by the time I found a business card, he did. He handed me a piece of paper with his name and a number scribbled in very neat penmanship. "My beepa..."

I gave him the card. "My home phone is on the back."

He studied it. "'Mitchell Crawford, Associate Edita, *Your World* Magazine...'" He pointed the card at me. "Yeah, *yo'* world." I giggled as he stuffed it in his shirt pocket.

I was at a loss for words, so I decided to be silly.

"You sure you'll be all right by yourself?"

He laughed – *again*. "Yeah. My boyz, they ova there." He pointed to two healthy guys – one a brother, the other Latino – talking and standing in the back.

I put out my hand. "Well, it was nice meeting you. I hope to speak to you soon." He shook my hand. I noticed how evenly cut and clean his fingernails were. I didn't want to let go. I didn't want to leave.

He beamed. "Catch ya lata. Peayce." He let "peace" draw out. It was so sexy.

As he went to join his boyz, I noticed his bowlegged strut and basketball booty. "Lord," I whispered to myself. As soon as he reached his boyz and they all turned to (I assumed) look at me, I made a beeline for the front door.

When I got outside, Gene was hugging Carl in front of B.D.'s bright red Honda. They held each other, Gene giving him a nice rub on his high, round butt. Carl then walked away, turning to say, "See you Monday night." Damn, they already set a date. Gene waved bye and turned to see me. I joined him as he plopped down on the hood of the car.

"So, where's the crew?" I asked.

"Babyface is at the corner talking to some child and B.D. went to the store so we can take some beverages to this party."

"Oh..." I was about to bust. Why doesn't he ask me what happened? Guess I'll have to steer the convo in that direction.

"Ain't we a fast worker. Going out on Monday, hunh?"

He lit a cigarette. "You know me. Skip the formalities and cut to the chase. That boy has a butt I'd hump any day in the week ending in *y*. And, speaking of a chase, did you catch what *you* were after?"

"Yeah..."

"Well?" he anticipated. "Tell me about it."

I thought he'd never ask.

"Well, we cruised each other..."

"And?"

"And he came over to me..."

He gave me a look.

"He didn't give me a chance to...," I began.

"Uh-huh, yeah, whatever, go on..."

"Well..." I didn't know where to start. "He has such a sexy voice..."

"Uh-huh..."

"Serious bedroom eyes..."

"Uh-huh..."

"He smiled a lot." Like I was doing right then.

"Yeah..."

"And he laughed a lot..."

"Yeah..."

"And he likes the way I sing..."

His eyes bulged. "You *sang* for him? My, this is serious. I betcha he didn't even have to ask, did he?"

I giggled.

"He didn't," he said. "Did he ask for the digits?"

"Yeah. And I asked for his."

"Well, I am impressed. Maybe now you can get plugged."

"Will you quit!"

We laughed.

"But don't get too excited," he advised. "You know how guys like him are. I wouldn't be surprised if he didn't call."

I wasn't listening to him, though. I was just too high. I got the fiercest guy in the bar! And I was also, like Gene, proud of myself. I was in command of our short but seriously flirtatious chat. I made him smile and laugh a lot. And, he said it was *jood* that I didn't have a man because he wants to talk to me.

Well, if he calls, he can talk and do anything else he wants to do to me. He had the hormones hopping. He was just what the doctor ordered...

And *why* was he what the doctor ordered? Well, besides being a vision of lust, he's a B-boy – or banjee/banji/banjie boy, or block boy, or homeboy, or homie, or, as MC Lyte tags 'em, "ruffneck." For those who don't know who these fellas are – and, if you don't, just where have you been living, on another planet? – I'll gladly school you on the subject. This is something I love to discuss.

They are the boyz who stand on street corners, doin' their own vogue – striking that "cool pose" against a pole, a storefront, up against or on a car, leanin', loungin', and loiterin' with their boyz, just holding court like a king with a "40" to quench the thirst, tryin' to rap to the females, and daring anyone to stake their territory, to invade their domain.

They are the boyz you see every morning, afternoon, early eve, and late nite on the news, heads down and covered – but nothing can hide the handcuffs.

They are the boyz who stand like a tree – body erect, but somewhat arched, slanted to one side, their arms stretched and reaching like branches. Their eyes are icy cold; they look through you, sizing you up and cutting you down. Their smile is a wicked, wavering one. At one moment, it seems both inviting and harmless; at another, cunning yet calculating.

They are the boyz who dress to thrill. Their heads – clean, close-cropped, or in a funky fade – are wrapped in bandanas, scarves, stocking caps, or sports caps, which are usually worn front, tilted downward, loose, or backwards on the head for full effect. They style and profile in their baggy jeans or pants falling somewhere between their waists and knees, barely holding onto their behinds, their undergear pulled up over their waists. They kick the pavement in sidewalk-stompin' boots and low- and high-top, high-priced sneakers, oftentimes worn loose, unlaced, or open, with their trousers tucked inside.

They are the boyz who move to a rhythm all their own – the swagger in their step, the hulking strut that jerks their bodies to and fro, front to back, side to side, as if they are about to fall. Their arms sway to their own beat. Their hands are right at home in their pockets.

They are the boyz who, whether they are in motion or standing, are always clutching their crotches. In fact, it seems like their hands are surgically attached to their dicks, as if they are holding it in place and fear it will fall off (or are they reaching for something that isn't really there?).

They are the boyz who walk like they are marching off to war – a war that many of them are, unfortunately, fighting against each other and themselves.

They are the epitome of cool.

They are the epitome.

They are *cool*.

They are the boyz who are filling our prisons, where many pump iron to pump up their bodies, when they should be in school pumpin' knowledge into their brains.

They are the boyz who are loud and boisterous; they speak to be heard, not so much to be understood. They are cantankerous and obnoxious; they know everything, and don't even try to tell them they are wrong. They are cocky and egocentric; the world doesn't revolve around them, because they *are* the world. They are self-centered and self-absorbed; they are all true men, 101 percent, and it's all about them.

They are the boyz who are walking stereotypes, walking statistics for commentators, forecasters, academicians, and politicians to discuss and dissect, to berate and blast, to write about and write off.

They are the boyz whose main challenge in life is to gain or sustain props (that's respect). So, don't even think about looking at them the wrong way or looking at them, period, when they don't want to be looked at, for it is over for you. They'll cap you, take you out, snuff you, to prove who is runnin' this motha-fucka.

They are the boyz who just don't give a fuck.

They are the boyz who are the true hip-hopsters, the gangstas, the menaces 2 and of society, the troublemakers, the troubleseekers, the hoods, the hoodlums, the hood-rocks, the MacDaddys, the Daddy-Macs, the rugged hard-rocks...

You get the picture.

We've all seen 'em and one thing is certain – they scare the shit out of a lot of folks, especially The Man and his Woman. They are White America's hellmare – those Big, Black Brutes, those Common Crimi-nals, those Violent Vagrants who have made the streets unsafe, taken the value out of "family values" — since, the logic goes, so many of them make babies but don't care for them — and just, in general, brought down the quality of life. When they are coming down the street, a path is not only cleared for them, it is *cleaned*. And they love it...

"Dat's right, step outa da way, you betta move ta da otha side of da fuckin' street, you white bitch, you ain't impo'tant, I don' want yo' fuckin' purse or yo' pussy...

"Mr. Mutha-Fuckin' Wall Street, I don' need yo' wallet or gold money clip, it ain't about you, it's about me, you cracka jack motha-fucka..."

Here arc "men" who throw their masculinity around for the entire world to not only see but swallow (pun intended). Of course, it is a rather grotesquely exaggerated take on manhood. But, when you are on your way to growing into a man (at least in years) and nobody has told you how to be one and almost all the "men" you see around you walk, talk, dress, and act like this, how else do you prove that you are a man but by joining them? Yes, you too have to be one bad motha-fucka, the one they'll fear the most. It's a man thang, nothin' but a man thang, and only the roughest, the toughest survive.

Banjeeness has become a boyz2men rite-of-life for many preteen/teenage/postteen males in the so-called inner city. And, the vibe these fellas give off is an overtly "straight" one. But B-boys do come in all ages (uh-huh, forty-year-olds nursin' a "40"), persuasions (the girlz are down, too), mutations (white boys like the down-with-the-homies-phony and Great-White-Aryan-Muscle-Boy-Hope Marky Mark), and orientations. For many Black heterosexuals, though, there is no such thing as a homosexual, so most would faint if you were to even suggest that a B-boy could be gay. The general rule is that, even if there are homosexuals in our community, there *should*n't be, and those willing to acknowledge that we do exist feel comfortable with us only as flaming faggots (a la Blaine and Antoine of TV's *In Living Color*). Given our history in AmeriKKKa, it has been a struggle defining what manhood means in a society that does not afford us the right to be men.

So, the worst thing for any Black man to be is a cocksucker or someone who takes it up the ass. *We* "want to be women" because we can't handle the harsh reality of being a Black man in America or dealing with a "strong sister," as if sleeping with other men is going to change one's sex or sexual orientation. God forbid if *we* bend over for a Caucasian — that is the ultimate symbol of subjugation, a throwback to slavery, and proof to some that homosexuality is something "the white man forced upon us." In fact, the nation's prisons, which many consider the white man's modern-day slave system, are responsible for helping to perpetuate this "pathology." *We* are worse than females who may be bitches or ho's, for at least they are good for something – pimpin' and puttin' out.

And *we* are a "threat" to the Black family – even though all of us come from Black families, and head or have our own, whether they be blood- or bond-related.

Because homosexuality is still a no-no, an unmentionable topic in most households and churches, too many of us spend our lives in the closet. And, one of the best ways to do that is to adopt the B-boy stance. And B-boys, with the indirect support of the community, fool themselves into thinking that, because they are so hard, because no one knows and probably won't be able to figure them out, they can't be homosexual. They just like to suck dick or have their dick sucked by another man is all; they just like to fuck other men. Hey, they can get an erection with a woman, maybe even have a baby (now *there's* a badge of masculine honor), so they must be straight. They are real men, unlike us, the faggots they fuck. But, as Teddy Pendergrass once vocalized: "You Can't Hide from Yourself."

Gene calls B-boys many things (most of them too vulgar for even me to repeat), but three of his labels are priceless. There's "homie-sexuals," "homoboyz," and his fave, "perpetrades": guys who "look" straight, "act" straight, may even think they're straight, but ain't. Since so many B-boys are trapped in this syndrome, Gene doesn't see how anybody could find them appealing. He admits their aura screams sex – lusty, animalistic, ravenous sex – and they do know what to do between them sheets (he has tasted a few himself). But an orgasm can last but so long. And, for people like me, who are looking forward to being "married" someday, they ain't exactly husband material. How can you build something with someone who lives for the moment, who can't or won't grow up? As Gene once remarked: "I want a man, not a boy!"

Still, I find them irresistible.

It took some time for me to notice they could be, though. Like most people, I was intimidated, put off by them. That in-yo'-face, gruff-and-grandiose air would always make me think, "Who the hell do these guys think they are, walking around like they own everything and can run anyone?" I guess because I have always been a softie, a sensitive, sensuous guy who cries at the drop of a hat, I was also somewhat jealous of this quality. But I soon came to find it sexy. It was certainly a smug kind of confidence, but it grew on me. That head-nigga-in-charge atimatude made me wish they would take charge of me!

The next "characteristic" that caught my eye was what Gene calls their "tail waggin'." As mentioned before, B-boys wear their pants hanging off their asses. Most of them have juicy behinds to begin with, so when they bebop down the street, it just jingles and jangles – and *that* is a sight to see. I am convinced that most B-boys, whatever their orientation, really enjoy the attention that their asses attract; I mean, why advertise like that if you don't want it to be seen and salivated over? When you think about it, this is very homoerotic. Homosexuals are often accused of "flaunting" their sexuality (a tired charge, since straight folks bombard us every day with images that glorify their sexuality), but B-boys, who are supposedly a heterosexual lot, seem to do it more, especially in this area. Needless to say, my head began turning a lot to gawk. Of course, this was something I had to do very carefully. Even if the one I was lusting over was gay, they might have kicked my ass for looking at them that way, anyway. I managed to do it well, though, and went from being just an ordinary homosexual to a butt man. It was then that I began daydreaming about having a B-boy.

But the curiosity boiled to the point of deep-seated desire by the spring and summer of 1991. It was the year of new jack cinema: boyz from the ghettos, dealin' and doin' drugs, carousin' and killin' up a storm, getting any and all the pussy they wanted. After seeing one of these flicks, I'd find myself starring in my own version at night, complete with opening and closing credits, soundtrack, narration, and special effects:

In *New Jack Booty,* I was a simple, naive schoolteacher who lectured his students on saying no to drugs, while I was cautioned by my own peers about saying no to a fine crack kingpin. Does my conscience prevail over my carnal instincts? In a word, *No.*

In *Hangin' Out, Over, and Under the Homeboyz,* I am picked up in a bar by one homie, agree to go to his house to have some fun, and we are joined by two of his buddies. They pass me around like a "40," taking turns sipping and gulping me down. And believe me, this one always made me wake up in a hot sweat.

In *Lovin' Large,* this hulky, bulky thug kidnaps me, the "bitch" of a rival, and demands that my hubby, a big-time drug lord, come up with $1 million in a day or he'll kill me (doesn't sound at all pleasant, does it?). Well, while we're waiting for hubby to decide whether I'm worth saving, I'm doing some serious sleeping with the enemy. I love it so much, I don't want to leave him and he feels the same way. Twenty-four hours later, he tells my now ex-boyfriend that he can keep the mill, cuz he's got something money can't buy, and we blaze off into the sunset in his Jeep.

But the one that gave me some seriously sticky nights was *Boyz under My Hood*. Talk about a romance: My car breaks down on a highway and this tall, dark, handsome B-boy with a bald head (shades of Raheim?) stops to help. He checks under the hood of my car, and then asks if he can check under mine! Of course, I let him, and his monkey wrench turns me out! This dream was too real. When I'd wake up in the morning, I could still taste him, smell him, and feel him in bed with me. While this made me smile the entire day, it also made me mad as hell. I wanted it, for real.

So, after all of this, I couldn't take the hunger anymore. I had to find myself a B-boy to satisfy it or I'd bust. And, when I met Raheim, the fantasy in full-bodied flesh had finally come along. All I could think was that he could definitely be Mr. Boyz under My Hood. He would be The One.

But, of course, I had said this before.

My very first taste of "banjeedom" happened at a club in Queens called Hector's, which, if the truth be known, is one of the most underrated places for homosexuals to hang out in New York. I think that its location (even the queens from Queens trek to the Vill to partay) and the fact that it is dismissed as a spot for Latinos (there are still so many folks who actually take *West Side Story* to heart — that these speak-no-English people are all carrying switchblades, just waitin' for the chance to slash you up) have kept it virtually hidden from many who, if they knew it existed, would make the journey.

I was one of those people. I didn't even know there were gay clubs and bars in Queens. Hell, I went to St. John's University for four years and I met only one homosexual there. (Of course, I was still somewhat in the closet at the time — as, no doubt, were all of the Italian Stallions I went to school with.) And Queens has that middle-class-America look and feel to it: the picturesque, modern, two-story homes; the well-mani-cured, blinding-green lawns (even in the winter, no less); the doghouses in the yard; the patios and porches on which you're bound to find a rocking-chair grandma or grandpa; and tree-lined, freshly cemented streets and sidewalks that are probably the cleanest in all the city.

In other words, it is not the kind of area one might expect to find men who put on face, fashions, and falsies to lip-synch to Donna Summer or Barbra Streisand.

But Hector's is there, and, since Gene dragged me there one night a few years ago, I've been back at least once a month. The only problem (besides its being so far from Brooklyn) is that it is so cramped. There is a sign that greets you as soon as you walk in — "OCCUPANCY BY MORE THAN 175 PEOPLE IS UNLAWFUL" — but not even half that number can fit into the joint without folks standing on top of and up against each other. For some, like yours truly, this close proximity can be a bonus — you can't help but brush up against others, and I've had my share of "brushers" who seem to linger a little too long in front of or behind me when they are passing by. (I don't mind being felt up as long as the guy doing the feeling is worth a feel or two, too.) But sometimes I can't help but wonder what would happen if a fire broke out or somebody started shooting. I generally get those fears, though, when I'm on my way there or after I've danced the night away, for one cannot help but get caught up in the crowd's festive mood. Everybody is there to have a good time. The music is good, the drinks are plenty, and the boyz are fine.

But it is the show that is most fab. Hector's puts on the best drag show I've ever seen, and most of the credit goes to the comically crass Roxie — a six-foot-two, robust, rousing female impersonator. He serves as the "hostess" and opening act, usually bowling the children over with some classic disco tune or contemporary hit, wearing some outrageously tight-fitting yet elegant gown or suit, with feathers, headbands, and glistening glitter and gold draping him from head to toe, and death-heel pumps that even RuPaul would stumble in.

After his number, he brings out his guests for the evening — but not before he reads the audience. He is one drag queen I would not want to cross. Not only is he, like Gene, venomous, but he is quick and sharp. It is the stuff of legend, it is probably all myth, but children have been known to fall out of Hector's ready to kill him for basically making them look like asses. I do recall one night where this one child was crying like his life was over because Roxie lit him up for criticizing every single performer who came on...

"Miss Thing, this is my show, OK, *my* show, so if you think you can do any better, we'll find a garbage bag that can fit you, some makeup to hide, not beautify, that crater face, and a wig to cover that sorry drip-drop curly perm, and you can bring your two-thousand-tons-of-unfun, Magilla Gorilla ass on!"

Naturally, the whole place rolled with laughter. Even Gene, who makes it a habit of not giving others their props in the reading department because he knows he is the king, cracked up — especially when, after this fool tried to come back, Roxie snapped: "Honey, reading is *fun*damental, not *for* the mental!"

On the night in question, Roxie was in the middle of the dance floor in the middle of yet another one of his fierce reads (the victim this time being a woman who claimed not to be a lesbian but couldn't explain why she was present) when Gene, who was off on the other side of the place gabbing with some of his fans, returned to me with some interesting news.

"See that boy over there?" he asked.

My eyes turned to the left to see a very narrow-headed, stringy-brown-haired, sad-eyed, floppy-eared Caucasian. He couldn't possibly be the one we were talking about, I told myself, but I just had to be sure.

"Him?" I asked, pointing at this man.

"Hell no!" he exclaimed. We both looked at the guy, then at each other, and screamed: "Eeeek!"

"Puh-leeze, he looks like Spuds McKenzie!" Gene declared, as we both laughed. *"That* is a face only a mother could love! It's the guy standing in front of the bar."

This time I couldn't miss him. He was the only one in that area; everyone else had formed a circle around Roxie on the dance floor to watch the show. And he was a sight: maybe five feet ten with a solid medium build, very dark brown skin, a long face, big eyes, and a neatly trimmed mustache and beard. He had on a gray Howard U t-shirt, fine-fitting blue jeans, and a white-and-blue cap. Several rings were on his left hand and a thick gold rope chain sat on his chest. There was a blank look on his face. His hands were in his pockets.

"Yeah, what about him?" I said, liking what I saw very much.

"Well, he's got his eye on you."

"On me?" I was thrilled yet surprised. He was, to be sure, a hard-core B-boy, but they never look twice at me (if they look at me at all). When I set my sights on roping a B-boy, I discovered that most don't want to be bothered with folks who aren't like them. I ain't "hard" in the slightest sense, so I naturally asked: "Why does he want to talk to me?"

"That, I don't know," Gene began, "but one of his friends asked me if I was your lover. So, don't be surprised if he makes a move. I just wanted to warn you."

"Warn me?"

"Yes, warn you. For the past eight months the only thing I've heard from you is 'I want a B-boy.' And, well, it looks like that chance is standing over there. Maybe after he gives you a little and you find out that they ain't all that, you'll come to your senses."

Gene was convinced that my craving for a B-boy was due to my dealing with so many "soft" men in the past. Almost all of my ex's didn't know what they wanted — from me, from us, from themselves. Typical ball-of-confusion folks. They were constantly putting me through changes. A B-boy, he argued, is the exact opposite of these men: They know what they want, when they want it, how they want it, and go after it. They are very sure of themselves and, based on what I've dealt with before (so-called straitlaced types), would provide me with the great adventure I was looking for.

But Gene felt (in fact, he prayed) that this yearning would be just a quick phase.

"I know, I know you think I'm crazy...," I admitted.

"I will be convinced you are if you go home with him," he said, as Roxie was bringing the show to a close. "If I haven't seen him on *America's Most Wanted,* I'm sure I will soon."

I chuckled. "You are so farce–"

"No – smart," he shot back. "Indulge at your own risk, honey. I'll be in the back if you need me."

As he went back to his fort, the crowd began to clear the dance floor and Mariah Carey's "Can't Let Go" came on. As I stood there, thinking how much I hate this song and the person who sings it, someone eased behind me, then into me, pushing, and hands grabbed my waist.

"Wanna dance?"

I couldn't speak. A sigh was caught in my throat, but even that couldn't escape. I turned around – his hands still securely holding me – saw that it was him, smiled, and nodded yes.

He led me to the middle of the floor, where we joined several other couples, and pulled my body into his. I placed my hands around his neck and rested my head on his chest. He cupped my ass and grinded into me. I was *gagging*.

Every time Mrs. Sony said she couldn't let go, he squeezed me tighter. I was *gasping*.

I was in another world. So *this* is what it feels like being in a B-boy's arms. His voice, which reminded me of Avery Brooks's, brought me back to earth.

"Wha's ya name?" he asked, still holding me by my buns.

"M-M-Mitch..." I pulled back a little to look at him. He was just a couple of inches taller than me.

"Royal," he said, not even returning my glance.

There was silence for a minute. I was too busy enjoying this to talk now. But he wasn't.

"Ya wanna git outa here?"

His question threw me off. I didn't know what to say.

"Le's go ta yo' house ... I got my Jeep outside..."

I still didn't know what to say.

He pulled back from me. "Well...?"

I looked into those dark brown eyes. "Well...? OK..." I didn't sound too sure.

He let me go, went into his pocket, and pulled out what I thought was a piece of paper. "Ya got a ticket?"

It was for the coat check. I let out an "Oh," and gave him my own. "Be back," he smirked. I walked behind him to find Gene. As Royal disappeared from view, Gene came out of nowhere.

"He didn't waste any more time," Gene said, dragging on a Marlboro. "I saw ya'll getting really close. What's up?"

I didn't want to tell him that I had reluctantly agreed to go to my house with a total stranger after dancing with him for no more than six minutes for what might surely be a one-night stand, so I lied. "Royal wants to get something to eat."

"Hmmmm, I *bet* he does," Gene responded, not exactly convinced. He looked at the gold Piaget on his right wrist. "Well, it's two o'clock now. You better be home by six. If you're not, I'm coming over to your house with the police to make sure you aren't the fifteenth murder victim to grace the front page of the *Daily News* this year."

Thanks a lot, Mama Gene, that's just what I needed to hear.

I forced a smile. "Don't worry. I'll be fine."

"OK." He hugged me and was off. And, like clockwork, Royal reappeared. He helped me on with my coat and we left.

Royal didn't have much to say as we drove to my place in his black Cherokee (when I saw it, I was reminded of my homeboy dream). I did most of the talking (or should I say, asking?). But he had plenty to say when we got there.

Before I could turn on any lights and offer him something to drink, he grabbed me from behind and just took me. He told me what to do, and I did it.

"Aw yeah, I wan' some o' dis ... yeah, take off my shirt ... play wit my chest ... yeah, lick me ... lick my cable ... git on yo' knees ... unzip it ... take dat shit out ... go ta work on it ... yeah, suck dat dick, suck it good ... no, don' stop ... right dere ... ooh, yeah, money, I'm gon' fuck ya real good ... git on dat bed ... stick dat ass out ... yeah, give it ta me ... ooh, yeah, i's so nice an' tight ... yeah, ya like da shit hard, don'cha? ... yeah, tell me i's good ... ah da shit is so good..."

And, if I did or was about to do something he didn't want me to, he let me know...

"Stop squeezin' my ass ... don' suck my nipple ... don' fuckin' bite me, you fuckin' crazy? ... don' feel me like dat ... nah, don' kiss me..."

I think it was the last thing that really got me. I fail to see how any man can really get busy with whomever he is with unless it all starts with a kiss. But some B-boys like Royal (and non-B-boys) definitely see a difference between fucking a man (which for some constitutes "fooling around" or "getting off") and kissing (which some save for the females or don't do at all). For them, you ain't a real man if you kiss another.

For me, though, if it ain't in the kiss I ain't down with it. But, of course, there's a first time for everything, and that night with Royal was it. I was too through having a B-boy in my bed, fucking me over and over like there was no tomorrow, that the fact that he didn't want to be smacked on the lips didn't matter. The fact that he didn't even ask me what he could do to make me feel good wasn't important. I loved his being cold and in control. Yes, Royal was the King: whatever he wanted to do (or didn't want to do) was fine with me.

And, at least I didn't have to teach him what to do and how to do it (this was the case a few months later with B-boy number two, Ricky – but more about him later).

Like I predicted, Royal was a one-night stand (and, to date, my first and only). He wouldn't sleep over, saying, "I don' do dat." (I should've known – he didn't take off his cap or gold during sex.) It was like six in the morning when he left (and, like he said he would, Gene called). I didn't want it to be just a one-time thing, though; the shit was the best I'd had in years and I wanted it again – and again. So I asked for and got what I assumed was his beeper number. I called him a dozen times, but he never called me back. I saw him in the Vill several months after that, but he, of course, couldn't (or more than likely didn't want to) remember me.

By that time, though, I had been "dating" Ricky, an eighteen-year-old stud I met via a 900 number (970-RUFF). After Royal, I was having no luck meeting another B-boy and my juices were working overtime. So I placed an ad on their bulletin board phone line:

"Hi, this is Mitch. I'm looking for an African-American B-boy to turn me out. If you are eighteen or over, and ready for action, call me at..." (I would never leave my number on a public access line, but I was desperate.)

During a total of two weeks, five people answered. Four were Caucasian, and, besides not being able to understand English, none of them seemed to understand why I wouldn't talk to or meet with them. One arrogantly argued that I should because "all black men want white men." After I nicely said, "Sorry, but you ain't the one, because you are white," he called me a nigger, and, I'm sure, was responsible for the crank calls I received for the next two weeks.

Then, after I had almost given up, Ricky called.

Ricky was a true-blue B-boy. He always dropped by unannounced. He'd strut his compact and cute chocolate frame (he was an inch shorter than me but bigger and beefier all over), and face (he had that fresh nature-boy look a la Tevin Campbell) around my apartment like a peacock, like he was running things. And I let him have his glory. I let him get off on his little manly man high.

But he was, for lack of a better phrase, "young, dumb, and full of cum." He was a kid who didn't know much but was eager to learn – and I taught him.

He didn't know how to kiss. I told him he must have been watching too many soap operas. He would just grab me by the neck or face and push his mouth into mine – like *that* was supposed to turn me on. After he took out those fake gold caps, I showed him how to let his lips caress, linger, and taste. I also showed him that you can kiss more than a person's lips. By the time our affair ended, we couldn't get into anything unless my lips and tongue made the trip all over his body – except his ass (in fact, it was a good four months before he let me fondle him there). He saw that exploring the body can make you (and the sex act itself) hotter.

He also didn't know the meaning of the word *foreplay*. In the beginning, sex for him was "Slam, bam, thank you, Sam." The first time we did it, he wouldn't take off his socks (Eeeek!), and just knew that he was Bronco Billy and I his saddled steed. After I getty-uped him out and off of me, I explained that sex is not some athletic sport, where the faster and harder it is done the better it's gonna be (well, at least not all the time). And it ain't all about fucking, either. Two people can share in other ways, such as taking a shower together, cuddling, massage, or frottage, which he liked a lot (as a tyke who was still going through that "girl stage," this reminded him of doing it with a female).

He remained cool about all of these lessons. I guess it was what he wanted. And I was obviously blowing his mind. Why else would he keep cuming back for more? He was willing and able to try anything – well, anything except get fucked.

And this is the reason he stopped visiting. Not that he got tired of me begging for it (which I did do a lot). He did give it up – but what happened afterwards ended what we had.

It was on one of our usual "Fuck Fridays." He was basking in the glow of his third climax in an hour and it was my turn. I was used to him deep-throating me and, just before my own climax, releasing me and watching me squirt all over his stomach. But this time, after several minutes of some serious sucking (he said he never did it before me but it sure as hell didn't feel like it), he let go and said:

"Fuck me."

*"What?"* I knew I was dreaming.

"Fuck me," he repeated.

"Are you sure?" I asked.

"Yeah. I been thinkin' 'bout it. I wanna do it."

The grin on my face made me look like the Grinch Who Stole Christmas. I was finally gonna get some of that ripe-for-the-plucking virgin booty, which sat so high and mighty on his waist.

I got him ready with my tongue (which had him throwing a serious fit) and a quarter tube of lubricant (he was tighter than a bra on Dolly Parton). I let him put the condom on.

"Tell me how you wanna do it," I said, ready to go.

"Wha'cha think is da bes' way?"

Shit, *any* way, I thought, as long as I get it in.

I then recalled my first time. "If you sit on it, you can guide it in and you can look into my eyes."

He liked that idea, so I got in the receiving position in the middle of the bed. He stood over me, his feet parallel to my thighs, and, holding on to my shoulders, lowered himself down, very slowly. There was pain; his face couldn't hide it (he was trying so hard to take it like a man). I kissed and talked him through it, telling him to relax, take it easy. The coaching worked: he was sitting on it in a couple of minutes. He then closed his eyes and, with his palms on the bed, got used to this new feeling by churning those hips slowly, breathing and sighing heavily.

By the time I said, "You lead, I'll follow," he had already pushed me back against the pillows, folded and locked his legs under my thighs, and started riding me like a cowboy.

He was lovin' it and I was too (it was the first time in over two years that I was getting mine). He rocked, I rolled. His moans, my groans, our screams were so loud that I heard someone outside my second-floor apartment say, *"Damn,* somebody is gettin' theirs up there!"

Not once did he say to stop or slow down, even when I grew larger inside of him. And when I exploded, he exploded, too – right in my face.

He collapsed in my arms. Fifteen minutes later, he wanted it again. And I gave it to him again, this time on his back with his legs elevated. While tonguing me down, he called me everything except a Child of God: "Mitchy," "Baby," "Honey," "Lova," "Boyee," "Homie," "Nigga," and my two personal faves, "Daddy" and "Motha-Fucka."

And, an hour later, he wanted it *again.* This time we did it on the living room sofa: he, on his stomach; me, doing the same getty-up I had chastised him for months before. But he didn't mind at all. In fact, he wanted, begged for it *ruff* – his ass whacked hard, his hands pinned behind his back, being placed in a semi-headlock and ridden like a wave.

I thought he was about to say, "Let's do it again," as I held him on the sofa – I was enjoying it all, but I was ready to pass out – when he whispered in my ear: "I love you."

I didn't know what to say, but I knew that I couldn't say, "I love you, too," because I didn't.

I know it hurt him when I mumbled: "That's sweet, baby... I love ... being with you. Now, let's go to sleep." He had this look on his face, a look I recognized because I had worn it many times before: he realized that the feeling was not mutual.

After we slept that night away, he got up the next morning, kissed me good-bye, and never came back.

I often wonder what would have happened if I had just lied to him. Maybe I could have grown to love him the way he thought he loved me. Maybe we could have become "lovers." But how can an eighteen-year-old really know what love is? And, of course, I reasoned, he *would* think that was what he felt — I had just fucked him silly, giving him pleasure he'd never known. But you always "fall in love with" or "love" your first.

If I were to ever see him again, I'd tell him that I was so sorry, that I hope I didn't break his heart. I really should've known that that could have happened. I went through the same thing when I was his age. He was only a kid and did look up to me. I was probably the very first person he had spent that much intimate time with. A few months after we began our affair, he started opening up, telling me his dreams (he wanted to be, of all things, a fireman). He did have a sweet, soft side, being a little boy in a man's body. And, the few times he did spend the night, he'd sleep in my arms like a baby.

But — and I know this is going to sound mean — I just saw him as a fantabulous fuck buddy. We really had nothing in common except sex. As soon as he walked in the door, we went right at it. There was rarely a "Hello" or "How are you?" And, after it was over, I'd say how good it was; he'd reply, "I know"; and then, not long after, he'd get up and leave, his last words being: "See ya!" Yes, we had a serious lust thang goin' on, but how serious could I *really* be with him?

I wanted a B-boy so he could bring out the freak in me, and both he and Royal did that beyond my wildest expectations. I wanted my B-boy experience, though, to fall somewhere between "get the goods and be outy" (Royal) and "let love get in the way" (Ricky). I wanted more than just a one-night stand but nothing so deep that the word *love* could be spoken.

But you can't always get what you want — and, like Royal and Ricky, Raheim would show me that.

"This is Mitch…"

This had to be the twelfth time I had answered my phone at work in the last fifteen minutes. It was always like that every other Friday when we were closing an issue of *Your World,* known as the *"Time* magazine for teens." Used as a teaching tool in some four thousand high school social studies classrooms around the nation, *Your World* takes whatever is in the news at the moment – be it the Persian Gulf war, the presidential election, the L.A. rebellion, or the recession – and shows young people why these issues and events are important to know about and how they affect their lives. Of course, the most popular topics are those that they can identify with directly, such as the one we were presently tackling, popular music. The staff agrees that the last issue of the year should always be a light one, since most of the kids are restless and looking forward to the last day of school. But we also do it to give ourselves a break after a year of stretching our imaginations to the hilt, trying to make some sense out of this very complicated world to those who are inheriting it.

But even when what we are covering appears simple and is fun, problems arise. I had received four calls from our fact checker, Deborah Garcia, saying that some of the figures in our feature, "How a Song Becomes #1 – And Stays at the Top," weren't adding up. Apparently the writer, a freelancer, had conflicting stats in both the story and a sidebar on how many albums (or rather cassettes and compact discs) an artist must sell to be certified gold or platinum, and what artists had racked up the most citations in 1992. In another piece, "Does Music Have a Color?," the concept of "crossover" was being trashed, but our golden boy Elias Whitley – a genuine, snot-nosed, yuppified Yalie – believes it is not a bad thing. After all, "white people are the creators and purveyors of American music; just look at Elvis," as he wrote on the checking copy of the article. Puh-leeze. There would be no pop music if it weren't for *us.* Seems we're supposed to be comfortable just being "blackground." Even though we create the soundz, white folks commit cultural banditry and are given the real kudos and cash for it (just look at all the R&B and blues greats who die penniless). So, my response to Elias was a simple one: "Yeah, right, tell that to the *real* King, Little Richard."

Elias and the other white editors except Denise Garafola – an Italian-American woman who defines herself as neither a liberal nor a conservative but a realist – also believe it is wrong to outright accuse "mainstream" record companies and radio stations of racism: "It's about money, not race." (Uh-huh, that's also what they said about African enslavement.)

And, to top everything off, our art director, Leonard Schwartz, was having a serious nicotine fit, because photos of Whitney Houston that Arista Records was to be sending over Thursday afternoon hadn't arrived yet – and the magazine, already in galley form, was going to press at noon on Monday. And the very last thing I wanted to do was fall up in here on a Saturday or Sunday to make sure that photos fit and that all the *i*'s were dotted and *t*'s were crossed – especially if Raheim called and asked me out.

Ever since we'd met on Saturday night, I couldn't stop thinking about him. Yes, he'd given me his beeper number, but I certainly didn't want to be the one to call first. I didn't want him to feel that I was sweating him, that it was all about him (even though that *was* the case). Every time the phone rang, either at home or at work, my heart jumped – and every time, after I answered it, I was terribly disappointed. I was beginning to believe what Gene said: Raheim was nothing but a player, a guy who scores points with his homies by just collecting as many phone numbers as he can, and just letting those poor, dreamy-eyed fools who were stupid enough to give it to him think that he was really interested. But I had a strong feeling that Raheim would call and make Gene gag.

Which brings me back to the phone call. It was Gene, whom I had talked to briefly just a few minutes before.

"No, it is not *him,*" he announced.

"Funny, very funny," I shot back, not in the mood for his sarcasm or jokes.

"Look, dahling, I know that I gave you the pleasure of hearing my angelic pipes just a few moments ago, but I had to call back with some news hot off the press," he said, waiting for me to bite.

Oh no, I thought, not another update on the continuing sexcapades of Simply Dope Records' male vocal and rap groups: hard-as-steel, rhymin', and harmonizin' brothers who, like some of their peers in the

industry, kick it to the females in their songs and videos but actually
bust the move with the fellas. Gene should know – he is the vice
president of public relations at Simply Dope and has had several of
these boyz. At the moment, things had really heated up between two
different groups: A member of a vocal quartet had been caught by
another member of the same group – his lover – in a conference room,
on a table, knockin' da boots *down* with one of their labelmates, a
rapper. The wronged party and the rapper came to blows, and the
couple had an ugly split, with the "adulterer" being thrown out of their
apartment. (Guess who he moved in with?) But the drama was just
beginning: The breakup had caused a major rift in the group, with the
other two members taking sides. They were supposed to go on *MTV
Jams* this weekend but none of them would budge. Gene said he'd call
back if he heard if they made peace.

"Gene, I really don't have the time to gossip with you," I retorted
matter-of-factly. "As you know, I am up to my armpits in work."

"Yes, I know. Give me a little credit here. I wouldn't bother you
unless this was important."

"Fine, what is it?" I asked, uninterested. I was reading yet another
silly comment on a checking copy of the "Does Music Have a Color?"
feature that said some of the language used was "inflammatory" and
"divisive." Some folks just hate the truth...

"Well, thank you for giving me your undivided attention," he said.
"It just so happens that Angela Martin, that fierce artist who designed
the cover of Mac T's latest CD, has quit."

"What? You're kidding?" Angela and I went to the same high
school and graduated together in 1984. Almost nine years went by
before Gene reintroduced us at a Simply Dope press party where they
were introducing new artists. One of these groups ended up in our
Music issue. I wasn't particularly moved by their work, but Gene was
unrelenting. Simply Dope really lucked in when they found him. He
can talk a reporter into doing a story on a performer he doesn't like –
and I am a witness.

"No, I am not kidding," he assured me. "It seems that that mugly
boss in the art department, Franklin Styles, was trying to get into
Angie's panties but she wasn't having it – particularly since, number
one, she is a lady, and, number two, she is a lesbian..."

"Excuse me, but this sounds like gossip to me," I observed.

"I am getting to the point, OK? She quit last week, and, instead of
hiring a new full-time artist, they want to give a few new jacks a break.
So, I thought you might know somebody. I mean, the pay is small but
the exposure is big."

I couldn't think of anyone off the top of my head, but it was something to keep in mind. I could pass the info on to others before word got around (which, if Gene had anything to do with, it would). "That sounds really good. Thanks for the tip. I'll see who I can dig up for you guys."

"Well, do it fast, because they will be announcing it in the press in a couple of weeks, and you know how all these wanna-be-in-the-music-biz homies and homettes are. They will be faxing in fake résumés in droves..."

"Yeah," I laughed. "I'll let you know. Now I really got to go. Someone else is on the other line."

"My, could it possibly be ... *him?*"

"Will you quit! I gotta go. We'll talk later."

"OK. *Ciao.*"

"Bye." I immediately clicked to my other line, praying it was him. "This is Mitch..."

"Hey, it's Michi" — that's *Mee-shee,* as in Michelle Snipes, our front desk receptionist and one of four colored folks (myself included) working at *Your World.* "There's a package here for you."

Finally, I thought, Whitney's pictures. At least that would be one less thing to worry about. I told her I'd be right down to pick them up. I strolled past the smoking lounge, where Leonard was busy puffing up a storm, and the vending machines in the outer hallway, where Denise was getting what had to be her fourth chocolate bar so she could "keep up her strength." It wasn't even noon yet and she, too, was having a fit.

I took the elevator instead of walking up the one flight. *Your World* is located on floors eight and nine in your average multistory Manhattan office building. When I got to the front desk Michelle was, as usual, on the phone. A voluptuous, diminutive 29-year-old with caramel skin and a fade that made her Nefertiti's twin, she was one fly sister (yes, even we homosexuals know beauty in women when we see it). The few times my 24-year-old brother, Adam, visited me, they flirted with each other terribly. He said that she'd be his ultimate fantasy, an "older woman" (funny how "older" means five years for some people but ten or twenty for others). But she only has eyes for the man she says will be her husband one day — Wesley Snipes. There are no less than a dozen pictures of him on her desk. I've told her that they could be related, but that doesn't matter to her. As she argued, "Puh-leeze. If we are, that will make it even better!" She's going to have to take a number though, for Gene and I are way ahead of her in that line.

Before I could open my mouth or look on her desk, she reached over a framed postcard of Wesley from *Mo' Better Blues* and pointed

toward the waiting area. I nodded thanks and approached what I
correctly assumed was a messenger. He was the only person there and
his back was to me.

"Do you have a package for Mitchell Crawford?" I asked, walking
around his parked ten-speed bike and the bench he was seated on to
make the transaction.

He stood up and, as I took him in, from head to toe, I *gagged*. It was
Raheim. He was wearing a white tank and black Spandex, both
hugging him so well they seemed to be holding his physique hostage.
Dark sunglasses sat on the top of his bald head, and there was a very,
*very* wide grin on his face.

"Day-am, it's about time. I thought you ain't want this," he said,
handing me a large white envelope.

"Th-th-thanks," I stumbled. I couldn't even talk right. Mitch, get
a*hold* of yourself!

"Guess you ain't expec' ta see me, hunh?" he winked.

"Yes, uh, no, I mean, yeah, I sure didn't, uh, expect to see you, right
here, right now..."

Get it together, Mitch, you're still stumbling...

"Yeah, I bet," he chuckled. He took his knapsack off his back,
reached in it, and pulled out a notebook. He took a pen that seemed
right at home above his left ear. He placed them both in front of me.
"Sign."

I was so caught up in him that I was oblivious to what he was saying.
"I'm sorry?"

He snickered, pushing the notebook closer to my chest and inching
the pen toward my right hand. "Sign, so I can be outy."

"Oh" was all I could vocalize. I took the pen and, as he held the
notebook, signed my name, the company, and date. I handed the pen
to him and he put it back over his ear, dropped the notebook in his bag,
and flung the knapsack over his back. He did it all with such ease that
all I could think was *I wish you would handle me like that...*

When his hypnotic eyes returned to mine, though, all I could say
was: "Thanks ... thanks a lot."

"You already did." He folded his arms, his left fingers seductively
stroking his thick mustache and goatee. I let out a laugh, covered my
mouth, and dropped my head to ease the tension. I was really hoping,
though, that he would cease with that serious sexy gaze and let me
relax. But he didn't.

He flexed his arms, which were muscle sharp, and clasped his hands
behind his head. Not once did his eyes leave mine.

"Do I make you nervous?" he coyly asked.

OK, OK, don't blow this one, Mitch, take your time...

"Of course not," I argued in a hushed tone.

"Well, you ain't got much ta say..." He leaned in closer. I almost fainted.

I giggled. "No...," I began, trying to find the right words. "It's just that, well ... this is a surprise."

"Well, I'm full of 'em..."

Ha, I *bet* you are...

"An' if ya like this one, I got anotha fo' ya tanite."

My eyes raised. "Tonight?"

"Yeah. You ain't doin' nothin'...?" It wasn't really a question; it was more like an expectation.

I grinned. "Uh, no, I'm not ... I'm free tonight."

He pointed to me. "Jood. I call ya at home, at like seven..." He dropped his head another inch toward me. His breath brushed my nostrils. Dentyne never smelled so good. "A'right?"

How could I say no?

"Sure," I answered.

"Cool." As he squatted to pick up a silver link chain from the floor, I watched his tree-trunk legs fold, then extend. They were as oily and shiny as his black boots. I sighed heavily.

"Check ya lata. Peayce." He winked and made his exit, my eyes fixed on his bubblicious butt as he arched his back to lift and pick up his bike with his left hand. He bounced past Michelle — who was, of course, still on the phone — and, swinging the chain with his right hand, bebopped on the elevator, which seemed to have been waiting for him. "Stay sweet, sweetheart," he called out to Michelle.

"You, too, baby ... and don't hurt nobody," Michelle cooed, looking up from her conversation.

"Ha, I'll try not ta," he chuckled as the elevator door closed.

I was frozen, again. I couldn't move until Michelle, finally off the phone, said: "Chile, do you know him? Oh, whatta man! He is *p-h-y-n-e* fine!"

I made my way to her desk. It was only a few feet away but it felt like forever getting there.

"Yeah, I do," I stated proudly, resting my body against the ledge of her desk. I was sweating.

"Lord *have* mercy," she testified. "He is a full-course meal, honey, plus the entire dessert tray."

I knew I was really looking silly then. I was blushing so hard one might've guessed that I had already had a taste and knew what she was missing.

And Michelle picked up on it immediately. "Don't tell me that Mr. Ebony Man is your latest?"

"No, but after tonight, who knows," I grinned, playfully tossing my head right to left.

"Hush yo' mouth!" she screamed, as the phone rang. She picked up the receiver and placed her left hand over the mouthpiece. "Well, you have a good time for you *and* me." She waved me away and continued: "Good morning, *Your World,* may I help you..."

I waved back and literally danced down the stairs, swinging the envelope in the air and never missing a beat. I just couldn't believe this. I had been waiting to hear from him all week and he pulls a stunt like this. This was a good sign; this was fate; it was meant to be. We'd been waiting for the photos and he just appears out of nowhere with them, delivering them to me personally? Somebody wake me, I'm dreaming...

As I floated down the hallway, Leonard saw me and flew out of the smoking lounge. "Mitch, are those the pictures?"

"Oh, yeah," I said, like it was no big deal they had finally come. "They just arrived."

"Damn, it's about fuckin' time," he coughed. He took the envelope from me and ripped into it. "These bastards better have been worth the wait."

I smiled. "Don't you worry, Len, they were."

*"A messenger?"*

Leave it to Gene. He couldn't admit that what Raheim did was sweet. He couldn't admit that it was somewhat romantic. And, most of all, he couldn't admit that he was wrong about Raheim not contacting me.

He had to criticize the way the man earned a living.

"Well, you two will be one dynamic duo — Tenspeed and Brown-shoe," he laughed.

I wasn't laughing.

Gene knew very well how hard it is for us to bring home the bacon in this U.S. of A. They say we are just lazy, that we don't want to nine-to-five it, that we have "chips on our shoulders," that this is the land of opportunity and anybody can make it — all you have to do is work hard.

*Bullshit.*

After over thirty years of Head Start, affirmative action, quotas, and set-asides, people (meaning white folks) like to think that the playing level is even for all, and it ain't so. I'm a perfect example: I watched too many incompetent Caucasians snag jobs while I, valedictorian of *both* of my college classes, graduated jobless.

With the odds still stacked against us, many of us can't be lawyers, doctors, businessmen, journalists, and engineers. But all of us don't have to be — or want to be. There was a time in our community when the "handymen" were really respected. It certainly wasn't easy for them to make a living back then — these jobs were usually the only ones available to them, since white folks couldn't (and to some extent still can't) see Negroes in positions where they weren't breaking their backs or getting their hands dirty. But these men did their jobs with dignity, they took pride in what they did — and so did we. Unfortunately, they have been replaced in too many communities by the drug dealer as a role model.

While all of my ex's were professional men, I haven't dated this type of man exclusively. (One usually goes out with those in one's social circle.) I've always said that a good man is a good man, and if he should come along and doesn't work on Wall Street or isn't a partner in a law firm, so what?

Besides, Raheim *is* a BMW — that's Black Man Working — and, what's more, he's making an honest living. It is very easy for a guy his age to be doing something illegal. I pointed this out to Gene as I went through my bedroom closet draped in nothing but a towel. It was 6:45, and I had been looking for something to wear for a half hour. Nothing was catching my eye.

"Yeah, or he could be working at Mickey D's," he countered.

"Gene, you are being so shallow," I argued, throwing yet another rejected outfit on my bed. "Even if he flipped burgers for Ronald McDonald, why should that make him undateable?"

"All I'm saying is that it makes things easier if you're with someone whose income or status is equal to yours," he explained. "You avoid the trap of doing for another man. And, you don't have to wonder who is gonna pick up the tab."

"You already have me involved with the man and we haven't gone out on our first date yet," I said. I knew where Gene was coming from, though — he had lived that story. But I still felt the need to defend Raheim and all the other men like him who are not in glamorous, high-prestige jobs. "People make the world go 'round, and even the jobs you and I wouldn't do, somebody somewhere has to do, and may even want to do."

"Yeah, like killing cockroaches or picking up trash," he snorted.

"That's right. My stepfather is a mailman. Ain't nothing exactly special about it, but he has been happy at what he does. And, even though I grew up seeing him as a homophobe, I also saw him as a hard worker, a flawed yet decent man.

"And, besides, you know what they say about blue-collar men," I continued, trying to choose between white and blue overalls. "They are really good with their hands."

"*That* I would most certainly agree with," said Gene, who has had his share of construction workers and UPS delivery men. "Ha, there's nothing like a stupid man with good hands! But, I would hardly call what Homie does blue-collar. He rides around on a bike all day. That ain't work, that's exercise..."

"It's work, Gene," I snapped. "He's one less Black man on an unemployment line, and he looks too good in his uniform."

"I would imagine that that is probably the most important thing for you," he assumed.

"Damn skippy!" I declared.

"Why am I not surprised..."

I looked at the clock — 6:50! Time was a-goin' and I had to be, too. "It's getting late. I got to get ready for him."

"Child, we know you are ready," he said. "I can hear your booty sizzlin', and I'm sure you got a jimmy right by the bed."

"Stop!"

"Considering his shoe size, though, I hope for your sake it's double-extra-strength."

"Gene, will you quit! Let me go."

"Fine, but I'm sure you won't be saying that later tonight. Talk to ya later. *Ciao.*"

Gene knew me very well. There was a three-pack of Zulus (yes, they are "designed with the Black man in mind") and a tube of K-Y lubricant on the night table by the bed. These are, after all, the '90s; one must be armed at all times. So I never leave the house without a condom and always have one near my bed so that, if I bring someone home (which hasn't happened since King Royal), the mood isn't spoiled trying to find one.

But I also did some other things for the evening Gene didn't know about. The house was clean (I had just done it the week before, from top to bottom), but not clean enough for me now, so I ran a mop over the kitchen and bathroom floors and vacuumed the living room and bedroom. I dusted the furniture, and even rearranged my record/tape/CD collection, putting more of the current titles out. I did it all hoping Raheim would be coming over, but you'd think I was about to have a party. I didn't know what he had planned, but I sure wasn't going to be caught off guard like I was earlier in the day.

And, not only did I take a 45-minute bath, I rubbed my body down in coconut oil. I also dabbed an aphrodisiac I bought from this Muslim fella in those private areas so that, if Raheim wanted to get busy, he'd be greeted by an earthy scent. The Muslim, of course, nearly choked when I told him that I needed it to turn on a man, not a woman as he suggested. ("Oh, you one a dose sweet mehn," he sighed.) But in the end it didn't matter, just as long as I gave him the five dollars for it.

I was able to do all of this cleaning and coifing because I left the office early. I gave the final OK on the cover picture of Mrs. Bobby Brown at noon, skipped lunch, and closed all the feature stories by three. On my way out the door, Elias was trying to give me more grief over some of the racial issues explored in the stories, but I told him to get over it.

I should've been exhausted, but I was too hyped. By the time I had hung up all the clothes I wasn't going to wear, put on my blue overalls, blue denim shirt, and black boots, and topped it all off with a black belt to show off what little curves I had, the phone rang.

It was 7:00 on the dot.

"Hello?"

"Wha's up?"

Yeah, it was him, and he was right on time. He spoke in a hushed, trailing tone. The bass was even more boomin' over the phone, sending chills through my body. Again, I wanted to say, "You – that's what's up," but I refrained.

"Raheim?"

"Who else?"

"Hi."

"So, ya ready?"

"Yes, I'm ready. I just finished dressing."

"Day-am." He snapped his finger. "I wanted ta catch ya in tha tub. I'm 'round tha corna."

"You are?" I was almost embarrassed.

"Nah, jus' jokin', jus' jokin'," he chuckled. "I go'cha, hunh?"

He sure did. I giggled. I sat down on the bed and crossed my legs. "So, what's on the agenda?"

"We gonna see tha Tina Turna movie."

That's right, tell me how it's gonna be. I was glad he wanted to see Tina. The word of mouth was that it was great. But it had just opened and chances were that it would be stupid crowded. When I relayed this to Raheim, he was not moved.

"Don' worry, I got it taken care of," he snickered.

"OK. Where do you want to meet?"

He told me where (in the Vill) and the time, and I knew he was buggin'. There was no way that we were gonna see the eight-o'clock show if we were meeting at the theater fifteen minutes before it was supposed to start. But I kept my mouth shut. I didn't care, so long as we got together.

"Don' be late," he said.

"I won't." I then thought of my talk with Gene. I wanted to ask whether he'd be paying. He must have read my mind.

"An' don' sweat it, I go'cha back..."

I breathed a sigh of relief. "Thanks. I'll see you soon."

"A'right. Peayce."

I was so excited that I started humming that Pointer Sisters song as I hopped off the bed and into the bathroom. I decorated my lips with cherry ChapStick, then checked myself in my bedroom mirror, which hung on the back of the door. "OK, Mitch, let's work it," I said. I grabbed my keys and wallet off the night table, turned off all the lights, and headed out the door.

It was only a fifteen-minute ride to the Vill from my third-floor brownstone apartment in Fort Greene, Brooklyn. The area has been put on the map thanks to Spike Lee and his 40 Acres & a Mule empire. His presence has helped attract some very talented brothers and sisters, most of them artists (musicians, filmmakers, and writers), as well as Caucasians trying their hardest to be liberal and cool living amongst the Tribe.

Fort Greene also happens to be the unofficial home of New York's Black gay community. In fact, in some circles, it is referred to as "Faggot Greene" or "Homo Hills," after a high-story co-op in the area named Clinton Hill. I've lived in the Fort for three years and met my ex in the area. You get cruised wherever you go — in the streets, in stores, even in the train station, where I was presently being eyed by this gorgeous guy who could've been Mario Van Peebles's twin. I would've normally returned the gaze and given him the green light to come on over, but I had Raheim on the brain. After the A train rolled into the station, he gave up on me and set his eyes on another fella, with body back but a face like a brick. I guess Pretty Boy was really hard up for a date.

I got to the triplex at 7:30 and the line was already around the block. I didn't find Raheim standing on it and so I figured that we'd have to catch the next show. The matron, a pecan-colored, petite young lady with auburn curls and gold door knockers larger than her ears, stood inside the door pointing people to the line. The expression on her face was not a happy one. I stood a few feet away from her and the crowd near the box office, where a poster of the film was displayed. There were the stars: Angela Bassett at the mike looking rather troubled as Larry (oops, sorry, he's Laurence now) Fishburne eases up to her right cheek. The tag line: "Who Needs a Heart When a Heart Can Be Broken?"

I was thinking how the poster would probably make a great birthday gift for Gene, who would be a very young thirty-five in just a few weeks, when my eyes caught the outline of a bowlegged fella coming up the block, his hands in his pockets. He was dressed *down* in baggy but huggy white jeans, and a black-and-white-striped checkerboard shirt that was unbuttoned, giving one a nice view of a chest that was outlined by a white sleeveless undershirt. He was easing on up the road in unlaced black boots. He sported a black "X" cap.

My heart started to race – it was Raheim.

As he bebopped his way up to me – all he had to do was *walk* and it turned me the fuck on – all heads turned.

"Wha's up?" he asked, standing but a few inches from me. He had a gold hoop in his left ear and a stud in his right. His goatee was trimmed and thin. A black leather Africa medallion hung directly below his Adam's apple.

He was *ovah*.

"Hi." I was trembling.

"You look *jood,*" he grinned.

I smiled. "Thanks. I guess I don't have to say that you do, too."

"Yeah, you can." His grin got wider. I laughed.

He went into his shirt pocket and pulled out the tickets. "So, ya ready?" he asked.

I nodded yes and proceeded to get on the line, but he grabbed my arm as I headed that way.

"Where you goin'?" he asked.

"Where am I going? To the back, where else?"

"Why? We don' hafta do that no mo', ya know?"

I looked at him quizzically. What's going on? I expected the matron to wave us away, but as soon as we reached the door, she opened it, and the frown I assumed was a permanent facial feature turned upside down.

"Hey, Cuz, this is Mitchell," Raheim said, handing her the tickets.

"Hi, I'm Diana, Raheim' s cousin," she replied. Her voice was deep yet feminine. She ripped the tickets in half and gave us each our receipts.

"Hi," I said. She looked me up and down, and then turned to Raheim. "Well, well, well, we never change, hunh?"

He blushed. I did too.

She pointed us to the stairs. "Ya'll enjoy the movie."

"Thanks," I said. "Nice meeting you."

"You too," she nodded. "I'll talk to you later." She pointed at Raheim, who chuckled.

As we got popcorn and soda from the concession stand, Raheim explained how Diana, his mother's sister's daughter, always got him in to the shows early. He usually came with his boyz, Derrick Carter, a.k.a. D.C., and Angel Lopez, the two guys I saw at Harry's the night we met.

"So, you dumped your boys for me, hunh?" I asked as we settled in the middle of the very last row of the theater, which consisted of five two-seaters.

"Yeah, but if I don' have fun, they back on tha list nex' week," he winked.

My smile said all that needed to be said.

The theater filled up quickly. It amazed me how many B-boys were in the audience with their B-girls. I guess the ladies wanted to see the film and dragged their husbands or hubbies to see it. It didn't seem like the ideal movie date: while a love story, it tells the women in the place that they don't have to take no shit from their men. I just knew that some of the fellas wouldn't be getting any later tonight.

The atmosphere in the place, though, was lovey-dovey: as the lights went down, the couples began cuddling up. Raheim also caught the cue – he slouched down in his chair, placed the popcorn and his right hand between his legs (which were wide open) and his left arm around my seat, letting it drop to my shoulder. With the soda in my left hand, I, in turn, moved a little closer and waited until after the public announcements and coming attractions to place my right hand on his leg. I let it spread out on his thick thigh ten minutes into the film (I didn't want to seem too anxious).

Sitting next to him was too much, but I managed to keep my eyes on the screen. And, not surprisingly, I loved the movie. It was a Hollywood melodrama musical, no question, but the music was slammin', the drama effective, the choreography kickin', and the costumes fierce. But it was the stars who made it. Like no one could do La Baker like Lynn Whitfield or Lady Day like La Ross, nobody could've done Tina like Angela. And Laurence was evil to the core as Ike. It was strange watching the man who gave African-American fathers their due in *Boyz N the Hood* doing a 360-degree turn with Ike, but that is the essence of powerful acting. And the chemistry between him and Angela was electrifying, especially during their brief but hot sex scene (which had me stirring in my seat and Raheim groping himself). I thought, If they are not nominated for Oscars, there is no justice in this world.

I couldn't get over, though, how much Laurence looked like my stepfather. Even the way he said Tina's real name, "Anna Mae," reminded me of how Anderson Walker calls his wife, my mother, "Annie." Unlike the character Fishburne became in the film (he didn't play Ike, he *was* Ike), Anderson ain't an abusive husband. He can blow his top, but he understands that swinging at his wife is not going to make him more of a man, or make him feel better, or, if he is angry at the world, help him get even with it. Besides, my brother and I wouldn't go for that, and neither would my mother, who, even though she is an inch shorter than me, would kick his ass. She has a black belt in karate

and taught my brother and me how to box. And, of course, she knows
how to swing a frying pan.

It was this issue in the film that got Raheim and me past the goo-goo
eyes and small complimentary talk as we sat across each other at BBQ,
a chicken-'n'-rib joint that has become a favorite homie hangout thanks
to its cheap prices and location (it's smack-dab in the middle of the
Village, surrounded by New York University's "campus"). Surprisingly, Raheim wanted to go to the BBQ that is in the heart of the East
Village (its clientele is far from banjee). But I wasn't up to walking.

"I don' know ... I don' think he did all that stuff ta 'er," he said,
placing more ketchup on one of his half-eaten cheeseburgers.

My eyes raised. Did he say what I thought he said? It was noisy in
the place, so I moved in closer. "What?"

"You know, there mighta been times when she ain't ask fo' it..."

I dropped my turkey burger on its plate. I couldn't believe my ears.
"Meaning she asked to be hit ... *sometimes?*"

He shrugged. "Well, you know how women sometimes ac'..."

"No, I don't. Why don't you tell me?"

"You know, females nag 'n' nag, get on yo' fuckin' nerves," he said,
taking a very big bite out of his burger. "That shit can drive ya crazy..."

"Or drive you to smack the shit out of them?"

His hands went up. "Yo, I ain't say that, a'right? All I'm sayin' is, if
he was such a bad motha-fucka, why she stay wit him all that time? She
shoulda lef'..."

"Why should *she* have been the one to leave?" I argued, my voice
going up. "She wasn't doing anything wrong, *he* was. And, besides, how
could she leave? He had all the money. She was terrified. When she
finally did leave — and mind you, she ran away, she didn't just pack her
stuff and walk out the front door with the kids, because she knew he
would probably kill her — all she had was the clothes on her back,
change, and a credit card in her purse..."

He cut his eyes at me. "You off yo' soapbox yet?"

That shut me up.

As he picked up his napkin and wiped his mouth, I tried to look
unbothered. I glanced at his plate: he had finished a burger already. I
then looked at and picked up my single turkey burger, which had only
one bite in it.

He sat back, rubbing his belly. "Regardless of wha' anybody say,
there are two sides to a story, an' 'til we hear his, it ain't right ta be
doggin' tha brotha," Raheim argued. "You a reporta. You know you
gotta have *all* tha facts, right?"

He was making sense and I couldn't help but laugh. "Right."

"Thank you," he bowed. "Now, you betta stop runnin' yo' mouth an' start eatin'."

"And what if I don't?" I asked, very sassy.

He looked around, moved in close, and glared at me. "I'm gonna eat it an' then spank yo' ass when we get ta yo' house."

I was gagging – not because he said it but because the idea intrigued me. He'd invited himself to my place. I had never wolfed down food so fast in my life.

We went straight there from the diner, stopping just to get some beer for him and Bartles & Jaymes for me. It was around midnight when we got to my place, and, as I let us in my apartment, he was in the middle of another tale about his life as a messenger.

"I was like, 'No, motha-fucka, I don' daliva packages ta people's houses, an' even if I did, I ain't goin' ta yo' place,'" he laughed.

"You didn't say that, did you?" I asked, turning on the hall light and locking the door behind him.

"Hell, yeah," he answered, following me into the kitchen. "He was on my dick. I woulda snuffed his ass, but I was on a run. Ev'ry fuckin' day somebody is sayin' shit like that."

"Well, walking around half-naked, you're gonna attract a lot of attention," I observed, imagining him in his uniform.

"Hey, I'm jus' doin' my job, ya know?" he said, putting the bag on the countertop and leaning against it. "That shit is ... wha' they call it? Yeah, sexual harassment."

"That isn't sexual harassment, Raheim, and you know it," I argued, taking a bag of pretzels out of the cupboard. "And you know you love it when people say stuff like that to you."

"Yeah, an' you should know 'bout that, hunh?" After his comeback, I turned around to find him just a few footsteps away in the living room, his arms folded across his chest with a very smug look on his face. Damn, he's so ovah all he has to do is *stand*...

"And what does *that* mean?" I loved playing this game...

"Nothin'," he replied, flopping his fine behind on my black Jennifer Convertible sofa bed. The only person who has ever slept in it is Adam, and his six-foot-three, 265-pound frame is too large for the mattress. Raheim glanced at and then picked up a picture of him that sat on the black coffee table my mother brought me as a housewarming present.

"Who this?" he asked, studying Adam, who was clad in black bikini briefs. The photo was taken at Action Park last summer.

I knew what he was thinking. "No, he is not my ex-lover," I consoled, passing him his beer. "He's my brother, Adam."

*"This* is yo' brotha?" As he took a swig of beer, he looked at the picture again and then looked up at me as I returned with my drink and the snack. "Day-am, wha' happened ta you?"

Many people wonder what happened to me. Adam is a carbon copy of our father, who was killed in Vietnam in 1972, just two weeks before he was expected home. Big, brown, and brawny. Most people can tell we are brothers, since we do look alike in the face — same slightly slanted eyes, thin brows, and long lashes, same full lips, same small forehead, same "taped" ears. But they also assume that I am the younger one, since I'm smaller. When we were both in high school, I got a serious complex because folks always joked about my size. But Adam was really big about it. He had no hang-ups calling himself my "little brother" and still doesn't. That always made me feel better.

"What can I say," I began, settling beside him and leaning over to see the photo. "He got the body, I got the brains."

"Hmmmm, look like I'm gonna hafta try botha ya'll out befo' I make up my mind," he said.

I tapped him on the leg, then reached for my drink. "Sorry, he's straight. But I ain't." I sipped sensuously. He laughed.

He put the picture down and went into his shirt pocket. He took out a cassette tape and walked over to the stereo. He squatted down over my floor-model Aiwa and placed the tape in one of the cartridges. He pressed Play and, still squatting, made his way back over to the coffee table, where he planted his beer and elbows. He folded his hands. There was a silly grin on his face.

I didn't even ask what we would be listening to — I knew it was going to be some mood music. I immediately recognized the elegant intro of Luther Vandross's version of "I Who Have Nothing" with Martha Wash. I couldn't help but grin, too.

"Like this song?" he asked, trying to look cute — and doing a very good job of it.

"Yeah," I lied. I did like the song but felt that both Luther and Martha were holding back.

"Sing," he announced.

I nearly choked on my drink. "What?"

"Sing," he repeated matter-of-factly.

I was floored. "Right now?"

"No, nex' week," he laughed, rising off his knees and sitting back down next to me, very close. "Yeah, now."

"I can't," I blurted out. I sat up on the couch to get away from him; he was turning me on so much.

"Why ... cat go'cha tongue?" He eased up, and was now all in my face. While his breath was kickin' with Bud, there was something sweet about it. I caught my breath.

"It's just that ... well ... I don't really sing, and, well ... you make me nervous," I stuttered.

"So you admit it, hunh?" he asked. "Tell me somethin' I don' know. You gonna sing ... fuh me. C'mon."

I gasped as he slid his left arm around my waist and almost carried me off the couch. He ushered me from around the table and, with that arm still holding me, cupped my ass with his right hand. His eyes held mine.

I got the message: I placed my hands on his shoulders and, as he stooped and slowly drew me into him, clasped the back of his neck. As my head made contact with his chest, I began to sing. Just like that.

Damn, what is he doing to me?

This was the first time I was asked to sing outside of a church and actually did it (with a little coaching, of course).

It was also the first time I slow-danced with a man without moving. For the entire song, we stood still but it was motion. Silent motion. Spiritual motion. Our bodies melting into each other.

And he smelled so good and felt so good that he made me want to sing.

"That was jood, Baby," he said, his lips brushing my ear as Luther & Martha faded out and Boyz II Men counted down to "Uhh Ahh."

"Thank you," I giggled, his tongue tickling my ear.

He called me Baby. That's right, with a capital B.

The real slow-dancing began. No, let's call it serious crotch rubbing. By the time the Boyz had repeated the title for the twentieth time, it had intensified to the point where our Uhh's became heavier and the Ahh's louder. We were both erect and, it seemed, on the verge of climaxing. I was wet and panting, and Raheim was about to bust out of his jeans when he whimpered, "No, Baby, not yet," slowing down the pace.

As Marvin Gaye began pleading for "Sexual Healing," it didn't surprise me when he said...

"So, you gon' gimme somethin' fuh my bir'day?"

Of course, I knew where this was leading, so I decided to play it dumb.

"Your birthday was last week," I answered. "It's too late."

"Baby, it ain't neva too late."

He called me Baby, *again*. And I liked that answer. I waited a few seconds, though, before I came back.

I peered up at him. "So ... what do you want?"

This time I got those incredibly white, straight teeth and the dimple. "You know," he beamed, squeezing my butt with both of his hands. "Some o' this."

I gazed into those eyes that had me hypnotized. I grabbed him by the neck. I kissed him on his chin. Then his right cheek. Then the left. Then his nose, making him giggle. Then his left eye, then the right. Then I zeroed in on his thick lips and...

How do I describe this kiss? Well, remember that TV show, *Love, American Style,* where, whenever folks puckered up, fireworks would go off? Well, when our lips met, it was like the Fourth of July. My head started to spin. The body heat, my temperature went up. I felt so light yet so heavy. It felt like I was floating. I felt so free.

By the time the kiss was over, I realized that Raheim had gotten off my belt, which was on the kitchen floor, and his hands were inside my overalls. And, for a guy who was supposed to be in a trance, I wasn't doing that bad either: I had tossed his hat (where it landed I didn't know), and managed to get off his shirt, which now draped the stereo. My hands were all up his undershirt.

"Day-am, Baby, yo' lips so juicy," he breathed, licking his own.

I would've said the same thing but I wasn't conscious when our lips met. So I planted another one on him to see if I could say it too. And I could.

"So are yours," I repeated. I stopped plucking his nipples and began stroking his head.

"Don' le' go, Baby," he whispered. He lifted me up. I knew what to do: I locked my legs around his waist, and, as we kissed again, he walked us into my bedroom. We fell on the bed and it was every man for himself.

By the time he undressed me and I unwrapped him (he may have seen this as his belated birthday gift, but he was really *my* present), I heard Marvin declare:

*Let's get it on...*

We did.

 As Sade sings, it's never as good as the first time.

To be honest, the only thing that made the first time different from any of the other sexcapades Raheim and I had is that it was just that — the first. But, there were other, important firsts that occurred that night (which we will get to later).

After six whole days of aching, craving, wishing I had him in my bed, I had him — and I couldn't control myself. I was overwhelmed, overjoyed, overwrought, just over him. My hands, lips, tongue, and teeth explored his terrain with a vengeance, leaving no nook or cranny, corner or crevice unconquered.

So, what did he smell like?

When I (finally) asked him what he was wearing as I inhaled him, he said, "I don' wear nothin'." Yup, that's just the way he smells. And the aroma is indescribably infectious. Everyone has their own body odor, and, unfortunately for some, being Sure ain't enough to suppress it. But one whiff of Raheim and my nose was opened. His scent permeated my nostrils and made me tingle all over. And it just made me want him more.

And what did he feel like?

While his physique was as solid as a rock, it was also as smooth as a baby's bottom. His clear skin didn't have a bruise, a blemish, or a blotch anywhere — not even on his big pretty feet. And the only cuts to be found were those that defined his manly muscle legs, manly muscle thighs, manly muscle arms, manly muscle hands, manly muscle abs, manly muscle chest, and manly muscle back. Uh-huh, a brick ... *howse*. I had a field day giving him a massage — rubbing, prodding, and knuckling as he called, "Ooooh, Baby, yeah..."

And, what did he taste like?

Well, let's say that I finally knew what the folks meant by "the blacker the berry, the sweeter the juice." He was the flavor of, not a

Hershey's bar, but a Häagen-Dazs dark-Belgian-chocolate-on-choco-
late-ice-cream bar. (Now *that's* sweet!) He was finger-lickin' good.
All-natural — no additives or preservatives — *mocha chocolata ya ya*. And
there was no need for dessert toppings, not even whipped cream or a
cherry (although we did experiment later on), because he was, as
Michelle surmised, a full-course meal plus the entire dessert tray — and
did I chow down!

I had to be feasting on him for an hour when he pleaded with me to
stop (I assumed he couldn't take the inspection anymore, which he did
pass with flying colors). But then he pushed my head toward the one
thing I was saving for last. I hadn't really gotten a good gander of it
until then, and, when I saw it in all its glory, I *gagged*. His shoe size *was*
a great indicator. No doubt thanks to my navigation, he was as long as
a Charleston Chew and thick as a cucumber. It looked so yummy, I
had to bite.

And it was just like M&Ms: it melted in my mouth, not in my hands.

As I licked him like a Charms lollipop, he begged me to swallow
him. *("No, Baby, don' fuckin' teeze me ... suck it!")*

And, when I did, he begged me to stop *("No, Baby, no...")*.

And, when I went all the way down on him, my nose tickled by his
neatly shaved and succulent-smelling pubic hair, he began trembling
uncontrollably, his teeth chattering as if he were caught in the cold,
snorting and stammering like Porky Pig.

I knew he couldn't take any more when he threw me off of him (I
wouldn't let go — I was greedy, what can I say?), screaming something
that sounded like Pig Latin. And then he came.

And came.

And came.

I swear to God, he must have been shootin' for a good minute and
a half. And I mean shootin'. Yeah, he's got a loaded weapon, an Uzi if
you will, and, if you tug it the right way, it'll getcha.

And he did get me. I couldn't get out of his path. He managed to
christen the comforter on the bed and my dresser drawer, which was
at least three feet away from the bed. Almost all of this happened
without his hand's help. That dick had a mind of its own.

I picked up the towel I had left on the night table earlier that evening
and wiped him, the dresser, and the bed up. When I thought the coast
was clear, I climbed in between his raised legs and lay on top of him. I
kissed his face as his body continued to jerk.

*"Oh, Bay-bee,"* he moaned, folding me in his big, strong arms. He was
still shaking. His eyes were still closed.

"Yes?" I asked, getting comfortable.

"That was *so* jood ... I ain't neva cum like that..."

I had heard that one before, but I bought it this time. (How could I not? It was the first time I had ever seen anyone cum like that.) He slobbered a kiss on my forehead. I was too happy with myself.

We took a little nap. It seemed like the natural thing to do. We slumbered for only maybe fifteen minutes, but it seemed like hours. I didn't feel him get up. I was awakened by a familiar feeling between the cheeks below my waist.

"I wanna fuck you..." He was on top of me. He already had my legs spread.

"You do?" I asked, being rather coy.

"Hell yeah, Baby, you know I do," he exclaimed, his arms slipping under mine, locking me in that position, and poking me with his sweet sticky thang. He opened his left fist to reveal a Zulu. "An' ya know ya wan' me to..."

Yeah, I knew I did. But, he was a big boy. We're talkin' *big*.

Sucking that chocolate joystick was one thing; being invaded by it, I knew, would be quite a different experience. I didn't think I could take it. And the idea that he might break me in two was a big possibility. He sensed my uneasiness.

"Wha's up?" he said, somewhat concerned.

"Well..."

"You ain't got tha package...?" He started to ease off of me.

"No," I protested, pulling him back. "Package" is what they call AIDS on the street. "It's just that I ... well ... I haven't done it in a while..."

He rolled off me and onto his left side. "How long?"

I sat up on my right side. "Like six months."

"Six months? *Day-am!* I ain't neva gone that long ... six days, maybe..." He paused. "So, wha'cha sayin'?" By the look on his face, I knew he thought I was going to say no.

"Yeah, I do want to do it," I said, brushing his chest. "I just want you to be patient with me, that's all."

"No prob," he shrugged. "I ain't gonna hurt ya. If I do, tell me, a'right?"

"OK. But I am pretty tight."

"Ooooh, I *like* that," he grinned, pushing me on my back. "But we can get ya a little loose."

And did he ever. It was then that I knew those thick lips, which were so incredibly cotton-ball soft, weren't meant just for kissing mine. He nuzzled my neck, nibbled on my ears, grazed the arch of my back, sucked my hard nipples, grooved across my torso, searched the insides of my thighs, trailed my spine, puckered my belly button, and, the thing that really had me going, parted my cheeks, making this baby's back go whack! He enjoyed this too, saying between blows, licks, and slurps, "Shit, Baby, you so fuckin' tay-stee..."

What made all of this even more mind-boggling was that I didn't expect him to do any of it. I mean, B-boys ain't exactly known for being giving. They usually like to be taken care of. Serviced. *Served.* My experiences with Royal and Ricky convinced me of this. But, of course, I had a lot to learn.

It all made me squeal and shriek with pleasure – and beg for it. "Oh, Raheim, fuck me ... please fuck me..."

"Ya sure, Baby?" he anticipated. We were right back in the position we started in.

"Yes...," I sang, throwing it at him.

His expression reminded me of how I looked when I was about to bust Ricky's cherry.

He positioned me in the middle of the bed and turned me on my back. He pushed my legs up and out. I tried to relax as he continued opening me up, this time using his long, thick, left middle finger. I was prepared for pain, but it didn't hurt at all.

I watched as he put the condom on himself in ten seconds flat.

"A'right, Baby, help me," he said. He proceeded to enter me, slowly. I braced myself again but was shocked when, a couple of minutes later, he moaned: "Ah yeah, Baby, I'm all in."

I couldn't believe it. *"What?* You, you're kidding?"

"Nah," he assured me. "An' you feel *so* fuckin' jood."

I held on to his shoulders and relaxed as he began to expand, sliding in and out of me. He grew larger and larger *and larger,* and with each thrust, our groans and grunts came together, each set louder than the ones before. I *loved* it.

"Oh yes, Raheim ... fill me the fuck up...," I cooed.

"Aw yeah, Bay-bee ... Le'me get all up in dat bad boy ... Ya like it, hunh?"

*"Mmmmm-hmmmm..."*

"Uh-huh...," he giggled.

He grabbed me around the waist and lifted me, so that we were sitting up. It is then that I *really* felt it. It all took me by surprise.

*"Oh, Raheim!"* I cried, not exactly in pain but flustered by the friction.

"Cool out, Baby, chill now ... jus' work it..."

After a little maneuvering, I found the right spot – and the feeling it gave me was unlike any I ever had before. I lost all control and started to, as he advised, work it. I gyrated my hips, up and down, left to right, using reflexes and muscles I never knew I had. I locked my legs around his waist and my arms around his neck. I licked his face and his bald head. He *loved* it.

"Yeah! Work dat dick, Baby ... Day-am you so fuckin' wicked...," he strained. He started whacking me on the ass. That really turned me the fuck on.

"*Sssss,*" I hissed. "Ooooh, whip it on me, Raheim, yeah..."

"Uh-huh, Baby, I'm gon' whip dat shit ... I'm gon' rock yo' ass..."

We tumbled back down. He drove his fists into the bed and proceeded to rock me, bumping and banging, grinding and galloping. I pulled my legs all the way back 'til they touched the bed. I grabbed a meaty handful of his ass, pushing him in deeper, *deeper,* inviting him to go where no man had gone before. We smacked between our sighs and cries of satisfaction.

"Uh-huh, Bay-bee, take dat dick!"

"Oh yes, Raheim..."

"Ha, ya want it, don'cha Baby?"

"*Yeeeaaaah! I want it, I want it!*"

"Oh yeah, Bay-bee ... ya wan' me ta take it, hunh?"

"*Take it, Raheim, take it, yeah!*"

"Ha, don' worry, cuz I'm gon' take it ... ya jus' gotta give it up ... now, give dat shit *up!*"

I did.

The scene was reminiscent of *The Exorcist.* Our faces were distorted, our eyes retreating to the backs of our heads. Our words were unintelligible, our hollering horrifying. Our breathing was so hot it was like fire. The headboard of the bed was drumming its own beat on the wall. The lamp on the dresser next to the bed fell to the floor. I could feel my blood pumping through me like raging waters out of control. I saw that his was, too; his veins were bulging through his skin. My body was twisting as if I were possessed. I clawed his back, digging my nails into his skin. Uh-huh, I was Linda Blair.

But when it was all over, he growled like a tiger; I purred and scowled like Eartha Kitt.

And then we came. And came. And came.

And with all that cumin' came a couple of other firsts: being fucked so jood, so right, that it alone made me climax. And, what's more, we reached it together. And it certainly wouldn't be the last time with Raheim.

I was the one having convulsions now. Not even Raheim's sweaty weight, pressed against me as he went through his own spasms, could hold me down. It was a good five minutes before I actually came down.

We were still for some time, just stirring. He then climbed off of me and out of bed without a word. I watched his big beautiful body strut out the door. The bathroom door hit the towel rack behind it. He took a leak.

I sat up and reached for the lamp, which I then remembered was on the floor, and just clapped my hands twice as the room light came on (that "clapper" gadget is a miracle). I wiped myself off, threw the comforter off the bed, and sat up. After the toilet flushed, I knew he was going to come back to the bedroom, throw on his clothes, tell me how he had such a great time, and that he'd call me (and, of course, they never do). He appeared in the doorway.

"Day-am, why ya turn on tha light, Baby?" He hit the wall switch off.

I didn't even have the chance to respond: he pounced like a panther, tickling me. When he finished, I was lying on top of him. He started spanking me.

"Stop!" I yelled.

"Huh, ya know ya like that shit, you freak," he said with glee. "Yo' ass is so fuckin' jood. I'm gon' have some mo' when I wake up tamorrow."

When he wakes up ... *tomorrow?* He was staying!

"Well, don't you want to get under the covers?" I asked, grinning and reaching to pull down the sheets.

"Nah," he mumbled. "They jus' get in tha way."

No argument from me. He spread out, his hands clasped behind his head and his feet touching the corners of the bed. I placed my legs parallel to his thighs. I rested my hands on his shoulders and was about to lay my head on his chest when...

"Yo, ain'cha gonna kiss me g'nite?"

I smiled. I did.

Which brings us to the last first of that night: I went to sleep with a smile on my face.

Wouldn't you?

 I also woke up with a smile. How could I not? That sleep was the deepest I ever had, the most peaceful. We were in the exact same position that morning as we were the night before.

My smile became wider after Raheim pulled me up to him, kissed me (yeah, the breath was stale but so what), and said: "Gimme some mo' o' that honey dip."

I knew exactly what that meant.

He slid from under me and put me on all fours. And, when it was all over, he was playing drum major on my ass and I hit an octave that made the dogs outside bark.

He collapsed on me. He smothered me. I *loved* it.

I looked at the radio/alarm clock on the nightstand and saw that it was only 7:45. What a way to start the day.

We caught some more z's. I woke up three hours later, very refreshed and very hungry.

"Mmmmm, I'm starvin'," Raheim mumbled, squeezing my thighs with his own.

"Well, what do you want to eat ... besides me?" I giggled.

"I don' know ... wha'eva ya got."

"Well, I'll fix us something."

"Sounds cool. I'm gonna take a showa."

He rose off of me and helped me out of bed. He held me. He kissed me.

Ahhhh. Delightful, delicious, delovely.

I walked behind him, my hands on his hips. I just couldn't get over his body — it was an immaculate conception. As he reached the bathroom, I gave him a nice slap on his ass.

"Yo, I do tha spankin' 'round here," he said.

"Well, you shouldn't have it all exposed like that."

"Uh-huh, keep talkin' shit," he grinned, closing the door behind him.

"There's an extra set of towels on the hamper," I called out into the door. I heard him pull the shower curtain back and the water turn on.

I skipped into the living room. I cleared the coffee table, dumping our beverages and putting the bowl of pretzels in the refrigerator. I took his shirt off of the stereo and put it on. It smelled just like him. My heart fluttered.

I picked up my belt from the kitchen floor and tossed it into the living room. It landed on the sofa.

I stood against the refrigerator, wondering exactly what I would cook. After such a grand night and morning, I decided to make a breakfast bonanza.

When Raheim walked into the living room he was greeted by plates of bacon, pancakes, and toast, and cartons of milk and orange juice, all set out on my dining table (which was really my grandmother's bid wiss fold-up that I got years after she died). It sat on the other side of the room, opposite the sofa.

"Day-am, Baby, this smells jood," he said, pulling up a chair and clanking the silverware. "This is wha'cha call breakfast."

"I waited 'til you came out so I could make your eggs," I yelled from the kitchen, standing over a hot skillet. "How do you like them?"

"Uh, ova easy."

Uh-huh, just like me.

Even though the hot oil, grease, and water were splattering all over the stove, the floor, and me, and the dirty dishes, pots, and pans were piling up, I didn't care. I usually clean up as I go along, but this time all I was concerned about was filling this man up the way he filled me up.

He didn't say a word as I fixed his eggs, and when I brought them to the table, I could see why: he had already stuffed down eight slices of bacon, three of the six slices of toast, three of the eight flapjacks, and was now guzzling down some o.j. – straight from the carton. He looked so p-h-y-n-e in my brother's white terry-cloth robe. He glanced up at me as I placed his eggs on his empty plate. He looked too cute when he was caught.

"Sorry, Baby," he said, putting the juice carton on the table. "It was almos' finish anyway..."

"That's OK," I said, taking a seat across from him. "I see that we have been enjoying the food."

"Hell yeah," he testified, drops of juice on his lips. Oh, how I wanted to lick them up.

As I made my own plate, he gobbled up his eggs. I watched him in amazement: he could certainly put it away. His not chewing his food, though, had a lot to do with it. They say you can tell a lot about a man from the way he eats his food. Raheim was no exception. And my body was a witness.

"Wha'cha lookin' at me like that fo'?" he grinned.

I guess I was staring. I reached for the syrup. "I was just thinking..."

"Thinkin'...?"

"Yeah, thinking how sorry I am that I let you shower by yourself. I wanted to help." It wasn't what I was really thinking, but it sounded good.

"Oh yeah?" he asked.

"Yeah..."

"You crazy," he laughed.

We ate the rest of the food in silence and over smiles. After he was finished, he drank the rest of the o.j. – yes, from the carton – and got up from the table.

"I gotta trek," he said. And as he rose, so did his love thang. It was just a-swingin'. In the daylight it looked even bigger and juicier. As he went into the bedroom, I followed it and him.

This was good-bye and I hated it. I didn't know what to say. All the usual lines – "I had a good time," "Hope I see you again," "Will you call me?" – didn't seem appropriate. While he dressed, I tried to be busy. I opened the window shades. I picked my own clothes up off the floor and hung them up in the closet. I took off his shirt, placed it on the bed, and put on a red St. John's University t-shirt and Fruit of the Looms. I remembered his tape, the thing that started it all. As I took it out of the cartridge, I saw his "X" cap behind the stereo speaker by the sofa. I put it on.

When I returned to the bedroom, he was tucking his jeans into his boots. I handed him the tape.

"Thanks," he muttered, taking it but not looking up.

I stood by the doorway. Say something, Mitch. *Say something*.

I didn't have to. After he put on his shirt, leaving it unbuttoned and outside his pants, he summoned me over with his hand, tapping the space between his open legs. I walked over. He palmed my buns, pulling me down. My knees fell on the bed.

"Well?" he asked.

"Well what?"

"You wearin' my hat."

I was. I took it off and placed it on his head. He chuckled.

"Why are you laughing?" I was a bit uncomfortable.

"You jus' actin' so silly." He fixed the hat to his liking, then pulled me in closer. "Thanks."

"For...?"

"Fo' a jood breakfast..."

"Well, you're wel–"

"...an' an even *jooda* bir'day present."

I blushed.

He grinned. "You bring out da dawg in me, Baby. I need ta have a bir'day ev'ryday..."

"Oh yeah?"

"Yeah..."

"Well, there's no law that says you can't."

His eyes flickered. His dark eyebrows jumped. "Oh yeah?"

I smiled. "Yeah..."

He looked at me and dropped his head. He looked at me again and then laughed, covering his face with his hand.

I pointed at his chest. "What's wrong ... cat got *your* tongue?"

He was still speechless even though his mouth was wide open. An "A'right..." finally come out. He rubbed his goatee.

I was enjoying this and decided to try him. "I'm sorry, but was there a part of that statement that you didn't understand?"

"Oh, no, don' *even* go there," he advised. "I heard you, I heard you right ... guess it's gonna be my bir'day again tanite."

I felt like doing a cartwheel.

I smiled. "Do you want me to cook?"

"Hell yeah, Baby, you can cook yo' ass off."

"What do you want to eat?"

"Anything, Baby."

Uh-huh, and you can *have* anything, baby.

We kissed. And kissed. And kissed.

"No, Baby, I gotta go," he mouthed, getting just as hot as I was.

"OK," I sighed, reluctantly releasing him from my grip.

I walked him to the door. He unlocked it himself. Just before he stepped out, he said: "Call ya lata. An' don' be givin' up my stuff ta nobody."

We both grinned.

"I'll be Black," he called as I watched him walk down the stairs. I watched him walk out the lobby door. I ran inside the bedroom and watched him walk up the block. As soon as he disappeared from view, the phone rang.

I picked up the receiver and spread out on the bed.

"Hell-o," I sang into the receiver.

"Uh-huh, I can just tell by that Kool-Aid smile comin' through the phone that he knocked dem boots," said Gene, who, I knew, was ready to take notes. Damn, Raheim hadn't even been gone a minute. Gene must have ESP.

"Yeeees," I sighed.

"So, how was it ... as if I didn't know?" he quizzed.

"Well..." How does one explain the unexplainable? How can I make him understand that it was the best — no, the joodest — I ever had? I discovered something that I knew would say it all...

"Let's just say that it was so, *so* jood that I ended up tearin' the sheets."

*"You what?"* I knew Gene had jumped out of his seat.

"You heard me," I said, slipping my fingers through the rips and holes I made. "He turned me out so well I had to turn myself back in."

"I see ... and what exactly does *jood* mean?"

"Better than good..."

"I see..."

"I fixed us breakfast. God, can he eat. He just left..."

"Oh ... so he stayed the night?"

"Yeah. I didn't think he would but he did. And, he'll be back tonight. I'm just too happy..."

"Well, I'm happy you're happy..."

"Don't do it, Gene," I snapped.

"Don't do what?"

He knew exactly what. He says that line from *All about Eve,* his favorite movie, every time he's being sarcastic. "We know you ain't happy about it," I accused.

"Come on, Mitch, if you had a fab time with him, I *am* happy for you," he argued. "But you know how you can get. A man gives it to you, uh, jood, and all of a sudden you're falling..."

"I'm not falling," I protested. "I'm just having a great time."

"Well, just remember that that's all it is to him."

After I gave him the 411 on Raheim (i.e., *how* he turned me out) and he told me about his third date with Carl, I thought about everything. I didn't think I was being anxious about Raheim, whose scent was all over the sheets and all over Adam's robe, which I was using as a pillow. After going without for six months, he took care of my appetite and then some. *And then some.* I wouldn't mind having him around for a while. Maybe we could get together every weekend. I'd cook and sing. He'd bring the music and his thang. He could keep my bed and booty warm. And, maybe we could become "friends."

I got more than I bargained for.

We spent the rest of that weekend — and every day during the next two weeks — doin' the wild thang.

It didn't matter when: morning, afternoon, evening, midnight, twilight...

It didn't matter where: in the bed, on the floor, on the sofa, over the sofa, on the coffee table, in a chair, over a chair, on the kitchen counter, in the bathtub, on the toilet lid, on the subway (off-off-peak hours, a la *Risky Business),* at the beach, in the park (uh-huh, doin' it after dark, oh yeah!), in a club (we didn't just dance the night away)...

It didn't matter how: lying down, lying up, lying over, lying under, bending down, bending over, upside down, right side up, sitting down, standing up, standing on my head, standing on my hands, doing a split, head over heels, heels over head (what can I say, I am very flexible).

It didn't matter the weather: rain or shine; hazy, hot and humid; cool, crisp, and calm...

It didn't matter if he didn't want to do it (which *never* happened) or I didn't (which did happen sometimes, but he always changed my mind, because I can't say no ... if he asks me).

Yes, the shit was always jood — so jood it'd make you wanna slap yo' mama.

I *thought* I knew what good sex was. But after Raheim, it was obvious that most of the sex I had during my first ten years as a sexually active homosexual was not. Compared to Raheim, all the men I loved before were just going through the motions. They couldn't get it up or get it goin' on like him.

Why?

Well, sex with Raheim wasn't just a physical act (although the physical certainly made it all the better). It was an out-of-body experience. He not only made my body come alive, but touched my spirit and soul. And this was all due to his sexitivity. He was the first lover I ever had who knew exactly *what* to do to me, *how* to do it to me, *when* to do it to me, *where* to do it to me, and *why.*

Every time we became One, I knew what my aunt Ruth meant when she said: "Heaven ain't just a place up in the sky. It's right here on Earth."

Amen.

**10** And, as a result of all this extra-ordinary curricular activity, I didn't have time to do much of anything else.

Which is why, exactly two weeks and a day after Raheim and I rose from our first night's sleep...

...the house was a complete mess. My mother, if she were to have dropped by, would have flipped. The floors needed washin', the furniture polishin', and the carpet vacuumin'. I did dishes only when I had no choice (meaning they had piled up in the sink, on the counter-top, and on the stove), and, at that moment, I had no choice. And there were clothes all over the apartment – in the bathroom, in the living room, in my office, even in the kitchen. I hadn't done laundry in over (you guessed it) two weeks, and both of us were running out of clean underwear...

...and...

...I hadn't returned any of the two dozen phone calls I received. They were all still on my machine. I had gotten three more between Saturday night and Sunday morning (give me some credit – I was at least keeping track of them). Raheim was still asleep while I listened to the latest...

"Yo, Mitch? It's Adam. Where the hell have you been? Everybody's been tryin' to get you. If you don't call me, I'm comin' over there to make sure you're all right. Ma is worried. I am, too. Speak to you soon. Later. Peace."

"Hello, Mitchell, this is your mother. This is the third time I'm calling you this week, and you know how I *hate* talking to these things. I'm going to church this morning. Please call the house and let us know you're OK. Love you, baby. Bye."

"Miss Thing, I know you there hangin' with the homeboy, so pick up the fuckin' phone ... Hello? *Hell-oooo???* Be like Aretha, and call me, before noon. Like, yesterday. *Ciao.*"

The last message was from Gene, who, I knew, was really pissed with me. The two times he managed to get me on the phone – and it figures that he would be the only one out of the bunch to accomplish that – we made plans to hook up. But, because of you-know-who, I didn't show up. The really bad thing is that I didn't even bother to call and let him know I wouldn't make it or say I was sorry for standing him up. Gene is known for being fashionably late whenever we go out, but that's because he has to make an entrance. I am never late for anything. I've never made plans with him and not kept them – and, knowing how he really felt about my rendezvous with Raheim, I knew he couldn't wait to read me.

After promising myself that I'd get back to everyone when I got to work, when I got home from work, or after Raheim and I took care of bizness (which even I knew wouldn't happen), it was time to face the music. So, after I busted the dust, practically polished the kitchen, and dumped all the garments lying around the house into a laundry bag, stopping to examine his undergear (Everlast ... uh-huh, it's not just a brand name) and smell every piece of his clothing (not even the musk and must could hide his scent), I sat on the sofa and dialed.

My mother wasn't home from church yet (it was just eleven, and early-morning service had just ended), so I left a message on Anderson's machine (my mother bought it for him one Christmas, but she refuses to touch it or learn how to use it):

"Hi, Mom, hi, Anderson. Just wanted to let you know that I am OK. Sorry, I've been ... a little busy lately. We'll talk later today, I promise. Love you two. Bye."

Next was Adam. He, too, wasn't home. Or was he? With him, you never know. Being the stud that he is, he might be ensconced at the moment. I left a message for him, too:

"Hey, little brother. Don't call out the National Guard, all right? I've just been so busy ... and you know what that means! His name is Raheim. We'll talk later. Love ya, big boy. Bye."

Last but not least was Gene. I was about to dial his number when the phone rang.

"Hello?"

"Well, it's about time. We finally get a real voice..."

It was B.D., a.k.a. Barry Daniels. When I first saw Barry, I wanted him bad. You hear me, *bad*. It was at a Kwanzaa party in the Bronx in 1990 that Gene and I attended to ring in the new year. B.D. is your classic pretty boy. He's what the elders would call "redbone" – very, *very* light-skinned, so light that back in the day he could almost pass (for white, that is). He has a small round face, hazel eyes, high cheekbones, a head full of brown wavy hair, and pretty pink lips. He's a couple of inches taller than me and has a serious medium-sized build. His legs, arms, and chest are packed.

But he is really stacked in the back. I couldn't take my eyes off of his butt — two bowling balls that you could serve a buffet on. Later that evening, I asked how he got such a great bod and booty. Besides his career as a dancer (at the time, he was with Alvin Ailey; he recently left to start his own "gay-identified" company, Nia, which means "purpose" in Swahili), he started pumping up as a preteen because he was getting chased home from school every day (he grew up in a small town named Calendar in South Carolina. "Not only was I a fine high-yella boy — and I knew it — I was also a faggot and proud of it," he chuckled. "But they weren't havin' it." Gene wasn't surprised he was from the South: "Child, they don't make butts like *that* in the city!"

My chance to meet him came when the clock struck twelve. After a silent prayer, everyone began hugging and kissing. B.D. was only one of a few people, though, kissing folks on the lips. I couldn't wait for him to get to me.

The kiss was nice. *Really* nice. But then he opened his mouth.

It wasn't his high-pitched, squeaky voice that turned me off (my voice ain't that deep, either). It was what he said with it. While he had a very interesting way of putting things (like his comment about his lovely looks), he fit the stereotype of a guy with a body and no brains.

Some examples:

He thought that having a "garage sale" meant you were selling a garage.

He thought that a "bookworm" is a person who loves to read books about worms.

When I told him that *Henry V* was one of my favorite plays, he replied: "Oh ... so parts I, II, III, and IV were no good?"

I know, I know, sounds too silly, right? Well, that's B.D. Dense, dense, dense. Brain dense.

"So what if he's not all there?" argued Gene, who felt that I should've taken him home that night. But you feel like you have to protect B.D., since he is so naive and childlike. And I would've felt guilty just plugging him (which is what I wanted to do). I didn't have the heart to do it (if anybody knows how it feels to be used, I do).

We did sleep together, though — he wanted to when he visited me at my house two months later (asking him for it was one thing; him asking me was another, and I sure as hell wasn't going to say no). He told me I was his "type" — a smaller, shorter guy to take charge of him. I had no problem with that. It was a one-time thing and it was really good. (He was another one who loved to do it all night, and, being in a long-distance relationship at the time that was on its last leg, I sure didn't mind catching up.) But we both decided that it would be best if we were just friends, which was easy, since we already were before that cold yet hot winter night. My brother, who thought we would make a cute couple, couldn't understand how we could just be friends. But most of the people gay men end up calling their "friends" they have been intimate with.

I'm convinced, though, that B.D.'s being dense is all an act – after all, it just gets him more attention. And, because he is so fine and doesn't look his age (he's thirty going on twenty), it makes people even more curious – baffled, but curious. I know I was.

One thing he *isn't* dense about is men. So, I knew he was dyin' to hear what Gene couldn't tell him about Raheim.

"Hey, what's up, you muscle queen," I joked.

"Don't even try it, Miss Honey," he warned. "Good to know you've finally decided to *cum* up for air."

"Don't *you* try it," I shot back, propping my feet up on the coffee table. "So, what's going on?"

"Hmph, I think the more appropriate question is, what has been going *up?*" It was Gene. I then realized that they were talking to me on Gene's speakerphone; that would explain the echo. They live only a few blocks from each other.

"Hey, Gene, I'm sorry, babe," I apologized. "You know how it is..."

"Oh, yeah, I know how it is, being dick-whipped," he calmly stated.

"I am not!" I exclaimed, flabbergasted.

"Ah, methinks the lady doth protest too much, don't you?" B.D. asked Gene. I just knew he had one hand on his hip, the other pointing to the phone.

"Damn straight," answered Gene, who I knew was puffing away and sitting on his brown leather sofa. "I don't know why he's gonna deny it. All the evidence points to it. And when you see this boy later today, you'll know it's the truth."

What were they talking about? "Excuse me?" I asked.

"Have you forgotten that today every homosexual in America is supposed to celebrate being a fag?" asked B.D. "We got six front-row seats, honey, and you and Raheim are invited."

"Oh, boy, I did forget," I admitted. It was Gay Pride Day and we always spend it together.

"Of course you did," retorted Gene.

"Well, after I do the laundry and some shopping, we can hook up..."

"Uh-huh, I've heard *that* one before," said Gene.

"But I don't know about Raheim...," I added.

"What, may I ask, is the purpose of celebrating this *joy*ous occasion if you don't have your man beside you?" B.D. asked.

"He is *not* my man," I corrected him.

"Then, what is he, then?" he continued. "You've spent every waking minute with him for the past two weeks, you've neglected your best friends..."

"Probably his family, too," Gene interjected.

"Oh no, you better *not* have been neglecting my boyfriend," B.D. warned. He was talking about Adam, whom he met at my twenty-fifth birthday party. Almost every guy at the party, including Gene, was lusting after him. But B.D. was the only one brave enough to walk up to him, start a conversation, *and* ask for his number. When Adam politely told him no, B.D. gave him his number on a piece of paper that said: "Call me when you've stopped being straight so we can get crooked."

See, he ain't *that* dense.

"Now that I'm thinkin' about it," he continued, "bring Adam instead. Maybe this could be his initiation."

Gene laughed. "Now *that* I would love to have a front-row seat for..."

"Look, I know Raheim has some things to do today, that's all," I explained.

"Yeah, like you," said Gene.

"No. But I'll see if he can meet us later on in the day."

"Well, he better do his damnedest to," advised B.D. "I think we deserve the chance to meet this chocolate-drop daddy. And, if he had any sense, he wouldn't let you loose on Gay Pride Day with thousands of men in the Village for the taking..."

"Funny, very funny," I said.

"We can meet you at our usual spot at like, say, five o'clock. By that time, the parade should be over," Gene said.

"And, Babyface will be joining us," added B.D. "He'll get off work at around five."

"Good," I said. "I'll see you guys later. I have to make breakfast."

"Oh, so you *have* to, hunh?" queried B.D. I could just see his eyes blinking nonstop. "Uh-huh, she *has* been dick-whipped."

"Will you two stop!"

"Well, I surely don't want you to get in trouble," giggled B.D. "See ya later, alligator."

"Yeah, bye, bitch," added Gene.

"I love you, too," I laughed. "Bye."

I hung up the phone and started on Raheim's special Sunday breakfast: Cream of Wheat, oven cinnamon toast, ham, and scrambled eggs with cheese, which his grandmother would make before she dragged him to church when he was "little." (Trying to picture him as "little" is hard, since, like Adam, he's been six feet since he was thirteen.) He hadn't had the meal in years, so when I surprised him with it, he freaked out. He said it took him back to the old days. For me, it was just another way to keep him satisfied.

It was over meals like this that Raheim opened up — a little. Being a B-boy, he's got the defense up; he's got to always keep people guessing — and on their guard. Every time I asked a question he didn't care for, he'd tense up — and clam up. But the way to a man's heart *is* through his stomach, so during our first two weeks together I did manage to find out that...

He was born and raised in the "boogie-down" Bronx. Now lives in Harlem. No siblings. Mother works "fuh tha city." Father? Whereabouts unknown. Is exactly six feet and 215 pounds. Has been a security guard, a salesman at a clothing store, and now a messenger for a year and loves it. ("It's betta than standin' 'round all day on my feet.") He's a high school dropout. Why? Won't say.

His likes? Sex (what a surprise), basketball ("Nex' bes' thang ta fuckin'"), Louis Farrakhan ("He tells folks like it is — especially them crackas"), Janet ("Tha's my girl. She got mo' class than all them Jacksons"), Chuck D. of Public Enemy ("He should run fuh president"), rap music ("Wha's not ta like?"), Michael Jordan *("He's* tha man"), Wheaties ("I can eat 'em all day"), and rainy days ("They jus' make ya wanna cool out").

His dislikes? White folks ("Wha's ta like about 'em?"), Caucasians who "act like us" ("Those motha-fuckas should be happy they white an' get ova it"), queens ("Yo, if you a fuckin' man, ac' like one"), Wednesday ("It's tha longest day of tha fuckin' week"), cops ("They don' pratec' nobody but themselves"), and Michael Jackson ("Yeah, motha-fucka, it *don'* matta if you Black or white, do it?").

I was chuckling about that last item when I heard the familiar sound of him taking a leak with the bathroom door open. After I placed the eggs, ham, and toast in a microwave dish and put the hot cereal on a very low boil, I headed for the bedroom. I found him on the floor, wearing only white briefs, doing one-arm push-ups. He was on number eighteen and had eighty-two more to go. His exercise regimen usually begins earlier in the day, like around six-thirty. It lasts about forty-five minutes. He starts with some basic stretching (standing and sitting up, on his stomach and back). He then goes into stomach crunches and push-ups, 100 each. When he does them, each movement is accented by a grunt that is similar to the kind he lets out when he's inside me, warming up. And of course, it is a sign of things to come: by the time it's all over, he's worked up a fierce appetite — for food and me.

I love to watch him pull, push, and pound, to see his cheeks fill up and let the air out like a balloon, and the sweat just a-droppin' off him like drizzle. It turns me the fuck on. I jumped over his legs, slapping him on the back, and took my usual position straddled in the middle of the bed.

"Ya need ta bring yo' ass down here an' work out, too," he said, not missing a stroke.

"Good morning to you, too, Pooquie," I smiled. Pooquie was the name of a black teddy bear I slept with for most of my childhood (in fact, he was the only "man" I slept with until I was sixteen). Like that teddy bear, Raheim is so cuddly and comforting. "Wha'tha fuck is a Pooquie?" was his first reaction to the name, but now he doesn't mind it — so long as I don't call him it in public.

"Uh-huh, wha'eva," he replied on number twenty-nine.

"God knows you do it enough for me and you," I argued. "Besides, I do enough exercise with you, and you wear me out. Ha, keep it up and I'll be bowlegged like you..."

"Don' gimme that cute shit, a'right," he said on number thirty-seven. "You got a nice little bit of a body, Baby, but it can be even betta."

I perked up. "Oh yeah?"

"Yeah," he breathed on number forty-four.

"OK." I got off the bed and bent down by his head. When he came up from pushin' number forty-eight, I slid myself under him. He stopped, placing both palms on the carpet.

"C'mon, now, Little Bit, I'm tryin' ta work out, now," he protested. *Little Bit*. Hmmmm, I *love* that...

"What do you think *I'm* tryin' to do?" I let both hands trail down his torso, which, I knew, drove him wild.

"C'mon now, don' start no shit," he huffed, trying to remain stable.

I tugged on his briefs, his dick popping out. "I like to start shit," I proclaimed, groping him and attacking those lips. He eased on top of me.

The Cream of Wheat burned — and so did we.

It is amazing how many white people there are on Gay Pride Day in the Vill.

Most heterosexual Americans view the lesbian and gay community as being white and male. This idea, for the most part, was created and is confirmed by (straight and gay) media images in which people of color and women are almost invisible ... like Gay Pride Day, the last Sunday in June. It's hard to find a colored face on local and national news coverage.

But, on any other day in the Vill, that ain't the way it is. For, while Greenwich Village is still touted (along with San Francisco's Castro Street) as "home" for the world's homosexual population, being the birthplace of what many consider the gay civil rights movement, the majority of the people who claim it as a safe haven, a place where they can be themselves without fear, are young men of African and Latino descent.

One hardly ever sees lesbians of *any* color. And those white gay men who do frequent Christopher Street seem to fall into two categories: (1) regulars at the strictly all-white bars (they don't say it but you know it), or (2) those "Looking for Mr. Mandingo," who seem to swarm like bees. In fact, I can't even begin to count the number of times I've been assaulted (not approached) by white men. After their indecent proposal, I'd throw my drink in their face or punch the shit out of them, all the while explaining that: (1) they have no right to touch me without asking; (2) I cannot be bought; and (3) I love color *au naturel,* not sun-soaked, cancer-causing tans, so I wouldn't be interested in going home with them anyway. Since they are used to getting what they want (after all, they *are* white), they protest: "But you misunderstand ... I'm not racist. I enjoy ... I *love* Black men." Yeah, *right.* Sorry, but I ain't bein' nobody's fetish or flavor of the night.

This patronizing, paternalistic attitude spills over into the world of activism, be it political, social, or cultural. I've worked, mostly on a volunteer basis, for a half dozen lesbian and gay groups, and every single time I've come up against this. Whenever I said something sensible (which was all of the time), you'd think I'd farted. Folks would frown, surprised that I could not only think but express my thoughts. And, when I had the unmitigated gall to run for office at a few of these organizations, I was told, both directly and indirectly, that in order to get white support, I couldn't be "too Black" and that I'd have to find myself a white boyfriend. Of course, I wasn't having it.

There are, though, too many gay men of color (and one is too many, in my book) who believe the hype: in order for them to be recognized for their talents, to do work for or be christened a "leader" of their own ethnic group, to be viewed as a part of the (white) gay community, they have to walk, talk, and sleep white.

Which makes Gay Pride Day such a farce. We all come out (pun intended) for this big, big, *big* party, looking somewhat like a "community," showing the world that we embrace "diversity" and denounce bigotry and indifference (after all, we have to if we expect to be seen as a *real* minority group, right?), when we know it's all a show. White homosexuals can be just as (if not more) racist as their heterosexual cohorts, and the nonrelations between the races and the segregation in the Vill are proof.

But everybody loves a party – especially us homosexuals. So we celebrate the Stonewall Uprising of 1969, when some of the children had all they could take from the cops raiding their predisco den of escape. It all starts with a parade that ends all parades. They say the freaks come out at night and, having hopped many a club in my day, I can say that that is true. But on Gay Pride, you get *the* Freaks, OK? We're talkin' the Three-Thing Circus: drag queens, transvestites, and transsexuals, all made up (or made down) to prance, prance, prance. You got your tattoo and piercing fanatics; and, of course, your leather men and women, who, I know, are hot walking around in their getups in ninety-degree weather. Heterosexuals point to all of these people when they argue that our "lifestyle" is sadistic and sick. But these folks are only a small part of the community. And, while many heteros will certainly deny it, these folks can also be found in the straight community in greater numbers.

It was five-fifteen and the Freaks were still traipsing down Christopher (the parade is usually way over by then) as I stood off of Seventh Avenue in front of Tiffany's, that infamous 24-hour diner where you can bet the person next to you or across from you is a homosexual. You see it all: the humble beginnings of a love affair, the dramatic endings of a love affair, the before or after meal-ticket transaction between a trick and his treater of the moment, and those one-of-a-kind, chance meetings – like the one that happened between Gene and me in 1989.

It was my first time in the Vill. I had heard about it in high school and college but was scared to go. Why? First, I had no one to go with. I had no gay friends (or, at least, none I knew were gay), and my brother, my closest friend in the world, might have accepted his brother as a homosexual but he sure as hell wasn't going to fall up in a gay bar with him.

Second, I had read a lot of books, magazines, and journals about being gay, but I had not actually experienced what they called the "gay life." I'd never been in a social setting with other gay people. Maybe then, I argued, I would see images of myself that I didn't find in any of the literature I came across. The Vill seemed to be the place to go for this exploration and education. It cost nothing but a token (the subway) and, so I was told, never closes.

It was a summer-on-the-horizon late afternoon in June that I went. I was too through to be around so many men who looked *and* loved like me. And what's more, most were so p-h-y-n-e, all that and a bag of chips to boot. I just walked and walked and walked – and cruised and cruised and cruised. It seemed all a tease, though; none of the fellas I made eye contact with tried to talk to me (maybe I was looking a little too desperate). And I guess my following half of them around didn't help matters (I guess I scared them away). But I was feeding on it all – by the time I looked at my watch, I realized that I had been out and about on my feet for four straight hours. Time *does* fly when you're having fun.

I was hungry, so I ducked into the first place I saw. I took a seat in a booth by the window so I couldn't miss anything. I didn't see the waiter place a glass of water and a menu on the table – or hear the stranger's voice.

"This is your first time, hunh?"

I did hear the tap on my table. I turned to see a man sitting in the two-person booth across from me. He had wide-set brown eyes, a big forehead, a pinched nose, and big juicy red lips. His skin was copper-colored. His black curly hair was trimmed on the sides and in a low fade on top. He was wearing what I would learn are his usual rags: a silk shirt (this one white), slacks (this pair black), and casual shoes (black penny loafers) with no socks. He was attractive.

"This is your first time, isn't it?" He tapped on his own table with a spoon.

"What do you..."

"Here ... in the Vill?" He picked up a cup and sipped. It looked like coffee was in it.

"Yeah ... how do you know?"

He snickered. "Child, the way you droolin', it's got to be. You'd think you never saw a man before..."

"Well, of course I have," I said, sticking up for myself. "It's just that..."

"You've never seen so many in one place, right?" he winked.

"Right..." I smiled. At that moment, I was so tickled that someone had finally talked to me that I decided to keep the convo going. "I take it it's not your first time, hunh?"

He coughed. *"My* first time? Ha, I haven't heard *that* one in years!"

"Would you like to join me?" It came out of my mouth so fast that I didn't even realize what I had said until he scooted over, bringing his coffee, newspaper, and black hat with him.

"Eugene Roberts, but everybody calls me Gene," he said as his arm extended across the table.

"Mitchell Crawford." He had a firm grip for such a slim fella. He was a few inches taller than me.

"So, do you always invite strange men to join you for a bite to eat?" he asked, sitting back.

"No, but you seem harmless," I reasoned.

"Ha, looks can be deceiving, my dahling," he grinned, as the waiter came over to take my order.

We sat at that booth for the next three hours, just talking and talking and talking. He took me on a tour of the Vill – I was so wrapped up in the boys that I failed to check out any of the bars, video peepshows, and bookstores. That night I went home with him, but I slept on his living room sofa alone (there was a little attraction there, but it was really based on my overall reaction to the Vill and his ordinary flirtatious character). Over the next few weeks and that summer, we became best friends as he showed me the ropes – taking me to all the hot nightspots and introducing me to new people.

One of those people was Courtney Lyons, a cute-as-a-button brother clocking in at six feet, five inches, with dark brown dred-locs, almond eyes, plump cheeks, a lean frame, and, like me, skin the color of a brown paper bag. Born in St. Croix and reared in Philly, he's a N.Y. assistant district attorney (you know they just *gag* when he comes into the courtroom). He is known as "Babyface," since he has that fresh-faced look (like he just stepped off a bus from the backwoods of Alabama or Mississippi). Like B.D., he is thirty. Unlike B.D. and Gene, he is always on time (he knows that time is indeed money). And Gay Pride Day was no exception.

He sneaked up behind me, lifting me up off the ground. I let out a shriek. I recognized his scent (Borsalino).

I pulled on his hands. "You better be careful, B.D. might get jealous."

"Hey, what he don't know won't hurt him," he smiled.

B.D. and Babyface have been "boyfriends" for a year and a half. Gene believed it wouldn't last a month and I had to agree. They have absolutely nothing in common. B.D. is loud. Babyface is soft-spoken. B.D. is dense. Babyface is very worldly. B.D. loves to party hearty. Babyface is a homebody. B.D. loves to work out at the gym. Babyface? You couldn't drag him to Jack LaLanne's. B.D. is into Jody Watley and Patti LaBelle; Babyface is into Dinah Washington and the Duke (of course, B.D. thought it was John Wayne). The only thing Gene and I saw that could link them was a difference: B.D. is a bottom, Babyface a top.

That, for some, would be enough.

Babyface, though, says that it is precisely those differences that made him fall in love with B.D. It was a first-sight thing for him. B.D. is everything he wishes he could be – outgoing, outspoken, and just plain *out*. After they met at Gene's thirty-third birthday bash, he courted the boy like mad for six months – sending him flowers, candy, gifts. B.D. didn't know how to handle it. No one had ever done that for him before. He says that Babyface's persistence – as well as "his dick that won't quit" – encouraged him to give the man a chance. And, now, to Gene's utter dismay, they are like lovebirds.

I always wondered, though, how Babyface feels about me. Like I do with B.D. and Gene, I hug and kiss him on the lips when we greet each other. But Babyface gives me more than a peck – which gives me a shiver.

"Damn, that kiss doesn't say hello, it says *hell-o!*" I said, pushing him away.

He just blushed. "So, where's Grumpy and Dopey?"

I slapped him on his hairy chest, which was exposed. He was wearing an Africentric short-sleeve shirt, blue jeans, and brown sandals. "How can you call your own boyfriend Dopey?"

"How do you know I was calling *him* Dopey?" He stood there, twirling his black leather shoulder pouch with that baby-boy smile. All I could do was laugh.

As if on cue, I heard B.D.'s voice coming through the crowd of people on the corner. One always hears B.D. before they see him. He and Gene were walking arm in arm, like sisters. One would assume that they were, given how they kee-kee with each other. Gene had on that mustard long-sleeve shirt-and-pants set I love; B.D. was his usual trampy self in a white bodysuit and sneakers. Babyface scooped him up in his arms and kissed him, the only surefire way to shut B.D. up.

*"Puh-leeze,* B.D., didn't I say for you two to at least wait until we were indoors?" announced Gene, who had his back turned to them. They continued to smooch.

"Will you quit," I said. "You're late, as usual."

"You know it," he proudly stated. "You know how I am."

"Yeah, I sure do. So, is person number six Carl?"

He rolled his eyes and sighed. "Yes, it is. But he won't be here 'til six-fifteen."

"Six-fifteen, hunh? How punctual. Well, you finally bring him out of the woodwork..."

He leaned against a parked car. "Never mind him, what about person number *five?"*

"He should be here any second now."

And, as if he knew we were talking about him, Raheim appeared. I had never seen so many people gasping for air, gawking with their eyes, grasping their cheeks, and gagging at the mouths. A pathway was cleared for him as he bebopped his way toward us, but by the time he stopped in front of me and said, "Wha's up, Baby?," a semicircle had formed around us. And for a good reason: he was wearing orange bikini briefs, black boots, and an orange Syracuse U cap. Gold hoops were in both ears and a thin gold chain choked him. A black leather bag was on his back, sunglasses on his face, and his skin was glowing. I felt overdressed in a white BGM (yes, Black Gay Man) t-shirt and black jean shorts.

"You certainly are dressed for the occasion," I said with a nervous laugh, squeezing his hands.

"I ain't had nothin' else ta wear, Baby," he explained. "An' you know why."

Yes, I did. Did I mention that I didn't have the chance to do the laundry? While I'm sure that Raheim had other clothes at home, there was an outfit in the dirty clothes that he really wanted to wear. "If I can't wear it, I ain't wearin' hardly nothin'," he told me as we stretched out on the carpet in the bedroom after, you know. And he wasn't lyin'.

While Raheim didn't seem bothered by the attention he was getting, I was — and so was Gene. I knew he would have something to say to the crowd — and he did.

"Ex*cuse* me, but what the hell do you mother-fuckers think this is?" he yelled into the air, causing a couple of Caucasians just a few footsteps away from Raheim, their eyes bulging and tongues wagging, to jump. "This is *not* an auction block and he is *not* for sale!"

All three of us broke out into laughter. I turned to see B.D and Babyface, but they weren't behind us. They then came out of the restaurant. B.D. was beside himself.

"My, my, my, my, *my,*" he said, walking straight up to Raheim and holding up his hand for Raheim to kiss, which he did. "I'm Barry, Barry Daniels. But everyone calls me B.D...."

"Yes, which stands for brain *dead,*" Gene piped in.

He turned to Raheim and held out his hand. "I'm Eugene. Everybody calls me Gene. Sorry about that outburst. Hope I didn't offend you..."

"Nah," Raheim said, shaking his head. "It's better you did it, cuz I woulda busted in some faces. I love ta see white folks put in they place."

"Ah...," Gene observed, glancing at me. "I think we'll get along just fine..."

Babyface gave Raheim one of those serious handshakes like a brotha on the corner. "I'm Courtney. They call me Babyface."

"Hmmmm ... B.D., Babyface, Gene ... and Little Bit," Raheim pondered, stroking his clean-shaven chin.

*"Little Bit???"* said the Three Musketeers in unison.

I shrunk, trying to hide behind Raheim.

"Well, *Little Bit,* a table is ready inside, so let's go," said B.D., who swung his arm around my shoulder and marched me to the door. Once inside and a few feet away from the others (Babyface was saying something about not being bold enough to wear such an outfit in the street, to which Gene replied: "Why would you, you pole, you don't have much to show!"; Raheim giggled), B.D. let it all out.

*"Now* I see what all the fuss is about," he began. "Girl, *he* is what you call a manwich. I'm sure that his Ball Park frank really pumps when ya'll get cookin' and them chocolate pound cakes must be as moist as a Duncan Hines triple-layer. He is just a mouth-watering morsel of masturbatory motivation."

*"A what?"*

"Oh, we're ready now," he said to the host, a short, rotund Greek gentleman who showed us to our booth.

"He's a what?" I asked again.

"That man is too, *too* fine, honey, even Stevie Wonder could see that," he went on. "He could keep me cumin' for days, which I'm sure you already can attest to..."

I nodded my head in disbelief. "You have a dirty mind."

"Well, you sure as hell ain't been teachin' him his ABCs," he argued, as we sat down.

"No, I haven't," I said as Raheim took off his bag and handed it to me. *"He's* been teaching me."

"Wha' I been teachin' ya?" Raheim asked.

I placed my leg over his thigh and tasted his lips. "All the right moves."

"Well, *all* right!" B.D. exclaimed.

All eyes were still on us — or, rather, Raheim — even after we ordered. I was still a little self-conscious, all of these folks basically dissecting him/us with their eyes. But Raheim took it all in stride. In fact, he was so relaxed that he was what you could call the life of the party. I assumed I would have to steer questions in his direction or bring up subjects I knew he would want to talk about. But, to my surprise, he took command of the conversation — filling us all in on how he was almost mobbed coming to meet us; complimenting Babyface on his shirt, which led to a discussion on Africentrism; asking Gene about his job and some of the rap acts he handles; and basically driving B.D., who grilled him like a cheese sandwich, crazy with his charm.

I sat back and enjoyed it all, squeezing him here and tickling him there. At one point, I was sitting in his lap. B.D. and Babyface also got in on the foreplay — especially when the food came. B.D. and Babyface had salad plates and fruit. Babyface teased B.D. something awful with a strawberry, and B.D. did some very suggestive things with a banana. Raheim and I shared a chocolate shake — spooning and brushing what was left on our mouths with our pinkies, tongues, and lips. These were what you would call Kodak moments.

Of course, Gene was disgusted by it all. But his tune changed when Carl, looking sharp in a lime green shirt-and-short set and open-toe sandals, showed up at 6:15 on the dot. Carl had already eaten, but he was hungry for something else — so he started feasting on Gene's neck. The look on Gene's face — obviously enthralled but trying to play it cool — made us all cry laughing.

By the time we fell out of there, the parade was finally over but the crowd hadn't dispersed. In fact, there seemed to be more people than earlier. We all walked in our separate duos — Gene and Carl were first, shoulder to shoulder; B.D. and Babyface were second, hand in hand; Raheim and I took up the rear, me holding on to his left arm. We were so into each other that we didn't pay any mind to the passersby still flipping over Raheim (and wondering, I'm sure, how I roped him).

I occasionally glanced at the exhibit booths on either side of the blocked-off streets, hawking products and services by and for gay folks. One disturbed me: an S&M table with the works of Tom of Finland on display. I have to admit that the man was talented. But has anyone noticed how all of the men of African descent he created are really, *really* dark? And that most are in submissive slave roles? I'm pretty sure that was not by accident. One of these drawings was blown up into a giant poster: a naked brother, hanging from his wrists off a tree branch, being lashed with a long bullwhip by a white man wearing only knee-high leather boots. And *both* men are enjoying it – they are cuming. Yeah, right: the nigger enjoys getting his back, ass, and legs ripped apart. There were no brothers sitting at that table, and if there were, such an image surely would not have been chosen. (Or would it have?) I then remembered that Gene had confronted the people at that table about the very same picture the year before. They didn't care if it was offensive; it's a freedom-of-choice-and-speech issue, they argued (uh-huh, my ass). It's obvious what they think of us and what they would do to a fella like Raheim, who caught the eye of a Mr. Clean–look-alike standing by the table. He started slapping a short whip against his leather pants and licking his lips. Knowing what was going through his mind – and knowing how many times what he wished he could do to Raheim *did* happen to African males during slavery (females weren't the only ones beaten and raped to satisfy the sadistic sexual proclivities of Massa) – made me want to throw up. I moved in closer to Raheim (who was inching along at a snail's pace, oblivious to what was going on, since he was grooving to his girl's new single, "That's the Way Love Goes"), and hurried him past their setup.

As the song was going off, I spotted a white man out of the corner of my eye who seemed to be following us. He was as pale as a sheet, had beady blue eyes, no lips, stringy black hair, wore Coke-bottle black-framed glasses, black jeans, a black Megadeath t-shirt, and old white Pro-Keds. There was a 35mm camera hanging on a strap around his neck. When we reached the end of another block, I didn't see him behind us anymore. But then Raheim jerked toward me.

"*Yo*, wha'tha *fuck* is wrong wit you?" I could tell by the look on his face that the man must have touched Raheim, more than likely on his shoulder, which is where he was hitting himself as if he were trying to rub some dirt off.

"I'm sorry but I was just trying to get your attention," he smirked. "Are you a model?"

"No, I ain' no *fuckin'* model," snarled Raheim. A crowd of folks were stopping to watch.

The man grinned. "You should be. You are so ... striking. You can make lots of money with, uh, a body like that. I'd love to be the first to do you."

"Sorry, but I am the only one who does him," I stated coldly. Others around us snapped their fingers including B.D., who said, "Read him!"

"I can take some shots of you now and after you see how photogenic you are, you can come to my studio and pose for me," he said, messing with the mechanisms on his camera. "I can pay you if money is a problem..."

I tugged on Raheim. *"You are the problem. We are not subjects for you to exploit, so walk."*

He hurried in front of us as we began to walk away, holding up his camera ready to shoot. "Now, just give me a hard look to start..."

I jumped in front of him, throwing my hands over the lens. *"What part of that statement did you not understand? Walk!"* He sucked his teeth, mumbled something under his breath, cut his eyes at me, gave Raheim a serious once-over, and walked.

People around applauded, but I could tell Raheim was shocked at what I did, embarrassed that I stuck up for him. But he listened intently as I explained that Mr. Snapshot was just another one of those bastards who takes pictures of *us* for *them*. I've heard too many stories about men of color being lured into the "studios" of white photographers. They end up seeing their face, body, or both everywhere, but they don't see a damn dime. Meanwhile, Mr. Snapshot rakes in the dough off of those photos for years.

And that whole "pictures for money" scheme makes me think of one thing: Jeffrey Dahmer.

"So, you was pratectin' me, hunh?" he questioned.

"Yes," I answered. "If anybody is going to take pictures of you, nude, half-nude, or otherwise, it's gonna be me."

"Oh yeah? You got a cam'ra?"

I pinched his nose. "I don't need a camera."

"You so fuckin' crazy, Little Bit," he laughed.

There were six other Mr. Snapshots (all white) who asked to shoot my Pooquie. And, as we stood against a police barricade in front of Killaretha's a few hours later with the crew, sipping on Slurpees (the sun had finally gone down, but it was still hot as hell), number eight came up to us: a light-skinned fella, maybe in his late thirties, who was my height and size, but had small eyes, cropped brownish red hair, and a goatee.

"Excuse me..."

Both Raheim's and my hands went up.

The man returned the gesture. "Please, I know you've probably been asked the question a million times today, but I'd really love to publish your photo in my magazine."

"What magazine?" I asked, uninterested.

He had a copy, which he handed over with a business card: "Graham Gardner, Editor & Publisher, *The Baldwin Bulletin.*" The publication was the size of a newspaper, maybe forty pages. Perry Watkins — the first person to successfully challenge being discharged from the military because he is homosexual — was on the cover. The headline read, "The Forgotten Warrior." After I checked to find Graham's name on the masthead, I leafed through it as Raheim asked questions while slurping.

"So, wha' kinda magazine is this?"

"It is by and for gay and bisexual men of African descent," he explained. "After watching too many publications that are supposed to be about us ending up being for others, I stopped complaining and decided to do something about it..."

"I hear that..."

"This is only our second issue," he continued. "Our third will be out in about a month, and these photos will be featured in our summer-in-the-city spread from around the country. You two would be a great lead photo."

"Wha's that?"

"The first page of the spread, which will be given to just one couple."

"Ge'tha fuck outa here." Raheim looked down at me and nudged me with his knuckle. "So, Little Bit, wha'cha think?"

Graham smiled. "Little Bit..."

"Looks good," I said to Raheim. "Do you want to do it?"

"Hell, yeah, if it's gonna get us a whole page. We gonna be stars." He scooted from behind me to place the Slurpee cup in the garbage.

"OK," I said, pulling Graham to the side, "but you can only use our first names."

"Can we use your nicknames? The readers would love it."

"OK. I call him Pooquie, P-O-O-Q-U-I-E. But don't tell him about it. I want it to be a surprise."

"Gotcha," he replied, scribbling away.

When Raheim returned, Graham captured us in a variety of poses — most of them staged by B.D. Graham had approached him and Babyface first, but Babyface said no. So did Gene and Carl, who, just before we began our photo shoot, said their good-byes for the evening.

I told Gene we had a lot to talk about. "Yeah, we do," he replied, "but who knows if we'll be able to get you on the phone again!"

After we had a mini-argument (which B.D. enjoyed watching) about him wearing his glasses (which he did take off), Raheim and I were snapped in front of a brick wall, embracing each other, looking serious. In the next take, we were all smiles, with Raheim hunched over and folding me into him. After much prodding from B.D. and Graham (and a few pecks from me), Raheim picked me up and twirled me, as Graham got some action shots. "Mahvelous!" screamed B.D. "What fun..." It was.

After it was over, B.D. and Babyface left. I gave Graham my address so that he could mail us a copy when it was published.

"And, by the way, we're looking for writers," Graham said.

Raheim pointed at me. "Yo, ya got one here."

Graham smiled at me. "Great. Hopefully, we can expect to hear from you."

"Yeah," I mumbled.

"Thanks, brothers," he said. "We'll be in touch."

As Graham walked away, Raheim stretched his arms, looking somewhat content. "Always gotta help out tha brothas."

"Yeah...," I said, putting the card in my pocket. I wrapped my arms around his waist. "So, did you have fun today?"

He sighed. "Yeah ... but I ain't think I would..."

"Why?"

"Cuz, Baby, I ain't know how they would see me," he explained. "I mean, I guess I thought they was gonna be all stuck-up. You a journalist, they all got important jobs an' shit. I ain't nothin' but a messenga..."

"You are a *great* messenger, Raheim," I corrected. "And that's not what defines you. You are funny and up-front. They liked that. I can tell."

"Yeah?" His facial expression told me he still wasn't sure.

"Yeah ... is this why you were Mr. Personality today?"

"Huh?"

"You were talking up a storm. You talked more in the past few hours to them than you have to me in the past two weeks — and *I've* been slaving over a hot stove for your ass!"

He blushed.

I pulled his face down to mine. "You don't have to impress anyone. Not even me."

I kissed him — *down*.

"So, tell me what you thought of them," I said, holding on to his shoulders.

He put his left arm around me and talked with his right. "Gene is a'right people. Babyface, he a real cool brotha. Ha, B.D., he jus' wack. An' he got back, *woooo, bay-bee!*"

"Excuse me?" I shook him as best as I could.

"But it ain't like my Baby's." He gave it a squeeze.

Just then, folks started running toward the dock.

"Oh, the fireworks must be starting," I assumed.

"So, you wanna see 'em?" He was looking off behind him.

I grabbed his face and turned it around. "No ... let's go home and create our own."

We did.

 Isn't it great having a man around the house?

I have had overnight guests. I've even had a gentleman caller spend the weekend with me. But Raheim was the first man who became a "regular."

He made himself right at home – and I loved having him around...

I loved finding him at the house when I got home – sitting on the stoop or messing with his bike (oilin' it, pumpin' it, washin' it, or just standin' by it lookin' so jood).

I loved that hello kiss.

I loved to massage his shoulders as he unwound, telling me about his day.

I loved to watch him as he relaxed on the couch, watching me in the kitchen as I made dinner.

I loved to see him eat. And eat. And eat. I never had to worry about there being leftovers.

I loved it when he'd help me with the dishes (even though he'd usually park himself on the counter and keep me company).

I loved to hear the *bang, bang, bang* of his feet, stomping around the house as if he paid the rent.

I loved hearing that bold voice, booming from one end of the house to another...

"Hey, Baby? We got any eyedrops?"

"Little Bit? You read this shit 'bout Dinkins? They givin' tha brotha hell..."

"Day-am, Baby, that smell so fuckin' jood."

...or up close...

"Little Bit? It's time ta get busy..."

And, like Aretha, I *jump to it.*

I loved to hear him laugh – I could sense it traveling from his funny bone to his mouth, which would open wide, the sound boomeranging off the walls.

I loved to sing to him (and why not – he filled my heart with a song).

I loved it when we maxed on the sofa in each other's arms, me sitting on or in his lap, watching TV, listening to music, reading, or just gazing...

I loved to watch him undress. "Wha' *you* lookin' at?" he'd always say, as he stripped down to his birthday suit. And I'd always smile: "You."

I loved it when he'd let me undress him.

I loved it when he'd rip off my clothes – *Ooooh yeah...*

I loved wearing his (for me) giant shirts, either to lounge around or sleep in (of course, I'd never sleep the whole night with it on).

I loved it when he'd walk around the house naked, his thang just a-swingin' and his booty just a-bouncin'.

I loved helping him wash away his day-old funk, soaping and lathering him from head to toe, using my hands as a washcloth and my breath as a towel.

I loved rubbing him down. And up. And all around.

I loved to lie in bed in his favorite position: he, on his stomach; me on top of him; both of us naked.

I loved to sleep with him.

I loved hearing his heart beating against my chest or back, his light snore, his heavy yet peaceful breathing, the faint sigh that escaped as he shifted his weight, the "Little Bit" and "Baby," sometimes whispered, sometimes mumbled, as if he was making sure I was still there.

I was.

I loved to sleep on top of him. I loved to sleep underneath him. (I really had no choice – he was such a space and cover hog that, if I slept beside him, I'd end up in a corner of the bed).

I loved it when he woke me up with a kiss on my lips – or a bump 'n' grind to the booty.

I loved the smell of him in the morning – the nighttime mix of sleep, sex, and self created one ardiforous aroma. I'd cling to him, taking him in before he worked out and then hopped in the shower.

I loved sitting on the toilet lid or standing in the doorway, watching him brush his teeth; gargling with Scope; shaving and shaping up his head (sometimes I'd help him), mustache, and goatee; standing in a towel, Adam's robe, or nothing at all.

I loved preparing him for the day. Yeah, I helped him pick out his outfit, socks and all, and ironed if needed. And, yeah, I made sure he didn't leave without the most important meal of the day (no, not me!). Even if it was just Wheaties, I'd have the bowl, the spoon, the milk (in a glass because he ate them plain), and a banana (his favorite fruit) waiting on the dining room table. And let's not forget the morning paper, usually *USA Today*. He liked to know what was going on in the world, not just in New York, which, he argued, the dailies couldn't even cover well.

Yeah, it was all ready for him – with a smile.

I loved kissing him good-bye – which took some time – wishing him a good day, and watching his bike and booty take leave up the block.

And, as I got myself together, got myself out of the house, and did my ten-to-six shift, all I could do was look forward to the end of the day.

*I couldn't wait to get home to him, because I had so much work to do...*

I didn't ask Raheim to be my "live-in lover" (B.D.'s description of our relationship). It just happened. And, while it isn't exactly obvious, Raheim did "contribute" to the household.

Besides making mine a happy home and knockin' da boots *down,* he was also a very handy handyman.

Arguing that "you be waitin' fo'eva on that fuckin' supa" (which was true), he fixed the drip in the kitchen sink, the rattle of the toilet bowl, the rolling mechanism of the bedroom closet door that usually got stuck, and the finicky front-door lock. He also hooked my stereo up to my TV ("Le's have some stereo-motha-fuckin'-phonic sound up in tha place") and, in three hours flat, dressed in nothing but a baseball cap and a pair of tattered, droopy jeans that exposed his underwearless booty, stripped and painted a small wooden cabinet that he found sitting in front of a thrift shop in the neighborhood. It cost ten dollars. He thought "it would go great in that corna" – meaning the space between the sofa and the stereo. He was right.

And, when I couldn't get a jar or bottle of anything opened, you know who did it for me.

Of course, nobody's perfect, and there were things that I could've done without.

He'd finish making himself *mo' fine* in the bathroom and "fuhget" to put the caps back on the toothpaste and mouthwash, and the lids on the deodorant, oils, creams, and lotions; wash the hair that came off his head and face down the basin; clean the tub; and pick up his towel.

He'd leave his clothes everywhere.

He'd pee with the toilet seat down. Sometimes I would have a wet seat – and a wet floor.

He'd play his music really loud, and I wouldn't have cared if the lyrics were a bit more "lyrical." *("I need a gangsta bitch"?)*

And, the thing that *really* got on my nerves: drinking the rest of the juice or milk or iced tea or soda or Deer Park – and putting the empty carton or container back in the refrigerator.

My mother would complain about most of these very same things while I was growing up, all of it directed at Adam. After she remarried, Anderson got chewed out for it. He argued, though, that that's just the way real men are (I guess I wasn't a real man, since I didn't do these things). He'd tell her: "Annie Baby" – he called her that when he was trying to get sweet on her – "it's just to remind you of me." A sour statement, yes, but my mother would confide in me that, while she was wiping that toilet seat or picking up his funky drawers, she would smile. Why? Because it was her man who did it. *Her* man. And she loved it.

Well, I could identify. Raheim's bad habits were, I had to admit, unique, because they were his. And, while I bitched to him (but mostly to myself) about them, I loved it. And, I reasoned, all of these things make up who he is – and would, hopefully, bring me closer to unfolding the mystery of Raheim.

And he was a mystery to unfold.

Raheim told me that he was "full of surprises" — and he wasn't lyin'.

One night, we were on the sofa — him sitting on the left side, me sprawled across it and his thick thighs, my head against the headrest. He was skimming through *The Source.* I was trying to get through the last fifty pages of Terry McMillan's *Waiting to Exhale,* half humming, half singing a tune (which one I don't know), when he snapped his finger and blurted out...

"I know who you sound like..."

"Oh yeah? Who?"

"Randy Crawford."

I was floored. "Randy ... Crawford?"

"Yeah. You don' know who she is?"

Yes I did. Randy Crawford (no relation to yours truly as far as I know) is so jood, she could sing the ABCs and give you goose bumps. In Europe, she is a bona fide star. But because she can't be boxed into any one musical category (she's tackled it all — pop, soul, blues, jazz, dance, even country and rock), the great marketing moguls don't know how to promote her to the very shortsighted, image-conscious record-buying American public. So, unless you are a vocalese aficionado or happen to be a real music lover (which many claim they are but aren't), you've probably never heard of her.

When B.D. and I were getting to know one another and he asked me who my favorite singer was, he, of course, didn't know who Randy was — or that he was a she. ("A woman named Randy?")

But Raheim knew.

"My moms, tha's all she listens to," he explained. "Randy's her fav'rite."

"Really? Mine too."

"Yeah ... she would sing along, but she don' sound half as jood as you, Little Bit."

"Thank you."

Smack.

Silence.

"So, do you have a favorite Randy Crawford song?" I asked.

I could tell he was thinking: he put the tip of his left thumb in his mouth and slightly shook his head. I was praying that he didn't say "Street Life," the song most people associate Randy with. No question it is one of her greatest performances, but it certainly isn't her greatest.

"It hafta be 'Someone ta Believe In.'"

The man must have been reading my mind. Randy's reading of that Brook Benton classic is itself a classic. So I started to sing it.

When I got to the second verse:

*Someone to come home to, after a weary day*
*Someone who'll understand me*
*When I'm lost for words to say...*

he put down the magazine, resting his left arm across my chest. His head went back. By the time I finished, he had shifted his body so that I was between his legs, my head against his right arm.

"Thanks, Baby. You can sing that ta me anytime."

I did.

Besides hearing me sing, Raheim loved to read – something Gene found hard to swallow. For Gene, the "B" in B-boy stands for brainless. "Most of those children can't put a subject and a verb together," he'd often argue. But Raheim turned out to be a serious page-turner. He must have studied at Brotha Hakim's School of Speed Reading.

I discovered this one evening while I was mulling over a story for *Essence* that was due the very next day (I know I don't have to explain why it wasn't done). And it almost didn't get done that night, either: Raheim was a big distraction, wearing a tan thong that let his booty hang all out and barely cupped his dick. He kept looking over my shoulder, thrusting his wiggling chest (oh, that drives me wild!) and hard nipples in my face. So, when I knew I was about to give in, I made him sit in a corner of my office out of view with the two African-American gay anthologies on my desk: *In the Life* and *Brother to Brother*.

Four hours later, I was done – and so was he.

"You read *both* of them that fast?"

"Yeah. It was nothin' but some poems an' essays an' stuff," he said, as if it was no big deal.

So we retired for the night and talked about what he read and it was obvious that he did read both books from cover to cover: he was reciting verses from poems and lines from the essays as if he had the books opened in front of him. And, he expounded on what he read, looking to me for guidance in case he misinterpreted or misunderstood something.

He didn't.

He was very insightful. He had a field day reading my mountain of freelance articles. He'd always have something interesting to say about every single one. ("Baby, why you do it this way? Why you ain't talk ta so-and-so? I ain't know that...") He laughed at my attempts to be "down" when it came to the few stories I did on rap (I didn't mind the criticism, though — it was always followed by a kiss). I convinced him to start reading to me, everything from the day's paper to my Black History calendar. He was so animated. So academic. So adorable. He could get really riled up about some things. One night, I cut out all the articles from that day's paper that I knew he would trip on. He spanked me for that. Yes, it was worth it.

His love for reading also explained his being so smart. I know folks throw that word around a lot, but it fit him perfectly. And it wasn't only because of his knowledge of current events (he could talk about the war in Bosnia or health care reform). He could've been a returning champion on *Jeopardy!*

That's right ... *Jeopardy!*

The night of this startling revelation, we were in our favorite position in bed. I was flipping the channels on the TV set and came to the show. Raheim told me to leave it on, so I did. And, for every other answer Alex Trebek had, Raheim had a question (which he'd reveal after popping on his left thumb). You'd think he was Encyclopedia Brown.

Alex: "The exact address of the White House."

Raheim: "Wha's 1600 Pennsylvania Ave?"

I knew that.

Alex: "The only two factors of a prime number are itself and this number..."

Raheim: "Wha's one?"

I couldn't remember it at the time, but I knew it when I heard it.

Alex: "Ben Franklin wanted this to be the national bird instead of the bald eagle."

Raheim: "Wha's a turkey?"

Hmmmm...

Alex: "It is the hardest substance known made in nature."

Raheim: "Wha's a diamond?"

A-ha...

Alex: "This is the world's second-largest but most bountiful river."

Raheim: "Wha's tha Amazon?"

OK...

Alex: "In soccer, this player is dressed differently from the referee and the other players."

Raheim: "Who's tha goalee?"

He would know that, being such a fitness freak.

Alex: "Daddy longlegs."

Raheim: "Wha's a spida?"

He would know that one, too – he *is* a daddy longlegs. But then...

Alex: "It was Cinderella's first name."

Raheim: "Ha, wha's Ella?"

I should've known *that* one.

Alex: "The age that Jesus Christ was crucified."

Raheim: "Wha's thirty-three?"

Now how did he know *that?* Just the night before we had a rather hot debate about God, during which Raheim confessed to being an atheist. ("If there was a God, half tha shit that be goin' down wouldn't be hap'nin'.") Grandma must have also dragged him to Bible study.

Then came "Final Jeopardy." The subject: Fables.

*Fables?*

How hard could this be, I asked myself, as Raheim got up to get a drink, returning just in time for the unveiling of the answer:

"The Pied Piper led rodents out of this German town."

Raheim looked at me. I looked at him. He sipped his drink, sitting on the side of the bed, and smiled. "Wha's Hamelin?"

He was right – and none of the contestants guessed it.

Here I was, a journalist, a person with not one, but two degrees, and I knew only a few of the sixty-one answers. Raheim knew at least a third. I always thought that if you could guess four or five questions a show, you were doing OK. Not anymore.

Was I embarrassed? Yes. But, more than anything, Raheim's being so intellectual made him so much more intriguing.

Yes, it turned me the fuck on.

But, while I felt that I was getting under that street-tough image, I didn't know what life was like for Raheim outside of my apartment. I only knew that he lived with his mother in Harlem. I had never been to his job. And the few people he knew that we bumped into when we weren't behind closed doors he didn't introduce me to. Several of them (particularly one in the Vill) raised my ire by being too touchy-feely with him.

So, when he informed me the Thursday before Independence Day that he was going to be spending the weekend with his boyz, the reporter in me turned on.

"You mean ... what are their names again?"

"D.C. an' Angel..."

I really couldn't stand being away from him for a day, God forbid a whole weekend. So I thought of something quick.

"Why don't you invite them over here?"

"Ova here?"

"Yeah, you all can hang out here."

His expression was similar to the one he had when I asked him to join me and the crew on Gay Pride Day. "I don' know, Little Bit..."

"C'mon, I'll get a chance to meet your friends," I said. "You met mine and they liked you."

"Uh-huh," he sighed.

"And, if you haven't noticed, you practically live here," I continued. "I mean, you can have your boyz over if you want."

He was silent.

"If you all want to watch a game, videos, whatever, it's fine with me..."

Still silent.

"I can make you all some of my famous burgers..."

I sensed his defenses weaken.

"And afterwards, you can have *my* buns ... please, Pooquie ... *please?*"

I gave him that coquette look while gently stabbing him in the dimple with my finger. Yup, he gave up.

"A'right, a'right ... we will..."

"Good ... and don't be worried," I consoled. "I'm sure it's going to be fun."

It wasn't.

"Hello?"

"So, do you have the forty ounces ready?"

Yes, it was Gene. I left his July fourth barbecue (a cookout on his fifth-floor terrace that was also billed as a belated birthday party) early so that I could prepare for Raheim and his boyz. After giving the house a swift sweep and shine and setting up the goodies on the coffee table in the living room (snacks which included a bowl of Wheaties), I tried to relax by sitting on the windowsill in the bedroom, where I would be able to see them as they arrived. I had on the air conditioner, but my nerves were so shot that I was sweating. I had the speakerphone on.

"Gene, please, I am in no mood for your jokes," I said.

"Do you hear me laughing? They sure as hell ain't comin' over there to have cocktails."

"First of all, they are bringing the beverages. Second, because someone dresses and acts a certain way, that doesn't make them a hoodlum. He may be rugged, but Raheim has such a great mind. He is not a hoodlum..."

"Oh, I'm sorry ... he's an intelligent hoodlum."

"And neither are his friends. I mean, birds of a feather do flock together."

"Uh-huh..."

"I'm sure they are going to be as much fun as him."

"Well, if all of this is so, why are you so nervous?"

Damn you, Gene. That's a best friend for you – they always know when something is wrong. While I wasn't exactly nervous about meeting his friends, I did know that Raheim wasn't too keen about it. Why? Was he ashamed of me? Did he think they wouldn't like me? Or that I wouldn't like them and my opinion of him would change? I hate to admit it, but in preparation for this event, I had practiced speaking "harsher" (like "Yo" and "Wha's up") and acting "harder" (the crotch thang and the bad posture). I'd even thought of buying myself a banjee outfit of some kind so I would at least look like them. But I came to my senses: putting on a front would be a dumb thing to do, since they would be able to smell a fake a mile away and it wouldn't sit well with Raheim.

I was thinking of how to respond to Gene when Ice Cube's "It Was a Good Day" became louder and louder, got closer and closer. The music was coming from an equally loud white-colored Jeep Wrangler that pulled up in front of my brownstone. I immediately recognized the bald head in the passenger side of the front seat as the roof closed.

"They're here!" I screamed.

"Child, will you calm down," advised Gene.

"Oh, I hope this goes well," I breathed.

"Just be cool. And be yourself. Call me later. *Ciao.*"

The downstairs bell rang. I zoomed to the intercom and buzzed them in. I put my ear to the door. I heard the voices ("Yo, close da do', nigga!" "Shut up, nigga!" "Yo, dis neighbahood betta be cool, cuz if somebody fucks wit my shit, I'ma hafta clock 'em") and the footsteps stomping up the stairs. One of them, probably Raheim, played a beat on the door with his knuckles, which made me jump back. I inhaled and exhaled deeply and opened it with a smile.

They were certainly a bunch to behold. My Pooquie was in the front, lookin' too clean in cap, tank, shorts, and high-top sneakers, all white. D.C. was on his right side; his arms were folded across his chest. He wore an identical outfit in gold that matched the caps in his upper front teeth. Angel was perched against the other side of the door, wearing a similar black outfit. All three had silver hoops in their left ears and smug grins on their faces. The scene could've been a cover jacket for a hip-hop or harmony group's compact disc.

"Wha's up, Baby?" Raheim asked, as he grabbed my waist and smothered me with a slobbery kiss. Raheim had never kissed me in public or around other people unless I initiated it, and when I did, he was always a little apprehensive. So I was shocked by this act of affection.

He let me go, chuckling, and did the honors. "Baby, uh, Mitchell, dese my boyz, D.C. an' Angel."

I tried my best to do that special B-boy handshake – you know, the one where you shake, rattle, and fold? Raheim and D.C. giggled; Angel smiled.

"Please, fellas, come in," I said, stepping out of their way. D.C. walked in with Raheim almost arm in arm, talking loud (they reminded me of Gene and B.D., even though I'm sure they wouldn't call what they do together kee-keeing). D.C. was an inch shorter than me but almost twice my size. His skin was mahogany. His eyes were light brown, his nose thin, his full lips a glossy brown. His ears were tiny like Raheim's. His goatee and mustache were thick. His curly brown hair was faded on the sides, cropped and styled on the top with a small part on the right side. Despite his decorated teeth, the giant nugget on the middle finger of his right hand, and the gold rings that adorned each finger on his left, he was a triple "S" threat: short, stocky, and sexy.

Angel was correctly named at birth. His face – dimpled on both cheeks – was almost square, his eyes dark brown, his lips pink, poked, and puckered (ready to be kissed). His skin was a shade lighter than mine, and he sported a Marine cut and a thin mustache. His ears were flip-floppy like Will Smith's. He was an inch or so shorter than Raheim but just as healthy; his legs and arms were gorgeous. I could tell there was a bad-boy quality in him – how else could one explain the smirky smile he gave me as he entered the apartment.

And, like Raheim, they both had back *back*. Birds of a feather...

D.C. and Angel parked it on the sofa, Raheim in the black easy chair near the entrance to the kitchen. I already had the TV set pulled out from the other corner of the room for their enjoyment. As I approached Raheim, he handed me one forty-ounce bottle of Colt 45 from the large brown paper bag he carried in, placing another two in front of him on the floor.

"Here, Baby. Put dese in da fridge an' get us some mugs," he said, patting me on the behind as I made my way into the kitchen.

"I know you wettin' *dat* pipe, *day-am!*" squealed D.C., slapping Angel five.

*Wettin' dat pipe?* I would later learn that this was another way of saying fucking. The pipe – a.k.a. the ass – he was referring to belonged to me. Which is why Raheim shot back...

"Watch it, motha-fucka. You betta not even think about it, cuz ya know I *fuck* you up..."

"Yo, I'm jus' complamentin' ya, brotha..."

"Yeah, *right...*"

Raheim popped in a video as they continued jibing about who they were about to watch (Michael Jordan, my Pooquie's idol) and, I assume, some guy that D.C. had tried to rap to earlier ("I'm tellin' ya, cuz, dat motha-fucka was all on yo' dick"). Raheim only yelled from the living room once to see if I was all right. And I only interrupted them once – to ask how they liked their burgers (both D.C. and Angel, medium; my Pooquie, well done). I didn't know what to say; I felt out of place in my own house. I tuned them out and didn't tune back in until the food was ready. And the conversation was not exactly stimulating.

"Nigga, yo' mama so dumb she thought St. Ides was a church!" cracked D.C., both feet on my coffee table.

Angel, sitting up on the edge of the sofa, laughed hysterically while holding his very flat belly. "Yo, man, you ain't gonna let 'im say shit like dat an' not come back..."

"Nah, you know I got somethin', cuz," Raheim replied, taking his plate from me and winking. "Thanks, Baby." He turned to D.C.: "Nigga, yo' mama so old she got Jesus' beepa numba."

"Oh yeah, well yo' mama so hairy dey thought she was King Kong," snapped D.C., taking his plate without a thank-you.

"Nigga, da's so sof'," said Angel, graciously accepting his food with a smile. "Dis really looks good. Smells good, too. Thanks."

"You're all welcome," I said, but only looking at Angel and Raheim as I returned to the kitchen.

"Dat ain' sof' an' you know it," argued D.C., just a-chomping.

"It is compared ta dis one, so check it out," Raheim said, as he helped himself to the fixins – lettuce, tomatoes, onions, cucumbers, chips, mustard, relish, mayo, and ketchup – on the coffee table. "Yo' mama so ugly dat if dey stacked 'er brick by brick she be a housin' projec'."

"You simple nigga," D.C. bellowed, missing Raheim's head with his open hand.

It bothered the hell out of me that I had three of the most beautiful men I'd ever seen in my life in my living room calling each other the *n*-word with such glee. Raheim particularly surprised me, being so Africentric. He had never used the word around me before. Since I had raised the issue before with B-boys (like Ricky) and others and they could never get past their own limited views, I planned not to say anything.

But D.C. forced me to.

"Yo, Mitch, da food was kickin'," he said, rubbing his belly and glancing at me as I stood beside Raheim, my fingers tapping the back of his head. "Da nigga can cook his ass off."

I knew he thought he was paying me a compliment. I knew he didn't think he was offending me. But I had to let him know otherwise.

"I'm glad you enjoyed it, D.C.," I started, trying to choose my words correctly. "But I'd appreciate it if you didn't call me that."

All motion stopped in the room. I could feel Raheim tense up. D.C. eased up, eyeing his way around Raheim, to face me.

"Call you what, G?"

I focused on the stereo. "Call me nigger."

He sucked his teeth. "I ain' call you no nigg*er*."

"Sounded like it to me..." Raheim inched backwards to nudge me. I knew he wanted me to back down, but I wouldn't.

"Man, I called you nigg*a*, ya know, like one o' da boyz," D.C. explained.

"What difference does it make?" I asked. "It is just a variation of nigg*er*."

"Yo, it ain't da same," D.C. brooded, sitting up on the couch, somewhat flustered. "It's diff'rent when we use it."

"We? We who?" I demanded. "We all don't use it..."

He cut me off. "Yo, I can tell you ain't down wit it. You jus' don' undastan'. But ev'rybody don' think like you, a'right? It ain't nothin' but a word, ya know? But, no offense, G."

We could have left it like that. But it was my house and I felt that I should have the last word.

"Well, all I know is, anybody who uses it must think they are what the white man says they are – and I am not."

D.C. glared at me. *If looks could kill...*

It didn't bother me that no one talked to me after my exchange with D.C., because no one was talking to me before it. But Raheim no longer acknowledged me with a smile or squeeze or pinch. They all went on enjoying some game. When they left an hour later, Angel was cordial – he gave me a grin and a good-bye. D.C. didn't do either, and Raheim, who had the boyz wait for him downstairs, told me why as he stood and I sat on the sofa.

"Ya know, Little Bit, you ain't had ta dis my boy..."

*"I dissed him?"* I asked. "I think the shoe is on the other foot. He insulted me."

"He ain't insult you. Tha's jus' tha way he talks."

"Well, it ain't the way I talk, and I'm so sorry that I bruised his fragile ego, but I don't like being called that."

"You heard wha' he said," Raheim countered, talking with his hands and pacing back and forth slowly. "He ain't mean it like you think."

I, too, started doing the hand action. "I'm sorry, Raheim, but for me, there is only one way to take that word, regardless of whose mouth it comes out of. In fact, I'm surprised at you for using it."

"Baby, it ain't nothin' but a street thang," he argued. "D.C. was right; you don' undastan' an' you shoulda jus' kep' yo' fuckin' mouth shut."

I folded my legs, placing my elbow on my knee and my fist under my chin. "I see ... so I can't speak my own mind in my own house, is that it?"

He placed his right hand on his hip; his left hand he pointed at me. "Yo, if you gonna say *stoo*pid shit like that..."

"Stupid?" I got up and stood in front of him. "Don't *you* think there is something wrong with taking the name that thousands of *us* have been killed with – both physically and psychologically – doing a little spelling change, and using it as a term of endearment when addressing your so-called brothers?"

*If looks could kill – again.*

I backed up. For the first time since I met Raheim, I was afraid of him. I felt he could do me harm. I rubbed my forehead, because I felt a migraine coming on. I didn't know what else to say. And neither did he.

"Fuck it ... I call you lata," he waved, turning and walking up the hallway and out the door. I wanted to go after him, to haul his ass back in the house because (1) I didn't want him to go and (2) he hadn't answered my question. I would soon discover, though, that running away *was* his answer when things got a little too hot for him.

I could hear the engine of the Jeep in the back of the apartment. I briskly walked into the bedroom and looked out the window. They were already halfway up the block. I sat on the windowsill for the next five hours, staring at the phone, waiting for it to ring.

It didn't.

It was our first fight.

I saw it more as a disagreement. We had words, we spoke our minds. But I am one to finish what I start, nip it in the bud at the moment, and move on. Raheim is the one who took off.

And did he take off.

While I wanted to hear his voice, I didn't want to talk about what happened over the phone. I was still steaming. So, I was kind of glad he didn't call the night of the fight.

But after one night turned into five days, I was freaking out.

I missed him. I hated coming home after work, because there was no one to come home to. There was no one to cook for. Clean for. To comfort and keep.

There was no one to relax with. No one to read with.

No one to rock and roll with.

I couldn't stand being in the bedroom or, rather, the bed. I would keep reaching out for him. He was all over the sheets and pillows. I tried to catch my z's in the sofa bed, but I did more tossing and turning than sleeping.

Yes, I was dick-whipped.

And I know this is going to sound crazy, but I even missed walking into the bathroom finding his towel on the floor or the toilet seat down – and wet.

The days went by so slow. He had become my life during the last few weeks. My whole world revolved around him. I was hooked.

He was turning this argument into something bigger when it didn't and shouldn't have to be. I was angry that he took the easy way out, making me suffer like this. He was obviously trying to get even with me, leaving me hanging like a dangling participle. He wanted me to beep him and say I was sorry. He wanted me to feel guilty.

And I was starting to.

"Don't you *even* think it," warned Michelle, as we sat in a booth at a diner a few blocks from the job. She took me to lunch to make sure I didn't sit at my desk watching the phone or waiting in the lobby for Raheim to show up.

I played with my french fries. "But maybe..."

"*May*be you should have thrown *all* their asses out," she said, pointing at me with her fork. "Dr. Feelgood ain't got no right telling you what you can and cannot say in your own house. Why, *why* do these mother-fuckers think they can run you just because they turn you out every which way but loose?"

"I just had to be so flip," I argued. "I guess I wasn't a good host."

"No, you weren't," she said, snacking on one of her own fries. "You were a waiter."

"What?"

"Think about it," she began, picking up her Coke. "All you did was take the orders, prepare the feast, and serve it. Hell, they could have come here if they just wanted to eat a burger. You didn't even get a tip!"

She was right. The more I thought about it, Raheim was not the Raheim I knew that afternoon. He was grandstanding big time to impress his friends. All that smoochy-smoochy stuff, "nigga" this and "nigga" that, boastin' and bassin', and crazy crotch cocking (he and D.C. didn't take their hands off of their dicks until the meal was served) – he never did any of it with me. This Dr. Jekyll & Mr. Hyde trick was not cute.

"You invited them over to get to know them, not to be ignored," she continued. "He knows he was wrong, that's why he hasn't called and probably won't."

I leaned back in my seat, throwing my napkin on my plate. "I don't know ... I just want to talk to him about it."

"Ha, you wanna do more than talk!"

I laughed for the first time all week.

She touched up her makeup. "Look, you're going through with-drawal. The dick was good and you want it again, badly. But don't sweat him like that. He's just one man, honey, *one*. And there are plenty others out here."

I had received the same pep talk from Gene, who, not surprisingly, wasn't surprised at what happened ("You can take the boy out of the hood, but..."). Michelle, though, was expressing her opinion without bias. As much as he protested, Gene didn't like my being involved with Raheim. Michelle could care less who I was seeing so long as they were treating me right. Michelle is a terrific confidant. While many straight sisters claim that they love gay men because we are sensitive, honest, sharing, and make great friends (qualities straight men for some un-known reason seem to lack), they also draw the line at talking about the one thing we have in common: men. Most of my heterosexual female friends are not comfortable discussing my love life or theirs. And even those that do are wary about me hanging around or out with their latest date or husband. I met one friend's Prince Charming – whom she was courted by for two years – on their wedding day. In her white gown (which was the joke of the ceremony, since everybody, including the groom, knew she was far from being virginal), she said she didn't introduce me to him before because she was afraid I would want him. Puh-*leeze*. First, contrary to what many straight folks think, gay men do not want every man they see. Second, this man was over three hundred pounds and was barely an inch taller than me – a weeble-wobble, if you will. And, third, even if I were a ho, did want him, went after him, and got him, what would that tell *her* about *him?* I've met many married men – bisexual, gay, even "straight" – who straddle the fence. The straight sisters just don't understand – we faggots can really give them the lowdown and rundown on men. We know where many of them are when they ain't with you. Can we talk, can we talk here?

Michelle understands this. She has never had these hang-ups and doesn't see us as competitors. In fact, she says I'm the brother she never had (she is the youngest of six girls). And, in the three years that we've been at *Your World,* she's become a sister.

After a little more counseling (and a little man watching), we got back to the office at around three – just in time for the staff planning meeting to discuss the agenda for the new school year. Finally, after walking around all week as horny as a toad, I would be able to vent some of my frustration. Elias always gives me an excuse to read his ass royally. I guess, like Raheim and Gene, I love putting white folks in their place – especially if they are trying to put me in one.

I went to my office (which was really a cubicle), checked my messages (there were none), grabbed a pad, pen, and copies of the proposal I'd drawn up (thank God I did it in May, because it surely wouldn't have gotten done in June with Raheim around), and headed for the big conference room on the ninth floor.

They were all waiting for me around the big table. On one side: Editorial Assistant Phillip Cooper, a 22-year-old Eddie Murphy clone (minus the wacky wit) from Staten Island and recent Morehouse grad who is darker than Raheim and long and lanky like Babyface, wearing denim jeans and a shirt, a yellow sports tie, and blue Nike open-toe sandals; and Assistant Editor and Demi Moore–look-alike Denise, the 24-year-old gung ho girl from Los Angeles, pretty in pink skippies and a summer dress. On the other side: Associate Editor Elias, twenty-five, a Steve Urkel in whiteface, in his blue sports coat (no matter the season he always wears it), white shirt and blue bow tie, Gap khakis, and loafers; and Managing Editor Andrew Goodman, the fortyish Robert De Niro double in lightly tinted Ray Bans that are for both seeing and show, wearing that drab corporate uniform – dark blue suit, shirt, tie, suspenders, and shoes.

And, at the head of the rectangular table, Editor-in-Chief Steven Goldberg, a frumpy fifty-year-old native Arkansan who looks just like Ed Asner. And he's obviously watched too many episodes of *The Mary Tyler Moore Show* and *Lou Grant*. He has brought that character to life in what he calls the "newsroom." He has Mr. Grant's mannerisms, his voice, even his dress, down pat. He's temperamental but tender; demanding but fair.

Unfortunately, Steven is still a white man and, as such, sees the world through a white man's eyes and, as such, is just as ignorant as the rest of the white men at *Your World* about anything and anybody that doesn't fall into the realm of their white male world.

Case in point: our first meeting, which would be my interview.

It was September 1990. I was told about an editorial assistant position on this youth publication by the placement office at Columbia. It was a job I would kill for – half of my published clips were covering youth issues – but I had been killing myself all summer long, going on two interviews a week, with no luck. I even schlepped 3,000 miles across the country to the National Association of Black Journalists' (NABJ) Convention in Los Angeles – spending most of my graduation gift money – only to be told, "Don't call us, we'll call you." Of course, no one ever called (which is, I later learned, the experience of 99.9 percent of those who attend the job fair).

So, I sent my stuff off to the editor not expecting to hear from him. But three days later Steven called, and the very next day I was in his office. It is big, spacious, and ugly: yellow-colored walls, brown carpeting, a wall unit complete with a makeshift stereo, TV set, and VCR in one corner, a red leather sofa and antique grandfather clock in another, a running machine (which I don't think he ever uses) near his high-ceiling windows, and the many plaques and citations the magazine has won over the years hanging all over the walls. The room was on an angle so that his desk sat up, allowing him to look down on anyone seated across from him. The Illusion of Power.

"It is such a pleasure to meet you," he said as we settled into our chairs. "I've been going over your résumé over and over again, and I am so, *so* impressed."

Translation: I'm used to seeing people who look like me with a résumé like this, but not one of you.

He prefaced many of his comments and questions with other loaded statements:

Regarding the content of my clips: "Many of these feature stories document inner-city life so well. I guess growing up in that environment helps you cover it better, hunh?" (No, mother-fucker, I didn't grow up in the projects, dodging bullets and crack dealers every day...)

Regarding most of my work, which was and still is done with African-American publications: "I'm sure you'll find that we'll expect more from you than your other editors." (Expect more of me, hunh? Like the others didn't expect the best? Kiss my beautiful Black ass...)

Regarding my passion for covering the African-American community: "I hope we can count on you to be objective when doing that." (Uh-huh, objective – that means seeing things the way you do, right?)

I'd heard different versions of the same comments before. But it was obvious that I was the first person of color he'd considered for a position on *Your World*. The man was a wreck. And I didn't make it any easier for him.

When it was my turn to do the asking, I was ready. "So, how many people of color work at this company?"

His face cracked. "You mean ... minorities?"

"To you, minorities, but I am not minor in any way. I am a person of color."

He cleared his throat. "I see ... well, to be quite honest with you ... out of a staff of seventy-five ... there is one..."

That "one" turned out to be Alex Chin, who didn't count, for three important reasons: (1) he was an advertising intern; (2) he would be leaving, to his dismay, two weeks after I started; and (3) he did not see himself as a person of color. He was playing that assimilation game to the hilt: trying to hide that thick Chinese accent, doing the water cooler thing, making sure he said good morning to Steven every single day, and wearing the ugliest polka-dot ties (like the other ad people) I'd ever seen in my life. After witnessing his act, I promised myself that I would not get caught up in that syndrome. Besides, the one thing I loved about the job was that there was no dress code. And, if someone expects me to dress up for work every day, they'll have to fork over much, much more money than I earned. I only bring out my Sunday best if we go to a conference or awards ceremony.

After I grilled him some more on employment policies, their affirmative action program (which was nonexistent until I got there), and the history of the magazine (he was *Your World*'s first assistant editor when it debuted in 1977), Steven showed me around and introduced me to the entire editorial staff (Andrew being the only one still on the magazine) and Leonard the Art Director, who was smoking a cigarette at his desk (they didn't have a smoking lounge back then). After he huddled with the posse for five minutes, Steven offered me the job. But I waited a week until I looked over the publication to say yes (after sweating for four months, I wanted somebody else to sweat). I knew very well that, while I was overqualified for the job, they needed some color up in the place and I fit the bill. Judging by the stares I got, there never had been a Black face working in the office before (even the mailroom, really the only spot in the corporate world hierarchy where brothers are assured a job, was all-white). I was the trailblazer, the fly in the buttermilk. And, of course, it took folks time to get used to my face. Sometimes I'd be mistaken for a messenger or the man who fixes the printer. And while I don't think I am "threatening," security was called twice during my first month by two unidentified employees who complained of a "suspicious" man lurking about. None of this stuff happens anymore – even though some folks still look at me as if I am from outer space.

Michelle came a month after me, then Deborah a year later, and in April, Phillip, whom I met at NABJ's '92 convention in Detroit. After we tried him out as a freelancer, I encouraged him to apply for the entry-level position and he got it. I was too glad to have another brother around. Steven made a point of having me speak to all of these folks before they were hired (I guess he wanted to make sure they knew they wouldn't be the only ones).

Besides those rare "Meet Our First Negro" occasions, I see Steven only three other times during the year – the Christmas party, my annual evaluation, and the summer meeting. Any other time, my "conversation" with him is never by phone or in person; we send messages through the computer system. I can't say I know him or like him; he's just the head-white-man-in-charge. But I will say that I admire him, for one reason and one reason only – he had the good sense to hire me.

I sat next to Denise (Phillip on her left), with Steven at my right and Andrew directly across from me. The "majority" on one side and the woman and "minorities" on the other. What a sight.

Steven first went into this long song and dance about how pleased he was with the past year's issues – people were still talking about our coverage of the Vietnam War (I contributed a personal essay about my father) and abortion. He announced what the six "mainstay" themes of the year would be: two issues on different regions in the world (this time South Africa and Puerto Rico), one each on the environment ("Waste Makes Haste"), science (astronomy and the space program), economics/politics (health care), and history (the Holocaust, in conjunction with Steven Spielberg's *Schindler's List)*. Another five are "open doors" – whatever news events break during the year we cover. The other five magazine slots (including the first issue of the year) are devoted to social topics, which we basically hammer out in the meeting.

Since he was the newest staff member, Phillip worked with Andrew (or so I thought) on his proposal, which was a well-thought-out outline on alcohol and how it is America's most popular yet dangerous addiction. After we all agreed that it should go on the list, Phillip glanced at Elias and thanked him for his guidance. Because of Andrew's schedule, he couldn't help him at the time. But why didn't he come to me? I gave Phillip a thumbs-up sign, but he brushed it off. OK...

During her presentation for "A Woman's World," I was glad that Denise had story ideas on the first person on Earth (an African woman) and how, as she put it, "the women's movement came hundreds of years too late for African-Americans." Elias felt the issue would be nothing but "male bashing," and had a serious problem with one of the stories: sexual harassment. "It happens to men, too," he claimed. True, but it is not socially acceptable or institutionally entrenched like it is for women. Despite his objections, that package was accepted.

I was next.

I started passing out copies of the proposal. "I believe the time is right for us to tackle gays..."

"Mitch, haven't we been through this before?" asked Elias, who, I knew, was not at all interested in hearing my speech from the last two years, just fashioned differently. He just hates "gay" anything being brought up. Could it be that he is gay and doesn't like talking about it for fear that someone will figure him out? My "gaydar" (yes, we homos can usually "detect" who is and isn't) tells me so. Gene, who assumes everyone is gay until proven guilty ("Hell, straight folks assume everybody is straight, so what's good for the goose..."), believes he is, too. And I do have some "evidence": Michael Weinstein, the blond-haired-blue-eyed-bubblehead in the art department, says he sees Elias at least twice a month at the Igloo, a bar in New Jersey. I don't fault Elias for not being "out" on the job; I'm not either (even though sitting in an office surrounded by pictures of half-naked men like Bo "Knows" Jackson and Roger Craig a la Calvin Klein tells it all). But at least I didn't avoid the subject altogether and sabotage every effort to shed some light on a group of people who are so misunderstood.

"Yes, we have, which is why it is being brought up again," I snapped. "Now, if you don't mind, I was speaking."

I explained that we cannot continue to ignore the topic because it may cause some teachers to cancel their subscriptions and appall or anger some parents (and students). Lesbians and gays are coming out of the closet more and more, and gaining mainstream prominence. The issue will talk about the struggle to be viewed as a minority group; legal issues surrounding gay-rights bills and protection from discrimination in housing, employment, and adopting and raising children; famous homosexuals in history; the controversy surrounding whether to "teach" young people about it in school; and how the homosexual community is very diverse, racially, culturally, and sexually. The news peg: the twenty-fifth anniversary of the Stonewall uprising in Greenwich Village.

Phillip chimed in first. "Well, I have two major problems. I don't understand that part about diversity. Just look at the news: you don't see any Black homosexuals, because they are all white. And if you start talking about civil rights, you're going to have a whole lot of Black people angry."

I did understand his concern about the civil rights tag. Even I didn't appreciate the way white homosexuals try to link the struggle African people faced in getting the rights they should've had from jump street with that of lesbians and gays (like *they* know). I pointed out that we would illustrate the difference: for African-Americans, it has been a question of *o*ppression; for homosexuals of all colors and strides, it has been *re*pression.

I didn't understand – or, rather, appreciate – his other so-called problem. For brothers like him (he is flamboyantly heterosexual and is engaged to a Spelman beauty queen), homosexual activity may go on in the community – in fact, some may even participate in it – but we as African people can't be homosexuals, because it is not a part of our culture. It's a white thing. I wanted to reach across Denise and wring Phillip's neck for saying that – but I didn't.

"That comment, Phillip, is precisely why we need to do this," I argued. "There are too many misconceptions about lesbians and gays. Even supposedly enlightened folks like you define a community by stereotypes and myth. We have the chance to challenge this and educate people..."

"Educate people about what?" he chuckled. "People will look at the cover and say we are trying to turn their kids gay, introduce them to what they see as a sexual preference, a chosen lifestyle..."

*"Sexual preference"? "Chosen lifestyle"?* I hate those two phrases. Yeah, right, I prefer to be a homo instead of being...? I choose to be gay rather than...? How come we don't hear folks say, "I prefer to be hetero," or, "I choose to be straight..." This ain't what I "prefer" and it ain't a "lifestyle" I "chose." It's who I am. It is my life.

Elias nodded at Phillip and then turned to Steven. "He's right. I've been saying the same thing for the past two years. Besides, didn't we cover most of that stuff in the AIDS issue last year?"

Denise jumped in; I knew I could count on her. "No, we didn't, and we have to stop thinking of gay coverage as AIDS. As journalists, we can't be afraid to take this on just because it is going to ruffle a few feathers. I say, now or never."

"Hold it, people," said Andrew, who, speaking for the first time during the meeting, had risen from the dead. "We are going down the same road on this. I think we all agreed last year that we had to do this and that it was all just a matter of packaging, and I think Mitch has done a great job of doing that. What do you say, S.G.?"

S.G. ... How corporate. How tired.

Steven sat back in his chair, slapped his hands, folded them, and looked at me. "I am impressed with Mitch's presentation, particularly the articles on the origins of sexual orientation, and gay-bashing. We'll get a lot of flak, but a lot of praise, too. But we'll have to work real close with the marketing and P.R. people on this one, like we did with abortion. I say, let's go for it."

The thrill of victory for me — the agony of defeat for Elias. I knew he would hate working on this issue, and I couldn't wait.

Elias, though, was about to strike back — his proposal was aptly titled: "Was Dan Quayle Right?: The Disappearing American Family." In his William F. Buckley tone, he reeled off a barrage of statistics about "illegitimate" births (my aunt Ruth says any baby born into this world *is* legitimate), absent dads, single-female-headed households and welfare mothers (he said what percentage are Black but not those that are white), and skyrocketing divorce rates and "children run amok," which he tried to blame on "the working woman" (making Denise roll her eyes).

As he ended his pompous circumstance monologue — which was only missing "America, the Beautiful" as a score — he grinned at me. "So, Mitch, I know *you* have something to say."

I placed my folded hands on the table. "Yes, I do have something to say: it sounds great."

He and everyone else in the room gagged.

"What?" he asked.

I smiled. "It's well researched and it grabs you. Catchy title. The only problem is that the focus is all wrong."

A silly grin swept across Denise's face – she knew what I was up to. And Elias looked as if I'd slapped *his* face (which, to be honest, I felt like I had).

"Wha–, wha–, what's wrong with it?" he stuttered.

"Well, it assumes that there is a model that we all should follow to be an American family and there isn't," I explained. "We're talking about life here, not *Father Knows Best* or *Leave It to Beaver*. We shouldn't be marginalizing and belittling the lives of a majority of the American public, just because they don't live up to that fictional family model of a mommy, daddy, two kids, a dog, a house, and a car."

Before he had the chance to respond, Denise added her five cents. "And, it seems to me that your proposal is basically a camouflaged attack on the, ahem, lack of values, as you put it, in communities of color. Nowhere did I hear you say what percentage of white women are on welfare or white men are skipping out on their kids. And, by the way, most women work because they *have* to..."

You go, girl...

I could see Elias just shrinking before my eyes. He tried to regain his composure. "The fact is that these problems are more prevalent in the black community. And, even if it is a glorified media image, the evidence shows that kids are better off with both parents. That's part of the American Dream."

"Oh, yeah, it's a dream all right," I argued. "Just like the idea of the melting pot, it is a farce. Look, there's no question that a child raised by two parents may be better off economically, but just because there are two parents doesn't mean life is going to be grand."

"What do you mean?" asked Andrew, swiveling in his chair.

"The attitude is that marriage is the answer, but there are a hell of a lot of screwed-up kids coming out of these homes. Look at all of these women killing their husbands because they are abused, and all these adults now coming forward and saying they were abused by Daddy, while Mommy ignored it all. Talk about dysfunctional families. I would rather a child be raised by one parent in a loving secure home than in one where there is turmoil."

"But these nontraditional families are *not* secure...," countered Elias.

"And whose fault is *that?*" I accused. "This country claims that it believes in the family, but our social policies tell a different story. Where's the across-the-board, affordable child care? Why are we sending so many jobs out of the country, especially those for people with little or no labor skills? Why are we building more jails and not pumping that money into educating these kids and cleaning up their drug- and crime-infested neighborhoods? Because of these warped priorities, families without both parents in the home suffer and the problems you mentioned arise. I say we celebrate the family, yes, but not just one type. No matter what type of unit you come from, you can succeed. Half of the people sitting around this table came from so-called nontraditional homes — and look at us now." I was talking about myself (single mom, stepfamily), Phillip (single mom) and Denise (single dad). I motioned to all of us.

Phillip, though, didn't like being used as an example. "I'd appreciate it if you wouldn't include me."

"Why?" I asked.

He looked at the ceiling. "Because, unlike you, I don't like making my personal life an issue at work."

I knew that Phillip was self-conscious about growing up without his father; we had talked about that. But everyone at the table knew, because he had written about it in a powerful feature story–essay that helped convince Andrew to give him a chance as a freelancer. "Well, it isn't something you should be ashamed of..."

"And, I wish you wouldn't assume anything about me," he advised.

"Um, Steve, I think we should sit on this one," Denise said, obviously feeling the tension, since she was sitting between us. "And, I think that Mitchell should come up with an alternative proposal for a family issue."

Elias, who was enjoying it all, did a double take. "Well, what's wrong with mine?"

"I think we just went over that," frowned Denise. *"Your World* should be breaking new ground, not following the status quo. There has always been more than one type of family, and it's time we really look at them and how they function in society."

"I think that's a good idea," added Andrew, who, although he was a card-carrying member of the Republican party, didn't care for Elias's overzealous conservative views. "The debate should be fresh, not this same old family-values crap."

Elias was beside himself. "I ... I..."

"I agree," said Steven, who had been scribbling notes the whole time. "Mitch, you'd have to do it this weekend, so we can read it over in time for the three-o'clock schedule meeting on Monday. We'll use some of the material Elias has gathered but reshape it. Hmph, if all goes well, it might be the right issue to start the year off with. Think you can do it?"

What a stupid question; he knew I could. "Yes, Steve. Everyone will have a copy Monday morning." Triumphant once again.

The meeting continued for another half hour (during which we discussed and approved Andrew's proposal on the elderly). After it was over, I went up to Phillip to apologize. But he, once again, brushed me off: he nodded, said, "Fine," and walked out the room behind the Caucasian Crew.

Denise was just as puzzled as I was. *"What* is up with him?"

"I don't know," I sighed. "We were relatively close before, but now that he's working here, he keeps his distance. And he won't talk about it."

"Now, I am only a white woman and I really wouldn't know about these things," she said, grabbing my arm as we came out of the room, "but could it be that he might think being chummy with you won't get him in good with the good ol' boys?"

Good question. It had crossed my mind, but I'd reasoned that this is his first job out of college, he's a little shy, and has to get used to his surroundings. But when he barely says, "Good morning," or even, "Fuck you," to me, something's going on.

"I fear it could be, but let's pray it isn't," I giggled. "The last thing we need around here is another white man *—especially* if he is in blackface."

"You said it," she laughed.

"And thanks for drawing your guns in there," I added.

"Believe me, it was no problem," she stated, as we got to the elevator, where Phillip was laughing, apparently at something Elias had said. A minute ago he was icy. Hmmmm...

I wasn't going to let his cold shoulder, though, down my high. It was only five, so I decided to start work on the family issue outline at the office and, after an hour, finish it at home. But I got so into it — revenge is so, so sweet — that when I looked up it was almost eight o'clock and it was basically done. So I finished it and printed out a copy to check over the weekend.

I hopped on the subway, loving every word of the proposal and enjoying Oleta Adams. Gene had got me a copy of the advance cassette of her second album, hoping it would cheer me up. It did — a little — but there were certain songs that made me think of Pooquie, such as "Hold Me for a While." How I would love to sing it to him in my arms. It was playing as I turned the corner of my block.

I tripped on a high note Oleta was hitting — as well as my own feet — when I saw him sitting on my stoop. Since it was dark, he was a neon sign in a white bodysuit and Nikes. A white visor was on his head that said, "Mel's Messengers." He was gulping down a liter of Sprite. His legs were wide open. He was very solemn.

I walked inside the gate, where his bike was parked and locked on the fence. I stood there, holding my brown leather carrying case against my chest. "Hi..."

"Hey...," he mumbled.

Oh, it was so jood to hear his voice again ... even that simple little word.

Silence. Sips. Stares. Slurps.

"How long have you been here?" I asked.

"Since six," he answered, putting the cap on the now-empty bottle and tossing it in the trash can without looking. It was at least six feet away. Good shot.

I looked at my watch. It was going on nine-thirty. "You've been out here all this time?"

"Yup."

He had to be telling the truth, because he seemed so subdued.

"Do you want to come upstairs?"

His expression didn't change. "If ya want me to."

I wanted him to.

My apartment door hadn't even fully closed when he had thrown my case on the floor, grabbed me, spun me around, and lifted me, and had his tongue down my throat. My body came alive again. I felt a rush. My heart skipped three beats. He ripped off my shirt and shorts, but this time he knew I wouldn't put up a fight. I tore off his suit.

An hour later we cooled down in bed, curled up like a pretzel, as I sang to him (yes, Oleta).

Taking *out* Elias and taking *in* Raheim.

A perfect ending to a perfect day.

**16**

"Little Bit..."

For a quick second, I thought I was back at the old house in Bed-Stuy, and my mother was getting me up for school. She was the only person who woke me with a gentle tap against my spine. (Grandma always caressed my face; Anderson would bellow: "Get up, sleepyhead!") She'd already have my blinds open, small beams of daylight peeking through. And, with her bright, brown-sugar face, strawberry-smelling breath, and pleasant smile, she'd announce: "You better come on, honey, because your brother is already at the table, and you know that boy can eat!"

But she never called me Little Bit, and, when my eyes opened, I should've known that it would be my Pooquie leaning over the bed. He was already dressed in three-quarter-length brown pants and tank, and a pair of brown sandals made by a street merchant on 125th Street in Harlem earlier in the week.

"C'mon, Little Bit, get up," he said.

I squinted, looking up at the clock on the night table. It was only nine o'clock.

"Why, Pooquie? It's early..." I yawned.

"I gotta go someplace..."

"Where are you going? What's going on?"

"It's a su'prise," he smiled, standing at the bedroom door. "I'll be Black."

A surprise? I couldn't imagine what else he had up his sleeve. He had already apologized in his own way ("Baby, I'm sorry I came outa my face at you like that.") He still hadn't answered my question concerning the *n*-word, but I wasn't that interested in the answer now; I was just happy he was back and I didn't want to trouble the water. Our quiet time had returned: relaxing on the sofa, watching select episodes of *The Cosby Show* (I have all of them on tape); taking turns reciting chapters from *The Autobiography of Malcolm X,* a book he surprisingly never read; singing a little Randy for him; and doing some serious honey dippin' as Rachelle Ferrell, Will Downing, and Chanté Moore provided the theme music (the best part of making up as far as I'm concerned).

But he even became much "handier" around the house. While I fine-tuned the family issue outline, he offered to do the laundry and, to my surprise, all of the clothes came back their right size and color. He also attempted to make dinner. It was a simple meal — fried chicken, Rice-aroni, and corn-on-the-cob — but he almost burned the rice, forgot to season the chicken, and undercooked the corn. I enjoyed watching him prepare it (simply ovah in purple briefs and tank) more than I did eating it. But all was not lost: the night was topped off with a fierce massage, which he gave to me. All right for Dr. Feelgood.

Knowing that it would have to be something special for him to get up and out so early on a Sunday (yes, on the seventh day, we rested), I happily hopped in the shower and dressed. I put on my new white t-shirt (my "make-up gift" that asked, ISN'T GOD THE GREATEST?), green shorts, and sandals. I went into the kitchen to whip myself up a little breakfast and saw that he had eaten and washed his bowl, silverware, and glass. But he left the banana peel on the counter. I laughed as I tossed it in the garbage can. Some habits are hard to break.

As eleven o'clock rolled around, I was sitting up in the bed, going over the outline one more time, when the bell rang and someone called my name. I stuck my head out the window. It was Raheim.

"Le's be out," he said, as he stood on the steps, tossing some keys in the air.

"Out where?" I yelled.

"How many times I gotta tell you, it's a su'prise, day-am. Hurry up. We double-parked."

"OK."

I snatched my wallet off the night table and then realized what he just said. *We? Double-parked?* While I didn't harbor any animosity toward D.C. or Angel, they were the last two people I wanted to see. I peered out the window, but the white Jeep wasn't there. Raheim was talking to someone seated in the back of a dark gray, four-door Toyota Camry. Because I was on the third floor and the car had tinted windows, I couldn't see who it was.

I came downstairs and found him leaning against the gate in classic B-boy profile: arms folded against his chest, head cocked down, and eyes raised.

"You so slow," he accused.

"Sorry."

"So, ain'cha gonna ask me?"

"Ask you what?"

He pointed to the car, grinning. "Tha wheels."

I shrugged. "OK, I'll ask. Whose is it?"

"It's Angel's. He le'me hold it."

"Uh-huh. And, now, for an even more important question: do you have a driver's license?"

He flashed it. The picture was a mug shot.

He returned it to his back pocket and reached for the gate. "So, le's be outy..."

I grabbed his arm. "So, who is in the car?"

He grinned. *"You'll see..."*

I didn't like the sound of that.

He bebopped over to the driver's side, opened his door, and unlocked mine. I got in and was, to say the least, surprised.

"Hi," said the cheerful little voice, which came out of the mouth of a boy no older than five. He was wearing a seat belt and the same outfit Raheim was. In fact, he and Raheim could've been identical twins: same glowing skin, same oval face, same deep-set eyes, same bite-sized ears, same dimple, same wide winning smile. There was one major difference: he had a cropped head of black curly hair.

I sat down and turned to face him. "Hi. What's your name?"

"Rah-heeem Jewn-yore," he enunciated proudly.

I put out my hand. "Well, it is nice to meet you. My name is Mitchell."

"Mitch-hull? How do you spell that?" he asked.

I told him.

He mouthed the letters and tapped his temple with his left index finger, going over the spelling in his head. "I got a cousin that name!"

"Oh, really," I laughed, glancing at Raheim, who was also laughing.

"Yes," Junior replied. "And the man at my camp, his name is Mr. Mitch-hull. Do you know him?"

"No."

"Oh," he said, somewhat disappointed. "Do you know anybody with my name?"

I glanced at his father and smiled. "Yes, I do..."

"A'right, ya'll," grinned Raheim, Sr., as he took the car out of park and looked in the rearview mirror. "We got a lota things ta do taday. Li'l Brotha Man, sit back an' be still."

"OK, Daddy," Junior answered and complied. "Mitch-hull, please put your seat belt on."

"Yes, Junior, I will." And I did.

Well, isn't this lovely, I thought. Raheim just springs his son on me without warning and forces me to accept the situation by bringing me out with them for a day on the town. I could've pulled him aside, refused to go, but what good would that have done? Besides, Junior seemed like a delight. He was a chip off the old block when it came to looks and charm. But unlike his daddy, he talked – *a lot.*

As we headed for Queens Plaza to do some shopping for him, Junior volunteered his résumé without me asking...

"My name is Raheim Errol Rivers, Jr., and I can spell it ... R-A-H-E-I-M ... E-R-R-O-L ... R-I-V-E-R-S ... J-R, peer-e-od ... I can write my name ... You got a piece of paper and a pencil? ... My birthday is June 5, 19 ... 19-8-8 ... I was born one day after my Daddy ... I live at 9-9-1 1-2-7 Street, number 3-A ... that's in Har-lem ... My zip code is 1-0-0-2-5 ... My phone number is 2-1-2, 2-2-2, 4-5, 3-1 ... I am five years old ... I'm left-handed like my Daddy ... Some of the kids, they tease me about it ... Daddy says they jealous ... I know my ABCs and my 123s ... Betcha I can count higher than you ... I will be in the kinder-garden ... It starts in ... in ... Daddy, when do I go to the kinder-garden?"

As Junior went on and on and on, there were questions I wanted to ask, but he couldn't answer them – only his father, who was busy driving and not paying Junior or me any mind, could. Why didn't Raheim tell me he had a son? Is Junior the reason he dropped out of school? Who does Junior live with? Junior's mother? Raheim and his mother? And, has Raheim lied to me – or, rather, not told me the whole truth about his life? Was he – or is he – married to Raheim's mother? And, since he has a son, does this mean that he is not gay? Of course, there are a lot of gay men who have children – and some of them are married to women who don't know they are. In order to do that heterosexual "lifestyle" thang right, they court women, which can naturally result in their producing children. Others are lucky enough to adopt children, something I plan to do one day. But judging from the evidence in front of me, I knew that Raheim did not adopt this child (Daddy planted that seed and Junior's momma spit him *out).* And, if he turned out not to be gay – something that I assumed was so – that would certainly change things. I had (unknowingly) dated so-called straight and bisexual men before, and it's nothing but heartaches.

I also didn't know what was Raheim's motivation for this "su'prise." Did he really have a close relationship with his son and just wanted to include me? Or was he using Junior to try to score points with me? I really prayed that it wasn't the latter. I would hate to think that he is another one of those brothers who makes the deposit but let's the sister handle the account – another example, in the immortal words of Elias, of "declining family values."

After being on our feet for nearly three hours – during which Junior got a few pairs of pants, some shirts, a pair of sneakers, socks, and a cap, asking me before any piece of clothing was purchased, "Mitch-hull, do you like this?" – we had lunch at a food court that contained at least two dozen restaurants and fast-food joints, including Mickey D's (where the Rivers men got Big Macs) and a Wendy's (where I settled for a chicken sandwich). The place was jam-packed with stressed-out parents, hip-hop teens, and screaming kids. After he finished his food – inhaling it just like his daddy – Junior skipped over to a playground that sat in the middle of the eating area.

"He is so cute," I said, watching him go. "Just like his daddy."

Daddy, lounging back with his behind on the edge of his chair, blushed.

I picked at my sandwich. "So, why didn't you tell me about him before?"

"You ain't ask."

There was that cocky smile.

"Funny, Raheim..."

"I was gonna tell you..."

"Oh, yeah ... when?"

"At tha right time..."

"And *this* was the right time? Just making him appear out of the blue?"

He eased up in his chair and put his arms on the table. "I ain't know how you was gonna reac'."

"Come on, Raheim, we have spent a hell of a lot of time together and..."

"I know. Taday's our annivers'ry."

I jerked back. "Anniversary?"

He lifted his head. "Yeah ... don' you rememba?"

I sure didn't. It was exactly one month ago that we went on our first date. I was shocked – not only that it had been a month, but that Raheim knew and he referred to it that way. He got me.

It all became clearer. "So," I began, "is this my present?"

"Part of it. Li'l Brotha Man today ... me tanite."

I blushed – big time.

Junior came running back. "Daddy, I gotta go."

"You always gotta go," said Daddy, standing and pulling on his dick. He grinned at me. "We be Black."

I watched them walk off, Junior just beginning to master Raheim's bowlegged strut. Daddy and son. Hand in hand. I felt so proud.

My men.

Later that afternoon, as Junior took a nap in our bed, Daddy and I sat on the sofa and he gave me the 411.

"I was a MacDaddy back then ... I was clockin' most pussy. But that was befo' I found out wha' makes my shit really jump..."

He cupped my buns to emphasize his point.

"But there was this one girl ... Crystal. She ... I don' know. In a way, you remind me of 'er..."

*"Oh?* How so?"

"She small, little ... you know, like I could jus' scoop 'er up like you. .. An' she, ya know, looked out fo' me ... Anyway, I started talkin' ta 'er. I wanted it but she ain't want to..."

"Mmmmm-hmmmm..."

"She was a virgin, she was scared. I tol' her I wasn't gonna hurt 'er..."

"Like me..."

"Yeah, smart-ass, like you. Anyway, she finally gave it up. An' it was *jood.*"

"Oh, *really?*"

"Chill, Baby ... not as jood as wit you."

Smack.

"Didn't you two use a condom?" I asked.

"Hell, yeah. My moms knew I was gonna be gettin' mine, so she gave it ta me straight: 'If you gonna stick it in, put it on... '"

"And when *did* you start putting it on?"

"At like thirteen..."

*"Thirteen?"*

"Yeah, thirteen. Wha', is there a fuckin' echo in here? When *you* start?"

"I was sixteen."

"You been fuckin' longa than me, so wha's up wit you?"

"Uh-huh, and the experience shows, doesn't it?"

"*Any*way, like I was 'bout ta say, tha shit can break, ain't nothin' a hundred pe'cent proof, an' it did. At first I ain't believe she was pregnant..."

"Uh-huh..."

"An' then I ain't believe it was mine..."

"Typical..."

"But befo' I knew it, she was gonna have it an' I still ain't tell my moms. So I did."

"And?"

"An', she said either I take care of my responsability or she take care of me."

"Hmmmm, I like your mother. We need more moms like her today..."

"But I wasn't gonna turn my back on 'er. I jus' needed ta figure out wha'tha fuck I was gonna do. All my boyz was tellin' me ta jus' breeze it, she havin' it, not you. But when my Li'l Brotha Man was born..." His face lit up. It was probably the look all fathers get when they recall the birth of a son. "I held him ... I was so scared I was gonna hurt him, he was so fuckin' little. I ain't neva felt like that befo'..."

"Did you two consider getting married?"

"Why? I ain't love 'er. Besides, ain't no way I was gonna take care o' him an' her. Shit, I could hardly take care o' me. I was only sixteen."

"Is that why you dropped out?"

He nodded yes.

I asked, in a very roundabout way, why I was included on a day for them to spend together.

"See, I promised my moms I take him shoppin' weeks back ... but I met somebody," he gushed.

I rolled my eyes. "That's right, just blame it on me."

He chuckled. "Uh-huh, I am."

"Oh, no you don't, Daddy. I didn't keep you from him. I would have understood if you wanted to spend the day without me..."

"Yeah motha-fuckin' right. Tha way you on my shit? Tha way you beg fo' it?"

"Yeah, that's right, and I ain't too proud to beg!"

"Ha, fo' real tho' ... Anyway, ta ansa yo' question, I ain't wanna choose."

"Choose? Do you think I would make you choose between us?"

"An' I ain't wanna be away from you, eitha..."

"Don't feel like that," I said, clutching his biceps. "You two need time to be with each other. I am glad you let me meet him. I don't know if I can handle two of you, but I'll try."

That's right, Pooquie, show those teeth.

He rose off the sofa. "I betta trek. My moms wants him by six an' I gotta take Angel his car."

"Are you coming back?"

He pulled me up and held me by my waist. "Ya know it, Baby. You gonna cook?"

"Ha, you sure as hell aren't!"

"Wha'cha mean?"

"Oh, what part of that statement did you *not* understand? After last night, we'll just leave the cooking to me, Pooquie, OK?"

"Yo, I can cook. Tha kitchen jus' ain't where I can really do it – and ya know it." He started bumping and grinding.

"Mmmmm-hmmmm, whatever, *Daddy...*"

"Yeah, keep talkin' shit, a'right. I got somethin' fo' yo' ass."

"Uh-huh, and I want it."

We kissed – *down*.

He went into the bedroom and woke Junior. After they both took leaks, I met them at the front door.

"Mitch-hull, I'm goin' to Grammy's house!" screamed Junior.

I bent down to face him. He was a big boy for his age and would, no doubt, grow up to be his daddy's size. I tweaked his nose. "I know. I had a good time today ... did you?"

"Yes ... and I wanna come back."

"You do?" I glanced at Raheim. "Well, you can come back. Just tell Daddy, OK?"

"OK." He hugged me. That really caught me off guard. The kid liked me. "Bye."

"Bye bye," I waved, as he zoomed down the stairs.

"Yo, man, stop runnin'! I tol' you 'bout that shit, right?" yelled Raheim.

Junior stopped at the bottom step, looking back up with those innocent eyes. "Yes, Daddy."

"I'll be Black," winked Daddy, as he also took leave.

I watched them pile in the car and drive off. I was tingling all over. And, when Daddy, uh, Raheim, returned, he tangled me all over.

When Michelle saw me at work the next day, she knew we had reunited. "It's all over your face," she said. And she absolutely gagged when I told her about Junior: "You mean there's another one of him running around out here? Chile, I hope he is straight, 'cause I *will* wait the thirteen years!"

Of course, Gene was not thrilled about the return of Raheim or the addition of Junior, arguing that I was getting too involved. "OK, so your fuck buddy is back – but do you want to end up taking care of his kid?"

I was, without a doubt, enchanted with the idea of "taking care of" Junior and Senior. And I got that opportunity: Junior wanted to visit again, and his mother – who, in addition to raising a son, went to college part-time and worked full-time – needed a break, so he stayed with us the following weekend.

And I can honestly say that the apple doesn't fall far from the tree.

They both had birthmarks on the backs of their left thighs.

They both snored lightly.

They both had memories like elephants'. You could tell Junior something and he'd remember it, verbatim, hours later.

They both loved basketball. I had never seen a child so young be so into a sports game and know what's going on.

They both loved bananas.

And both of them could shovel it in, so I was glad that I made two big pots of succotash (a Pooquie favorite) and homemade chicken noodle soup, which Junior especially loved ("Camp-bell's don't taste like this!"). I also made my life easier by having plenty of Wheaties, milk, and orange juice for them. They not only had cereal for breakfast but ate it during the rest of the day. At least Junior doesn't snack on candy, I told myself. And, since his body wasn't filled with all those sugary sweets, he wasn't your superhyperactive, out-of-control kid.

In fact, he was an absolute joy.

He was mild-mannered and polite; he always said, "May I," and, "Thank you."

He never talked back or got out of line (I guess I wouldn't either, with a big daddy like Raheim).

He had his own special, cute way of saying things, like "Not nececelery," "Un-bee-wee-vuh-bull," and my favorites, "Yes, I'm am" and "No, I'm ain't."

And he even got on his daddy about being neat ("Daddy, pick up your towel"; "Daddy, put the milk thing in the garbage, not back in the fridge"; "Daddy, flush the toilet").

I figured that things would be awkward at first, that it would take time for him to really warm up to me. After all, going on an afternoon shopping spree is one thing; spending forty-eight hours under the same roof is another. But he not only liked me, he trusted me. This was made clear when he and Raheim arrived that Friday night as I was cutting my hair.

I am no barber, but because of the outlandish prices one can pay just to get a shape-up (some folks have the gall to charge $15), I purchased a pair of clippers. Because my hair is naturally straight (it's the Cherokee in me), it grows long instead of up and out. So I give myself a Caesar every other week.

Junior sat on the toilet lid, watching in silence. After I was done, I checked myself out in the mirror. I smiled at him. "So, what do you think?"

He smiled. "It looks jood."

I couldn't help but laugh.

"Mitch-hull?"

"Yes?"

"Can you do my hair like that, too ... *pleeze?*"

How could I refuse? Besides, Raheim was planning on doing it after I finished mine. But I knew that he was exhausted from making the trip to Harlem, so I happily obliged.

It took half an hour. The cut was like mine except that I gave him a part near his left temple. I was pleased with my creation; it was the first time I had really done another person's head (Raheim hardly had any to do). And Junior loved it.

"Oh wow!" he cried, as he looked at himself in the bedroom mirror, waking his father up with his screams. "This is jood! Thank you, Mitch-hull, thank you!"

Later that night, Raheim told me that Junior only let him do his hair — that is, until me. That made me feel jood.

Of course, he did like to talk a lot. ("Mitch-hull, how old are you?" "Mitch-hull, when is your birthday?" "Mitch-hull, do you have a brother or sister?" "Mitch-hull, what is a reporter?" "Mitch-hull, Daddy says you can sing. Sing for me, *pleeze?*") But sit him in front of the TV set and the only peeps you'd hear out of him were when he was giggling over the Road Runner outrunning Wile E. Coyote.

And, like those cartoons, the entire weekend was a riot.

Take Friday night. An hour after we all went to bed, Raheim began nudging me.

"What is it, Raheim?"

"I want some."

"What?"

"Gimme some, Baby, c'mon..."

"No."

"Why?"

"What do you mean, *why?* Your son is in the next room."

"So...?"

*"So?"* I thought it was understood that we couldn't address each other with our nicknames, that we'd have to refrain from being so affectionate and playful, and, most of all, that we would be knockin' no boots because of Junior. In fact, I wanted Raheim to crash with Junior in the sofa bed, because I feared that Junior would tell his mother or grandmother that Daddy was sleeping in the same bed with another man. But, as Raheim pointed out, there wasn't room for two people in the sofa bed. Besides, he told Junior that we were "roommates" and that he was giving up the sofa bed for him. That I could deal with.

But having sex? No way, José.

"He'll hear us, Raheim..."

"He ain't gonna hear us. When he's out, he's out. Anyway, we can be quiet."

*"We* can be quiet? Since when?"

"C'mon, Little Bit, I need it."

"No, I..."

Before I knew it, the hands were everywhere, his lips were all over mine, and the dick was poking me *there*. After a few minutes of some hot foreplay, I stopped him.

"Quiet?" I whispered.

"Yeah...," he breathed, still going for his.

"OK..." I surrendered.

We did it — and paid for it the next morning.

I was getting breakfast ready as Junior, all washed up and sitting at the table, greeted Raheim with:

"Daddy, your TV set was loud last night."

Raheim looked at me as I placed the box of cereal on the table. My facial expression said, "See, I told you so." Junior had already asked me about the noise and I told him his father was watching a movie. All Raheim had to do was go along.

"It was loud?" said Raheim, sitting down.

"Yes. It sounded like somebody was doing the wild thing."

Upon hearing that, I dropped the bowls on the kitchen floor. Thank God they were plastic.

Raheim patted him on the back. "I'm sorry, Li'l Brotha Man. If I watch TV tanite, it ain't gon' be loud, a'right?"

"OK."

Needless to say, the TV set was not turned on that night.

After breakfast, Junior said he wanted to see *Jurassic Park*. I didn't think it was a good idea. I heard the movie was really scary and particularly violent at the end, and that children under the age of eight shouldn't see it. Raheim, though, didn't see it that way.

"He ain't too young fo' it," he argued.

"Raheim, a person in their twenties reacts much differently to people being eaten by dinosaurs than a five-year-old."

"Wha'cha think he should see? Some *stoo*pid shit like *Free Willy?*"

"No, I don't." And I didn't. I, quite frankly, am tired of all of these white-boy-loves-and-saves-the-endangered-animal flicks.

"He's my Li'l Brotha Man," Raheim bellowed. "He can hang."

"Well, if he starts having nightmares..."

"He ain't gonna have no nightmares. My son ain't no punk. It's jus' a fuckin' movie. A'right?"

"OK..."

We took him and he screamed. Hell, I screamed. But Raheim screamed the loudest. And *he's* the one who ended up having nightmares. Two times that night he woke up, shaking and jumping, yelling, "No!" and scaring me. After the second nightmare, I cradled him like a baby and hummed him to sleep. He wouldn't admit he was dreaming about T-Rex; he said he couldn't remember. But both Junior and I, snickering behind his back, knew better.

And, on Sunday, I made one full-course meal: bar-b-qued turkey wings, spinach, rice and gravy, hot rolls, and a chocolate pie. Junior loved everything – except the spinach.

"I don't eat that," he frowned.

"Have you ever eaten it before?" I asked.

"Yes, and I don't like it."

"Don't you want to grow up to be strong like your daddy?"

"Yes..."

"Well, how do you think he got to be so big?"

Raheim spit out his food, laughing. I then realized what I said – and the innuendo behind it.

I held in a chuckle. "Believe me, Junior, it tastes great. I promise you. Try it, for me, OK?"

He looked at his father, at his plate, then me. "OK." He tried it and liked it so much that he asked for more.

But the Kodak moments to cherish were when Raheim, the Big Bad B-boy, was being tender with his son.

They exercised together – or, rather, Daddy did and Junior imitated his moves. I fell out watching Junior do one-handed push-ups on his Daddy's back – an event that turned into a piggy-back ride into the bathroom.

They took a bath together: Junior at one end of the tub, Daddy at the other. Junior played with his father's big pretty feet and my rubber ducky, splashed water about, and pretended to be allergic to soap. He tried to escape, but Daddy swooped him back in and scrubbed him down.

They wrestled each other on the bed and Junior, thanks to Daddy, remained undefeated. He pinned Daddy down, got him in a headlock, tied his hands behind his back with imaginary rope, and walked on his back and butt, his hands pointed to the heavens, proclaiming, "Mitch-hull, I'm still the Champ!"

They tossed Junior's football in front of the house as I sat on the stoop, loving every minute of their touchdown tagging and tackling. They also went "swimming" – the fire hydrant was open in front of my brownstone. They splished and splashed each other in matching yellow trunks. Raheim thought he was funny filling a bucket with water and drenching me, but Junior got him back for me – right in the face. With revenge in his eyes, Raheim chased us into the house and I ended up with a flooded bathroom.

And that Sunday after dinner, they went into the bedroom to watch television while I washed the dishes. It took me only ten minutes, but that's all the time they needed to fall asleep. Daddy was sitting up in the middle of the bed, his right arm around Junior, who was using Daddy's hard chest as a pillow (I've been in that position before). Both wore the same gold shortall. I turned off the TV and covered them up, since it was a little cool in the house.

As I smiled at them and remembered everything that happened that weekend, all I could think was:

*I wish I could have Pooquie's baby.*

"They are *so* cute..."

Denise and I were in my cubicle, editing three of the six family profiles we were overseeing for the revamped first issue of the year, renamed: "We Are Family: How the American Family Continues to Change and Challenge Our Society." Elias was too through; most of the points that he wanted to make were thrown out in the final draft. We would tackle welfare, but in its proper context. Denise dug up stats that said the majority of folks on the rolls are white and a third of all U.S. children will be on welfare before they are eighteen, making it clear that it is everybody's problem. And, instead of indicting nonnuclear families, we would analyze how media images influence our attitudes about what we think a family should be.

I was saving and printing out new copies of the profiles when she picked up the photo of Raheim and Junior on my desk. Raheim had given it to me when he came back to the house after taking Junior home the night before. It was taken at Junior's birthday party – the day we met. Junior, wearing a gold King hat, is sitting on Raheim's lap as he blows out his six candles. I took the autographed postcard of Wesley Snipes out of its gold frame (sorry, Wes) and put my men in.

"Yeah, they are cute," I agreed, grinning.

"So, I guess we're getting serious, hunh?" she asked, putting it back on the desk.

"Serious?"

"Yes. I mean, I am a heterosexual woman, so I wouldn't know about these things, but if a man introduces you to his next of kin, doesn't that mean he's going to, uh, pop the question?"

"Denise, you're a trip," I laughed. "We've barely known each other six weeks..."

"So? Some people have known each other six *days* and gone to the chapel."

"Ha, talk about a short engagement."

"Yeah..." She sat back in her chair studying the picture. "You know, since we are trying to shatter stereotypes with this issue, why don't we include this photo on the cover with some of the others we've chosen?"

"You think so?"

"Yeah, why not? We see single mothers all the time but not single dads. And from what you've told me, Raheim doesn't live up to the image of a love-'em-and-leave-'em father. Hell, the photo says it all."

I looked at the picture again. She was right. Of course, the difficult task would be to convince the rest of the staff. They would certainly argue that such a picture just turns the stereotype upside down, not inside out.

"I think it's a terrific idea," I admitted. "But you know what *they* will say."

"Don't worry about it. When Michael sees that picture, he's gonna love it to death. All you have to do is OK it through Mr. Raheim."

The phone rang.

"This is Mitch..."

"Wha's up?"

"Hey, I was just talking about you."

"Oh yeah?"

"Yeah. Where are you?"

"Tha Uppa Wes' Side, Baby, still waitin' on this fuckin' package. I wish these folks have they shit tagetha befo' I come..."

"I guess we can't have lunch, hunh?"

"Nah, Baby. But I see ya tanite. I got a su'prise for ya..."

"Another one?"

"Yeah. I'm gonna blow yo' mind."

"You already do that ... *Daddy.*"

Denise looked up from the notes she was reading and grinned.

I'd forgotten she was there. We both coughed a laugh.

"And ya know that," bragged Raheim.

"Listen, Denise and I thought it would be a great idea to use the picture of you and Junior for the family issue. How about it?"

"Sounds cool."

"Really?"

"Yeah. No big thang."

"Great. But don't tell Junior. Let that be his surprise."

"A'right."

"So, what time will I see you tonight?"

"'Round nine."

"OK."

"Little Bit?"

"Yes?"

"Who's tha man?"

I grinned. "You are."

"An' who is *yo'* man?"

I beamed. "You are."

"And ya know that. See ya. Peayce."

I hung up the phone, staring into space.

"Mitchell. Hello? Mitchell? *Earth to Mitchell?*" said Denise, waving her yellow pad in front of my face.

"Oh, I'm sorry." I wrung my hands. "He says it's OK. I can't wait to see Junior's face when he sees it in the magazine."

"Hunh, I can't wait to see Elias's face when we tell him about it at the twelve-thirty meeting."

"Me too."

The phone rang.

"This is Mitch..."

"Miss Thing, I know who it is," said Gene.

"Hi ... What's up?"

"I know you've been very busy with, ahem, Daddy and Junior, but have you asked anyone about the art position?"

"What art position?"

"Uh-huh, I figured you hadn't."

It hit me. "Oh shit, I forgot."

"Look, make some calls, like yesterday, 'cause they are about to look at this Caucasian child and the last thing I want up in here is a white man drawing caricatures of Negroes and thinking he's hip."

I chuckled. "Gotcha. Call me at home tonight."

"Thanks. *Ciao.*"

"Bye."

I made a note to myself, took the picture out of its frame, grabbed my own notebook, and turned to Denise. "Well, let's get this over with."

⊕

After Michael, who was filling in for Leonard while he was on vacation, gave us a progress report on photos for each article and sidebar, we discussed the cover. We all agreed that four different images should appear. Denise and I wanted one to be a homosexual couple and their child. Elias and Phillip didn't, since we would be covering it in the gay issue. Andrew, speaking for Steven, said that the inside profile of a lesbian-headed family "would be enough" (causing Michael to roll his eyes and hiss). Out of some twenty other photos, we chose three: a white (and naturally widowed) single mother and her twin two-year-old sons; an Asian couple and their teenaged daughter; and a Latino couple, the wife visibly pregnant. All four pictures featuring Black families had a single mother and several kids. Figures...

There was one slot to fill. Before people started going through the pile again, I pulled out the photo of Raheim and Junior and passed it around.

"I thought we wanted to avoid this type of thing, Mitch," observed Elias, as he and Phillip frowned at the picture. Phillip sat between Elias and Andrew on one side of the table, with Denise, Michael, and me on the other.

"What we want to avoid is the obvious," I argued. "And this isn't. How many times do you see a photo of a Black man with his child in print?"

"Almost never," answered Denise.

"Well, I don't know...," pondered Elias. "There isn't enough balance."

"Balance?" Denise and I said in unison.

"There's already one single parent on the cover – we don't need another one," he argued. "We should have another type." Phillip nodded his head in agreement.

"There are also two couples on the cover already, Elias, and you had no objection to them, so what kind of balance do you really want?" I asked, even though I already knew: white balance or, rather, dominance.

"People won't be able to identify with this," added Phillip.

"What does *that* mean?" I demanded. He was obviously hanging out with Elias too much – I would expect the golden-haired golden boy to say something stupid like that.

"How many single fathers are there? Not many..."

"Yes, there are, and no matter how many there are, they are out there..." I then realized that Raheim isn't a single father in the figurative sense; Junior's mother is in his life. But so what? The picture is great.

"Oh, they are *so* delightful!" exclaimed Michael with a melodramatic slap to his face. Andrew had just given him the photo. "We have to use it!"

Denise and I nodded at each other.

"We can't," protested Phillip.

"Oh *yes* we can," said Michael, pulling his "Catwoman" glasses down to his nose and glaring at Phillip. "It's a natural family event that all of us can identify with. It isn't staged or phony-looking. In fact, it is *the* best photo of the lot."

"I would have to agree," surmised Andrew.

"Well, we should take a vote on it. It's already past one," added Denise.

The vote: four to two. Majority ruled.

"I'll meet you in the lobby," said Denise, as she gathered her things up and headed out the door. We were going to have lunch. I nodded.

As Elias and Phillip walked out grumbling, Michael eased over to me. "Hmmmm ... Is this the gentleman you've been seeing?"

I giggled. "Yes."

"And this is his son?"

"Yes."

He put his right hand on his hip and poked me in the chest with the picture. "You better work, Mitch."

⊕

I was so happy about my men being on the cover of my magazine that I, once again, forgot all about Gene and the freelance artist position at Simply Dope. I remembered when I was home. I'd started going through my Rolodex when Raheim rang the bell.

"Wha's up, Baby?" he said, as I let him in.

"You."

Smack. Smack. Smack.

"What do you have there?" I asked. He was carrying what appeared to be a framed poster in a brown wrapper.

He pushed me into the living room. "Now, don' be so damn nosy. You'll see it. Now sit on tha couch, an' keep yo' eyes closed."

"Oh, this is my surprise?"

"No, it ain't, a'right? ...Jus' sit down..."

I did as I was told. I heard him take off his black leather backpack and the paper coming off the surprise. He placed it on the coffee table in front of me.

"A'right, open 'em."

I did and couldn't believe what I was seeing. In a silver frame and on a piece of tan construction paper was a dark pencil drawing of me, lying across the very sofa I was sitting on, naked, on my stomach, my right leg bent and extended up, the right side of my face resting on a pillow, which my arms are clutching. The look on my face said one thing: *I'm Easy.*

I was speechless. "I ... I..."

Raheim, who was standing over the drawing, bent down to face me. "Wha's wrong ... cat go'cha tongue?"

I blushed. "Yeah, you could say that. It is *fab*ulous."

"I know. Tol' you I blow ya mind."

I reached for it and held it. "Where did you get this done?"

"I ain't get it done nowhere. I did it."

I pointed at it. "You did this?"

"Yeah..."

"Serious?"

He became indignant. "Yeah, serious ... why? You don' think I can do somethin' like that?"

I looked at the portrait. "No, it's just that ... well, you never told me you *could* do anything like this..."

"What, I gotta tell you ev'rythang? Sometimes I wanna jus' show you."

Uh-huh, show me.

"When did you do this?"

"Uh, tha week I ain't come 'round," he mumbled.

"You were able to draw this without seeing me?"

"Hell, yeah. I know wha' my Baby look like ... all ova."

He sure did. He'd remembered the scar near my left ankle when I injured myself in gymnastics class in high school, and the dimple on my left butt cheek. And speaking of my butt...

"My behind is not that big, Raheim."

He plopped down next to me. "It is too—"

"No, it isn't," I pouted.

He swung his arm around my shoulder, pulling me close to him. "Baby, be*lieve* me, it is. You don' see wha' I see. Ha, you can't see it!"

I hit him on the chest. "Shut up!"

"But it's mine an' I love it," he said, sliding his hand around my back down to my seat. He motioned toward the drawing. "You like it?"

"I *love* it. Thank you."

After we lip-locked, I asked him about his talent. He said he had been drawing since he was six. He had a book of his work in his bag, all of it stunning. Most were snapshots of his 'hood: the details of the houses, stores, and people were so real. There was one of him, D.C., and Angel, striking that cool pose on a stoop. There was also one each of Junior and Crystal, which had the title SUNSHINE. "Tha's wha' she is," he explained.

I became jealous. "Mine doesn't have a title."

"Yes it do. Tha frame is cov'rin' it up." He took the drawing out and there it was: LONGIN' 4 LITTLE BIT.

"Why that title?" I asked.

"Cuz, stoopid...," he giggled.

I looked at the title and then the portrait. I smiled. "You missed me."

"Wha' you think?"

I smiled. "Uh-huh ... you better had."

"Wha'cha say? You talkin' shit again, hunh?"

He reached for me but I shot up off the sofa just in time. The phone rang – saved by the bell.

"Hello?"

"Well, any luck?" It was Gene.

"Any luck with wh– oh, I'm still trying."

"Look, dahling, I know you find it hard tearing yourself away from Rah, Rah, Rah, Raheim..."

I didn't hear anything else he said after that, because the lightbulb turned on. I looked at Raheim, who was taking off his black boots, and at my portrait.

"Gene, I have a great lead for you. I'll call you back in fifteen minutes."

I hung up the phone and returned to my seat.

"Pooquie...?"

"Uh-oh..."

I rubbed his head. "What...?"

"Don' even play that inacent shit. You want somethin'..."

I moved in closer, resting my right hand on his left shoulder. "I don't want something from you. I want to do something for you."

"Oh yeah?"

"Yeah." I told him about the part-time job at Simply Dope and he freaked out. I had never seen him get so excited about anything – well, anything except, you know...

But his excitement was quickly doused by his own self-doubts. "They ain't gonna gimme no job like that..."

"Why you say that?"

"I ain't even got a high school diploma, Baby. They prob'ly want somebody in college..."

"If they did, Gene would've told me. They want someone with talent, someone they can work with and work hard ... and that's you, Pooquie."

"I don' know..."

"Look, we'll call Gene and talk to him about it, OK?"

He looked defeated, his head back on the sofa. "A'right..."

I dialed Gene's number, then sat back down, stroking Pooquie's face and neck. "Hi, Gene. I have someone for you."

"You do? *Fab*ulous! Who is he ... or she?"

"It's a he, he's sitting right here, and his name is Raheim."

Dead silence.

"This *is* a joke, isn't it?" he queried.

"No, of course not. He can draw his ass off. He has a small collection of his work sitting in front of me, and he gave me a poster-sized picture he drew of me. Wait 'til you see it. You'll gag. He is Talented with a capital T."

"My dear, what *that* boy is talented at is not normally done in a place of business ... unless we count a brothel."

"Will you be serious! I know you all can work with him. And, to correct you, that other talent you mentioned isn't talent ... it's a gift!"

"All right, Miss Thing, I hear you. Well, if the boy wasn't talented, you wouldn't be going to bat for him. Put him on."

I handed Raheim the phone. After his standard "Wha's up," he alternated between "Yeah," "A'right," and "Uh-huh." He then laughed out loud and handed me back the phone.

"Yeah, Gene?"

"I told Homeboy to come to my office at five-thirty. You'll tell him where to go. And I also told him to make sure he dresses for the occasion. In other words, he can't be showing off his ass in an orange loincloth."

I looked at Raheim, simply ovah in a dark green fishnet shortall. His green briefs – and everything else – were very visible to the naked eye. It wouldn't be an appropriate outfit, either. I laughed. "Don't worry, he'll be dressed for success."

"Thank you. He'll be a hard sell, since he hasn't studied in school. His work will have to speak for itself. But, when Monica and Arthur get a look at him, he'll probably be hired on the spot." Monica Wilbourne and Arthur Haile are the head artists at Simply Dope. I met them at one of their press parties. She is a fag hag and he is her hangin' partner. After Gene mentioned them, I didn't like the idea of Pooquie working under those two man-hungry mongrels. While she has a pretty face (a la Halle Berry), Monica is six feet tall and as skinny as a toothpick – literally. Everyone swears she's anorexic, but she denies it. Arthur looks like a brown-skinned Michael Bolton with freckles and a very bad weave. I knew they would be clawing at Pooquie. But if this opportunity led him to get his GED, I was all for it.

"Thanks, Gene. I'll talk to you tomorrow."

As I hung up the phone, I heard a bang in the front of the house. I went into the bedroom and found Raheim standing on the bed to hang up the portrait.

"Wait!" I yelled, making him stumble back on the bed, the portrait still in his hands.

"Day-am, wha's wrong wit you?"

I sat on the bed. "Shouldn't we hang it over the sofa?"

"There's a pic'cha there already..." And there was — a full-length framed poster for the film *Looking for Langston*. I didn't care for the movie, but the poster is hot — two nude, gorgeous brothers sleeping in a semi-69 position.

I poked and pinched his right nipple through a hole in the shortall. "Well, since it is a portrait of me nude and I'm on the sofa, I think it should go there. Besides, after you put it up, we can, you know, bring the drawing to life..."

We did.

Raheim got the job. Simply Dope's art department head, Franklin Styles, who overlooked Raheim's not having a résumé and not having an art degree, felt they should give new jacks like him a chance. Styles loved his "rare, raw talent." In fact, he loved it so much that he gave Raheim his first assignment right after he accepted the position: designing the cover of the CD single for a new female rap trio named Ax-2-Grind. Raheim brought the CD to the house; the song was called "R-E-S-P-E-C-T," which took brothas to task for referring to sistas as bitches and ho's. And, yes, they sampled Aretha *(Sock it to me, sock it to me, sock it to me...)*. Since I'm not an avid rap fan (my collection boasts only the catalogs of Salt-n-Pepa and Queen Latifah), I could hardly make out anything they were saying, so Raheim broke it down for me.

As Gene predicted, Monica and Arthur loved Raheim. Arthur wanted their introductory handshake to last longer than it should, while Monica wanted him to kiss her hand (being a gentleman, he did). Every word he said they gooed over. And everything they said to him was a compliment: "handsome face," "strong aura," "sweet personality," "sexy voice," "beautiful skin," "naughty eyes" — and, mind you, all of it was during the ten minutes they were supposed to be interviewing him. Raheim, of course, ate up the attention.

Raheim's having a full-time day job worked in his favor. They needed someone who would be available in the evening, and most of the kiddies they wanted to hire had to work or study after five.

But he didn't really need to come into their offices to work on any projects. I gave him a present to show him how proud I was: his own work space. I rearranged my office so that he had one corner and I had another. I got out the rickety yet usable architect table and chair that Peter, my ex, had left in my closet (along with a box full of other mementos, such as a few photos, love letters, and a fuck movie). I also bought him a work light. He was so thrilled with what I did that he decided to break it in that night. His deadline wasn't until the following week, so he had time; but he couldn't wait to get started. As he crafted and conceived, I milled around him, occasionally looking over his shoulders – and massaging them.

After about ten minutes, he couldn't take it anymore. "C'mon now, Little Bit. I can't concentrate if you doin' that..."

"I'm just trying to help you relax," I argued innocently.

But he wasn't falling for it. "You know that ain't wha' you doin', so stop."

"OK. If you need anything, call me. I'll be in the bedroom." I kissed him on the back of his head.

I got in bed to watch TV, but within half an hour, it was watching me. When I woke up, it was five in the morning. He wasn't beside me (or, rather, on top of me). I went into the den and there he was, fast asleep in the chair, his head resting on the desk. I got him to come to bed.

He had to get up a couple of hours later, so he was dead tired. I advised him to take the day off – the last thing I needed to hear was that he fell asleep at the wheel – but he said no. Besides, the concept was done and he wanted to hand it in. He wouldn't show it to me – he wanted me to see it in record stores. He dropped it off on his lunch hour, and that night, Franklin told Raheim that they would be using it. He got his first check: $400. While that may not be a lot compared to what other artists earned, it made Raheim, who had never sold a piece of his work before, an instant celebrity. Folks at the office congratulated him heartily – especially Monica and Arthur, who offered to take him out to dinner, but he refused ('cause I told him so). Even Gene, who was impressed with his talent, sent him a note, telling him to keep up the good work.

After surprising me so many times in the past few weeks – helping me around the house, letting me meet Junior, drawing my portrait – I thought that it was time I surprised him, as well as help him celebrate his new career. Raheim would often say that I had a "nice little bit of a body" (hence, my nickname) and that I'd look jood in a pair of Spandex – something I didn't find hard to believe but hard to do. While I knew I had a tight, toned physique, I wasn't too fond of walking around in the street with my thighs, buttocks, and crotch basically on display. Some folks got off on that, like Raheim. How else can one explain his coming to the Vill on Gay Pride Day in almost nothing?

But, if Pooquie wanted me to get them, I would. So, I went to a body shop in the Vill called Form Fit on my lunch hour to buy a pair. I wasn't in the place more than five seconds when a deep voice asked,

"May I help you?" I knew the face I would see would be a Caucasian one — they pounce on us as soon as we enter a store to make it clear that they know you, a potential criminal, not customer, are there. But when I turned around, I was pleased to see a brother. A bodybuilding brother. He was my height but three times my size. Beefcake *down*. A red bodysuit accented his bodacious brown bod. His face was shaped like a lightbulb, his jaw a sharp square. His short locs were in an onion bun. His eyes were coal, his eyebrows thick, his lips full and inviting. A gold hoop was in his nose and a silver cross dangled from his right ear.

"Oh, yes, yes, you can," I answered, a little taken aback by the sight in front of me. What an Incredible Bulk! "I'd like to purchase a pair of cycling pants ... for myself."

"Fine. Please follow me."

I went with him to the back of the store, where there were piles of them set out by size on a makeshift shelf. I started checking them out while he checked me out.

He struck a pose against a mirror on one of the three dressing room doors. "Do you know what you want?"

I glanced at him and smiled. "Well, to be quite honest, I don't. I've never worn them before."

"You're kidding. With a great shape like yours?"

I knew he was flirting — I was wearing a pair of black jeans and a gray Columbia Journalism t-shirt. The most he could see was the shape of my behind, which, no matter what kind of pants I wear, cannot be hidden. I blushed anyway. "Thank you. But you're the one with the shape."

"Thanks. Just leave it to me. I'll help you find something you like."

Uh-huh, I bet you will.

After he showed me a host of multicolored, psychedelic, and see-through items, I finally saw the one I wanted: basic black with a white stripe on both sides of the legs.

"Well, it wouldn't be the one I'd choose for you," he lamented. "I mean, it's so plain and ordinary. But I'm sure it won't look that way on you."

Do they give him a commission for saying shit like that?

"I guess I'll need a small," I said.

"No, you'll need a medium, believe me..."

"Well, I'm sure..."

He placed his hands on my love handles, gripping me tightly for a second, measuring my waist with his fingers. "A medium," he smiled, his fingertips lightly indenting my cheeks.

"OK...," I sighed, unable to take my eyes away from his.

He found the size and, with his hand pressed against the small of my back, ushered me to the dressing room. "If you need help, just let me know," he winked as he closed the door.

I was already hot, since it was ninety degrees, but he was making my temperature rise even higher. I felt a pang of guilt: here I was, enjoying this man's attention when I have Pooquie. But then it dawned on me: there's no harm in flirting, is there? Raheim probably does it when he's not with me — especially since, the few times we went out, I caught him all in somebody else's shit and he promised he'd never do it again. "It's jus' a nat'ral thang ta do, Baby," he argued. It didn't sound right then, but now that the shoe was on the other foot, it did. Besides, this man was a real hunk: I almost never catch the eye of guys like him.

So, after I disrobed (leaving on my shirt), tucked everything in its proper place, and got a feel for the pants, I emerged from the dressing room to do a little winking myself.

When he saw me, he licked his lips. "You look good."

"Do I really?" I cooed, prancing in front of the mirror.

"Damn straight. You have really nice legs and ... the pants, they fit you well."

I giggled. "Thank you."

I approached him as he leaned against one of the displays. "I don't know ... do you think they are too tight?" I turned around to give him a better view. He gagged.

"Uh, uh, no, no, not at all...," he managed to mouth.

"Fine. I'll take them."

He also convinced me to buy a white tank. As he rung me up, I gave him the third degree.

"So, how long did it take you to get a body like that?"

He smiled. "A couple of years."

"That's all?"

"Yeah. For guys our size, it's not that hard. Are you interested in pumping up?"

My eyes raised. "I might be..."

"Well, why don't you give me a call? I do personal training. We can come up with an exercise regimen you'll like..."

This time I didn't just think it, I spoke it. "Yes, I'm sure we can..."

We introduced ourselves as he gave me the store card with his name and home number on the back.

"Why do they call you Fox?" I asked.

"I can't tell you why ... I have to show you," he grinned, handing me my receipt and clothing.

I put the card in my back pocket. "Well, you might get your chance. Thanks for your help."

He came from behind the counter to open the door for me as I headed out. "Anytime. Come back real soon."

"I will," I smiled.

When Pooquie called me after lunch, I told him to meet me in the Vill after work – don't go to Brooklyn and don't go Uptown and take off his uniform. I wanted us to ride home over the Brooklyn Bridge on his bike. We had done it twice before. But this time, unbeknownst to him, we would both be dressed for it.

When I put on the outfit in the bathroom and was checking myself in the mirror, Michael came in.

"*You* had better *work,* Mitch! When *RRRRR*aheim sees you, he's gonna flip!"

The folks I encountered on my way to meet him, though, got to flip first. Several fellas and females stared me down. One guy, walking hand in hand with some girl, nearly broke his neck trying to get the back view. But their peekaboo glances were nothing compared to the whistles and comments I got in the Vill.

"*Day-am,* small fry, you betta shake 'n' bake!"

"Le'me freak ya, baby, *all* nite long!"

"I'd like to taste *that!*"

"Aw yeah, baby, I got somethin' fo' you!"

"Gimme yo' phone numba ... I'm in love wit ya!"

"*Whoomp, there it is!*"

I just blushed at all the statements, even though I knew I shouldn't have. I was being sexually harassed. I'd heard identical things said to women by men on the street. But I knew my admirers (if we can call them that) wouldn't see it that way. They believed they were paying me compliments. I played along, though, because it fed my ego. Things did get a little tense when this one guy tried to put his arm around me. I kindly told him, "Sorry, I got a man," to which he predictably replied, "How long ya *had* dat problem?" I couldn't help but laugh. He backed off, blowing a kiss in my direction: "Cool. But I hope yo' man knows wha'ta do wit you."

He does.

My man was standing on the next corner. I would recognize his back and butt anywhere. He was wearing the same outfit I was. His bike stood between him and a tall light-skinned fella with an Eraserhead fade and skinny legs. When he spotted me walking toward them, he smiled and cued Raheim.

"Hi...," I cheerfully said.

"Hey," Raheim mumbled.

"My name is Mitchell," I said to his friend.

He shook my hand. "Randolph."

"So what do you think? You like?" I asked Raheim, modeling.

He didn't answer; he was busy looking at a B-boy who obviously liked what he saw. He was scopin' me out, taking in the full view by walking around us.

And Raheim didn't like it. "Yo, man, you got a problem?"

The short, stout, honey-colored guy, who had a very long, unattractive face and unkempt, thick braids under a stocking cap, stopped in front of us. "I think you da one wit da problem, G—"

"No, motha-fucka, *you* tha one wit tha problem. Ain' nothin' ova here fo' yo' ass, so jus' keep walkin'..."

"Nigga, who *you* s'pose ta be? Ain' no-fuckin'-body say *shit* ta you. I wanna talk ta *him*, not *you*..." He took a few steps toward me. Raheim charged him. The bike fell to the ground as I jumped in front of Raheim.

*"Raheim, stop!"* I screamed.

*"I'll stomp this nigga! Move, Little Bit, move!"* he demanded.

"Yo, brotha, can'cha see they tagetha," argued Randolph, attempting to hold back our uninvited guest. "Jus' move it along, a'right?"

The guy pushed Randolph. *"Yo, ge'da fuck offa me, man!"* He started brushing off his clothes as if Randolph had contaminated him. "If dat's da way it was, dat's all ya'll had ta say. *Dis* punk-ass motha-fucka ain' had ta try ta break fly an' shit..."

"Nobody tol' you ta bring yo' punk ass ova here startin' shit," Raheim snarled, his eyes and temples jumping. My hands were on his chest. His heart was beating a mile a minute.

The guy put his hand inside his black jean jacket — did he have a gun? I moved toward Raheim, not taking my eyes off of his hand. He just kept it there. "Dat's a'right, G. I ain' gon' embarriss yo' ass no mo', cuz ya doin' it yo'self. You ain' nothin' but a *fuck*in' zero ... you ain' worth it..."

Raheim tensed. The fella looked at me, winked, and, grabbing his crotch, strutted off through a part of the crowd that had come to see the fight.

Raheim walked away from me as Randolph helped him pick up his bike. By then, the crowd had dispersed. After making sure the bike, Raheim, and I were OK, Randolph took off. Raheim leaned up against the pole and glared at me.

"Jus' wha'tha *fuck* you think you doin'?"

"What are you talking about?"

He pointed at my pants with both hands clasped. *"That."*

"My pants? You don't like them?"

"No, I *don'* like 'em."

"Why not? You're the one who said I'd look jood in them."

"Yeah, but I ain' tell you ta come out here an' show ev'rybody wha's mine..."

Show everybody what's mine?

"What you mean by that?" I asked.

"Wha'tha *fuck* I jus' say? Am I yo' man?"

"Raheim..."

*"Don' 'Raheim' me nothin'!* I ain' *even* tryin' ta hear that! Ansa tha *fuckin'* question."

I jumped back. I took a deep breath. "Yes ... yes, you are."

"Well, then *ac'* like it. You wit *me*. I don' need you comin' out here lookin' like you ain't, like you some ho..."

That was it.

"Wait one mother-fucking minute, Raheim," I began, my hands on my hips. "How *you* sound, telling me what I can and cannot wear. You are wearing a pair ... what does that make you?"

"Tha's diff'rent..."

"Uh-huh, you wear them because of your job, right? Bull*shit*. You can parade around half-naked, but not me, right?"

"That ain't it..."

"It is too, Raheim. What about your little see-through jumpers? What about your strolls through the fuckin' Vill in your underwear? You *might* be my man, but you *ain't* my boss and you *ain't* my father."

I huffed off toward the train station. He grabbed me.

I fought him. "Get *off* of me, Raheim, *get off.*"

"C'mon, Little Bit, be cool."

"'Be cool,' *my ass.*"

"Don' be like that."

*"You* should've thought of that before you talked to me like that."

"Hey, hey, hey, c'mon, jus' chill..."

"No, *no* ... don't *even* try to kiss me ... no, no, *no...*"

Yes.

The kiss was hard and hungry. It burned me. When our lips parted, I saw that he was leaning up against a red-brick building, holding me by my buns. I turned to see who was around us – no one. Just the bike. I just stared at his chest.

"Ya know, you so fuckin' hot when you angry," he whispered in my ear, licking it. I flinched but remained silent.

He squeezed me tighter. "I lose my head sometimes, Baby. You right ... I ain't had no right talkin' ta ya like that. Pleeze don' be angry... *pleeze?"*

He gave me those sad eyes like Junior and I couldn't help but fall for it. I wrapped my arms around his waist and my head sank into his chest. We stood like that for a while. The silence was broken when he said, "Le's go home." We hopped on his bike and went.

As the sky turned burnt orange and we trekked across the bridge, I thought about his behavior. He was being a little overjealous. It was, in a way, attractive. He was willing to fight over me, to challenge someone for even *looking* at his Baby. But, I told myself, he was crazy to do that: if Homeboy had had a gun, he could've shot Raheim — maybe even all of us — for dissin' him. Folks are killed every day over *stoo*pid shit like that.

And, besides, these ain't the days of chivalry and I ain't a damsel in distress.

Or am I?

"Yo, man, wha'tha *fuck* you call that?"

There was my Pooquie: sweat dripping from the top of his shiny bald head, falling down his face and bare chest. His hands were on his hips, but in no way were they holding up his gray sweat shorts, which hung loose and low on his waist. The expression on his face told me that he was not to be played with: the game would not continue until his beef was addressed. How I wished I could've walked onto the court with a towel (which I happened to have been holding), washed him down, and pulled up the trousers.

As he shot me a quick glance, though, I'm sure that that wouldn't have been the best thing to do — especially since he was surrounded by eight other guys, and I was watching this scene with at least a hundred other people. We were at the infamous West Third basketball-handball spot on Sixth Ave. in the West Village, where, every Saturday and Sunday during the summer, pick-up games can make you, a Jordan wannabe, an MVP for the day. While I've yet to see someone graduate from this arena to the NBA, the brothers are nonetheless outstanding players with boomin' brown bodies. You got your new jacks like Raheim, "tweens" (twenty-somethings trapped in the teenage zone), and "dunkin' daddies," men thirty-five and up who hold their own against the young guns.

Raheim was in the center of the court, the center of attention, raising hell about, from what I could gather, a foul that the referee — who was close to seven feet tall and sported a nasty Jehri curl — had the nerve not to call. While fellas in the game and folks watching immediately took sides, I was completely lost — as usual. Even though I grew up in a house where both my stepfather and brother lived for sports, I still, to this day, know hardly anything about basketball — or any other sport for that matter.

Let's just say that I was turned off by sports as a kid. Because I was fully aware of my sexual orientation by the time I was eight, the thought of being that close to another boy made me scared. (Now *that's* strange, hunh?) I just figured someone would detect I was gay. But most came to that conclusion anyway when they discovered I couldn't throw, catch, dunk, dribble, dodge, or hit any type of ball correctly.

So, after a few humiliating experiences (including one where, after I didn't catch a fly ball during a game of stickball, I was called a faggot in front of half the neighborhood), I avoided playing any type of sport by not volunteering for and not allowing myself to be volunteered for anything. In both elementary and junior high school, I tried everything from faking illness to cutting class so that I wouldn't have to participate in gym, which for me was boring. Just picture it: a bunch of nappy-headed, knobby-kneed, knuckleheaded boys attempting to play everything from volleyball to relay races in less than forty-five minutes as a thirtyish man brandishing a whistle and a clipboard, whom we also knew as a substitute science teacher, struggled to take attendance (forget about controlling and conducting the class). Oh yes, what fun...

But when I got into high school, I was introduced to a sport (if we can call it that) that allowed me to be athletic without adopting that moronic male-machismo attitude. I became a gymnast – or, as my stepfather jokingly termed it, "a B-level ballet dancer." He laughed about it, but I took it very seriously. For the first time in my life, I did simple exercises like jumping jacks and actually enjoyed them. I took a weight-training class and managed to put a little tone on my slim physique, giving my body (particularly my behind) a sharper look and feel.

And, I started to feel better about myself. After watching my brother get crowned the superathlete of the family and shoot past me in weight and height, I was no longer a "McDonald's french fry," as some neighborhood kids called me. I could finally complement (if not compete with) Adam athletically. I could stand on my head and spin like a top; do splits just as easily as I could walk; and, as Mr. Reid, my coach, would say, "make love to a balance beam." I won dozens of gymnast competitions around the city and state, and, with my brother, received a special citation from the mayor's office as one of the city's top high school athletes in 1984. I was so good that Mr. Reid encouraged me to pursue gymnastics professionally, but I didn't see that in my future. I mean, what kind of a career could I have expected? One shining but brief moment at the Olympics? And I didn't then and I still don't see any balance-beam babies clockin' the dollars that the heavyweights in baseball, basketball, and football do. Has anyone ever wondered what happened to America's All-American White Girl, Mary Lou Retton? I didn't think so.

So, setting my sights on a journalism career as I entered and tried to adjust to college, I concentrated on my writing and didn't continue any type of athletic activity (unless one counts sex, which did – and continues to – allow me to use my body in ways that blow the boyz' mindz). But I did start a new pastime that I haven't given up yet. I enjoy watching sports, but I don't follow the game – I follow the *guys*. I always have to let out some kind of sigh, moan, whistle, or scream if someone on the court or field catches my eye. It drives my brother out of his mind; he forbids me to watch any type of event with him, especially if he's joined by some of his jock buddies. (I know better than to do it around Raheim, for he'd have my ass – even though that would be enough motivation for me to do it.) Adam says (and I'm sure many others might agree) that my behavior is what one would expect from a homosexual. Well, what can I say!

Of course, with my interest in both journalism *and* men, you'd think I would've done the smart thing and opted for a career as a sports journalist. But that would not have worked. I can't concentrate on learning the mechanics of any game long enough before being distracted. And putting me in a locker room with dozens of sweaty, naked men would've gotten me into much trouble.

So, I "take notes" from the sidelines. And what are my favorite sports to watch? In reverse order, the Top Five are:

Bodybuilding: like Diana, I want muscles, and these fellas got 'em. Flex Wheeler can flex his pecs for me – and *on* me – anytime.

Tennis: in two words, MaliVai Johnson (whom, it turns out, Raheim favors). The sight of him in his tennis whites makes my heart dance.

Basketball: men in tanks and shorts runnin' up and down the court, with their bizness just a-jugglin' along with 'em. The Shaq? I'd slap my mama – *twice* – for five minutes with him.

Baseball: men in booty-huggin' uniforms base stealin', home-run hittin', and crotch grabbin'. I'd love to be Ken Griffey, Jr.'s bat boy!

But football is *the* one. Two dozen big, buxom men tussling and tumbling all over the field – and each other. It amazes me just how physical football is, not to mention erotic. The way they squat – feet spread wide apart in a bowlegged stance, torso arched, back bent, booty *all* the way up in the air while they are on their toes ready to soar – gets my juices flowing.

And the way they tackle each other. When Adam first started playing in junior high and would get all bruised, it really got to me (what can I say, I'm a sensitive guy). But it seemed that he and the others enjoyed that rough play, and, as I started going to his games and watching it on TV, I saw how "graceful" this violence is. You have to do a hell of a lot of maneuvering to strategically pounce another guy, wrap your arms or legs or body around him, and then press him down so that he falls – and believe me, I certainly wouldn't put up a fight, especially if the tackler was named Warren Moon or Jerry Rice.

And the noises they make as they slam their bodies and pile on top of each other sound like the grunts of orgasmic pleasure, not pain.

But the thing I love the most – and there seems to be more of it in this game than any other – is the ass slappin'. All those pumped-up and packed butts are just crying out to be smacked, and I know I wouldn't be able to resist such temptation. (Of course, I'd want to play one of those tight ends like a set of drums.) I'm sure most football players (like Adam) would say that it is just done to remind the person being "tapped" (his word for it) that, whether they have just fumbled or scored a touchdown, their hard work and team spirit is acknowledged and appreciated.

*Yeah, right.*

I see something totally different: the gleam in the eyes of those who take aim and make contact, and the look of masked gratification on the faces of those who have been "tapped" on the backside in front of hundreds, thousands, millions of people by another man. I've often wondered: if they have the guts to do this slip 'n' slide on the air for all to see, then what happens when the cameras are off? And, I'm sorry, but there is no way that all of these men are, as Adam has vehemently argued, straight. It is so difficult for any hetero man to believe that their sports heroes could be homosexual or even bi. After all, the majority of them are married, have kids, and are manhood personified. But I caught two of the "manliest" men on this earth – six-foot-two, 220-pound Mr. Reid and "wide-receiving," five-foot-ten, 190-pound Randy Richardson, our all-around high school athlete – doin' the nasty in the locker room and school gymnasium. I was also one of Randy's "male groupies" – and, contrary to what some might think, they do exist in the pro sports world. Just like their female cohorts, they have some very interesting stories to tell.

I saw both Mr. Reid and Randy as my "heroes" back then, but now that torch has been passed to Raheim. In fact, he has brought my sports-watching pastime to life. I've always wanted to date a guy who wowed 'em on the court and field like Adam, and it had come true in the weirdest way – my man was playing on the same team with my brother!

At the moment, though, Adam was trying to calm Raheim down.

"C'mon, brother, chill," Adam consoled, placing his hands on Raheim's shoulders. Raheim was about to charge the guy who had overstepped his bounds.

"Fuhget that, man," Raheim argued, trying to push his way around my brother. It wasn't an easy thing to do, since Adam is taller and thicker than him, a "chunk-a-munk hunk," as B.D. would say.

The ref blew his whistle and summoned the guy to join Raheim in the center of the court. The other teammates formed a circle around them, so we couldn't see what was happening. But when the group broke up a minute later, Raheim was left standing with the ball in his left hand.

He was awarded two free throws (at least I know something about the game). This, more than anything else he does, turns me the fuck on.

He dribbles the ball with his fingertips, but it's almost as if he isn't touching it, like he is making it bounce with some sort of telekinetic power.

He bends down, rising on his toes, and locks his knees together.

He sizes up the hoop.

He scoops up and clutches the ball in his left hand, which reminds me of how he palms me from behind when he wants some.

His eyes buck.

His tongue rolls out of his mouth – like a red carpet – and makes contact with his chin, making me shiver...

... and he shoots the ball with his eyes closed.

He says that, since he was ten, he has never missed – and that day was no exception. No one screamed as loud as I did.

After the hoots and catcalls, the game resumed but was over in another five minutes. Raheim and Adam's team won by eight points. As the two other teams made their way onto the court, two of the three most important men in my life (Jesus Christ being the other) made their way over to me after they congratulated each other on a game well played (they bumped chests as they hi-fived, then hugged each other while slapping the other's booty). I couldn't help but smile.

"Wha' you smilin' at?" asked Raheim as he reached for the towel I was still holding. He wiped his brow and patted his head and chest. "Ha, as if I don' know..."

I grinned. "What, I can't smile if I want to?"

He wasn't having it, though. "See, I know yo' ass real well. There's always somethin' goin' on in yo' head..."

"That is word," added Adam, who was hovering over a blue Nike tote bag, out of which he retrieved a green towel. He pulled off his white, sweat-drenched *White Men Can't Jump* t-shirt, causing several ladies around us to shout, "All right now!" and, "Hmph, baby!" As he dried himself off, he turned and smiled at them and they swooned. He returned his attention to me. "Don't try that innocent shit, 'cause it ain't gonna work."

Raheim nodded, then grabbed and pulled on his dick. "An' if anybody knows you ain't inacent..."

"Shut up, Raheim," I blushed. Adam let out a nervous laugh.

Raheim rubbed his stomach. "Well, I hope gettin' somethin' ta eat is on yo' mind, cuz I'm starvin' like Marvin."

"I hear that," agreed Adam, as he pulled a brown thermos out of his bag and started gulping down.

"Well, why don't we go back to the house?" I said, taking Raheim's towel and putting it in the no-frills tote bag I was carrying. "I can fix us all something while you guys take showers."

"Sounds good to me," Adam responded, passing the thermos to Raheim, who gladly took it. As he gulped, Adam reached in his bag again and took out a small chain with a million keys on it. "The car is parked around the corner."

"Well, le's be outy," said Raheim. They walked ahead of me and stopped to chat with those flirtatious female groupies. I wasn't about to join them — especially since I wasn't interested in them and they sure weren't ogling over me (next to Adam and Raheim, I was still a McDonald's french fry). So, I waited on the corner and scoped out the fellas who were scoping Raheim and Adam on the sly and throwing me most shade because I was with them. It was a good five minutes before they finally started heading toward me, but I didn't mind.

I *did* mind it, though, when Raheim, who was letting Adam do all the talking, allowed one of those heifers to feel his head — *my* head. And I let him know it.

"Wha's up wit you?" he asked, ducking the tote bag as I swung it in his direction.

"You know damn well what's up," I said, half joking, half serious.

He threw his hands up in the air — now he wanted to pretend that he was innocent. "C'mon, Baby, you know it ain't nothin' but a show."

"Yeah, well, I don't like anybody touching you like that. And you don't have to put on a show for nobody except me." I felt that I had put him in his place. I was proud of myself.

I took a few steps toward the car, a brown Chrysler Le Baron, and, as I was about to open the door, Raheim got all up in my face. We were so close that our lips were almost touching. His breath, somewhat stale, and his funk, musky yet sweet, all overtook me. I could see Adam, who was leaning on the driver's side, out of the corner of my eye tensing up.

Raheim grinned. "Oh yeah, I show yo' ass a'right."

I had to catch my breath. "We'll see about that." I bent down and climbed in the backseat.

He whacked me on the butt. "Oh, yeah, I *will.*"

"Damn, you two never quit, hunh?" asked Adam, as he settled in the driver's seat.

On our way to Brooklyn, Raheim traded dirty looks (the nice kind) with me while he and Adam talked about b-ball, Michael Jordan, working out, Adam's career (a gentle giant who loves kids, he's an elementary-school gym teacher) and Snoop Doggy Dogg and Dr. Dre, who, at one point, were rapping that it was "Nuthin' But a 'G' Thang" on the stereo. Even though the music was being played at a deafening volume, they were able to hear what the other was saying and carry on a lively convo (more than likely because the speakers were in the back blowing out *my* eardrums). And the way they were talking, you would've guessed that they were the best of friends, not that they just met several hours before. Adam isn't a B-boy, but he can hang with 'em. And the body language: Raheim gave Adam what we called "love taps" as a kid on his massive arms, while Adam gave Raheim "noogies" on his bald head.

The camaraderie didn't end when we reached our destination. After we parked the car, they walked up the block, into the building, and into the apartment shoulder to shoulder, almost arm in arm. This was just too good to be true – my brother liked one of my "boyfriends."

"Day-am, it's cray-zee hot up in here!" complained Raheim, as the heat hit him in the face. "Turn on tha AC." He disappeared into the bathroom.

"That's just like him to tell somebody else to do what he can do himself," I said, as I locked the door and dropped the tote bag on the floor. Adam silently parked himself on the sofa, legs spread apart with his head back. Yes, he practically covered the whole thing. I popped in Natalie Cole's *Take a Look* CD (after all that thumpin' and bumpin' in the car, I needed a change of pace), put the air conditioner on low-cool, and joined him on the sofa, practically sitting on his left thigh.

"So, what do you think?" I asked.

His head eased up slowly. There was a slight grin on his face. "About...?"

I nudged him in his arm – which was like hitting a wall – and motioned toward the bathroom. "Raheim..."

"Eh, he's all right," he nonchalantly answered, relaxing his head again.

"Please," I laughed, slapping him on his thighs and climbing over them both to get into the kitchen.

Silence.

"One thing's for sure: he ain't nothin' like those suckers you dated before."

I put the cold cuts I had just taken out of the fridge on the counter and turned. "What do you mean?"

"They were *suckers,*" he repeated emphatically, sitting up, leaning over, and clasping his hands. "They were pussies, they weren't real men. I could see right through all of them."

I was very amused. I came out of the kitchen, stood against the wall near the easy chair, and folded my arms. "Oh, *really?*"

"Yeah, those mother-fuckers were skatin' on you, playin' with you so they could get what they wanted and then make their exit," he explained.

"You make it sound like they were all dogs," I protested.

"They *were,*" he argued. I thought about it. All of them weren't dogs, but most of them sure acted like it.

There was Marc Livingston, a dead ringer for Dewayne on the TV show *What's Happening?* Like Dewayne, Marc was just as adorable and humble, and sported that trademark 'fro. It was 1984 and we were both freshmen at St. John's University. Our friendship started out of necessity – everyone else in the fall classes we had together was Caucasian. That following spring, while complimenting me on my legs, he confessed: "I sure would like to do more than just look at them." I let him, and we were a couple until the end of our junior year. It would have continued if I hadn't discovered that the person he often referred to as his "best friend" from his native Boston, Ernest, was really his boyfriend. Somehow, Ernest found my number, called, and demanded to know why I was sleeping with *his* man. Marc tried to irrationally rationalize his behavior – "I got involved with you because you seduced me" – and convince me to continue seeing him, because, as he argued, "Ernest would never know the difference." Needless to say, that friendship, along with the fucking, ended, leaving me with a broken heart.

Next came Edward Rochester II, a Morehouse Man with matinee-idol looks (a young Quincy Jones) and class for days. He was an absolute gentleman and knew how to romance you – candy and flowers, candlelight and wine. I had my suspicions that I wasn't the only one – I could call him only at work, because he didn't have a phone at his apartment, and he didn't feel right having me visit him, because he had two "straight" roommates – and it all finally got to me. One day I decided to pay him a surprise visit and guess who opened the door? Yup, his wife!

After him, there was Victor Townsend, a Cadillac-drivin', silk-suit-wearin' preacher who did the Holy Dance and called the Almighty's name out during sex ("Yes, Jesus, yes, Jesus...") as if *that* was whom he was having it with. He also, to my dismay, was a crack addict. And, when he couldn't milk me for any more money (unbeknownst to me) to support his habit, he staged a burglary at my house. You should've seen my face when the police told me they'd caught the culprit – and that he was my lover.

And the "boyfriends" who came before and after all this nonsense were Prince Charmings but men I just could not have. Mr. Reid, whom I consider "my first love," was twice my age and naturally "broke up" with me after I graduated from high school so he could hook up with another unsuspecting, naive, trusting student. And Peter Armstrong, who was my age, seemed like The One – he had the body, brains, *and* butt to prove it. And, he made me laugh out loud. But after an intense ten-month relationship (he helped me keep my sanity during my tenure at Columbia) that was leading up to the Big "C," he took a better-pay-ing job in Los Angeles. He wanted me to come with him, but I wasn't about to leave *Your World,* a job that I initially loved, two months after I had started – something he couldn't (or wouldn't) understand. So, we tried the long-distance thing for five months. Airfare between New York and L.A. ain't no joke, not to mention long-distance phone calls. So, the trip planning stopped, the calls went from once every day to once a week, and before you knew it, out of sight, out of mind.

Adam's point had much truth to it: this list was *not* a good one.

"OK, so they weren't all that," I admitted, snapping back to our convo. "Things happened. People changed, people moved on. They lied. Maybe I was a little too trusting..."

"Try stupid," he countered.

"OK, OK, stupid. But they all had their good qualities."

"Well, from what I can see, I like Raheim."

"Oh yeah? Why?"

He stood up and put his hands in his pockets. "For one thing, you can tell he don't bullshit and he don't take shit from nobody. Just the way he handled himself today. He's also supercool. You can talk to him about anything. And, he plays a mean game of basketball. Any guy who can throw down the way he can is my kind of man..."

I flashed him a look.

*"You* know what I mean," he added. "Besides, it's obvious that he is in love with you."

"What?"

"You heard me – in love," he repeated.

"What makes you say that?"

"Look at the way he acts, the way you both act. It's like, everybody could see it today. It was written all over his fuckin' face — and yours."

"It is?"

"What do you mean, '*it is*'?" he laughed, as he threw his hands up in the air. "What part of these statements do you *not* understand?"

I was gagging — I was just read with my own line.

He continued to drop the science. "Those punks you were with before walked around with their asses on their shoulders, thinkin' it was all about them. That's why I didn't get along with any of them. I *hated* that pretty boy. And that preacher? He ain't really had no God in him if you ask me."

"Adam, now..."

"'Adam,' nothin'. Bottom line is Raheim is real, straight-up real. And if ya'll ain't in love yet, y'all will be soon."

Just then Raheim appeared with only a light blue towel around his waist. "A'right, Schwarzenegga, you got it," he said to Adam, nodding toward the bathroom.

"I guess that's my cue," Adam announced. He winked at me and headed for the bathroom, smacking Raheim on the butt.

"Yo, Hercules, be careful wit that. Somebody might get jealous," he laughed. He bebopped over to me, smacked me on the lips, and went into the kitchen, taking some Gatorade out the fridge. As I watched him intently, I heard Natalie exclaim:

*I'm beginning to see the light.*

 Adam spent the night on the sofa – if one can call napping from five 'til nine spending the night. After dinner, Raheim moved the coffee table into the kitchen and he and I spread out on the carpet as they talked and talked and talked, and laughed and laughed and laughed. I was a little jealous – neither one of them was ever this chummy with me. I drifted off at around three. When I woke, I was in Pooquie's arms in bed. He said he carried me to the room. I told him he should've gotten me up for that.

But I was glad that they hit it off so well. It couldn't have worked out any better if I had planned it myself. I wasn't too thrilled with Raheim after our little fight about my Spandex, and didn't quite feel like joining him in the Vill the next day to watch him play ball. It slipped my mind that Adam shoots hoops there, too. If I had let my pride get in the way, I would've missed their meeting.

Adam and Raheim exchanged beeper numbers so that they could shoot the breeze and hang out. As they said good-bye, they hugged and patted each other on the butt (I also gave 'em both a rub). Raheim wanted him to stay for breakfast, but he had a million things to do before my mother's anniversary dinner later that day. As Raheim sat down in his red BVDs to his Wheaties, he was as giddy as Junior when he confessed: "Adam is so cool. If I had a brotha, it be him." I listened to him go on about Adam and I thought about what Adam said the night before. Could Raheim – could *we* – be in love? Or falling in love? I couldn't speak for Raheim, but it certainly didn't feel like it to me. Lord knows that I loved having Raheim around. But I couldn't be in love with him – I was still trying to get to know him. Besides, I wasn't looking for love – I wanted to have a good time, and *that* he was certainly giving me. Just because I'm having *the* best sex in my life doesn't mean I'm in love or going there – does it? I saw him as "my man" – figuratively speaking. I liked him, yes, but there were things about him that I didn't like, that turned me completely off. Like being selfish. Being domineering. Being pigheaded. Being possessive. Being arrogant.

And being ignorant.

"You hear 'bout this, Baby?" he asked, popping cereal in his mouth.

"Hear about what?" I was sitting across from him drinking juice. I had on his Jordan jersey.

"This..." He handed me the newspaper, pointing to an item about NABJ's convention in Houston. I wanted to go, but *Your World* couldn't (or wouldn't) foot the bill like it had the past two years. Martin Schultz in Human Resources told me that "there wasn't enough money in the travel budget." Uh-huh. But there *was* enough to send Elias to the Republican National Convention and Bush headquarters to cover the presidential election in Texas (both wasted trips) the year before, and the entire art staff to a four-day convention in San Diego in April. Cheap, shady mother-fuckers.

Anyway, Bushwick Bill (or Richard Shaw) of the rap group the Geto Boys had caused an auditoriumful of journalists to walk out of a symposium called "Hip-Hop: The Medium, Its Message, and Responsibility." He kept referring to women as bitches and ho's — even after several members of the audience, including NABJ president Sidmel Estes-Sumpter, criticized him and asked him not to.

"I can't believe this fool," I said, finishing the story.

"Wha'cha mean?" he crunched.

"How can he defend calling any woman a bitch or ho? It's simply ridiculous..."

"Tha's jus' how tha brotha talks..."

"Meaning?"

Raheim didn't blink. "It's where he comes from. If you ain't a part of it, you not. But if you a bitch you a bitch, if you a ho you a ho, and ya know it..."

I threw the paper down. "What?"

He gulped down his juice. "If you ain't a bitch, if you ain't a ho, that shouldn't botha you..."

"Oh," I began, trying to understand his illogical logic, "just like the *n*-word?"

He nodded. "Yeah."

"No, Raheim, you're wrong..."

"I ain't wrong. It's jus' a word, tha's all..."

I folded my hands across my chest. "Oh, *really?*"

"Yeah. Like if I call you my nigga. You shouldn't bug out, cuz I say it cuz you cool wit me..."

I became flustered. "I ain't your nigga, Raheim."

He gave me a sly smile. "You are."

"I am not!"

"Uh-huh ... you are." He popped a Wheaty.

"No, I am *not!*" I stormed over toward the sofa. He giggled his way over.

"You should see yo' face, Little Bit..."

I struggled with him. "Get off of me, get off..."

"Ooooh, I love it when ya get like that, Baby." His tongue made contact with my ear. He blew in it, whispering: "You my nigga, you my nigga..."

*"I am not!"*

"Yeah, my nigga..."

*"Stop, no,* I am not, I..."

There it goes again.

His hands were everywhere, his lips on mine. We tumbled onto the sofa. Good thing there was a Zulu right on the coffee table.

He always does that shit. I get pissed. He wants me to be angry – but not at him. He knows the sex is even fiercer when I am upset. We work it out by working it. He strings me like a guitar, just reels me in like a fish on a hook.

And I just keep cuming back for more.

After he finished munching on me and crunching on his cereal, he took a shower. He was spending the day with Junior. As I sat on the couch in deep thought, the phone rang.

"Hello?"

"Well, I was beginning to think that you didn't live there anymore ... just your answering machine."

I smiled. It was my mother.

"Hi, Mom. How are you?"

"No, how are *you,* baby? I haven't seen you in two months. You've obviously been occupied." That's code language for *There's a man in your life.*

"Yes, Mom...," I admitted.

"OK .... so what's his name?" Like she didn't know. While Adam had just met Raheim, I'd told him about him weeks ago. I knew that he'd already blabbed to her.

"Raheim..."

"Raheim ... how manly..."

"Mom, please," I laughed. Funny ... that's exactly what I thought when I first found out his name.

"How old is he?" As if she didn't know *that,* either.

"He's twenty-one."

"Twenty-one! My, my, my ... are we robbing the cradle?"

"Mom, I am only twenty-seven..."

"Well, six years can be a lifetime, you know?"

She should know – Anderson is seven years younger than she. But you wouldn't be able to tell by looking at them. He sure couldn't. If she hadn't been working the nightshift as a nurse, they probably would never have met. She was thirty-five; he was twenty-eight. He was our mailman. He came to the apartment with a package that wouldn't fit in the mailbox, she opened the door and BAM! Every weekday after that, when he'd deliver the mail, he'd stop by to see her. He'd have a rose; she'd have a hot homemade muffin or roll with piping coffee brewing. He was shocked to discover that she was a widow pushing forty with two boys. He didn't let the age difference get in the way. She was a bit apprehensive; it was the first time she had felt that way for a man since my father died, but she couldn't see herself getting serious with a man "who looks like he could be my son." But she got over it.

They dated for three years before they got married. He wanted to tie the knot after six months, but she wanted to be sure. She took a lot of good-natured ribbing from my aunt Ruth, who called her "Mrs. Robinson," and teased her about Anderson's age ("Well, you *are* in your sexual prime; at least *he* can keep up witcha!") and his being a mailman ("Ain't nothin' like the mail being brought right to your door, *hunh,* Annie?"). I knew Aunt Ruth would have something similar to say about Raheim being a messenger.

But it was my mother's turn first. "Like mother, like son," she said.

"I'm sorry?"

"We both have men in our lives who are younger than us – and they deliver."

"Mom, you are farce," I chuckled. But it was true, and I had never made the connection before. She has been a big influence on me. I remember her working two jobs and attending night school to get her nursing certificate. She was such a model of strength. So, like her, I am very independent, observant, giving, patient, and determined. But I've never sought out a man like hers. This was, though, one hell of a coincidence.

"So, are you bringing him to dinner?" she anticipated.

I knew how Anderson felt about homosexuality and I knew what kind of friction there might be if I showed up with my latest. I almost brought my ex three years ago, but I changed my mind at the last minute. If Anderson could not be fully comfortable around his stepson, then how would he act toward a total stranger? Anderson wouldn't make us feel uncomfortable just to be mean, but he *would* say something stupid. He can't help it — he's a heterosexual man. Like most straight people, his fear of and ambivalence toward homosexuality is due to not knowing any homosexuals and listening to heterosexuals who know *nothing*. He has come a long way since I came out five years ago, but I didn't feel like testing the waters and his tolerance right then.

"Well, he won't be at the party," I explained, "but he will stop by to pick me up after dinner."

"If you want him to come, he can...," she informed.

"No, Mom, that's OK. He'll be with his son today anyway."

"His son?"

"Yes. His name is Junior and he is five."

"Ah..." I could see her biting her nail, thinking. "And have you met his son?"

"Yes, I have. He is wonderful."

"Hmmmm ... and you've known Raheim how long?"

"Like a month and a half."

"And you've already met his son?"

"Yes..."

"Well, you and Adam didn't meet Anderson until we knew each other five months!"

"Mom, it's no big deal..."

"We'll be the judge of that..." "We" being her and Aunt Ruth.

"Do you want me to bring anything?"

"No, just yourself ... and Raheim."

"I will."

"See you at five."

"OK. Love you."

"Love you, baby. And tell Raheim I said hello."

"I will. Bye."

I hung up the phone, warm and secure in the knowledge that I was blessed. How many men could have such a conversation with a parent about what Aunt Ruth calls a "companion"? I know in the back of her mind that my mother is still praying that I will give her a grandchild in the "regular" way. But she has done something I never expected her to — accepted me with no strings. (Straight folks think we want to be accepted, even tolerated, but I know that I don't; all I want is respect.) And, sadly, I have my late uncle Russ to thank for that.

Uncle Russ (short for Russell) was my mother and Aunt Ruth's baby brother. He was my only blood-uncle, but even if he wasn't, he would've still been my favorite. Picture Sam Cooke, a shade darker, a little taller and stockier. He had a great personality and charm to go with his great looks. All the ladies — and men — loved him. Aunt Ruth said she always knew he was "different," but didn't know exactly what that difference was until his thirty-third birthday in 1987, when he died of AIDS. He did not want the family to know 'til he was gone. He led a very closeted life, even though it should've been obvious that he wasn't straight. He never married, never once talked about a girlfriend, and always had male "roommates," even though he had the financial means to live on his own. It wasn't until after his death that we discovered that the man he'd lived with for the last five years of his life was his lover, a burly, sensitive chocolate drop named Algernon. The few times the family visited Uncle Russ in Chicago, Algernon, who was a cordial and amicable host, slept on a cot in their den. Anderson and my mother took Algernon's "room," Adam slept in the sofa bed, and Uncle Russ and I cuddled up in what was really their bed.

Because of Russ's silence — and the family's silence surrounding his invisible life and death — both my mother and Aunt Ruth promised that that would not happen to me. When I told my mother, she said she already knew (they say mothers always know) and she was just happy that I finally decided to tell her. She was relieved. Aunt Ruth said she always knew too: "You had the same look in your eye that Russ did growing up. You were both trying to hide it." She also knew I was starting to experiment when I was sixteen. How? "Because," she laughed, "your pimples were clearing up and your butt was getting bigger."

Uncle Russ knew too. In 1984, the last time I saw him alive, he told me: "Don't ever be ashamed of who you are, Mitch, no matter what family says, no matter what friends say, no matter what the world says." I think he wanted to come out to me and wanted me to do the same. God knows that I was dying to tell somebody about my affair with Mr. Reid and I could've used some advice (like telling me to get ready for heartbreak). He didn't press me and I was afraid, like him, to just confide in someone. But if you can't turn to family, who can you turn to?

Uncle Russ didn't give my mother or Aunt Ruth the chance to try to understand because he feared they would reject him, so he lived and died alone. Anderson couldn't understand why, if he was so close to his sisters, he didn't come out. Uh-huh, typical. If you stay in the closet but lead a secret gay life and straight folks find out, they get upset. ("You could've told me ... I would've understood...") If you stay in the closet, lead a straight life, and then come out, they get upset. ("How could you drag a woman into this?"; "What about your child?") And, if you don't perpetrate a fraud and just come out, they get upset and wish you would've stayed in the closet. ("It's just a phase, you'll turn back soon";

"You better repent and live the way God wants you to.") It's easy to say how one will react if a family member reveals they are homosexual. And, because all of us, including lesbians and gays, are taught to hate homosexuality and homosexuals, many of us stay in the closet and don't risk losing our family, our friends, and our lives.

Since I've been out, my mother and Aunt Ruth have been there for me, learning as I learn, discovering as I discover. I think my aunt Ruth has read more about homosexuals and homosexuality than I have; sometimes she'll come up with something I've never heard of. I know that it's her way of making up for lost time. It is through me that she and my mother get the type of relationship they wish they could've had with Uncle Russ.

And I get the very best girlfriends a gay man can have to talk to about men!

Anderson Lionel Walker may be hetero-
sexist, but he is a good husband. He gave my mother the dream of her
lifetime: a home in the suburbs. Well, Longwood is really a miniburb,
a township; it's so small that you can ride right through it and not
realize it. The great thing is that it isn't far from the city. The bad thing
is that I have to take New Jersey Transit out of Port Authority Bus
Terminal in Times Square – and it ain't a joy ride. You'd never know
there was a schedule the drivers had to follow; they are always late.
And, on Sunday, the bus runs local only – meaning the half-hour ride
turns into forty-five minutes, because we make several pit stops through
Newark Airport. I usually tune into my Walkman or read a book to
pass the time. But it is difficult to concentrate when the bus is swerv-
ing and swirling off of turnpikes, mini-highways, and dirt roads, and
your churchgoers and juvenile delinquents are chattering away at
very loud decibels. I survived this ride like all the others – but this
time I knew I wouldn't have to ride back home the same way, by
myself.

The bus stops right in front of the Walker residence, and once you
see the house you understand why they decided to move from Brooklyn to the Garden State. It's a modest but sprawling dwelling, with three
bedrooms, a basement, an attic, and a two-car garage. It's exterior is a
light gray. A beautiful patch of brownish green shrubs and flowers
outline the front yard and garden, which Anderson proudly takes care
of – no one touches it but him. There is a crystal chandelier in the
dining area, a bright red-brick fireplace in the living room, and parquet
floors throughout that my mother has a ball cleaning. (As she says, "It's
good to shine floors that aren't in somebody else's house.") It was a
major steal at $95,000.

We all moved in in 1988 – and Adam and I moved out a year later.
After being more of a friend than a stepfather for the first five years
of his marriage, Anderson decided, now that he had a house, he could

really be a father figure – a.k.a. The Boss. He turned into Ralph Kramden: "This is my house, m-y house, *my* house! And *I* am the King!" We knew he was, for the most part, kidding: he was just very excited about this new environment, this new direction his life was taking with his wife. He wanted to be Heathcliff Huxtable. But he started bugging: expecting us to get up six, seven o'clock every morning to have breakfast as a family; having us do chores – on a schedule; and imposing a curfew, something neither Adam nor I could live with. He might have been concerned about us being in NYC, coming home on a bus late at night, but expecting us to be home by nine was wack.

Columbia U saved me; for Adam, it was a girlfriend with her own place.

I do make the trip at least once a month and stay the weekend, because the neighborhood is hear-a-pin-drop quiet no matter the season. The kids that live in the other dozen or so houses on either side of Harrison Drive even play quietly. I come to get away from the hustle and bustle of the city, the hectic pace of my job, and, yes, to wash those men out of my hair.

As I approached the walkway, there, standing on the front step of the door, was Aunt Ruth, just a-puffing away. I've told her about smoking two packs of cigarettes a day, but she won't listen. She says she does it to make up for her lack of a sex life. Her husband, my uncle Tweedle (don't ask me why they call him that; no one seems to know), is from the old, *old* school: sex is for marriage and marriage is for procreation. And, since they've already had their 2.5 kids, sex is no longer necessary. They do it, but not as often as she'd like. Once I told her to just divorce his ass if he wouldn't satisfy her the way she wants to be satisfied. But she gave me that tired old line: "I love that man." Sorry, but there ain't that much love in the world.

It's a shame that Uncle Tweedle (who was once again away on business) doesn't realize what a treasure he has. Aunt Ruth is a stunning 54-year-old, a dead ringer for Mary Alice, my favorite actress. She doesn't look a day over forty. There's not a wrinkle on her face or a strand of gray in her head full of naturally straight, long black hair. She usually wears it combed back, but that day it was in a serious bun that sat on the top of her head. She wore a plain white cotton dress with a large black belt and black flat shoes.

"What's up, Mother Sister?" I asked.

"Well, well, well ... if it ain't my Honeysuckle," she beamed, meeting me at the bottom step (there were only five) and embracing me. "Come here, chile, and gimme some suga."

Aunt Ruth has called me Honeysuckle since I was a kid because she says my lips taste like honey and they make you want to suck 'em. I guess Raheim would agree. I call her Mother Sister because, just like the character with the same name in *Do the Right Thing,* she is exactly that to everyone – the folks in her neighborhood, at her church, and in the family. You can go to her with any problem, and don't think you can hide it from her – she can see right through any disguise. Anderson calls her a plain old nosy busybody (but not to her face).

"So, what you doing out here?" I asked, pulling back and looking at her classy bun.

"Waitin' on you. Now that you're here, it's time to eat," she answered, stamping out her cigarette.

We walked into the house and were greeted by Anderson, dressed in a flowered brown blouse, tan dress shorts, and brown sandals that looked very familiar.

"Mz. Ruth, I hope you didn't put your cigarette out on my stoop," he said.

"No, I put it out in your garden," she mumbled, passing him and walking straight into the kitchen. "The petunias should be on fire right about now."

He sucked his teeth and looked at me. He smiled. "Well, Mitch, how's it goin'?" He held out his hand. It was sweaty.

"Good. How are you?"

"Fine, just fine." You could say that again. The older he gets, the younger he looks. Even though his hairline is receding a little, he still has a headful of short curly black hair – and everything else is in place. I'd be lying if I said that having sex with him hasn't crossed my mind at least once. But I had most of those thoughts as a teen. It was safer. Even after my mother married him, he still seemed like my peer, not my elder, because he looked the part. And I'd enjoy it when he'd lounge and walk around the house in his boxers, his cut-to-definition chest out to here and his round butt just a-sitting on his waist. (Black men, no matter their orientation, just have it goin' on there.) One day I accidently walked in on him taking a leak – and it was *big*. I was a sexually frustrated teenager, and he provided me with some serious wet dreams. Since my revelation in 1988, I'm sure he's wondered about that time and all the others parading in front of me half-naked. Once, he indirectly asked whether his skin parade had encouraged me to "turn the other way." My answer: "Don't flatter yourself."

"Where is everybody?" I said, turning to my right and peeking in the living room, which was empty.

"They're in the backyard. C'mon, let's go." He led me to the kitchen, out the screen door, and down the stairs.

"Well, look who's finally here!" yelled my mother, standing over a smoky grill that was full of meat.

"Annie, didn't I tell you I'd do that? You suppose to be sitting down," said Anderson, as he brushed past me toward the grill. I noticed the bottle of bar-b-cue sauce in his left hand – and the booty.

She slapped him on it as he went to the pit, making me jump. "What was I supposed to do, let them burn?" She turned to me. "Hey, baby. You just in time. The food is just about done."

I held her tight. She smelled of Passion, the fragrance I gave her for Christmas the year before. She hadn't changed either. She favors Alfre Woodard, number five on my Best Actress list (Ruby Dee, Rosalind Cash, and Cicely Tyson are numbers two, three, and four, respectively), except that her skin is a shade lighter, her face fuller, and she has long, dark brown hair, now styled in a fierce braid-twist combo. My brother and I took after her in the lips, eyes, and nose department. She's all but five feet six and has a figure like an hourglass. It was being shown off by a shoestring-strap orange sundress that fell just above her knees. She's got Tina Turner legs, what Anderson calls a "big ol' butt," and she admitted to my aunt Ruth two years ago that because she's got the equipment, she's still in the breast-feeding business. Hmmmm ... Because of their different heights (Anderson is just over six feet), I often wondered how they (and other couples like them) maneuver it in bed. But, considering who I was presently with, I had a pretty good idea. All things become equal on the horizontal plane.

As we held each other, I played with her hair. "When did you do this?"

She broke away from me, smiling. "A few weeks ago. It was the most grueling six hours of my life. Never again. You like it?"

"You look fierce!"

"Thank you, baby," she blushed. She pointed to my right hand. "And what's that?"

"Your gift." I handed her the small Bloomie's bag. She took out and examined the thin rectangular box, wrapped in gold paper with a white bow on top. I started playing with her hair again. It was so fly.

"Hey, Cuz, what's up?"

I looked to my left. My cousin Alvin Hardwicke, one of Aunt Ruth's twin sons, sat on one side of the brown wooden picnic table on the lawn with Adam; his brother, Calvin, on the other. While they are identical, it is easy to tell them apart. Alvin is the one with the sweet disposition and sex appeal (like his mom) plus a cool baritone voice. Calvin, like

Alvin, is an LL Cool J clone – but that's it. There's nothing in between his ears, and every time he opens his mouth my body cringes. He has the most groggy, throaty, irritating voice I've ever heard – sort of like E.T. He also has the personality of a rock.

And *he* is the gay one!

Well, that's what Gene tells me. He says he and Calvin had one hot little affair a decade ago which lasted for six months. ("After the things we did together, puh-leeze! If *he's* straight, *I'm* an arrow!") And then there's the aversion Calvin has for talking about anything gay, just like Elias. We know what that can mean. But both twins have my gaydar up: they are thirty, partners in their father's bakery chain (Tweedle's Tasties), and neither has been married, engaged, or even "hooked." If Alvin is gay or just conveniently bi (which some Black men find easier to be), I'd drop Raheim like *that* and run off to any island where kissing cousins of any orientation can live lustily ever after. Gene says that, even if Alvin plays the role like his twin, I could still get him. "No man can be had who doesn't want to be," he reasons. And the way Alvin was bear-hugging me, the possibility that he might want to be felt very real.

The hug raised Aunt Ruth's eyes as she set the table. "Now, now, watch it, Honeysuckle. I don't want you corrupting my boy..."

"Hey, Ma, how do you know I don't want to be?" Alvin asked, still clutching my waist. He looked too jood in tight blue jean shorts and a sky blue tank. Hmmmm, he might want to be...

"Disgusting!" shouted Calvin, eating some potato chips. He wore the same outfit, but he didn't *wear it* like Alvin.

"You're just jealous 'cause it ain't you!" Alvin snapped, still holding on to me. He then pecked me on the lips for full effect.

I *liked* that.

Calvin let out an "Argh!" like Charlie Brown. Everybody cracked up – except Calvin and Anderson.

"All right, all right, everybody chill and just sit so we can eat," said Anderson, who had his back to us the whole time flipping the meat.

Alvin didn't let go of me until we were seated at the table, and during the entire meal he kept touching me here and there. I knew he didn't really mean anything by it – or did he? He's always been a very touchy-feely person (I loved wrestling with him in bed when we were younger) and we hadn't seen each other in like a year. Whatever the reasons for this overt affection, I decided to join him – pinching his arm, slapping his back, poking his hard abs, and squeezing his thigh (allowing my hands to linger). No one seemed to be bothered by it except Anderson and Calvin. Maybe they were *both* jealous.

Calvin obviously wanted to spoil the fun, because he brought up a subject that made everybody at the table gag: gays in the military.

"What do *you* think about it, Mitch?" he asked with a slick grin. He was seated across from me.

"Well, what is there to think about?" I began, heaping a forkful of potato salad toward my mouth. "There *are* gays in the military."

Laugh out loud, everybody – except Calvin and Anderson.

"I don't see what's so funny," said Anderson, sitting on my left at the head of the table, a drumstick in his hand.

"There are gays in the military – always have been and always will be, no matter what kind of ordinance or law they pass," I lectured to no one in particular.

"Well, I don't think that that is right," said Calvin. "Clinton should keep them in the closet."

"I have to agree with you, Calvin," added Anderson. "How is a man supposed to feel, knowing a homosexual is taking a shower with him or sleeping next to him?"

I could tell where this conversation was going – we'd had it before. It always came down to the issue of masculinity. (Take his comment: "man" means heterosexual only; homosexuals aren't real men.) Some past examples:

Anderson: "Is it that you don't like women?"

Me: "No, I like them very much. Some of my best friends are women. It's just that I don't want to sleep with them."

Anderson: "Why do gay men want to be women?"

Me: "If I wanted to be a woman, I'd have a sex change!"

Anderson: "When you are, uh, with someone, who is the man?"

Me: "Whoever gets the condom on first!"

He knew I was going to lay into him again, and I did. "That so-called man is supposed to feel safe because there is a fellow soldier, albeit a homosexual one, next to him or her. They can do the job just as well as anybody else."

"But they may make a pass at a straight soldier," said Anderson. Calvin cringed.

I grinned. "That's right, Anderson, all we think about is sex, and all of us want straight men. Puh-leeze. Uh, have you ever heard of Tailhook? The way straight men act in the military, *we* should be on the defensive. They can't seem to control *their* sex drives. They may decide to come after us!"

Everybody cracked up – except Anderson and Calvin, who grunted, "Give me a break" under his breath.

"Look, it's not just for straight soldiers, it's for gays, too," countered Anderson. "Look at all the people who are expelled each year for being homosexual, and those that are attacked. If they weren't in the military, those problems wouldn't exist."

My hand went up. "Once again, you're allowing your ignorance to prevail over your more-positive aspects. You are excusing their fear and hatred, and granting them a license to ruin people's lives, even kill them. Bottom line is, any straight man who feels threatened by another man's sexuality is not that secure in his own *man*hood."

"Come on, Mitch, don't try that reverse-psychology stuff," said Anderson. "Gay people know they don't have a leg to stand on with this one. That's why they are trying to link their cause with us. And it ain't gonna work."

Not only was he talking about me in the third person, but he wanted to bring up the race thang. Well, I was ready for that one.

"*They* link their cause with *us? Who* is they and *who* is us, Anderson? What about those brothers and sisters in the armed forces who are homosexual? Are you telling me that one part of their identity matters and another doesn't? That their rights as African-Americans should be protected but not as homosexuals?"

"Well, well...," he muttered.

"Should they – should *I* – have to choose to make your life and others' easier?"

"What have those white gay people done for us?" he accused. "They are just trying to hijack our movement."

"*Whose* movement, Anderson? Weren't Black lesbians and gays hosed down? Chased and bitten by dogs? Clubbed by police? Denied the right to vote? Aren't we also, to this day, denied the right to *be?*"

"But you, you ... you can't compare being Black to being gay!" he blurted out.

"Oh ... *I* can't?"

It never fails. One of the reasons why this tired, nonsensical "Black vs. gay" debate has intensified is because homosexuals of African descent are often missing from the picture. People (meaning white homosexuals and Black heterosexuals) discuss this non-issue as if they are experts on being both Black and gay when we live it every day. And, they expect us to pledge our allegiance to one identity. Sorry, but this ain't that kind of party.

Which is why I relish the opportunity to set folks like Anderson, er, straight.

"Think about it, Anderson," I continued. "Discrimination is discrimination. No one is saying that the two are the same. I know I'm not, and hell, I should know. I know what both of them feel like. But I know when it happens to me for either reason, it is wrong."

Dead silence.

"So, anybody see that cover of Janet Jackson's new album?" asked Calvin. "I sure would love to be the hands touching her."

"Shut up, you fool," said Alvin. "Even if you had her, ya wouldn't know what to do with her." He knocked my knee with his and winked. What was he trying to say?

As everybody else started talking, I looked at Anderson. He nodded at me as he sipped his beer.

After dinner, he came up to me as I was watching Adam and Alvin in a game of one-on-one near the garage.

"So, who's winning?" he asked.

I managed a smile. "Adam, as usual."

"Oh ... Mitch, I ... I guess I did it again, hunh?"

"Did what?"

"You know ... all those things I said..."

I shrugged. "Well, you were just speaking your mind. There's no crime in having an opinion..."

"Well, it's one thing to have an opinion ... it's another thing to have an *informed* opinion."

I laughed. "Amen to that."

"I know it gets to you to hear me say crazy things like that. But believe me, I don't enjoy making myself look like an ass."

I grinned.

He searched my eyes. "Guess it's gonna take a little more time, hunh?"

I nodded. "Hey, that's all we got."

He put out his hand. As I shook it, he pulled me toward him and gave me one of those brotha pats on the back and butt. *Whoa!* I most gladly returned the gesture.

This somewhat tender moment was interrupted by Aunt Ruth's voice, blowing through the back screen door. "Yoo-hoo, everybody, I have a surprise."

Out she came with a triple-layer double-fudge chocolate cake in one hand – and another in the other.

"Now, this is Mr. Raheim Rivers, the guest and com*pan*ion of our dearest Mitchell," she said, as she pranced down the stairs on Raheim's arm. "Ain't he just the cutest chocolate thang you ever seen?"

Both Raheim and I blushed.

"Ruth, you're embarrassing him," my mother said, approaching him. "Raheim, I'm Mitchell's mother, Mrs. Walker."

"Nice ta meet ya." He took her outstretched hand and kissed it. He turned to me, looking too jood in his Africentric vest and three-quarter blue jeans. "You ain' tell me yo' moms was so fine."

"Did you hear that, Anderson? So fine!" my mother smiled.

"Yeah, I heard," he answered, coming up to Raheim. "I'm Anderson Walker, Mitchell's stepfather."

"Wha's up?" asked Raheim, as he and Anderson did the brotha shake. Raheim looked down and smiled. "Nice shoe."

Anderson looked down. They had on the same sandal. I knew it looked familiar. He laughed. "Harlem, right?"

"Ya know it," Raheim saluted.

One by one they fell under his spell. After Aunt Ruth and my mother forced us to stay awhile and stuffed him with food ("Lordy," Aunt Ruth testified, "this boy can *eat!*"), Raheim survived an hour of b-balling with Adam and Alvin, Calvin's cold shoulder, Anderson's curiosity ("So ... *you* are with Mitchell?"), my mother's *ooh*ing and *aah*ing (she squeezed the merchandise a bit too much, causing me to remark: "Uh, he's mine, lady, your man is over there!"), and Aunt Ruth's silly nature ("I betcha you been makin' a lot of deliveries at Honeysuckle's house, *hunh,* Raheim?"). Everyone was sad to see us go, even Anderson and Calvin, who, I'm sure, couldn't believe that I was leaving with Raheim and leaving him behind. I slapped Alvin on the butt and told him to come visit me in Brooklyn ("Cousin, I'm sure we can find something to do"). And I told Aunt Ruth and my mother we'd talk soon. They both looked at Raheim and each other and sang: *"Sure,* we will."

As we drove, Raheim told me how much he liked my family ("They all look like stars, Baby") and about his day with Junior at Great Adventure. The poor guy got sick on one of the rides. I thought he would be with us, but he was staying with his cousins in Newark. We had to drop off Angel's car and then take the train home from Harlem. We didn't get into Brooklyn 'til around midnight, but I didn't mind.

My mother didn't wait for me to call her to ask what she thought. She and Aunt Ruth compared notes right after we left. I discovered the blinking message on the machine after I shaved the few hairs growing on Raheim's head and he took a shower:

"Hi, baby, I thought you'd be home by now. Anderson and I want to thank you again for the gift. We already discussed it and we think we'll take the cruise in mid-September. We all enjoyed Raheim and we hope we see him again real soon. You two make such a *cute* couple. I'll be asleep by the time you get in, so we'll talk later in the week. Love you. And tell my son-in-law I said hello. (Chuckle.) Bye."

*My son-in-law?*

 Because Raheim was getting along so well
with my family and friends – he had chatted with my mother once and
Adam twice since the picnic, and even he and Gene, being fellow
employees, were on speaking terms – I felt that I should reach out to
D.C. and Angel.

I saw my chance when we were watching *Jeopardy!* in our favorite
position on his least-favorite day of the week. After guessing the last
"Double Jeopardy" question (Alex: "Gibberish, or the language of a
particular profession or trade"; Raheim: "Wha's jargon?"), he reached
for his knapsack, which was under the bed, and pulled out an invite to
a "B-boy bash" that Saturday, not far from my house.

"A B-boy bash?" I asked.

"Yeah, jus' tha posse kickin' it," he answered.

Pause.

"Uh, are Angel and D.C. going?"

"Yeah."

Pause.

"Well, do you think they might want to hang out here first?"

"Nah," he abruptly said.

"Raheim..."

"Little Bit, we been ova that, now."

"No, we haven't," I argued. "You get along with everybody in my
life. I just don't want there to be any walls between us..."

"Wha'cha mean?"

"I know you go out with them and have a good time, but you never
talk about it. They are your best friends. They don't have to be mine,
but we should all at least try to get along..."

"Why? You ain't Rodney King," he chuckled.

"I'm serious. Please, just ask them."

"Shit, why I gotta ask 'em? You ask 'em..."

"Me?"

"Yeah. You wanna get along wit 'em. You call 'em up."

I thought about it. My extending the invitation would at least show them – more so D.C. – that what happened in the past was water under the bridge.

"OK," I said, rising off of him. "Give me their numbers."

He shifted his body to the right along with his head. "Hunh?"

"You're right. I'll do it."

He looked at me for a few seconds and shrugged. "A'right..." He rolled out from under my bent knees. He sat on the side of the bed, picked up the phone on the night table, and started dialing. My nerves began to jump all over; was I ready to do this right now? I folded my legs in a yoga position and breathed deeply.

He handed me the phone. "Tha easy one firs'. Angel..."

As soon as I put the receiver to my ear, someone picked up. *"Hola?"* It was a little girl's voice. It was more than likely Angel's daughter, Anjelica, who is four. I met her the night we returned his car.

"Hi. Is Angel there?"

*"Si. Papi!"* she screamed, making my ear ring. I had finished popping it by the time he came to the phone.

"Yo..."

"Angel?"

"Yeah. Mitch?" He knew it was me.

"Yes. How are you?"

"I'm coolin'. Hey, do Raheim know you callin' me? I don' want da brotha ta think I'm tryin' ta put a move on ya."

I giggled. "Angel, you are so silly. Yes, he does. He's right here. I know you'll be coming to the B-boy bash on Saturday and wanted to know what you were doing before then."

"Nothin'."

"Well, I wanted to invite you over. You know, just to watch TV or something."

"Sounds cool. Wha' time?"

I didn't know, so I said the first thing that came to mind.

"Around eight."

"A'right. D.C. comin'?"

"I hope so. I'm about to call him."

"Well, tell 'im I'm comin'. He don' like missin' out on nothin'."

"I will. Do you want to speak to Raheim?"

"Nah. I shout at him lata. Good luck wit D.C."

"Thanks. I'll see you Saturday night."

"A'right. Want me ta bring somethin'?"

"No."

"Cool. Peayce."

"Bye." Raheim was right — that was easy.

He took the phone and dialed D.C. I started to sweat. He hung up the phone.

"What...," I began.

"His beepa," he said, folding his arms against his chest.

"Oh."

The phone rang. He picked it up and gave it to me.

"He-llo?" I asked.

"Yeah, somebody beep D.C.," he said. Over the phone, his voice reminded me of Al B. Sure.

"Hi, D.C., this is Mitchell, Raheim's friend."

Dead silence.

"Yeah, wha's up?" he grumbled.

"Uh, well, I just wanted to know what you were doing before the party on Saturday night..."

"Why?" he abruptly asked.

I looked to Raheim for help, but he was now against the night table, pondering the "Final Jeopardy" answer ("It is the longest suspension bridge ever constructed in the U.S.") and pulling on his dick. I swear, if he could, he'd probably suck it himself.

"Well, I wanted to have you over to the house."

"Ta do *wha'?*" He wasn't cutting me any slack.

"Well, uh, whatever you guys want to do ... watch a movie or maybe play cards..."

*"Cards?"* I'd hit on something. His snappy, bothered tone switched to a peppy, interested one. "Wha' kin'?"

"Well, what kind do you like to play?"

"Spades, all da way."

I was an undefeated champ in high school; we'd play on our lunch hour. "That sounds good. It's been some time since I've played."

"I hope you ain' fuhgit. I don' play no chumps."

"Don't worry, I'm a challenge," I said. At that moment Raheim had come up with the question ("Wha's tha Verrazano-Narrows?"), and he also did a double take after he realized what I'd said.

"Ha, we see 'bout dat," D.C. laughed. "Wha' time ya wan' me ova so I can teacha howta play?"

I was very amused. "Teach me?"

"Yeah. An' I don' take no pris'nas."

"You won't have to, believe me. You'll be the one begging for mercy, not me." By this time, Raheim was sitting on the bed with that "Wha'tha fuck's goin' on?" look.

D.C. giggled. "Uh-huh. *Da time?*"

"Eight."

"Cool. See ya. Peayce." Amazing ... they all have the same sign-off.

Raheim didn't like the smile on my face as I handed him the receiver to hang up. "Wha'tha fuck's goin' on?"

I laughed. "Don't get all excited. He's agreed to come over."

"Oh yeah?"

"Yes. We're going to play Spades."

Raheim plopped himself back on the bed, his head falling on my left thigh, and started laughing.

"What is so funny?" I asked.

"You gonna play tha Masta, hunh?"

"Oh ... is that who he is supposed to be?"

"It ain't who he s'pose ta be, Baby, tha's who tha brotha is. I hope you know wha'cha gettin' yo'self inta..."

"Even if he is the Master, he hasn't played me yet."

Raheim shrugged. "A'right ... you'll see..."

⊕

"So, ya ready ta git yo' ass whipped?"

It was D.C. He and Angel were right on time and both were looking very sharp – D.C. in an orange tank and shorts, black boots, and black "X" cap; Angel in yellow tank, blue shorts and cap, and Nike sandals.

I took one of the six bags of White Castle out of D.C.'s hands. "Sorry, but I don't get my ass whipped ... only licked."

"Hmph, I bet," he laughed, walking in the house and allowing his eyes to linger on my butt.

After Raheim greeted his boyz with brotha shakes, hugs, and booty pats, we all sat down to eat at the dining room table. They brought at least forty burgers. Like usual, Raheim and I shared a chocolate shake. Angel asked if he could play a CD – a group called the Barrio Boyzz. He was telling me how two of the fellas grew up in his 'hood when D.C. interrupted.

"So, I hear you from Bed-Stuy?"

"Yes, I am," I said, not looking up. I was putting ketchup on my fries.

"Well, you don' ac' like it."

"I don't act like it? How am I supposed to act?"

"You know..." He gobbled up another burger with two bites. "All da brothas I know from Do-or-Die ain't, ya know ... preppy."

I giggled. "Preppy? I'm preppy because I don't wear my pants down to my knees and my drawers up to my chin?"

Angel laughed; Raheim just ate.

"You funny," D.C. snickered. "But you ain' gonna be laughin' lata."

"Uh-huh ... where are *you* from?" I asked.

"Where else? Harlem." He pounded on his chest.

"Well, *you* don't look like it."

"Wha'cha mean I–"

"Well, all the brothers I know from Harlem ... uh, how do I put this delicately ... ain't short like you."

Raheim coughed on the shake and Angel, once again, cracked up.

D.C. became testy. "Wha'cha mean, short?"

I smiled. "What part of that statement did you not understand? You *are* the shortest man sitting at this table."

"Oh yeah? Well, I'm big in da right place." And he grabbed his dick.

I had to laugh at that one. But why, *why* does it always have to be about the dick?

This conversation continued for half an hour. Once you got behind his ruff exterior, D.C. wasn't such a hard ass. He and Angel talked about their daughters (D.C.'s being a three-year-old named Precious). After he disclosed that the only nonrap groups he liked were Mary J. Blige and Jodeci, I programmed *What's the 411?* and *Forever My Lady* to play randomly. Raheim bragged about my singing and coached me to give them a few bars of "You Remind Me." D.C. loved it ("Not only can da brotha cook, he can sang, too") but wanted to prove that he could, too. So, after much prodding, he got the others to do the chorus from *their* song, "It's So Hard to Say Goodbye to Yesterday." While they wouldn't win the Amateur Night at the Apollo contest, they were cute standing side by side with D.C. in the middle, their arms on each other's shoulders, singing it way off-key.

And then came our square-table discussion about Jodeci being "too hard."

"God knows they can sing," I began. "But that image ... I just don't think it's necessary."

"Yo, da brothas jus' know wha' time it is," D.C. argued. "It's jus' da life, ya know?"

"Well, I do like their music. But they are a bit too roguish for me," I argued.

"No, they ain't," piped in Raheim, sipping on the shake.

"What?" I asked.

"You heard. You know you like shit like that."

"I do not."

"Ha, you ain't say that shit las' nite."

I aimed for his thigh with my open palm, but he caught it, pulling me off my chair and tickling me.

I fought him. "Stop!"

"Uh-huh, yeah fuckin' right." He had me sideways, sitting on his lap. He kissed me. I almost got into it but then realized we had company – company that was doing the "woof, woof, woof" chant, egging Raheim on.

"A'right, Raheim, get a taste fuh me, man," winked Angel.

"Yeah, Brotha Man, squeeze dat ass fuh me," grinned D.C., as Raheim patted me on the behind and I eased back into my seat. D.C. gave Angel a high five.

"Shut up, motha-fuckas," said Raheim.

"Who you callin' motha-fucka, *motha-fucka?*" D.C. shouted.

D.C. and Raheim then lapsed into yet another "Yo' mama..." reading session – something that I absolutely would not participate in or listen to. So I announced that it was time to play Spades. But after we cleaned up the table (yes, they helped!), Raheim gave me the bad news.

"But I thought *we* were going to be partners..."

"Sorry, Baby, but me an' D.C. go way back as partnas."

"Yeah, way back," D.C. said, taking a seat on my right.

I took the cards out the box and started to shuffle. "That's OK. Me and Angel will do just fine."

"I don' see how, when he don' know how ta play," chuckled D.C.

I looked at Angel as he sat across from me. He gave me the same smile B.D. has when he doesn't have a clue. Uh-oh.

"Angel, do you know anything about this game?" I asked.

"A little," he explained, still sipping on his vanilla shake. "I know how it go, but I ain't really play before."

"Just as long as you have the idea of how it goes."

"Yo, I ain' got no time fuh you ta be teachin' nobody," said D.C.

"Do you mind?" I snapped. "I am trying to get a few things straight with my partner."

"Cool. But it ain't gonna help," he predicted.

I went over the reason why the game is called Spades – they are the only wild suit – and explained how it was similar to rummy or 500. I showed him how he could use his spade to cut other suits, and that, if he didn't have a particular suit and didn't want to cut me, he could throw off with another. I told him how he could play spades any time – especially if he had one or both jokers, plus the deuce of diamonds, which is the third-highest card in the game. The talk was no more than four minutes; I had done it before with others and it helped. Angel seemed to grasp it.

"Yo, can we play? If he ain' git it by now, he ain' neva gon' git it," said D.C.

"You know, I hope your game is as good as your gab," I chimed, putting the deck in front of him to cut.

"Don' worry, it is," he giggled, cutting the cards.

I picked up the deck and started to deal. "OK, these are the rules..."

D.C.'s eyes went up. "Rules?"

"Yes, rules."

D.C. slid back in his chair. "Wha'cha sayin'? You don' trus' us?"

"Yes, I am."

Raheim gave me that Pooquie look and grabbed my hand. "Baby, you don' trus' *me?*"

I smiled. "If you are his partner? No."

Angel fell out.

"Well, fuck you, too," said D.C., slamming his hand on the table.

"Yeah, wouldn't you just love to ... Derrick."

I knew that would strike a nerve – Raheim told me how he hates to be called by his first name. "Yo, don' call me Derrick," he advised.

"I'll call you whatever I want ... *Derrick.*"

He simmered.

I continued dealing. "There will be no coughing, no waving, no whispering, no winking, no sighing, no finger tapping, no knuckle cracking, no foot stamping, no clearing of the throat, no dropping of the napkin, no twisting of the ring, no pulling on the ear, no chain pulling, no brushing of the nose, no flipping of the cap, no peace signing, no black-hand-hi-fiving, and, one I'm sure you all will find very hard not to do, no dick tugging."

*"Day-am,* can we breathe?" D.C. had both arms on the table, looking at me in disbelief.

"I guess you can do that ... I want you to be fully awake when I win," I smiled, picking up my own hand.

"Yeah, jus' shut up an' play."

Angel and I got off to a rough start. During the first hand, he reneged (meaning he threw off on a suit – hearts – when he had them in his hand) and that cost us three books. Since we had bid five, we started the game fifty points in the hole. The second hand we couldn't even make board (the minimum bid of four books) and went back again, to a total of minus ninety points. The third time around, we bid a blind four – meaning we had to make four books or we went back another eighty points. But we made it on time. We were then minus ten. But they already had 232 points (500 points won the game). And D.C. was, of course, quick to declare victory.

"Y'all wanna hang it up? I undastan'," he laughed.

"This game is not over yet, D.C.," I said. "We can come back, and we will."

"Ha, we see."

An hour later, the game was close: we had 430 (mainly due to my tenacious competitive spirit) to their 495. All they needed was a board to win the game. I was going to make sure they didn't. But when I saw my hand – six diamonds, four hearts, two spades, and one club, none of them face cards or high trumps – I knew we were sunk.

I was ready to concede defeat by bidding a board when Angel announced: "I got seven books."

It was the first time during the game that he'd had more than two in his hand.

"He ain't got no seven books, cuz I got five," said Raheim.

"Yeah, an' even if he did, he wouldn't know he had 'em," added D.C., as he and Raheim laughed it up with a hi-five.

"You sure you have seven?" I asked, somewhat skeptical myself.

"Yeah, I think so," he said, unsure.

"Man, you betta know, not think," warned D.C.

I looked in my hand. I couldn't help him; he would be on his own. And if he couldn't do it when I was pulling for him, how could he do it alone? But, we had nothing to lose – except the game – since a board would give it to them anyway. So, I decided we'd go for broke.

"Give us a seven," I told Raheim, who was keeping score.

"Baby, you cray-zee! Y'all may as well take a board an' leave it at that," he advised, rubbing my left foot, which was sitting on his chair between his legs.

I tugged on my foot, brushing him in the crotch. "We are taking a seven. I have all confidence in my partner."

"She-it, you betta have mo' dan dat," grinned D.C.

"Word," agreed Raheim.

Angel took the first two books – both of his aces (clubs and hearts) walked. His ace of diamonds, though, didn't – D.C. cut it. Uh-oh.

Raheim and D.C. then ran the next four books. That could've been the game, but they had to be greedy. They'd bid a seven, also, so one of us was going in the hole. There were only thirteen books in the deck.

But then Angel's queen of hearts walked. Maybe we weren't out of it after all.

Angel then shocked us all. Knowing that D.C. was cutting diamonds and Raheim was probably cutting everything else, he had the top three spades and ran them. Way to go!

But we still needed another book, and it seemed Raheim and D.C. were cleaning up the rest.

"Well, I know dis is ours," said D.C., as he put down his last card, the ten of hearts.

I put down mine: a six of diamonds.

Raheim looked at me, tickled my foot, and put his five of clubs on the table. "Well, ya'll may as well give it up ta us."

Angel looked at his card. "I don' think so."

He put down the jack of hearts. We won.

D.C. went, as Raheim would say, ballistic. "Ge'da fuck outa here! No! *Day-am!* I don' be*lieve* dis shit! Yo, Raheim, wha'da fuck happened?"

"I don' know, man, I thought we had it," said Raheim, bewildered.

"Yo, ya'll musta cheated," accused D.C.

"You know we didn't," I said. My arms were around Angel's shoulders, his around my waist. He had, like I, jumped up for joy over us winning. After a clumsy embrace, I had smacked him on the cheek.

"Yo, I wan' a rematch," demanded D.C., who gathered up the cards.

"Now, now, now, do you really want to have your ass whipped ... *again?*" I asked, easing back into my chair.

He shuffled the cards violently. "Uh-huh, talk shit now. Dat was jus' luck. We *had* dat shit. An' we gon' git it back."

I turned to Angel, who had also sat back down. "Shall we?"

"Hmmmm, why not," he giggled.

We played again and whomped them – 508 to 312. D.C. wanted to play again – he just couldn't accept the fact that he wasn't the Master – so we did. And we stomped them *again* – 527 to 179. During the third game, we managed to set them back four straight times. The only reason they finished near 200 was because they were able to take several blinds to get out of the whole.

"Three strikes, you out, brotha," said Angel.

"Wha*t*eva, motha-fucka," D.C. grunted, sitting with his head back.

I nudged Raheim in the crotch with my foot, but he pushed it away. He glanced at me. "Sore loser," I mouthed. I slapped D.C. on the thigh. "Listen, D.C., I know you'll probably think I'm bullshitting you, but you are the very best player I've ever known."

His head came up. "Yeah?"

"Yeah ... you are tough. Those were the best games I've ever played."

"Yeah?"

"Yeah ... maybe one day we can be partners and really kick some ass."

He laughed, sat up in his chair, and held out his hand. "Yo' game is a'right, too, brotha."

I grabbed his hand and pulled him up and hugged him. He was caught off guard but returned the hug. As I had with Angel, I patted him on the butt. He also obliged, saying: "You cool, you cool."

"C'mon, y'all, we gotta be out," said Angel, rising out of his chair and looking at his watch. "It's one o'clock."

D.C. slapped his right cheek. "Oh shit."

"Y'all go downstairs, we be there in a minute," Raheim said blankly, still seated at the table.

"Cool," said Angel. "I'm ready ta dance. It's time ta celebrate."

"Motha-fucka, you ain' got nothin' ta celebrate. He did all da fuckin' work. You ain' do shit," argued D.C., picking his car stereo up off the coffee table.

"Yo, I helped," answered Angel.

"Yeah motha-fuckin' right," D.C. shot back.

"Well, we see. We can do it again nex' week an' see who is still champ," Angel boasted.

"Man, you tell *any*body dis shit went down an' you ain' gonna *see* nex' week," D.C. joked.

They continued prodding each other as they headed out the door. I went into the kitchen to place the cards back in the tool drawer when Raheim cornered me against the counter.

"Wha'cha call all o' that?"

"All what?"

"Huggin' all on them ... an' kissin' Angel?"

"I didn't kiss him, Raheim, it was just a peck on the cheek."

"Ain' look like that ta me."

I laughed. He didn't.

"You're serious? Come on, we were both excited about winning."

"Well, I don' want you kissin' on nobody, not even a peck," he huffed, walking over to the fridge, where he planted his left fist.

I smiled. "You're jealous."

"I ain't jealous," he snapped.

I went over to him and placed my hands under his tank top. He flinched. "Yes, you are, Pooquie, and you don't have any reason to be. It's silly."

"Yeah, wha'eva..."

"Whatever, nothing," I countered, pulling him around to face me. "I'm just really happy that we all are having a good time. And you didn't think we could."

He wouldn't face me. I gently grasped his chin and turned his head. "You know you my man ... don't you?"

A grin grew into a smile. "Yeah."

We kissed.

"Oh, I love it when you get like that, 'cause you are *so* hot," I whispered, kissing his chin.

He giggled. "Don' even try usin' my line."

"I'll use whatever I want ... *Daddy.*"

Smack, smack, serious smack.

"Now, let's get out of here. I wanna dance with my Pooquie." I stabbed the dimple. He headed off to change his clothes. And I just stood there smiling my ass off.

I finally felt like one of the boyz.

 From the moment I walked into the third-floor apartment in the six-story housing project, it was obvious what a "B-boy bash" was. Every single person was (or, like me, came with) a B-boy. And, if you didn't fall into either category, don't *even* try to bum-rush the show. When we arrived, two guys who looked like B-boys were being escorted to the stairs and then thrown down them by a rotund bouncer who accused them of being "wannabes." It was not a cute scene.

But in the somewhat dark, musky-hot (*where* was the air-conditioning?), incense-maryjane-smelling, loftlike living room were a good seventy brothas who were the real thing. Ranging in age from fourteen to forty, all were in some state of banjeedom: unlaced boots or sneakers, droopy pants, exposed undergear, shirtless chests, cabled necks, gold-capped teeth and adorned fingers, and backwards or sideways tilted caps. Some looked like they'd just escaped in their jailhouse-striped gear. Others were carrying wooden canes, as if they were in some sort of fraternity (I would later find out that they were). Like they do in the bars and clubs, most were standing against the walls (there was nowhere to sit), posturing and posing, staring at no one or no one thing in particular but trying to outman each other. And even those that danced had to do it with cool. Their feet never left the ground, their bodies strutted back and forth in a rockabilly motion, their hands were glued either to their sides or their dicks, their heads swayed up and down but stayed cocked, and their faces remained expressionless, as if they weren't enjoying what they were doing.

*This is a party?* I asked myself, surveying the scene. *Seems more like a Narcissists Anonymous meeting.* I also thought of the title of a recent Aretha tune: "What You See Is What You Sweat."

As was the case almost anyplace we went, Raheim knew just about everybody. It took us a good half hour to get in the party, because folks were stopping him all around us (and, of course, he didn't introduce me to any of them). Raheim had on his usual, get-loose party gear – a black tank that says COOLEY LOVE, black jean shorts, white boxers with clubs (visible since his pants were way off his waist), and black boots. But he added an extra item to this ensemble: a white head rag with black polka dots. I was surprised when he came out of the bathroom with this on. He had never worn one before – at least in my presence. He really looked like a gangsta. I didn't question it; I figured the reason for it would be revealed when we got to the party, and it was. At least two dozen other fellas were sporting their own head rags, one in the style of an American flag. I laughed, wondering how ex-prez George Bush would've felt about someone wearing that treasured symbol on their head.

After the boyz and I found a spot of our own for the evening, Raheim grabbed my arm: "Le's dance, Baby. This my song." Of course, it was "That's the Way Love Goes." We hit the floor and people gave us room. Raheim was always surprised that I knew all the latest dances and could keep up with him. In fact, he'd gag when I'd slide in and under his legs and over his head. He had a lot of energy (not to mention stamina) and could dance all night. If he wanted to, I didn't mind. And after the triumphs of that night – beating D.C. three times but also gaining his respect – I was more than ready.

No matter the song, no matter the style (house, dance, rap, reggae), we jumped and humped and bumped. No, let's say we sexed it up. I ground my behind into him with such a vengeance that Raheim claimed he came (talk about dirty dancing). But at three different times during the night, he worked this same groove with other people – two of those times with one person I didn't know and didn't care for. I remembered him from Gay Pride Day. Like then, this ho, who was a lighter version of me, ignored me, as if I wasn't standing right in front of him, his hands all over Pooquie. Uh-huh, as the song he shook his hips to declared, he was down with O.P.P. And Raheim, while he wasn't exactly returning the attention, once again allowed it to go on. I felt like a fool. I also felt like wringing that trollop's neck with Raheim's shirt, which I was holding. Angel must have sensed that I wasn't pleased. He asked me whether I wanted to dance. I said no. He told me not to worry, that Raheim only had eyes for me.

"David still on his shit, but Raheim ain't havin' none o' dat again," he explained, sippin' on gin and juice. "You think he get da message it's ova..."

"What do you mean, 'get the message it's over'?"

He looked as if I had just caught him with his hand in the cookie jar. "I uh, uh ... maybe Raheim should tell ya..."

"Oh, no, Angel, finish what you start," I demanded, preventing him from walking away by holding on to his arm. "Were they ... are they involved?"

Seeing no way out, he confessed. "Dey was ... las' summa."

My blood began to boil. I went to the bathroom to cool off. What the fuck is his problem? He gets bent out of shape if I so much as shake hands with his boyz, but he flaunts his ex right in front of my face, gyrating and pulsating as if they were still together. By the time I waited on line and splashed cold water on my face, I decided that I wasn't going to be overly jealous like him. But then I walked back into the room and almost lost it. David, wearing black sneakers and a black bodysuit that seemed to be glued to his frame, was now imitating me, throwing his big ass all up in Pooquie's dick. Raheim would kill me if I came out of the house looking like that, but that is obviously what he likes — he was holding on to David's waist, enjoying the ride. I wanted to cut in and cut them both up.

What made the whole thing even worse was that they and the two dozen other couples on the floor were groovin' to Buju Banton's "Boom Bye Bye" — a song which encourages folks to kill homosexuals. How can a room full of faggots even allow a song like that to be played at a party? I wanted to find the host and voice my concern. But that would've done no good — he was one of those going wild on the floor. And what a queen! There were, to my surprise, many there — big bad boyz you'd never think would say "Miss Thing" or "Miss Honey" but who acted as if they invented those phrases, not to mention the limp wrist and vogueing. The concept seemed weird to me: why have all that body, all that bass, and act like that? All of these children had their eyes on the more "masculine" fellas in the house. But there certainly seemed to be more "man-on-man" pairings, which made me giggle at a question Anderson asked me years ago: "How do you know if someone is a, uh, top or bottom?"

Anyway, this death-dancing scene, along with the gross popularity of the *n*-word (Raheim and his boyz caught themselves several times before saying it at my house but joined their peers in the nigga chanting as soon as we arrived), was a bit too much self-hatred for me. I wanted to leave. But I just stood near one of the four giant speakers that was in each corner of the room, out of Raheim's view, not being banjee or queenie at all. After two more monotonous-sounding reggae records, the deejay finally cut me some slack by mixing Whitney and Chaka's versions of "I'm Every Woman" — and I had to do a double take. Raheim was doing the electric slide with David and company, mouthing all the words to the song, pointing to himself and slapping his chest *e-ver-y-time* the divas declared they were every woman. Now *that* was a sight worth seeing. *You're* every woman, it's all in *you*, hunh, Raheim? I couldn't help but laugh out loud.

Then one of my songs came on – the dope house mix of "Ain't 2 Proud 2 Beg" by TLC – and I wanted to dance. I peeked over to see if Raheim and David had resumed fuckin' each other and they had. Now that heifer had his hands inside Pooquie's boxers, which, like his pants, were so low you could see his pubic hair and a good chunk of his ass. Raheim also had a handful of David's butt. I didn't want to make a scene, and I knew I would if I went over to them and butted in (pun intended). I searched for the other boyz, but they were both occupied: Angel was shaking it with one of the only other Latino fellas at the party, and D.C. had some cute, chocolate muscle boy who was shorter than him up against a wall, just workin' it. So, I just bopped in place.

"Wha's up?"

For a second I thought it was Pooquie, because of the bass-boomin' voice. But my eyes focused up – way up – on a B-boy, maybe thirty, who had been steppin' with seven other frat boyz earlier in the evening. One wouldn't know there are gay and bisexual men in fraternities, since most are in the closet. Babyface, who is a Kappa, and Adam, who is Sigma, say some frats do use homosexual activity as an undercover rite of passage to promote "true brotherhood bonding," but won't accept those who identify themselves as gay. I certainly didn't expect to see any at this party. And, to be taller than Pooquie and just as built, this guy was not clunky on his feet at all. It takes a lot of skill and flexibility to do those moves – especially with a cane – and he was doing them with ease.

He had a clean head, which a Chicago Bulls cap barely sat on top of. His eyes were glassy and gray. His goatee was shaped in a box, with no hair between his chin and rosy lips. His nose was broad just like his shoulders. His legs were long and sleek. His red tee was over his left shoulder, and his black-and-red Spandex clung to him nicely. His nipples were sharp. It looked like he had on no underwear. His thang was hangin' kind of low and, judging by the outline in his pants, was *big*. His high-top black-and-red Air Jordans were unlaced.

As B.D. would say, he was tall, light, and lovely. And he made me nervous.

"Hi," I mouthed.

He nodded at the floor. "Dance?"

"Uh, no, no thanks," I said, wishing he'd go away. He was tempting me. I continued bopping.

He moved in, down and closer. "Ya sure? Looks like ya do ta me..."

"Well, I'd like to but ... I'm here with my man."

He grinned, showing a gap in his upper front teeth that was very sexy. "Uh-huh, an' where he be?"

My heart sank as my eyes fell on Pooquie and David. "He's ... he's dancing."

"She-it, he dancin', leavin' a fine lil' thang like you by yo'self?" He checked me out from head to toe. "You wearin' dem shorts, small fry..." I felt outdressed in a light brown blouse, sandals, and brown shorts which, of course, couldn't hide my ass. Hmmmm, that line sounded familiar. Do all these B-boys use it?

I smiled. "Thank you, but..."

"You wanna dance, baby, so c'mon ... I ain' gon' hur'cha."

He grabbed my arm and took me to the floor. I didn't put up a fight. Hell, if Raheim can dance with whomever he wants, why can't I?

At first I wouldn't let him touch me. At least if Pooquie saw us, he wouldn't be able to say that I was flirting. But it just became a natural thing for him to do. Our bodies blended into each other's well. I allowed him to slide his hands along my waist, then my legs, while I held on to his shoulders, tracing the brand on his arm, curious as to what it felt like. He smiled and whispered: "If ya like da way dat feels, I got somethin' else for ya." I asked what frat he was in. The Q-Dogs: Omegas. By the time the song went off, I had my arms around his neck while he rocked us, enjoying the feel of my rump. Yes, it was turning me the fuck on and he knew it. "Oh yeah, baby...," he groaned, grinning up a storm. I blushed.

It figures that "Rump Shaker" was coming on next – and that Raheim would appear out of nowhere.

He jerked the guy away from me, knocking me against the wall and causing folks around us to run for cover. "Nigga, wha'tha *fuck* you think you doin'?"

The fella threw up his hands, pointing at Raheim. "Motha-fucka, wha'da fuck you think *you* doin'?"

Raheim got all up in his face, putting his hands on his hips. "You ain' got *no* fuckin' bizness puttin' yo' hands where they *ain'* s'pose ta be!"

"Nigga, pleeze, you got a claim on ev'ry *bitch* in da fuckin' place?" He pushed Raheim.

Their hands went up and they went for theirs, rumbling and tumbling to the ground, tussling on the floor right in front of me, fists flying and falling on hard flesh. Up against the wall, I couldn't watch. I ran out of the room against the traffic running to see the fight. I bumped into D.C.

"Wha'da fuck's goin' on?" he asked, the vodka so strong I could smell it on his breath.

I was hysterical. *"Raheim is fighting in there!"*

He took off. "Aw she-it!"

I kept moving along, shaking, ending up outside the apartment in the hallway. I was distraught, as the four or five people chatting in the hall could see. One fella approached me and asked if I was all right. I told him I would be. He gave me his handkerchief so I could wipe my face. I thanked him.

A few minutes later, the guy I danced with came out. He held some tissue up to his eye. Was it black? He bent down to face me as I sat on the top step of the stairs.

"When you wan' a real man an' not some fuckin' chump, le'me know, small fry," he said, dropping a card in my lap. "I know how ta trea'cha." He puckered up and tried to kiss me, but I moved my head away. He snickered, mouthed a kiss, rose, and strode down the stairs. After he had gone, I tore up the card and threw it toward the open window.

Five minutes later, Raheim appeared with D.C. and Angel. He was nursing a bloody nose. I freaked out.

I got up and ran to him. "Oh my God, Raheim, are you all—"

*"Don'* fuckin' touch me!" he shouted, pulling away and heading for the stairs. I looked at D.C. and Angel. They both shrugged. Not wanting to wake up the whole building, I just followed him down. When we got outside, I placed my hand on his shoulder. He knocked it away.

I was dumbstruck. "Raheim, what's wrong with you?"

He threw his arms up, causing me to jump back. "Wha's wrong wit *me?* Wha'tha fuck is wrong wit *you?* Throwin' yo' shit 'round, all up in some motha-fucka's face an' causin' all shit ta go down. *Day-am,* I can' take yo' ass *no* fuckin' place wit'out you playin' me..."

I squinted. I noticed the bruise on his left cheek. "What?"

He paced. "I ain' bring yo' ass out here ta dance wit any nigga you want. Was you gonna go home wit him an' shit?"

"Oh, I see..." I tried to calm down but couldn't. The words came out angry. "I'm supposed to stand against a *fuck*ing wall and wait for you to finish dancing with whoever the *fuck* you want to, even your *fuck*ing ex, and then when you snap your fingers, dance when *you* want?"

Raheim turned to Angel and put his left hand in his face. "Mothafucka, you got a *big* fuckin' mouth."

Angel threw up his hands. "Yo, man, I ain' mean ta tell, swear ta God."

Raheim was not moved. *"Shut up,* motha-fucka."

"Raheim, don't blame him," I interjected. "You have only yourself to blame. He didn't do anything and I didn't do a damn thing wrong. You did all of this to yourself."

That's when he came for me.

D.C. jumped in front of him. "Yo, Brotha Man, now, don' do dis shit, a'right. Dey gon' call da fuckin' cops."

He was screaming at the top of his lungs as D.C. pushed him toward the Jeep. Smoke was coming out of his ears. *"Get offa me, man! I don' give a fuck! You betta stay outa my fuckin' face, you hear, bitch? I fuck you up! You got a whole lota fuckin' mouth..."*

I was afraid. When Angel touched my shoulder, I screamed and started trembling. I walked around in a circle, feeling lost, unaware that folks were watching, snickering. Raheim said he was going to fuck me up. He called me a bitch. A *bitch.* My whole body went numb.

After walking around the corner with Raheim, D.C. came back up to us. He grabbed Angel and they huddled together. After their little talk, they approached me.

D.C. was somber. "Uh, we gon' git you a cab."

They weren't going to take me home. I didn't hear anything else they said. I didn't say anything. D.C. went into the street and hailed one just like that. Angel opened the door for me. I got in. He closed the door. D.C. gave the driver money and told him where to go. Good thing – I couldn't talk. The cab took off.

Before I knew it, I was home. I got out. It felt like I was in a trance. I don't remember taking out my key. I don't remember opening the downstairs door. I don't remember walking up the stairs to my apartment. I don't remember getting into bed.

But, still clutching Raheim's shirt, I do remember crying myself to sleep.

"Your sisters are here!"

It was B.D. at my door, joined by Gene and Babyface. It had been seven whole days since Raheim and I had had what Gene referred to as a "domestic dispute" in the street, and I hadn't heard a word from him. It's not like I expected to. In fact, I was really hoping I didn't get a phone call or a tap on my door. I feared him. He wanted to hurt me that night. But why? What did I do? Gene, who found out that Raheim was not expected to come into Simply Dope that week, explained that Raheim dogged me out because I had the nerve to question his word, his authority. After all, he is my man; I should do as he says, not as he does. And his (and his brawl partner's) calling me a bitch – a possession, a piece of booty to fight over – was proof. When my mother and Adam called and asked about him, I told them he was OK. I didn't tell them what had happened.

I couldn't really concentrate at my job. I did what needed to be done – we were working on the next two issues, Puerto Rico and health care – without my usual bravado (i.e., putting Elias and Phillip in their places). I didn't even get excited about the family issue, which I put together. Of course, I was reminded of his face, because there he was on the cover with Junior. In fact, when Leonard returned from hiking in Colorado, he felt their photo was the best out of the bunch and that Senior and Junior should be on the cover, solo. I should've been thrilled, but I wasn't. Denise and Michael showed more enthusiasm over the finished product than I. Because I didn't talk about the party or how things went between D.C. and me, Michelle knew something was up, but she didn't press me.

I didn't feel like going out, but I didn't mope around the house. I was oblivious to his clothes and other items; I just blocked them out. B.D. said that I was still in shock and that a "serious sister session" would lift my spirits.

So, the crew decided they would all come over for dessert that Sunday to keep me company. We usually did this type of thing one day during the summer anyway. We all had hectic schedules – our work and vacation times were always different – and could only count on getting together on Gay Pride Day, which was at the very beginning of the season. So we made another date later on just to dish the tee over tea, coffee, juice, and sweet-potato pie, which I made. B.D. said that he could buy them from a bakery in Harlem this time so that I wouldn't have to worry about it, but it gave me something to do. They had arrived at six on the dot for our Brothers Brunch. Of course, it is kind of late in the day for it to be a "brunch," but who cares? The title fits the gathering perfectly and, besides, Babyface and I prefer it over "sister session"; Gene could care less.

I smiled at my guests. "Come on in, y'all. The hot water is boiling and the coffeemaker is percolating."

"Wait a minute," said B.D., giving me a hug and kiss and then going in the opposite direction toward the bedroom. "I have to see the shrine first!" He was wearing yet another bodysuit, this one a shade of violet known as queen's jubilee (figures, doesn't it?).

Gene, also dressed in his usual outfit (this time silver-gray), also said hello in our usual way. "Ain't no need to worry, hon. We is here."

Babyface, sexy in an olive short set and open-toed sandals, embraced me tight – and, oh, how I needed *that* – and then smacked me on the lips. "How you holding up, Mitch?"

"OK..."

"So *that* is the scene of the crime!" declared B.D., joining us as we headed toward the living room. "Girl, I just know that those walls got a *lot* to say!" I laughed, something I hadn't done in a while.

When we all met Gene in the living room, he was motionless. He was staring at my portrait hanging over the sofa.

*"That* is *fierce!"* exclaimed B.D., moving in closer to it.

Gene finally pointed at it and spoke. *"He* did *that?* Now, I know the boy can draw, but *that* is *fab*ulous!"

"It sure is," nodded Babyface, as he took his spot on the sofa. After he got drinks and cut slices of pie for them both, B.D. joined him.

Gene took his space in the imaginary doorway between the living room and the kitchen. He'd stand there and hold court for the entire evening. Give him an ashtray (I made one for him, putting foil in a bowl) and one of the pies (I'd made four; he took one off the stove and put it off to the side for himself) and he was set.

After I programmed the CD to play Aretha's Atlantic boxed set randomly, I took my seat in one of the folding chairs from the dining room table so I could face all of them. I didn't want to talk about *him* yet, so I shifted the convo before it stayed there. "So, Gene, B.D. just told me you are still seeing Carl."

Gene gave him a dirty look. "Some folks can never keep their mouths closed."

Babyface put in his five cents. "He was about to tell us in the car exactly what the problem is."

"Thank you, Perry mother-fucking Mason, for your input," Gene snarled.

B.D. held a spoonful of pie to his mouth. "Come on, just tell us."

Gene lit up a Marlboro and began to pace the floor. "Carl is a very interesting man. Has a good job ... he's a stockbroker. He treats me well. Buys me a lot of nice things and..."

"You have him buying you gifts?" I asked.

"And what if I do?"

"That is really tired, Gene," I lectured. "You know what Momma always said: 'Money can't buy you—'"

"Uh, do you *ever* get a nosebleed from taking the *high* road all the time?" he accused. "I got a newsflash for you, my dear: money can buy you anything in this life!"

"You are too much, Gene," said Babyface.

Gene continued. "Anyway, as I was saying, he is a good man. But there is a small problem."

I took a guess. "He's falling in, you know ... the *l*-word with you, right?"

"Hell no! If that was the case, I would've dropped him by now. Let's say that, while he is very affectionate and passionate, Carl shoots blanks when it comes to, you know..."

I got it. Babyface did too. B.D. didn't.

"When it comes to what?"

We all looked at him in amazement.

"You are nothing if not consistently absentminded, B.D.," said Gene. "Sex, you fool, sex."

"Oh..." He then put the two together and tried to come up with a mental picture. He reminds me of Edith Bunker when he does that. It finally dawned on him. *"Oh..."*

We all sighed.

Babyface sat up. "So what are you going to do?"

"Well, when I get tired of the thrill without the spill, I'll dump him," said Gene, without blinking.

"Gene, that's so cold," Babyface mumbled with a mouthful of pie.

Gene blew on his coffee. "Hey, that's life."

B.D. filled us all in on the progress his company was making. They'd gotten a grant from the NEA, and Bill T. Jones would be an advisor for their first season, starting in November. B.D. wanted me to sing during one of the dance routines. I told him I'd think about it. Babyface didn't have much to report. Same old story, same old song at the DA's office: almost all the people on the law side are Caucasian and those on the order side are of color. Then *the* topic of the evening got discussed when Babyface noticed the latest copy of *Your World* sitting on one of the speakers.

"Look, he don't need him!" declared Gene, chowing down on pie. "It's like I always say: if you ain't got a man, you got a hand!"

We all fell out.

He continued. "You laugh, but it is the safest sex you can ever have. And, you don't have to worry about throwing somebody out of your bed after the bizness has been taken care of."

"He should give him the benefit of the doubt, he shouldn't just brush him off," argued B.D.

"Who's brushing whom off here?" asked Gene. "It's been a whole week and that mother-fucker ain't even call. And mind you, this ain't the first time he's run off. This disappearing-act shit has got to go. Who the fuck does he think he is, David Copperfield?"

B.D. pointed his fork at me but looked at Gene. "I am not saying he should wait on him. All I'm saying is that Mitch, uh, Little Bit, should give him a chance, listen to what he has to say."

Gene was not being swayed. "Yes, he should listen to what he has to say ... and *then* kiss him off. If he does reappear like Houdini, you better be careful. If you think you hurtin' right now, he might really hurt you next time."

"Meaning?" I asked.

"Meaning that there may not be a D.C. to pull his ass back. Think about it."

I did. Could it happen again?

"Well, we didn't come here to depress him, we came over to cheer him up," said B.D. He grabbed Babyface's hand and snuggled up to him. "We have some great news."

I sipped my tea. "What is it?"

B.D. smiled at his man. "Should I tell them or do you want to?"

"You tell them, Baby."

When he calls B.D. Baby, it's just like Raheim.

"Well, Babyface and I have set a date."

"Set a date for what?" Gene asked sarcastically.

"Come on, Gene, don't *you* be so brain dense ... they're getting married!" I screamed, leaping off my chair and giving them both hugs and kisses. I aimed for Babyface's cheek, but he gave me his lips instead. Sly, sly fox.

"So, when is the date?" I asked, sitting back down.

"February fourteenth," smiled B.D., looking into his man's eyes.

Gene rolled his eyes. "How appropriate."

"Gene!" I snapped.

"So, what exactly does this mean?" he interrupted. "Planning to buy a house on Mulberry Street in the 'burbs? Getting his-and-hers mono-grammed towels? Giving *birth?*"

"No, it means we are no longer starving," Babyface matter-of-factly stated.

"'Starving'?" Gene and I sang.

Babyface got that litigator look. "All of us are starving ... for attention, for love, for understanding. I don't care what the sisters say: we take more shit than they do in this life, 'cause we are brothers in a white man's world, and there ain't no space for us. Never has been, never will be. All we want, all we need is someone to love us for who we are, to grow with us, so that the world ain't such a bad place. You got somebody in your corner, you lucky ... and blessed. And when you get that, you gotta know it, stand by it, and treat it with care. To nurture it. To build on it. I'm glad I got mine ... and I'm never letting it go."

"Oh, my Honey...," cooed B.D.

They kissed. I swooned.

But Gene gagged. "Are you *quite* through giving that *nau*seating testimonial?"

I got up and went into the kitchen. "Gene, must you always be so fucking cynical? Damn!"

"Look, I'm happy you two are happy. I am ... *really*. But you two *are* lucky. Most of the brothers out there are not like you, Babyface." He grabbed his dick in banjee mode. "They think with this head, not the one attached to their neck."

I returned to my seat with a slice of pie. "Yeah. I don't see how anyone can think they are gonna find love that way."

Gene sucked his teeth. "Oh, there's that word again!"

"Yes, there it is, *again,*" I snapped. "Some of us in this room do still believe in it, ya know?"

"Please, let's face the facts, hon ... all these mother-fuckers want is a good fuck and that's it."

"That's not all true."

"Well, we do know what's wrong with all the ones who want more than that, don't we?"

I knew what that meant: time to go down The List. We both looked at B.D. "Sorry, guys," he said, playing with Babyface's dred-locs, "but I don't have to worry about that anymore."

Gene turned to me. "Well, I guess it's just you and me, kid. Ready?"

"Ready..."

I started.

"They are confused ... don't know whether they are gay, straight, bi, or otherwise..."

"Or whether they are coming or going..."

"Afraid to be a man..."

"Afraid to be a *Black* man..."

"Afraid to be a Black *gay* man..."

"Afraid to *be*..."

"Bottom only..."

"Top only..."

"No dick..."

"No ass..."

"No job..."

"No integrity..."

"No R-E-S-P-E-C-T..."

"Married ... to a man..."

"Married ... to a woman..."

"Still living at home with his momma..."

"Don't have a home..."

"Won't grow up..."

*"Can't* grow up..."

"Cheap..."

"Conceited..."

"Stuck-up..."

"Liar, liar, jockstrap on fire!"

"Running the streets..."

"On parole..."

"In jail..."

"On their way to jail..."

"Jailbait..."

"Too old..."

"Dead..."

"Just plain oogly..."

"Don't know how to fuck!"

We all cracked up over that one.

"And the worst thing," began Gene, "the Ivory Complex..."

"Eeeek!" he and I screamed.

"The Ivory Complex?" queried Babyface.

I chewed and swallowed. "Yes. That's when they believe that a white man can save them..."

"From what?"

"From themselves..."

"Yes ... like Sydney...," added Gene.

Sydney Harrington was the very first friend – and lover – Gene had when he came to New York in 1977. He was Africentric before the word existed. They are, however, no longer friends. Since he "settled down" with a white man fifteen years his junior two years ago, Sydney dropped his chosen spiritual name (Malik Shakim Muhammad) and refuses to have anything to do with his brothers. To Gene, he has become a kept boy, living in a mansion in Connecticut and keeping house (like a good nigger) as Massa makes the dollars at his Fortune 500 company. As he explained to Babyface, Gene is convinced that Sydney got tired of fighting every day for what Caucasians automatically have as a birthright: life, liberty, and the pursuit of happiness. Unfortunately, he's livin' that life with shackles and chains on his neck, ankles, hands, mind, *and* dick.

Gene continued. "I hope he wakes the fuck up soon, for you know what they say: 'When you go too far away from home and you don't have carfare, you get stranded.' He fell for that 'your life can only be validated by a white man' nonsense. They ram that shit down all our throats ... pun intended."

It is true. I could count on one hand the number of images of brothers loving brothers I'd seen in my life. We (as well as other men of color) are often depicted in some passionate embrace with a white man, particularly in safer-sex ads. The message is insidious, insulting, and very clear: we don't fuck each other, we don't love each other, and, hence, we're better off fucking and loving a white man. No wonder so many of us believe Black men loving Black men is a revolutionary thing when it isn't. This multicultural bullshit has got to go – we all can*not* just fuck to get along.

"Well, are you saying that every single relationship between a brother and a Caucasian is based on that?" asked Babyface.

Gene frowned. "No, I am not. I do know at least one such couple where they are truly in, you know, the *l*-word. But they are together for the right reasons. Like those brothers who chase white women, some of us latch on to the first mugly white man who comes along, 'cause he ain't nothin' but a status symbol. And some of us think *they* are an alternative. But if you have your heart set on a Nubian king, why settle for anything less?"

Amen to that. As you already know, I am *not* an equal-opportunity lover. When I look into another man's eyes, I want those eyes, his total reflection, to complement mine – physically, emotionally, historically, and spiritually. I don't want to spend my days and nights being a spokesperson for all Black folks, educating my lover about me, about us, constantly challenging his arrogance, correcting his ignorance, and justifying my existence. I guess I should never say never – I said that about B-boys not too long ago – but no white man has ever turned my head. And if one did – and that is a very, *very* big if – I certainly would not hook up with him just to jump on the jungle-fever bandwagon (it is, after all, the "in" thing to do), nor would I be foolish enough to think our union is what Dr. King "dreamed" of, that it will promote better "race relations" (which, when you really think about it, do *not* exist), or "expand my horizons" and make me a kinder, gentler Negro.

Babyface sat up, but B.D. still held on to his arm. "Well, maybe they are tired of the games brothers play with each other, all the BS..."

"And white men don't play games?" Gene snapped. *"All* men do."

Babyface nodded. "That's true, but it ain't easy for two brothers, struggling to find themselves and be together."

Gene's hand went up. "Well, I'm sorry, but if you're with a Caucasian, you still Black. It ain't gonna make your life any easier or better. Sleeping with Ken is *not* going to make you Barbie!"

Babyface shrugged. "Well, all I'm saying is, if a brother finds something special with someone who is *not* a brother, I don't have a problem with that. I mean, people are not color-blind, but love is. That's my closing argument."

"Look, Counselor, court is not in session, so don't push it," warned Gene, pointing a finger at Babyface. They laughed.

"Well, I don't see what's so bad ... I did it once," admitted B.D.

All eyes – and opened mouths – fell on him.

*"You* would," Gene snapped.

"You never told me about that, Baby," said Babyface.

"Well, I didn't think it was important. I mean, it wasn't like we were boyfriends, even though he wanted us to be. It was a short fling. I wasn't interested at first. But I was curious."

"About what?" I asked.

"About, you know, *them.* Well, he really wasn't one of them."

"What?" we all sang.

"I mean, he was white but not American. He was an exchange student from Norway."

"Ah, so he was a frozen fruit," chuckled Gene.

B.D. rolled his eyes, pulling Babyface back against the sofa. "Funny, very funny. Anyway, he was after me — dropped notes in my locker, wanted to take me out to lunch or dinner, have coffee. And so I finally said yes. He was really a sweet guy. And handsome. He was on the football team, and wasn't in the closet at all."

"Folks knew about him?" I asked.

"Yup. And it had to be obvious that we had something going. He had SVEN LOVES BARRY written in Magic Marker on his locker."

"Get out of here!" I yelled.

"Sven?" laughed Gene.

"But I didn't feel that way about him. I mean, he was just an experiment."

I moved forward in my chair. "And did you take him for a test drive?"

"Yes."

*"And?"* we all anticipated.

"And ... it was better than I thought it would be."

"But, was it *bigger* than you thought it would be?" asked Gene.

*"Much* bigger!"

"Well, you lucked out."

"What's that supposed to mean?"

"That means that most of them don't have what it takes. They ain't hung like us..."

"Gene, that's the worst kind of stereotype," I argued.

"Call it what you want to, but it's true. Child, the white man ain't stupid. This" — he grabbed it once again — "has been our only weapon to fight his ass with. Why you think so many of us were castrated when we were lynched in the South?"

"Well, just because it is big doesn't mean it's going to be better," I reasoned.

"Now, I know *you* don't believe that," piped B.D.

"Yes, I do ... why?"

"In one word? Pooquie," he bellowed.

I blushed.

"See, you full of shit," he added, sashaying into the kitchen. "Pooquie is large *and* in charge!"

Gene took the floor again. "Well, bigger is better, but just because it is big doesn't mean the person it is attached to knows what to do with it."

"You got that right!" I agreed.

"And I must admit that, because no two dicks are the same, nor do they feel the same, a smaller one can do the trick," he continued. "It's all a matter of knowing how to work it. But the bottom line is, if you ain't swingin' low, you know where to go!" He pointed toward the front door. We cracked up.

He moved into the room and bent down, so we could all hear him whisper. "And, I've even been with some folks whose dicks look better than them."

"You are *so* farcical," I giggled.

"Uh, can we please change the subject?" asked Babyface, who had finished his pie and kicked off his sandals.

Gene sipped on his coffee. "What else is there to talk about?"

"I want to go back to The List," Babyface said.

"What about it?" I asked.

"Well, it seems to me that you guys can't win," he started, lying back on the sofa with his hands clasped behind his head on a pillow. "You have all of these things you won't tolerate in a man, but no man is perfect. We all come damaged in some way. No one is a complete package. We all have our issues."

I was interested. "So, you think our standards are too high?"

He sighed. "No, not too high. Just unrealistic."

"That's bullshit," argued Gene, his hands on his hips. "If I don't tolerate those negatives in me, why should I in someone else? Sorry, but I'm *not* featuring it."

Babyface got that litigator look again. "But you should see that negative as just one aspect of a person that he and you can deal with and maybe even overcome. We're all a work in progress. You're not going to find your Mr. Right if you're too busy looking for what's wrong."

"I would have to agree with my Honey on this one," added B.D., who moved Babyface's left leg so he could sit down. "I believe there are three types of men: Mr. Right, Mr. All-Right, and Mr. Right-for-You."

Gene lit a cigarette. "Oh, *really?*"

He put his teacup in his lap. "Yeah. Now, Mr. Right is the one we dream about every night. He's perfect in every way, but..."

"He doesn't exist," sighed Babyface.

"Right," nodded B.D., rubbing Babyface's chest. "Now, Mr. All-Right is the guy we usually fall for. He has some of the qualities that we dream about or that we are told a man should have, but, plain and simple, he is a dog. But they are always getting the play, because they know what to say *and* what to do..."

"I've known plenty of those," puffed Gene, striking a pose against the wall.

"Finally, there's Mr. Right-for-You. He is far from perfect. He could be fine, but he's got his ways. He could be ugly, but he is sweet and appealing. He may not be rich, but he's earning a dollar every day, working hard. Hell, he may not have a job, but he is trying. He may not have the body of life, but he does have one. He may not be as romantic or as charming or as cultured or as conscious or as together as you want him to be, but he is working on it. He's an ordinary man. A nice guy..."

Gene blew a circle into the air. "Uh-huh, and we know where they finish."

"Exactly. We're busy searching for Mr. Right, who doesn't exist, pass over Mr. Right-for-You because he is too nice, and settle for Mr. All-Right, who ain't worth the effort or time."

He sipped his juice. The room was quiet for some time.

"You know, B.D., sometimes you amaze me," grinned Gene. "As dense as you are, you will, once every blue moon, say something that makes me know that you *do* have a clue."

"Thank you," B.D. smiled. "It is sort of like the figment of our imagination becoming our reality. A good man *isn't* hard to find. Just like the sisters, sometimes we just don't know a good one when we see him."

I nodded. "Uh-huh, *they* think all the good men are gay and *we* can't seem to find any!"

"Yeah," chuckled B.D. "All I know is, if I had still went along with that checkpoint program, I would never have seen the good thing in front of me. My Honey."

He turned to his Honey for affirmation, but he was asleep.

"Well, there might not be such a thing as a Mr. Right, but God knows there is a Mr. Wrong!" declared Gene.

"But, hey, even they are not all bad," I reasoned. "It's like my aunt Ruth once told me: 'While you waitin' for Mr. Right, you can be getting some *good* stuff from Mr. Wrong'!"

We all screamed, hi-fivin' it up.

"So ... have you thought about what you're going to do about Pooquie?" asked B.D.

I breathed heavily. "There's not much I can do. I'm still upset and unsure. I can't say whether I would take him back, but ... I don't know. I'll just see what happens."

B.D. smiled. I knew Gene would say something smart.

"You know how I feel...," he began. "But no matter what goes down, you know you got me in your corner."

I nodded at him and smiled. He came over and hugged me.

B.D. put his cup down and got up. "Oh, wait, wait, wait, group hug, everybody..."

"Miss Thing, *puh-leeze,* this is *not The Golden Girls!*" said Gene in his best Bea Arthur impersonation.

He did it anyway. We held each other for a good minute.

I sighed. "Thanks, you guys. For being here and for that hug. I really needed that."

I did.

Then, *our* song came on: "Giving Him Something He Can Feel." I was Aretha, since I had the voice. B.D. and Gene were Cissy Houston and one of the Sweet Inspirations. We worked the moves right, since all of us had seen *Sparkle* dozens of times (En Vogue ain't had nothing on us). We woke Babyface up with our lip-synch show and he loved it — especially when I got all up in his crotch as Aretha cried: *Ya know, Baby ... I just can't get enough of your funky stuff!* I needed that release.

They all left an hour later. All of them told me to leave "it" alone — meaning the situation with Raheim. If it gets resolved, it does; if it doesn't, it doesn't. B.D. was right: I just needed to talk it out and deal with it. And I felt that I was ready to move on. Raheim turned me the fuck out, yes, but somebody else could. In fact, maybe it was time to think about what — and who — I really wanted. But that night, in bed alone, I knew what I *needed...*

Something I Could Feel.

 I wasn't surprised when I came home that rainy Wednesday night and found Raheim sitting on the stoop.

I had been thinking about him a lot those few days after the Brothers Brunch. Now that the shock was over, I was beginning to really miss him around the house. B.D. said he really knew what it was: "The electrical outlet is lonely – the socket misses its plug!" That *was* part of it. But there was an emptiness inside that I couldn't explain that I knew only he could fill.

I was also concerned: he was hurt in the fight and I wanted to know that he was OK. How I wish he hadn't pushed me away: I would love to have nursed his wounds. My concern turned into alarm when, that afternoon, Gene told me that Raheim dropped by the Simply Dope office on Monday and said he wouldn't be coming in the rest of the week because of a personal emergency. Did something happen to Junior? His mother? Him? I started to worry.

So, I was happy to see him – especially since, as I was on my way home, I realized that it was our second-month anniversary. But he wasn't happy at all. He looked like he hadn't slept in days. His eyes were puffy. His lips were poked out, like he was a little-boy-lost. He hadn't shaved in some time: an unshaped bushel of hair sat on his chin and I could see the outline of a beard. The bruise on his cheek was gone, but there was a Band-Aid near his left temple. He was dressed in black – jeans, boots, windbreaker, and a *Menace II Society* cap. He didn't seem to be bothered by the rain, even though he was getting soaked.

I came in the gate and sat down next to him, covering him up with my umbrella. It was one of those big beach jammies that keep you most dry. I wanted to invite him up and I knew he wanted to come up, but I wanted him to ask. I wanted him to speak first. He finally did – and it was the last thing I expected him to say.

"D.C. is dead."

I just stared at him. Did he say what I thought he did?

He turned to face me. His eyes tried to focus as if I were a block away, not sitting right next to him. "He's dead," he whimpered, his head falling on my shoulder. I grabbed and squeezed his right hand, which was on his knee, pulled him up with me, and led him into the apartment.

I had him get out of his clothes and get in bed. I fixed him some tea with lemon, because he had been waiting for me for an hour. As he sipped it, he lay on his side in my arms. I sat up and stroked his head as he told me what happened.

They — meaning Raheim, D.C., and Angel — had gone to another B-boy bash in the Bronx last Saturday. They were having a good time — until D.C. ran into his ex at the party. Jay, according to Raheim, "was a good fuck, but he ain't care shit 'bout D.C." Apparently, he was gassing D.C. for cash and clothes all the time, and, when D.C. wised up and realized he was being taken, Jay decided to get what he wanted elsewhere — from one of D.C.'s enemies, Rock. Rock was at the party, too, and he and D.C. stared each other down all night. Their eye-balling match became so intense that they almost came to blows. Both Raheim and Angel knew it was time to go, so they got D.C. and left.

But Rock wanted a piece of D.C. He and a group of his boyz followed them outside. He called D.C. every name under the sun, taunting him about Jay ("Ya jus' mad cuz ya couldn't handle it, cuz ... he needed a real man"), trying to provoke him, with Raheim and Angel urging him not to let that shit get to him — just get in the Jeep and let's be out. Unfortunately, Rock said something about D.C.'s mother. D.C. came for him and Rock, being the coward that he is, ran. After D.C. chased him for half a block, yelling for him to face his ass whipping like a man, Rock pulled out a gun instead of putting up his fists. D.C. froze. Raheim moaned. Angel and Jay begged Rock to chill. But Rock wanted D.C. to beg. "Yeah, that's right, get on yo' fuckin' hands an' knees. We see how fuckin' tough you are now..." D.C. pleaded with him not to shoot. Roc put the gun in his mouth — but didn't pull the trigger. He started walking away from D.C., who then ran back toward the Jeep. In front of two dozen witnesses, Rock fired the six bullets in his gun, four of them hitting D.C. — two in the right leg, one in his right shoulder, and one in his back. Rock and his buddies ran off; Jay couldn't believe what had happened and kept screaming, *"Oh, God, D.C., I am so sorry, I am so sorry..."* He'd obviously instigated the whole thing. Raheim wanted to put him in the Jeep and take him to the hospital, but the folks around him said not to. So he just held him and rocked him until the paramedics came. The doctor told Raheim, though, that even if he had gotten D.C. to them sooner, it would not have saved his life. In fact, she was surprised D.C. didn't die at the scene.

"So ... he was conscious?" I asked.

"Yeah," he sighed.

"Did you ... did he ... say anything?"

He put his left thumb on the tip of his mouth. "I held his hand ... it was cold ... I tol' him, 'Don' die ... don' die ... you can't, cuz we got a lota shit ta do ... fight ... don' give up ... help is comin' ... talk, man, talk ta me ... jus' keep talkin', man...'"

He suddenly laughed out loud, causing me to jump. "He say, 'Brotha Man, Brotha Man ... I ain't dyin' ... I ain't goin' nowhere.' He said, 'Precious ... my baby, my baby ... I'm here ... I'm here...'" Raheim snuggled closer, holding me tighter. I just snuggled and held tighter, too.

"Did they have the funeral yet?" I asked.

"Friday."

"Do you want me to go?"

He sighed, resting his head on my chest. "Yeah."

He didn't want to eat — not even Wheaties — but I forced him to stomach some soup. I offered him a massage; he didn't want it. I didn't try to kiss him; if he wanted to do it or anything else physical, he would let me know. Like the past few nights, he couldn't — or wouldn't — sleep. He stayed up and watched me. I called in sick for the next two days. He didn't want to do anything except stay in bed and be held. The TV was on, but he wasn't watching it, not even *Jeopardy!* He just stared into space. I stared at him.

He didn't want to talk, but sometimes he would just come out of nowhere with a story about D.C....

"Baby, I tell you 'bout tha time we almos' got inta a *stoo*pid fight ova whose kid was betta lookin'? Precious, she cute, but she ain't like my Li'l Brotha Man. We think they gonna marry."

"Until you come along, we always kicked ass playin' Spades. There was this one time where we played fuh money an' got like sixty dollas. And, one time we played it like strip poka. Ha, damn, Crystal and Laticia was angry, cuz they had ta walk 'round tha house that day wit jus' they bras an' panties on — an' it was cold as a motha-fucka!"

"He wants ta start a rap group. He says, 'If Vanilla Ice, Hamma, an' all them tired motha-fuckas can, we can, too.' We got equipment an' ev'rythang ta hook up a demo."

"He drive like he in tha Indy fuckin' 500. He got mo' tickets than anybody I know, but he ain't paid none o' 'em. It's no wonda they ain't tow his Jeep away yet."

He went up to Harlem the night before the funeral to check on Ms. Carter, D.C.'s mother (he was her only child), and get a suit and shoes. While he was gone, I called Gene.

"So, how is he taking it?" he asked.

"I don't know ... I know he's hurting a lot. They were best friends since they were little."

"Do you think he really knows he's dead?"

"What do you mean?"

"Well, he might be in denial."

"I think he knows it, but ... the last time he saw him he was still alive, although he was barely holding on ... and, he does talk about him in the present tense, like he is still here..."

"Has he cried?"

"I don't know if he has before, but he hasn't with me."

"He's in shock. The funeral is tomorrow, you say? It will all hit him then. Are you ready for it?"

"Am I ready? For what?"

"D.C. wasn't your best friend, but it may affect you – especially if he carries on. I mean, once he sees his body in the casket, it will be all over. You know how *we* can get at funerals."

Yes, I do. I've been to only three in my life – my father's, my uncle Russ's, and my grandmother's, Ada Mae Farmington – but I've seen it all. Folks crying oceans of crocodile tears. Having fits. Fainting. Running up and down the aisles of the church or parlor, tearing their hair out. Throwing themselves on the casket. Trying to get *in* the casket. After those experiences I decided that I did not want a funeral. It's a waste of time, money, and, most importantly, spirit. Some of the people who pay their respects didn't respect the deceased when they were alive, while others just want to turn the event into their own moment. I could just see Calvin Hawthorne, my obnoxious cousin, pulling such a stunt if I died tomorrow. Testifying as to how much he cared for me and how much he'll miss me – and then throwing himself on the altar. Oh, no, *spare* me the melodrama. I want people to remember me the way I was – and looking at my lifeless body in a box ain't gonna bring me back nor is it gonna make folks feel better, as the behavior at funerals certainly proves.

I then realized that I hadn't been to one since 1987 and that it could very well be an emotional experience for me. "Well, I'll just have to be brave...," I reasoned.

"And what's going to happen after the body is laid to rest?"

"I'm sorry?"

"Have you two talked about what happened at the party?"

"Now is not the time, Gene."

"Well, despite his grief, you two have to face it. Don't get sucked back in without knowing where you stand, Mitch. Help him through it, but make sure he knows that your shoulder don't come easy."

While I was still a little unsettled about the fight, I did know one thing: Raheim, facing probably the most traumatic experience in his life, had to turn to someone — and he came to me. Yes, actions do speak louder than words. If he was really that put out with me, if I was really the "bitch" he called me, he wouldn't have returned. He'd be with David or someone else. I was convinced that things would work out, that I wouldn't have to push. So I knew how to answer Gene.

"Regardless of what happened before, he needs me now. And I know if I needed him, he'd be there for me, too..."

Or so I thought.

 I was not family, or viewed as family like
Raheim, or a "friend," so I took a seat in the very last pew of the
storefront church in Harlem with the other nondescript respect-payers.
All God's Children House of Worship, the church home of Ms. Carter,
was small — not even forty by thirty feet — but I just knew that, come
Sunday, the joint was jumpin'. That's the way it was in most Black
churches this size. When I was a teenager in the youth choir at my
church, we'd travel throughout Brooklyn and Queens to churches just
like All God's Children, and those folks always praised the Lord like it
was their last time. That spirit is so contained that nobody can escape
feeling it; it intoxicates you like wine. There also seems to be a greater
sense of community, since they don't have hundreds of members
walking around, thinking they got the only private line to Jesus and
know the only way He can be lifted up.

The drawback is that most of these churches are not air-conditioned.
And it figures that, on that particular day, it was already ninety degrees
at eleven in the morning and only two of the four big floor-model fans
were working. One of the deacons had opened a few of the windows
in the back of the church — as if *that* was going to make it better. And
with the cheap cologne, perfume, and the very unpleasant smells from
the bathrooms mixing with the humidity, the air was thick and not the
least bit cute. So, while waiting for the processional to begin, I (like
dozens of other folks, young and old) kept myself cool and my nostrils
guarded by using one of the bent cardboard fans from the area funeral
parlor with a picture of Mahalia Jackson on the front and the Healing
Hands on the other. I also took off my black-and-gray pin-striped suit
jacket and unbuttoned my white shirt at the top.

I looked over the program, printed on off-white paper in purple ink.
HOMEGOING SERVICES FOR DERRICK THEODORE CARTER, JR. —
1971–1993. A very nice photo of D.C. without the gold tooth graced
the front. He really had a warm smile. I turned to the obituary, which

was only two paragraphs. There weren't many details about his life: his education, his employment, or his goals. It did say that he "found the Lord at an early age." Hmmmm ... I think all obits say that. I noticed that he was Ms. Carter's only child, and he and Raheim were born on the same day, just a year apart. And Raheim – identified as his "Best Friend and Brother in Christ" – was listed as one of those he left behind.

The organist took her seat and began to play. I think it was "Precious Memories." We were all asked to stand. Ms. Carter – I assumed it was her – walked in by herself. The same color, height, and size (not stocky but heavyset) as her son, she was dressed in a very tasteful solid-black dress, pumps, and a veil. Six people followed her: two women, probably her sisters; a hefty man, more than likely D.C.'s uncle, who had his left arm around the shoulder of a slim, sobbing teenaged boy who looked just like him; and a young woman and a darling mahogany-colored little girl in a white chiffon dress, black shoes, and white ribbons in her pigtails. I knew who they were: Precious and her mother, Laticia. Raheim, Junior, and Crystal were next.

Raheim told me Crystal would be coming and that she would be sitting with him. I didn't really have a problem with that. I knew that, for appearance's sake, it was best. I'm sure that both Ms. Carter and Crystal would've been suspicious of a strange man comforting Raheim and sitting with them. Knowing Raheim, I knew she would be beautiful, and she was. A round face, bright light skin and big eyes, brown hair in a serious weave, and red lips. She lit up the room even though she wasn't smiling.

*Sunshine...*

She had on the same outfit as Ms. Carter, minus the hat plus white gloves, and it hugged her svelte figure. She had a regal, dignified walk and came in with Junior on her left side and Raheim on her right. They were all holding hands. Both father and son had on the same black suit, white shirt, black-and-dark-gray block-pattern tie, and black shoes. Raheim stared straight ahead, his face blank. Junior smiled at me and I returned the gesture.

As the minister was about to give the invocation, Angel walked in. I knew somebody was missing. I tugged on his black suit jacket and scooted over.

"How are you?" I whispered, hugging him.

"Okay, I guess," he sniffled. His eyes were red. A handkerchief was in his right hand. "I, I almos' ain't come. Funerals, dey..."

I grabbed his left hand. "I know..."

He held my hand – tight – through the entire service.

I didn't pay much attention to the first part of the program. I was anxiously anticipating my Pooquie making his speech. Ms. Carter asked Raheim to read the obituary and deliver the eulogy. Even though he agreed to do it, he was scared shitless. He said he had a fear of speaking in public. That I found hard to believe. But I explained that Ms. Carter wouldn't have asked him if she didn't want him to do it and didn't think he could. And, I added, if the crowd intimidated him, he could look directly at me and pretend we were at home and he was reciting it to me. I helped him write and practice it the night before and he sounded jood.

"And now, Raheim Errol Rivers, Sr., will read the obituary," announced one of the deacons.

Raheim made his way to the pulpit, dragging his heels. *Pick up your feet, Pooquie.* He stood in front of the microphone and read the obit without looking up. His eyes then fell on me. I nodded and smiled. He looked at me the whole time.

"Uh, I wanna ... say a few words 'bout D.C. ... tha's wha' we called 'im ... he was like a brotha ta me ... he was cool ta be around ... he always made me laugh ... he was my bes' frien' ... they neva be anotha like 'im ... ev'rybody loved 'im ... I loved 'im ... an' I'm gon' miss 'im ... peayce, Brotha Man..."

I was so proud of him that I felt like running to the pulpit and giving him a big hug. But I stifled myself.

The organist played again. The song was familiar, but I couldn't place it until Angel started mouthing the chorus, tears streaming down his face. *It's so hard ... to say goodbye ... to yesterday...* I put my arm around his shoulder and helped dry his eyes.

Next up was the Reverend Carlton John James. He was a man of the cloth that you'd love to unclothe. He reminded me of Magic Johnson, only darker. His skin was flawless, his mouth wide and toothy, and his eyes small but commanding. When he stretched his massive arms, it seemed like they would never end, and his voice vibrated the pews. But that conked, slicked-back hairstyle had to go.

His sermon wasn't just about saving the tears ("Weep not for Derrick ... he is safe in the Master's arms!"), remembering and rejoicing in the life D.C. was given ("You have the memories ... cherish and thank God for them"), carrying on ("His life is over, but yours must goes on ... so live it to the fullest!"), and preparing oneself for Judgment Day ("Are *you* ready, brothers and sisters? Your time is coming soon..."). He also expounded on "the real reason D.C. died."

"Hate, brothers and sisters, and the worst kind at that ... self-hate. One brother getting so consumed by his own insecurity, his own instability, his own lack of identity, that he takes it out on his own. What are we, as a people, coming to, if we think blowing each other away will get rid of the pain? When are we going to stop turning *on* each other and start turning *to* each other? We are committing suicide. We need to replace this Black-on-Black crime with Black-on-Black love! And you can't love your brother, you can't love your sister, and you can't love yourself if you don't know Who has given you the gift of love!"

Even though he was, for the most part, preaching to the converted, I was glad that he was tellin' it like it is. (I didn't like his using the phrase "Black-on-Black crime" though; like "underclass" and "wilding," it tags us as a "pathology people.") But I wondered if Reverend James also preached as fervently and passionately against homophobia. Because of the hypocrisy of the Black church — it will only acknowledge us if we sing in the choir and stay in the closet — I do not attend regular services anymore at Mount Zion Baptist Temple in Brooklyn. Our pastor, the Reverend Dr. Alexander Pierce Gooding, not only denounced homosexuals in the pulpit, he declared AIDS our punishment sent down from God. I'll never forget what he said a week after 24-year-old Timmy Meadows, a dedicated, beloved member with a voice like Donny Hathaway, died of AIDS: "Cry for him, if you must, but cry for him because he chose to defy God's law and paid the price with his life." Of course, what made Reverend Gooding's ranting so sick was that he is, unbeknownst to his wife and six kids, bisexual (at least on the surface). In fact, he made several passes at me and, I am told, had several trysts with Timmy. What do they say about people in glass houses? My mother says that when she and Anderson make the trek back to Mount Zion each month, Reverend Gooding always asks about me. I *bet* he does. Thanks to assholes like him, AIDS is now an epidemic in our community and hating homosexuals is still a religious pastime.

After Reverend James's fire-and-brimstone ended, it was time to view the body. I stood up, but Angel didn't. I knelt down, tugging his hand.

"Aren't you..."

He shook his head no. "I can't, I jus' can't."

"Are you sure? I'll go with you."

"Yeah, yeah, I can't, I jus' can't see 'im like dat..."

He broke down again. I told the usher I'd go after I comforted and calmed him.

After he seemed OK, I made my way down the aisle. The casket was light brown. There were at least a dozen flower arrangements surrounding it, including a stand of white, yellow, and red roses in the shape of a heart that said, "D.C., We Love You." That must be the one Pooquie told me he, Angel, Crystal, and Laticia pitched in to buy.

Don't you just hate it when the person in the casket looks absolutely nothing like the one you knew? I flipped the day my mother and I went to check how they made up my grandmother: she was three shades darker and her hair looked like it had been fried. But D.C. looked like he was asleep. His skin wasn't drained of its natural color and his fade was neatly styled. A yellow rose was in his hands, which were clasped over his waist. The flower nicely accented his mink brown suit jacket and tie. I couldn't believe that just two weeks before, he was at my house and we were having such a great time. I touched his forehead. What a tragedy. A tear fell. As I returned to my seat, I noticed the hold Crystal had on Raheim. How I wished that could've been me.

I asked Angel once more if he wanted to go; he said no. I held his hand and watched as Raheim, Crystal, and Junior went up. Crystal had her head on Raheim's shoulder as he held her. She seemed more distraught than Raheim. She was sobbing but not loudly. Raheim just shook her lightly and, after she kissed D.C., guided her and a very confused-looking Junior back to their seats. Ms. Carter, if she was torn up inside, didn't show it. She got up, walked to the casket by herself, stared at her son for a good two minutes, kissed him, and sat back down. Jackie Kennedy had nothing on her. This was the most uneventfully quiet funeral I'd ever been to in my life.

After a final prayer, Raheim took his place with the other pallbearers, all of them young men from around the way. This was another thing Ms. Carter asked him to do that he wasn't too sure about. He was afraid he'd lose his balance, causing the others to drop the casket and send D.C. out onto the pavement. Of course, he was being paranoid. He performed his duty without incident.

After the casket was in the hearse, Raheim found me. God, he looked so jood in his suit.

"You did really good," I said.

He wiped sweat from his forehead with the back of his left hand. "Thanks."

"Are you OK?"

"Day-am, why ev'rybody keep askin' me that?" He realized he had snapped. "Lit— I ain't mean..."

I clutched his arm, causing him to look around. "I know." I let go, sensing his uneasiness. "So, do you want me to come to Ms. Carter's?

I mean, you do have your hands full with her and Junior ... and Crystal..."

He just looked around.

"I'll probably just be in the way," I decided. "Will you come over later?"

"Yeah."

"What time, do you know?"

"I don' know ... late ... like midnite."

Just then, Junior ran up to me.

"Hi, Mitch-hull," he said, his arms out for a hug.

I gave it up. "Hi, how are you?"

"I'm OK. But Daddy is sad."

I ran my fingers through his hair and looked at Daddy. "I know."

"Come on, Raheim, Junior, it's time to go," said Crystal, as she approached us. She looked at me and smiled. "Oh, hello."

Crystal and I were waiting for Raheim to introduce us, but he didn't. Seemed like he couldn't even move.

"Mommy, this is Mitch-hull," announced Junior, coming to the rescue.

We shook hands; hers were smaller than mine and even more delicate. "I'm Crystal, Junior's mother. It's nice to meet you. Junior talks about you a lot."

"Nice to meet you, too." We were the same height, but she had a lot more meat on her bones. I looked at Junior. "Well, I hope he says nice things."

"He does. He says he has a great time at your house."

"I do!" he concurred.

"Well, hopefully he'll come back before school starts."

Junior's face lit up. "I can?"

I tweaked his nose. I loved doing that and he loved it, too. "Yes, you can."

"A'right, a'right, we gotta go," said Raheim.

Crystal held out her hand again. "Thank you for coming."

"Please, you don't have to thank me." I didn't want to like her, but I couldn't help not to. *Sunshine...*

She grabbed Junior's left hand as he began waving with his right. "Bye, Mitch-hull."

"Bye." They all walked off. As Crystal stopped to fix Junior's clothes, Raheim quickly turned his head.

"Tanite," he mouthed.

I nodded.

"Thanks, Little Bit."

"Anytime, Pooquie."

After he spoke with Ms. Carter, Raheim, Crystal, and Junior, Angel walked me to the train station. He offered to drive me home, but I declined. He wasn't going to the cemetery, but would be at Ms. Carter's place later on, where Raheim's mother (who doesn't go to funerals) was holding court.

"Mitch?"

I was about to put my subway token in the turnstile. I turned. "Yes?"

He came toward me. "I jus' wanted ta let ya know ... D.C. ... he liked you."

"Really?"

"Yeah. Afta playin' cards, when we was waitin' on y'all ta come downstairs ... he said how you was really cool. He said Raheim was lucky ta be wit you ... jus' thought I let ya know..."

I smiled. "Thanks. Don't be a stranger. And take care of yourself."

"I will." We hugged and I took off.

I thought about going to work for a quick second but nixed that idea right away. I'd spend the rest of the day doing absolutely nothing. And I did. I ordered out for Chinese food (something I hadn't done in months), took a long, hot shower, flipped through the day's paper, watched Oprah and Montel, and went in and out of sleep on the sofa for most of the evening.

The bell rang and woke me up at one-thirty. I buzzed him up, opened the door, and turned on the water for his hot oil bath. I knew he would be dead tired. I heard the door close. He inched his way past the bathroom into the bedroom.

He didn't say a word. As he took off each piece of clothing, I hung it up. He slipped into his bath and came out a half hour later. I was sitting up in bed rereading James Baldwin's *Just above My Head* (which is his real classic gay novel) when he climbed in and buried his face in my chest, hard.

I didn't know what to say and I didn't want to ask if he was all right. I just held him and started to hum "It's So Hard to Say Goodbye to Yesterday." And the tears started to flow, my shirt soaking up his pain. His grip became tighter; he moved in so close that he suffocated me. By the time I finished, he was bawling like a baby. Deep moans and chilling cries of *"D.C.," "My Brotha Man," "No...,"* and *"Why?"* I just rocked him and rocked him and rocked him until he cried himself to sleep.

 I had stayed up for most of the night. I just wanted to watch Pooquie sleep. It made perfect sense that he wouldn't be able to until he allowed himself to grieve. The night before the funeral he wouldn't even get in bed. I dozed on and off, finding him in different poses – standing by the window, kneeling against or sitting on the windowsill, sitting at the night table. Just staring. It hurt to see him like that. I was glad that his body, his mind, and his heart were finally getting the rest they needed.

It was two in the afternoon when the phone rang. I managed to reach it despite being pinned to the bed by Pooquie.

"Hello?"

"Hello, Mitchell?" The voice was husky and hurried.

"Yes?"

"This is Carl."

Carl?

"Do I know you?"

"Oh, I'm sorry. I joined you and Gene on Gay Pride Day. Remember?"

Oh, that Carl. Yes, I did remember. But why was he calling me?

"Mitchell, I have some bad news."

"What is it?" I tried sitting up, but Pooquie had a serious hold on me. He loosened his grip – a little.

"It's Gene ... he was beaten up."

I broke away from Pooquie and sat on the edge of the bed. He grumbled but just turned over.

"Beaten up?"

"Yeah, last night in the Village. He was jumped by three guys."

I felt a migraine coming. "Where is he?"

"St. Vincent's Hospital."

I grabbed a piece of paper and pen off the dresser and wrote down the address and room number. I told him I was on my way. I clutched my pounding head. When it rains, it pours: D.C. was just laid to rest and now we have another life in the balance. I dashed into the bathroom, washed quickly, and threw on the first thing I saw (my kick-around stone-washed jeans and t-shirt from yesterday).

I didn't want to wake up Pooquie. He'd probably sleep the day away; he had some catching up to do. But I didn't want him to wake up and find me gone with no idea as to where I was.

So I taped the note on the bedroom door:

> Pooquie,
> Gene is in the hospital.
> I'll call you from there.
> Please don't snack.
> There's some Chinese food left over.
>                    Little Bit

I was lucky enough to catch a yellow Medallion cab going back to the city. "No, I am *not* going uptown," I answered the driver, a man with a Russian surname, as I got in. I wouldn't normally entertain such a question; I usually tell them to keep on going if that's the way they treat a paying customer, but I was in a hurry and not in the mood to battle. At least he was reasonably racist: sometimes they let you get in, ask you where you're going, then refuse to take you. When that happens, I nicely get out of the cab and leave the doors on the passenger *and* driver side open for them to close. Yeah, it is hard for Black folks (particularly men) to catch a cab in New York and other cities, but what can we do about it? It's just another indignity we have to suffer daily because it is illegal being Black in America. (What other group can count on being stopped and stomped by police for sport?) But I certainly don't think this particular problem warrants the attention of the NAACP. I mean, if they don't want our money, why try to force them to take it? For those brothers and sisters looking for relief, I've always had one piece of advice: if you can't hail one yourself, ask a Caucasian to do it for you. It works every time.

As we rode, I sat with my eyes closed, saying little prayers for Gene. "God, please let him be OK..." "Please give him the strength to pull through..." "Give me the strength to help him through..." "Bless him..." Why did this happen? Why to him? *Why?* Gene is my bosom buddy, the big brother I never had. Yeah, he's as hard as a nail – bossy, brassy, and bold – but he's really a softie underneath. I couldn't lose him. *We* couldn't lose him ... Oh shit! I hadn't called B.D. or Babyface. I'd do it from the hospital.

I found Carl standing outside Gene's room. He had obviously been at the hospital all night. His blue jeans and black shirt were disheveled, wrinkled, and bloody. His hair was matted. His face and hands were ashy. He embraced me.

"So, how is he?"

"Like I said, he was lucky."

"What happened?"

Carl explained that he and Gene were heading back to Gene's place at around three-thirty last night after hanging out at Harry's when Gene said he had the munchies. While Carl waited for him in front of the bar, Gene went into a store around the corner. When he was coming out, a group of guys were coming in. According to the cashier, one of them said, "Fuckin' faggot," to Gene. Gene, never missing a beat, turned around and proclaimed: "Ha, you're just mad because I won't let you fuck me!" For once he should've kept his mouth closed. One grabbed him from behind, putting him in a choke hold, while the others took turns punching and kicking him, all the while yelling, "Fuckin' faggot. We teach yo' ass." They finished the job by knocking him in the head with the bottle of Coca-Cola he purchased for Carl. Gene did put up a fight, but there wasn't much he could do.

While some idiots watched the incident from their windows, it was a group of folks on their way to Harry's who responded to Gene's cries and the cashier's screams, chasing the guys, who hopped in their Jeep and escaped. Someone memorized the license-plate number and handed it over to the police. Carl didn't hear anything, because he went back in the bar to talk to someone. When he came out, he expected to see Gene but didn't. He heard the commotion and ran around the corner and found Gene on the sidewalk. He was flat on his back. His face was blue and bloated. His body, wracked with pain, twitched as if he were having a seizure. Broken glass, M&Ms, and the Twinkies he'd purchased were splattered around him. There was a lot of blood. Carl covered him with his own body until the ambulance arrived.

Carl rode with him to the hospital. The doctor said Gene had a broken nose and right arm, cracked jaw and left cheekbone, busted lip and right kneecap, fractured ribs, a damaged testicle that might have to be removed, and a slight concussion. He was awake but weak. Because he didn't know our last names, Carl said he had to go to Gene's place and find my and B.D.'s number. That's where he was when he called me. B.D. wasn't at home, so he left a message on his machine.

Both Carl and I were crying. I held his hand as we sat in the waiting area.

"I feel like it's my fault," he sniffed.

I handed him a Kleenex and dabbed my own eyes. "It isn't. Don't even think that. It could have happened to both of you. To any of us. You didn't know."

He blew his nose. "He asked for you."

"Can I see him?"

"Yeah. Afternoon visiting hours are until five."

"Don't you want to go home, maybe change clothes? Have you eaten?"

"I ain't worried about that right now. I just wanna be right here for him."

I smiled. "You've been a really good friend to him. Thank you."

I hugged him. I took baby-steps toward Gene's room. I stopped at the door, took a deep breath, and then opened it.

He was the only one in the two-person room. His bed was by the window, in a half-staff position. Four very thin pillows were under his head. I walked slowly toward him.

"Carl..." His voice was frail, but it was him.

"No, no, Gene ... it's me."

He was facing the window and tried to turn his head, but it was obviously painful. I walked around the bed and pulled up the chair. He was hooked up to an I.V. His face looked tight and was still bloated from the blows. His nose and head were covered with bandages. Though they were coated with some type of cream, I could tell he had two black eyes. His lips were caked and red. His right arm and leg were both in a cast.

Damn, those mother-fuckers. Why did they have to come into *our* space? What were they doing in the Vill? If they were straight or bi, probably looking to get their dicks sucked, to pick a fight, or both (these are the same mother-fuckers who'll fuck your ass in the dark but kick it in the light to earn their props on the street). If they were gay – and, yes, contrary to what some think, gay people can be the perpetrators of such violence – more than likely trying to inflict their own self-hate on others. Where were the Guardian Angels and the gay "Pink Panther" patrol when you needed them? We had heard about gay-bashings all the time, even in the Vill. But Gene was the first person I knew to become a victim of these sexually insecure, intellectually degenerate assholes. It made me so angry I wanted to scream. I grabbed his left hand and smiled instead.

"Hi, baby. How you doing?"

"You got eyes ... what you think?"

Same old Gene.

"Carl told me what happened..."

He sighed. "Yeah..."

My tears started to fall again. "Oh, Gene..."

"Oh, no, don't *you* start. That's why I threw Carl out of here." He held my hand tighter and, with what little strength he had, pulled me out of my chair. "Come here..."

He held me. Yes, that's right, he held me. You'd think I was the one who had gotten beaten. He dried my eyes with tissues he already had in his hand. "I am always prepared," he said.

After I composed myself, I sat on the side of his bed and he told me what did and did not hurt. He even joked about one of his injuries: "Well, I guess Carl and I will be the perfect couple — we'll both be shooting blanks." We were laughing about it when B.D. entered the room.

"Oh my God! Look what they've done to you!" He was very bright in a yellow bodysuit and white sneakers. Does he wear anything else during the summer? He had a bouquet of flowers.

"How did they let *you* up here?" asked Gene. "I'm sure you had to play doctor with somebody."

B.D. grinned. "And I love you, too, darling. But watch it, or you'll have three black eyes." He hugged us both, and, as he put the flowers in water, we filled him in. We kee-keed so much that the nurse came by to tell us to keep it down. After she left, Gene said: "Children, hurry up and get me out of here. She looks too much like that broad in *Misery.*"

"Oh, Kathy Bates?" I asked. "She was great in that role."

"Uh-huh, and Miss Thing is too much like her. She wanted me to take some pill a little while ago and, when I refused, got all bent out of shape. She is not wrapped too tight. She is gonna come in here late one night and really turn me into a paraplegic by breaking my fucking ankles."

I cracked up. "You are too much, Gene."

And he was. I couldn't believe how he was handling everything. But I knew, like Raheim, he was breaking up inside.

Raheim.

It was almost five. He might be up. Since visiting hours were about over, B.D. and I left. Gene was glad to hear that Raheim finally let his guard down and let it out. "You know how those banjees are; they think that crying is for faggots like us, not them," he said. Both he and B.D. told me to send Raheim and Ms. Carter their best. Since I would be visiting him tomorrow, Gene requested some real food. He wouldn't be leaving the hospital for several days and the cafeteria was not the move. I promised I'd make something just for him.

I called the house as B.D. and Carl talked in the first-floor lobby. There was no answer. Raheim might have stepped out and forgot to put the answering machine on. I hoped he made sure the inside lock was on so I didn't get home and find myself robbed. He probably went back up to Harlem to check on things. Since we were all starving, we went to Carl's place in Soho so he could change his clothes, and ate at a diner not far from his place. Babyface, who was working, met us there. Carl is a nice guy – "a real live Mr. Right-for-You," as B.D. commented when Carl excused himself to call Gene. Even though Gene told him he didn't have to, Carl went back to the hospital with Babyface to check on him before evening visiting hours ended at eight. Hmmmm, looks like he is falling – and Gene certainly isn't going to like that.

It was close to eight-thirty when I put my key in the door. The house was dark but for the light from the TV in the bedroom. I found Raheim lightly snoring away in his favorite position – spread-eagled on the bed, naked. There was no tray or dish in the room, evidence that he might've put something in his system. I sat by his head and rubbed his back and butt. He woke up.

He yawned. "Hey, Baby."

"Hi. Did you get enough sleep?"

"I don' know ... I guess."

"I called ... you must have been asleep."

He nodded, holding the pillow tighter.

"Did you get my note?"

"Uh-huh."

"Did you eat something?"

"Nah."

"Why?"

He sighed. "Cuz ... I was waitin' on you."

"Well, you have to eat, Pooquie. Let me get you something..."

I was about to stand when he grabbed my arm and pulled me down. "Nah, nah, c'm'ere..."

"Raheim, come on now, you..."

He took ahold of me, started kissing me, and, before I knew it, my clothes were off and we were going at it.

The shit was *jood*.

"Well, I guess I don't have to ask if *you're* feeling better," I cooed afterwards. He sat up in bed, his hands clasped on my back. I was on my belly between his legs. My arms were around his waist, my tongue circling his belly button.

He stared straight ahead. "Yeah ... I ... I feel a little betta."

"I'm glad."
Silence.
"Little Bit?"
"Yes?"
"Thanks."
"For...?"
"You know ... fuh helpin' me."
"You're welcome ... I'm here for you."
"Yeah?"
"Yeah."
"Thanks, Baby."
I squeezed him tight. "Anytime, Pooquie ... anytime."

"I'll be Black."

Yeah, right. You'll be Black, but no time soon. That's the way it was the week following D.C.'s funeral. Raheim went from being My Crying Baby to being a crybaby. If he got his way, he was "a'right." If he didn't, he'd throw a tantrum and then step. Out the door.

He got upset because I cooked a three-course meal to take to Gene in the hospital. "Wha' he need a special dinna fo'?" he demanded, as I was preparing the roast chicken. "I don' want no fuckin' hero." You don't, hunh? Well, then, you won't eat.

He'd complain because I came home late from work, dealing with Gene's recovery and return home, B.D.'s dance company, and the Terrible Two at work (Elias and Phillip). "It's like you ain' got no time fuh me no mo', like you dissin' me," he'd say. Huh, you dissin' yourself.

He'd sigh really loud if he felt I was on the phone too long. Sometimes he'd try to prevent me from answering it, tickling me or trying to get frisky. But let him get on the phone with Angel (whom he would not let me speak to) or anybody else and he'd gab for as long as he pleased.

He'd whine because there was no more orange juice, no more Gatorade, no more Sprite, no more milk. And, every time, he said the same thing: "Yo, Baby, wha'tha fuck tha empty carton doin' in tha fridge?" You put it there, stupid.

He'd purposely say something with a sinister smile just to fuck with me...

"You my little nigga."

"Why you wanna be a bitch, Mitch?"

"See, Gene got so much fuckin' mouth ... tha's why he got his ass kicked."

But he really copped a serious a-ti-ma-tude when the sex ceased. When he felt like it, he'd go for his. But I wasn't having it.

"C'mon on, Little Bit," he'd push and push and push.

"Please, Raheim, I don't feel like it." And I didn't. I was dealing with a lot of shit. I needed him to be patient and supportive, not a pest. And fucking him − or, rather, letting him fuck me − was not a priority on the list.

After being turned down several times in several days − something I couldn't remember happening before, so I knew it bruised his ego terribly − he left the house as he had been doing all week without saying a word. When he returned later that night and got in bed, it was obvious that he "got his" someplace else. How could I tell? Well, I knew what Raheim smelled like, from head to toe, and the scent coming from his body as he got under the sheets was not just his own. It was another man's, too. Who was it? David?

Gene said that there was an easy way to solve my problem: don't let his ass back in. "He can't have you all to himself. He still feels alone and lonely because of D.C. and wants you at his beck and call, but you ain't his doormat."

We couldn't go on like we were − talking at each other and not to each other; sleeping on opposite sides of the bed, not even touching one another. But I knew that locking my door would devastate him. He was still grieving. I didn't have the heart to tell him to just walk − especially after I had already pledged to be there for him. I was really eating those words.

I knew that something had to give, though, when Raheim got up early Saturday morning, brought Junior to the house, and, five minutes later, jetted.

And he didn't come back until late Sunday afternoon.

The kid was his usual jovial self. He told me many a knock-knock joke. We sang songs ("Old MacDonald," "If You're Happy and You Know It...," "I've Been Working on the Railroad..."). I helped him read the only children's book I had in the house, *Bright Eyes, Brown Skin*. He loved the story so much that I told him he could take it home. We played blackjack − and he beat me every time. We played tic-tac-toe − I let him beat me most of the time. We went food shopping and he begged to sit in the cart seat. I obliged.

Of course, he watched lots of cartoons. He knew "Rabbit Seasoning" by heart (you know ... Bugs: "Would you like to shoot him now or wait 'til you get home?" Daffy: *"Shoot him now, shoot him now!"*), dismissed Popeye ("Mitch-hull, his lips don't even move when he talks!"), and just gushed over Pebbles Flintstone, who he feels is so cute (uh-huh, the brainwashing has begun). He wanted our Saturday night movie to be *The Little Mermaid,* but after the Pebbles thang, I scratched that. We saw

*Bebe's Kids* instead, with a giant bowl of popcorn and lots of butter. He loved the movie so much that he wanted to see it a second time.

He had a tape of Barney, who, quite frankly, scares me more than Freddy Krueger. (Give me Dino, the original purple dinosaur, anytime.) But I survived it, even though I almost threw up hearing that "I Love You" song so many times.

And he also made a friend in the neighborhood: a little boy named Simon III (and yes, he asked to be addressed that way). I sat on the stoop listening to my Walkman and watching them toss Junior's football, while Simon II, a married man with the face and form of Evander Holyfield, watched me. He tried to buss a rap ("I seen you 'round ... is dat yo' kid?" "Ya got, uh, nice legs, neighba. Uh, ya work out?" "So, when you an' me gon' git tagetha?"), but I refused to take off my headphones.

But, despite all this fun, Junior couldn't hide his sadness and disappointment. He wanted to spend the time with me *and* his father. He said that Raheim had done this type of thing before and that really bothered me. Children learn by what you show them, not what you tell them. Exactly what kind of a message did Raheim think he was sending Junior, just dropping him off at folks' houses on a whim? Every time the phone rang, he thought it was Daddy. Every time the bell buzzed, he thought it was Daddy. Every time he heard a car pull up or honk in front of the house, he thought it might be his daddy. Every time it wasn't, and every time he became gloomier. He slept with me Saturday night, because he felt so abandoned. And he, like his daddy had the week before, cried himself to sleep in my arms.

It was around six o'clock when Raheim showed up. Junior was napping. I was doing the dishes from the spaghetti-and-meatballs dinner he'd requested. I greeted Daddy at the door.

"Where have you been?" I demanded.

He dusted past me. "Who *you* s'pose ta be? My motha?"

I followed him into the living room. "No, I am not your mother, Raheim, but I think you owe me an explanation."

He stopped and turned. "I don' owe you *shit*. Ya hear me? Nothin'." He continued into the kitchen.

"Yes, you do," I said, watching him open the fridge and drink right out of the milk carton. "And, please, don't do that."

He stopped, looked at me, sucked his teeth, and kept on doing it.

I was ready to explode.

I turned my back on him and planted my palms on the counter. "Raheim, I don't care if you don't feel it is necessary to be nice to me, but the least you can do is be nice to your son."

He finished gulping and placed the empty carton in the fridge. "Wha'tha fuck is *that* s'pose ta mean?"

My tone was low with a hint of sarcasm. "What part of that statement do you *not* understand? He cried himself to sleep last night because of what you did."

"Wha'tha fuck I do?"

I turned to face him. "What did you do? You left him here."

"So..."

"*So?* Raheim, he wanted to spend time with you."

"He came here ta see *you*, not me."

"Daddy, Daddy..." Junior ran up to his father, clutching his left leg and holding up the copy of *Your World* with them on the cover.

"Yeah, Li'l Brotha Man, I'm busy," mumbled Raheim, not even looking at him and just brushing him off.

Junior waved the magazine. "But, Daddy, Daddy, look, look, it's me and you, it's me and you."

Raheim clasped his hands, holding them to his face as if he were praying. "Yo, I tol' you now..."

"But, Daddy..."

*"But, Daddy' nothin'! Now ge'tha fuck outa my face!"*

I was afraid – for Junior. His whole body was shaking. There was terror in his eyes. He looked up at his father as if he'd just told him he wouldn't be his father anymore. A tear rolled down his left cheek.

Raheim just stood there, his hands still in the air from when he pointed Junior the fuck out of his face. He knew he was wrong. He knew it. But he didn't say anything.

I came to the rescue this time. "Uh, Junior, why don't you go back in my room and lay down, OK?"

He just nodded and slowly moved. I don't think the little guy could talk even if he wanted to.

Raheim's hands came down. He folded his arms and dropped his head.

I sighed, my back against the counter and my right hand on my chest. "I think you better go in there, Raheim."

He looked at me. He looked at the floor. He put his hands in his pockets and eased out the kitchen into the bedroom. Ten minutes later, Junior came into the kitchen. "Mitch-hull?"

"Yes?"

"I'm goin' home."

I knelt down. We were face-to-face. "Well, I really enjoyed your company this weekend. Maybe we can do it again. OK?"

"OK." His voice was soft and unsure.

"Do you have the book?"

He nodded yes.

"Now, you do good in school, OK?"

"OK..."

I hugged him tight. I could tell he didn't want to go.

"Mitch-hull?"

"Yes?"

"I wuv you."

I grabbed him again. "I love you too, Junior."

I walked him to the door and called Raheim. I heard Raheim call Junior — from outside. I opened the door for Junior and watched him walk and wave down the stairs. I went to the bedroom and watched them walk across the street, to the corner, and into the train station.

I really did love that little boy. He was so special. But he has a father who can be so, so, so...

That night I had had it. After witnessing what he did to Junior, I decided that enough was enough. We were going to have this out once and for all. I wasn't going to take no for an answer. And if he didn't like what I had to say or like the way things would be around my house, then he could just get the fuck out.

Raheim didn't come back that night, but he did show up the following evening. And I was ready for him.

He walked in the house, cursing and carrying on.

"Fuckin' faggot," he said, storming by me and into the living room.

"What's wrong with you?"

"Jus' some fuckin' freak..." He was once again in the kitchen. While he was looking damn jood in his uniform, something I hadn't seen him in for some time, he still had a serious a-ti-ma-tude. The effect was not happening.

He was gagging because the fridge was empty. I did that on purpose.

"Yo, wha's goin' on? Ain't nothin' ta drink."

"Forget drinking, Raheim, we have to talk."

"You, you s'pose ta be takin' care o' shit 'round here."

"Yeah, that's right, I take care of shit while you don't do *jack*shit."

"Wha'?"

"You heard. I'm tired of you falling up in here like you own the damn place. All you think about is you, you, you. Well, what about me, Raheim?"

"An' wha*t* a*bout* you?"

"That's exactly my point. You're not the only one dealing with a lot ... I know it's been hard for you with D.C. and..."

*"You* don' know *shit."*

"Raheim, how do you expect me to understand, to help you if..."

He threw his hands up and stomped into the living room. "I don' *need* yo' fuckin' help!"

I sighed heavily and followed him. "Fine. But I don't like being disrespected in my own house."

He turned to face me. "Wha'tha fuck you talkin' 'bout?"

"You know exactly what the fuck I'm talking about. Let's start with you fucking somebody else."

"Huh?"

"Please, Raheim, I'm not stupid. You think I can't tell?"

He shrugged. "Yo, you ain't gonna gimme..."

"Gimme, gimme, gimme, that's all you know, and I'm sick of it."

"Then go to tha *fuckin'* docta."

"Look, Raheim, we can't ... I don't want to fight anymore. But I will not be dissed like that. I don't like being called a ho, I don't like being called a nigger, and I don't like being called a bitch."

He laughed. "Day-am, you can' take a fuckin' joke. You still trippin' on that shit?"

I was not amused. "Yes, I'm *still* trippin' on that shit ... and I also don't like you using the word *faggot* up in here either."

"I ain' talkin' 'bout you."

"Oh, *no?* Well, just what do you think a faggot is?"

"That motha-fucka was actin' like a fuckin' queen, tryin' ta get nex' ta me an' shit, followin' me. I ain' havin' that."

*"We* have shared a bed for the last two months, Raheim. If *he* is a faggot, what does that make me *and* you?"

His body tensed. His eyes bore down on me. "Wha'choo tryin' ta say?"

"I'm not *tryin'* to say nothin'."

He pointed at his chest, his face twisted. "Yo, I'm a man!"

"And what am I, just the faggot you fuck?"

*"I ain' no faggot!"*

"Oh no? Well, all *I* know is, I ain't the only one in this room."

I didn't see his fist — but I felt it.

One second my feet were firmly on the ground. The next, they were hanging over the left arm of the sofa. He had punched me on the right side of my face, sending me soaring over the coffee table.

Everything went dark for a second, even though my eyes had been knocked wide open. My head was pounding, my temples jumping. My mouth hurt — *bad.* It felt like I had several toothaches. I looked down and saw the blood on my white t-shirt.

I turned my head to the side. Raheim wasn't there.

I tried to get up, but the pain only intensified. I was dizzy. I pushed my body onto the sofa, holding on to it as if my life depended on it. I focused on the ceiling. I listened for any sound. There was the TV in the bedroom. Chatter. Laughter. A bus. A motorcycle. A few cars. Honk honk. Birds tweeting and flying. The crickets. The water faucet in the kitchen, dripping.

I gave myself a group hug. I cried on my own shoulder.

Oh yes ... we had definitely come to the end of the road.

I wasn't angry; I wasn't hurt (although my busted lip and chipped teeth were no joke). I was just *through*. I had tolerated a lot of things from the men in my life: cheating, deceit, drug addiction, stealing. But Raheim really put me through some shit, pushing me 'til I couldn't take anymore. Calling me a bitch, a ho, a nigger ... hitting me? Oh, *no*, my own mother never hit me. I will not be any man's punching bag.

I've seen many an episode of *Donahue* with battered women and I always believed they were stupid: how, just how could they get themselves into such a situation? They had to see some sign before they got involved with him, before they got married. One day they wake up and he just comes out swinging? But I could identify with the helplessness and broken trust, now that I was in their position − or was I? Raheim no doubt abused me, but does that make him an abusive man? Does it take just one hit? After the initial shock wore off, I was trying to make sense of it all and found myself doing the exact same thing many of those women did: rationalizing, in a way excusing the man's behavior...

*Raheim was under a lot of stress.*

*He witnessed the death of his best friend.*

*I had to share some of the blame; I provoked him.*

*If I had just kept my mouth shut...*

*I should've known he would react like that...*

Of course, I only felt that way for a quick second.

No one deserves or asks to be hit for any reason. I hated Raheim and I wished he was dead.

I could tell by the "Oh, shit!" that Adam couldn't believe it. But his surprise turned into vengeance. He wanted to fuck Raheim up. He had Raheim's beeper number, called, and, not surprisingly, the service was off. I told him not to tell Mom. I didn't hear from her, so I figured he didn't tell her. Thank God; he finally kept his mouth shut. This was not the type of news I wanted passed on, and I didn't need her to be worried.

Gene was livid. He told me to report it to the police, have them hunt his ass down, and charge him with assault.

"Gene, I don't want to do that."

"Why the hell *not?* You do the crime, you do the time, and Home-boy has got to learn that he don't own this fuckin' world."

"He was wrong, dead wrong, but ... I just don't feel right going to the police. He'll just be another Black man with a record..." All I could think of was *that* statistic — one out of every four brothers in their twenties is in prison, on probation, or on parole (mind you, no one ever talks about the three that aren't). I didn't want to add Raheim's name to that list.

"How do you know he doesn't already *have* a record?" Gene asked.

Good question. I didn't know.

Gene also advised me to change the locks on my door, and make sure all my windows are secure anytime I leave the house.

"Why should I do that? I never gave him a key and..."

"So? His shit is still there and if he decides he wants it, he sure as hell isn't going to knock on your door and ask for it."

"Gene, he might've acted stupid, but I'm quite sure he isn't going to break in here."

"It is better to be safe than sorry."

I told him I'd consider it.

"Go ahead," I said.

"Go ahead what?"

"Say it."

"Say what?"

"I told you so."

"Now, why would I want to say that?"

"Because you love being right and you know you want to."

"Well, you're half-right, my dear. I do love being right. In fact, I thrive on it. But why would I say, 'I told you so'?"

"Because you *did* tell me so."

"Tell you what?"

"That Raheim would hit me."

"All I did was tell you to be careful, that's all. And, come on, Mitch, what kind of a monster do you think I am? I might love being right, but being right is not more important than being there for my best friend when he needs me."

"I'm sorry, Gene. Thanks."

"Anytime."

I didn't want company. I just wanted to be alone. I'd just go to work and come home. It took a week, a little dental work, and some massaging exercises, but my mouth fully healed.

Then it was time for my heart to and I knew that would be easy.

I never wanted to see him again and I acted like it. I walked around with a stone face. The thought or mere mention of his name made me simmer. I cursed him. I prayed that what he did to me happened to him. I listened to, sang, and hummed Randy's "I Hope You'll Be Very Unhappy without Me" all day and night.

But my heart was singing a different song. And there was always something there to remind me ...

The portrait over the sofa.

The *Your World* cover photo.

Wheaties.

Bananas.

*Jeopardy!*

His Michael Jordan video.

His Dr. Dre cassette tape.

His *Source* magazine.

His construction boots.

His "X" cap.

His gold chain.

His silver hoop earring.

His Onk.

His sunglasses.

His gangsta rag.

His shaving cream.

His electric razor.

His hair clippers.

The condom wrapper by the night table.

His jockstrap behind the toilet.

His dirty socks under the bed.

The empty bed.

His smell, all over the house.

His sex, all over the house.

His spirit, all over the house.

*Him,* just all over the house.

And I – or rather my heart – couldn't get away from him by going out of the house. Is that him whizzing down Broadway on that bike? Is that him beboppin' up the street? Is that him shootin' hoops in the park? Is that him hangin' on the corner with the boyz? Is that him getting on the train? Is that him lookin' too p-h-y-n-e in those Spandex?

Is that him...? Of course, it never was. One day, though, I knew my
eyes were not deceiving me: he was standing on the corner across the
street from my job, sitting on his bike in his uniform. In the blink of an
eye, he was gone. I ran to the corner, checking out every direction he
could've gone in. Nothing.

The only place I actually did see him was in my dreams. The wild
thing is that I had never dreamt about him before (well, I didn't have
to). They were always replays of the good times we had together, in
color. It was like someone had videotaped our private moments and
was showing them in a theater. When I dreamed, it was Heaven; when
I woke, I felt like hell.

I needed closure, to end the chapter. I needed to see him one last
time. That would help me put it all behind me.

I thought of beeping him – but I remembered it wasn't working.

I thought of finding out where his job was and paying him a visit –
but I couldn't remember where he worked.

I thought of the part-time job at Simply Dope, called Franklin Styles,
and found out that he hadn't heard from Raheim in weeks; they'd had
to hire someone else.

I thought of going to Harlem and enlisting the help of Angel – but
I couldn't remember where he lived.

I even thought of calling the Psychic Friends Network – but I didn't.

I was going mad, you hear me, *mad*. What was wrong with me? I
couldn't stop thinking about him, shake him, forget him, even though
I wanted to. He haunted me. When I started hugging my pillow so tight
that I was squeezing the feathers out of it, and standing in front of the
mirror, doing that mood thang like Ms. Jackson in *Poetic Justice,* I knew
I had to get away. Michelle argued that I was, once again, going through
withdrawal; I had to get ahold of myself and get Raheim out of my
system. So, I took a week's vacation (something I had postponed at the
beginning of the summer so that I could be with him) and five of my
ten sick days when Labor Day weekend rolled around, and went to the
house in Longwood.

Anderson and my mother knew what was up. I didn't mention
Raheim at all, and he didn't visit or call. And when Anderson, of all
people, inquired – "So, how is your, er, gentleman friend, Raheim?" –
I just stared at him as if he were asking me about a total stranger. He
didn't press me.

I just spent the time lounging around the house, listening to Aretha
("Today I Sing the Blues") and watching cable: the Cartoon Network
(not even Bugs, my fave, cheered me up), HBO's *Def Comedy Jam* (the
homo jokes by all those closet cases had to go, and all that *"motha-fucka*

this" and *"motha-fucka* that" made me think of him), and BET (which I had to click off after just thirty minutes because too many of the chocolate drops in the videos, particularly En Vogue's latest, "Runaway Love," reminded me of him). Only the Fox show *Living Single* got me to crack a smile. (John Henton, a.k.a. Overton, the adorably dumb handyman, is *ovah,* and I would crack more than a smile for him any day!)

The second week I was there, Anderson and my mother left to go on their Caribbean cruise. I told my mother not to tell anyone I was at the house. The only company I wanted was Pooquie — as in my teddy bear. I found him in the back of the closet in my room, still fuzzy, furry, and missing one of his black eyes. I slept with him at night and carried him around with me during the day. He was great to talk to, because he never talked back to or at me.

But one afternoon Aunt Ruth dropped by. We hadn't seen each other since the anniversary bar-b-cue, so she was an unexpected yet welcome visitor. She knew the man and woman of the house had gone on their cruise, so my mother had to have told her I was there — she didn't use her key to come in.

While fall was a few days away, the temperatures were still in the low eighties, so we sat in the backyard. We snacked on her famous lemon cake and sipped some lemonade. After a little update on my "boyfriend," Alvin; his bothersome twin, Calvin; and Uncle Tweedle (who had been putting out more often — and putting it out jood), Aunt Ruth got down to the reason for her visit.

"I know something is wrong ... you've hardly touched your cake. And it's all over your face."

"There's nothing wrong."

"Mitchell *Syl*vester Crawford, you can fool some of the people some of the time, but you can *never* fool Mother Sister."

Sylvester — I *hated* my middle name. The only good thing about it is that it was my grandfather's first name. As a kid, though, I didn't like the idea of having the same name as a pussy — as in cat. And, every time Aunt Ruth or my mother would address me with it, I knew I was in for one thing: an interrogation.

"You're right. Nothing is wrong ... something is right and you don't even have a clue as to what it is."

I looked at her, puzzled. What the fuck was she talking about? She sat up in her chair and placed her folded hands in her lap, striking that Dorothy Dandridge pose.

"It's Raheim, isn't it?"

I didn't say a word. I just lowered my head a bit.

"You two had a fight, hunh? Probably the *big* one."

I wouldn't look up.

"He left and you haven't seen him in weeks."

Adam must have blabbed.

"And you feel you're in limbo. Well, you're not ... you're in love."

My head rose. My eyes met hers. "In love?"

"Yes, in love. Don't you know love when you see it? When you feel it?"

I thought I did. With Mr. Reid, with Peter. To an extent, the others in between them. But with Raheim? Love never felt the way I was feeling right then.

And that's because I never knew love like this before.

"Ha, you head-over-heels and you don't even know it. Now *that's* the power of love."

Is that why I've been trippin' – trying to get Raheim out of my system when I can't?

She grabbed my right hand with her left. "Whatever happened between you two – and you don't have to tell me about it, because it ain't none of my business – it happened. You can't change it. But you two can't throw away whatcha got ... it's in your eyes ... it's in his, I saw it."

My mother saw it, too. *And tell my son-in-law I said hello...* Everybody probably saw it – except me.

"You probably didn't expect it to happen ... probably didn't want it to happen ... probably didn't even *think* it could happen."

And *that's* the truth, Aunt Ruth. Me fall in love with Raheim? *A B-boy?* Puh-leeze, what do *they* know about love? I couldn't even imagine it, but...

"But it has happened. Love don't always come when you want it, it don't always come the way you want it, and it don't always come in the package you want it in. And it *don't* come easy. But when ya got it, ya better name it and claim it."

I smiled. I intended to.

 The undeniable proof that I was in love with and loved Raheim Errol Rivers, Sr., was waiting for me when I returned home after my two-week reprieve.

A large, tattered manila envelope was left on top of the radiator in the foyer of my building by the mailman. It couldn't fit in the box. It had a postmark date of July; it was sent third-class mail. There was no return address.

I didn't think it was important, so I opened it after I had unpacked, eaten, and was in bed for the night with Pooquie. (I'd brought him home with me.)

I'll never forget the moment. I pulled out the two magazines. There was a note attached to them:

July 20

Mitchell,

It was great meeting you. You're on page 20. Everybody on staff loved it. Hopefully we'll work together soon.

Peace,
G.G.

G.G. Who is that?

I didn't even bother looking at the cover of the magazine. I flipped to page twenty — and I nearly fainted.

The headline: HOT LOVE IN THE SUMMERTIME. In a full-page, close-up photo, Raheim and I were gazing into each other's eyes, my hands around his head. The caption read: "Pooquie & Little Bit ... Is This Love or WHAT?"

I dropped the magazine on the bed. I clutched my chest. My heart was skipping four beats. And from the boom box on the night table, the radio announcer said: "And here's something from the lady that helped us bring love home... from her debut ... Mz. Toni Braxton."

I studied the photo as the song played. I'd never heard it before. I didn't even know that Toni's album was out. But by the time she sang the last "breathe again" – and *breathed* – my tears started to fall.

"Pooquie & Little Bit ... Is This Love or WHAT?"

Yes.

While I knew that I would breathe again if Raheim didn't come back, I knew that I would breathe easier if he did. I also knew that, while there was no harm in hoping he did ring my bell again, I couldn't sit at home and wait. I would whisper a prayer for him and about him every day, knowing that, if he felt the same way, love would bring him home. He knows where I am; he knows where to find me.

Besides, I had to eat and pay my bills.

So, I went back to work calm and content. I was also pleased: they'd caught the three guys who gay-bashed Gene. He called me before I left the house to say that Carl went with him to the police station, where he identified two of them in a lineup; the other he couldn't, since he'd had Gene from behind in a headlock. But the cashier could. All three were eighteen, and would be charged with aggravated assault. And, while New York does not recognize gay-bashing as a hate crime, all three had been fingered by two other men who were beaten in separate incidents that happened in the Vill just weeks before Gene's attack. The multiple assault charges could result in each one spending at least ten years in jail. So, when I hopped off the elevator at work, I was in a great mood.

"What's up, girl?" I smiled.

Michelle got up from her desk to give me a big hug. "Well, you sure must've had a good vacation. You look good."

"Thanks. I *feel* good."

"Well, you won't for long."

"Hunh?"

She grasped my left shoulder and pulled me closer. "Now, I ain't one to gossip, so you ain't heard it from me ... but word is that Evil Elias is being promoted to senior editor."

*"What?"* Michelle had never been wrong about any gossip item she's passed on to me. She checks out the story herself, gathering up her own

evidence before spilling the beans. She's the Liz Smith of the office. I
wanted to believe that this was gossip, though: Elias Whitley, senior
editor of *Your World? My* boss? Somebody shoot me...

"I know this is a stupid question to ask, but are you sure?"

She handed me a piece of paper. "Exhibit A."

It was a memo that would be going out in the afternoon announcing
the "great news," as Steven wrote. A chill went through my body.

"One of the mail guys gave me the copy. I wanted you to know
before it came out ... and before Steven told you this morning."

"This morning?"

She handed me the pink message sheet. "Yeah. Exhibit B."

It said: "From: Steven. Wants to see you in his office at 10:45.
Important. Michi."

It was 10:40.

I stared at both of the papers. "I cannot believe this."

"You're not the only one. Call me after the meeting and let me know
what happens." She ran back around to her desk to answer the phone.
*"Your World..."* She gave me a thumbs-up.

I sleepwalked to my desk. Ain't this some shit. Elias Whitley ... my
boss. *My* boss. It just played like a soundtrack in my head, echoing.
This could not be happening. I trained that no-talent bastard. He
couldn't write for shit, didn't know how to interview people, didn't
know how to research an idea when he came to *Your World* – he
learned it all from the Master (even though he still isn't half the
journalist I am). He was just a hack of a hick from the Georgia hills
who'd published some ragamuffin neoconservative excuse of a college
paper that was the toast of the right-wing intelligentsia. The *National
Review* hailed it for "being a leader in the crusade against the fanatical
political-correctness movement sweeping our college campuses." He
was hired to bring what Steven referred to as "ideological balance" to
the staff. But as I told Michelle: "I didn't know being a simpleminded
ass was an ideology."

How, just how could *he* be promoted to senior editor? It didn't make
sense. *I'm* the one with the journalism degree – and a student Pulitzer
to prove it. *I'm* the one with the intense journalism background: a
million bylines and internships at two of the most prestigious publications in the nation (the *New York Times* and the *Village Voice*). *I'm* the one
who has expanded the magazine's scope, pushing to examine topics
never discussed before and gaining thousands of new readers. *I'm* the
one with the half dozen feature-writing awards and a citation from the
Department of Education's service department for excellent educa-
tional reporting and writing.

I couldn't wait to hear why all of this wasn't important, even though I already knew why. While some white men constantly complain that they are unjustly being passed over for jobs and promotions (not only are they qualified to do *everything,* they can always do it better than us), they still benefit from the oldest quota system on earth (cashin' in on white skin). "Merit" always seems to be an issue when we want to get ahead, but them? Right out the window. Elias's incompetence-yet-steady-advancement is proof of that. It makes all this media-induced white-male paranoia absurd. (Could it be that, for once in their lives, white men really have to compete with us and know they can't?) If white men want to be angry at any group, it should be white women – *they* are the ones who have benefited the most from affirmative action. We still have to be twice, *thrice* as good as Caucasians – I call it the "Michael Jordan Syndrome," having to do death-defying leaps and bounds – in order to get our props, and sometimes that's not even enough. So, who is really getting over?

Steven was on the phone when I entered his office. He waved me in; I shut the door and sat. He was in his usual corporate uniform. His tie, which was an ugly lime green, looked familiar. Isn't that the one Elias gave him last year for his birthday?

He hung up the phone. "Well, good morning, Mitch. You look good. I guess you enjoyed your vacation?"

"Yes, I did, Steven, thank you."

"I guess you're wondering why I've called you in here so early on your first day back."

"Yes."

"I know we said we'd do your evaluation this week, and we will ... later this week."

I'd completely forgotten about it. We'd postponed it because I wouldn't be in.

He cleared his throat. "I wanted to speak to you personally about a decision made regarding the staff."

I played it off like I knew nothing. "Oh..."

"Yes ... it is good news."

Yeah, right.

He smiled. "Last week, Elias was promoted ... to senior editor."

He waited for my reaction.

"And...?" I asked.

"And, well, as you know ... there is only one such position on the magazine."

Yes, I know. He had announced it two weeks before I went on hiatus. Everyone knew it was created to accommodate our growing staff. And, of course, just about everyone predicted I would get it.

I sat there like I was thinking, when I really wasn't. I knew exactly what to say. "Hmmmm ... so are you telling me that another senior editor position will be opened up?"

His eyes bulged. "What?"

"Well, I am also up for promotion and I do have more experience than he does. And, I've been with *Your World* longer. Is that it?"

"Uh, Mitchell ... uh, no, that's not it."

"Well, what is it?"

"Only Elias will be a senior editor."

I wanted to scream but didn't. I just sighed. "I see ... so, what does this mean?"

Steven stood up over his desk and put his hands in his pockets. If he thought that was going to intimidate me, it didn't. "Mitch, I really respect you ... you are a valuable employee. *Your World* is a better publication because of you ... you are special."

Uh-huh, I'm not like the others ... I'm a special nigger...

"...but Elias is management material..."

"And I am not?"

He walked around from the desk, talking with his hands. "It's not that you aren't ... it's just that he has more of the qualities a manager should..."

Uh-huh, like white skin...

My voice was tempered. "Well, the position is senior editor, Steven, not managing editor, so I don't see your point. What exactly are the qualities he has that I lack?"

"Well, I would rather not discuss that right now."

"Why? Isn't that why I am here?"

"Well, yes, but I'd rather go over your own performance in depth later this week. In fact, we can pick a time for that right now."

"There's no need to do that."

He did a double take. "Why?"

"Because my performance has already been evaluated."

"What do you mean?"

I couldn't resist. "What part of that statement do you not understand, Steven? What's the sense of going over something we don't need to? You've already told me what you think of my performance – and it isn't good enough."

His face became flushed. "I didn't say that, Mitchell."

"You don't have to. The message is clear."

He was gagging. "Now, now, Mitchell, I believe you are taking this the wrong way ... you don't understand..."

Hmmmm ... it's a white thing, so I guess I wouldn't, hunh?

"Well, let's see if I am..." I got up out of my chair, startling him, and stood in front of him. "There is only one senior editor position. Elias has it. I am due for promotion. Means I ain't gonna get it – even though I deserve it. Is that about right?"

"Uh..."

"Sorry, Steven, but I am nobody's fool or Guy Friday. This is 1993, not 1793. Dem days are done."

"Mitch, I, I think we'll have to talk about this when you're not so hostile and accusatory..."

I smiled and clapped my hands. "Not once have I raised my voice or come at you in a nasty tone, Steven. Ah, if it was Elias saying all of this, he'd probably be seen as an individual who stands up for what's right and has the utmost self-respect, dignity, and integrity."

I'd pressed the right button; his face turned beet red. "Uh, uh, surely, Mitch, you, you're not suggesting..."

"Not suggesting ... just stating."

"Mitchell ... you know that I see you as a journalist, a great journalist who *happens* to be black ... your color doesn't matter."

Uh-huh. How many times has he said that nonsense? The last time, he was relaying some bullshit story about his mammy's son. *He is one of my best friends and he is smart, just like you, Mitch. He's a great guy who happens to be black.* Uh-huh. After letting him slide so many times, I let him have it. "Correction, Steven ... my mother had a child who *is* Black and just *happens* to be, at this point in his life, a journalist. And, if my color *didn't* matter, we wouldn't be having this conversation."

His mouth fell open, but nothing came out. He walked over to his desk, flipping his calendar. He forced a smile. "Uh, let's make that appointment, shall we? How's Friday at eleven?"

"Unless you are putting me in a senior editor's position, I'll be here Friday at eleven – to hand in my resignation." I turned, walked to the door, opened it, and smiled. "Oh, and have a nice day."

I didn't have a chance to think about what I did. We had an editorial meeting at eleven o'clock.

All the usual culprits were there – Elias and Phillip, all too cheerful, on one side of the table; Denise and I, very solemn, on the other; Andrew at the head.

After Elias's flip comment about Michael Jackson and the child-sex-abuse allegations ("Well, thank God we didn't put *him* on the cover of the music issue!"), they went over some of the stories they were doing on the elderly and Elias announced the lineup for the Holocaust. Everything sounded fine until...

"Oh, and we are not doing the slavery story."

I looked up from my planning book. "Excuse me?"

"We're not doing the slavery story."

"Why?"

"Because it doesn't fit."

I looked at Denise. Her face said it all: *I've already been through it with them, so now it's your turn.*

I accepted the challenge. "Yes, it *does* fit, Elias. It is a piece that focuses on, not just slavery, but other forms of genocide throughout history. People think what the Nazis did was an isolated incident, but there are other examples of it, in different forms."

Phillip jumped in. "Oh, come off it, Mitch ... don't you think you're stretching it just a little here? I don't see the link."

Uh-huh, Uncle Thomas (as in Clarence) strikes again. I lit into him. "Tens of millions of African men, women, and children were categorically chosen to be chattel because of *who* they were, stolen from their homes and families, packed like sardines in slave ship holds, and died on their way to what would have been a life of barbaric bondage and savage servitude, and *you* can't see the link?"

He was gagging. Denise let out a soft giggle.

*"We* – you *and* me, Phillip – wouldn't be here if our ancestors didn't survive both horrors..." He began seething.

Elias jumped back in. "Look, slavery was a tragedy, yes, but..."

"It was *not* a tragedy – we're not talking about a plane crash. It was genocide. The Middle Passage was a holocaust."

Elias became flustered. "You can't use that word to describe it."

"Why *not?* It fits what happened."

"That is really insensitive, Mitch. You, of all people, I would expect better from."

My eyes shot up. *"Oh?"*

"Yes, being so politically correct."

That was it. This mother-fucker was going to get it now.

I looked him dead in the eye. "That has to be *the* most *un*brilliant thing you have ever said, Elias. Don't you even assume you know what's going on in my head; we know you *look* stupid, but let's not act it, OK? I have never strived to be politically correct – whatever *that* means. It's just a matter of being correct – something you know *nothing* about."

"Uh, maybe we ought to continue this discussion on this particular issue later," interrupted Andrew. Why is he always coming in on the tail end of things?

"Slavery is an issue that...," Elias began.

My hand went up. "Correction: it was a *crime* ... like *the* Holocaust," I interrupted.

Elias slapped his hand on the table, his glasses falling down his nose. "Slaves were taken from Africa to work in America, but..."

"*Three* corrections: *no* slaves were *taken* from Africa ... peaceful, innocent human beings were kidnapped. And, I wouldn't exactly call what they did *work.*"

Andrew slammed his hand on the table. "OK, OK, you two, quit!" He caught his breath. "We will discuss this later this week, understood?"

I didn't say a word. I just looked at Elias. Come noon, he is officially my boss. *My* boss.

It was then that I knew that I had done the right thing in Steven's office.

⊕

I'll never forget Arnold O'Neil, a chunky, deliriously sweet 54-year-old professor at Columbia who could've been St. Nick's brother. He was the first white man I ever knew who admitted that we have a harder time in this life, and that we have the right to be fucking angry about it. He also said that I had a lot of talent – "more than most of the white folks I know who have been in the business all their lives" – and that, if I should ever feel that my talents were not being appreciated and that I was not being respected, I should have a "fuck-you fund" saved so that I could say, "Fuck you," and just pick up and leave and have a nest egg to live on while I find another job.

That was basically my plan. I had over $10,000 in my "fuck-you fund." That, along with my regular account (which included insurance money I received because of my father's death) and freelance opportunities, would allow me to live comfortably for some time. Surprisingly, feeding Raheim didn't put a dent in any of these tills. He did contribute sometimes, but he didn't really need to. I always purchased food in bulk quantities. Even though it's cheaper, I often find myself giving away portions each month to the homeless shelter a few blocks from my house. Of course, that stopped with him (and Junior) around.

After the meeting I received my copy of the "great news" and informed Steven by electronic mail and on paper that if he *really* respects me as an individual and *really* values me as an employee, he would take what I said *very* seriously. Anything other than a senior editor position (or something equal to or higher than it) would be "totally unacceptable." I would be taking the rest of my vacation time (a week) and would return on Friday for either a promotion and pay raise or my paycheck. I sent a copy of the letter to Martin Schultz in Human Resources.

But, because I was well aware of the Ways of White Folks, I didn't have much faith in Steven seeing things my way. So I packed up my shit, most of it pictures, posters, postcards, research files, and writing aids. I had enough samples of my clips at home, so I didn't plan to take any more copies of the magazine. Within an hour, my office was bare. I dropped the three medium-sized boxes off at the mailroom (you didn't think I was going to carry those mother-fuckers home, did you?) and, with Raheim and Junior's picture under my arm, left.

I hadn't even been in the house five minutes when the phone rang. "Hello?"

"Did you quit?" It was Denise. "I went by your desk and it was cleaned out."

"It looks like it."

"Well, thanks for tellin' us." It was Michelle. They were on a conference call, more than likely in a conference room.

"I left both of you notes."

Michelle sucked her teeth. "Yes, a note. How nice."

"I'm sorry, I just had to get out of there."

"So, what happened?" asked Denise.

I gave them the story.

"You have a lot of guts, Mitch," declared Denise.

"Shit, it wasn't his guts he was waving," exclaimed Michelle. "It was his dick, all up in that old fart's face."

"Michelle...?" Denise and I said in unison.

"Puh-leeze, you know that's what they scared of ... they know you shoulda had it, but *no*..."

"Well, I am a white woman and I wouldn't really know about these things," began Denise, "but I think you've been the victim of race discrimination, darling."

"Darling, I think you're right," I laughed.

Michelle smacked her gum. "So, what are you gonna do ... besides quit?"

"I don't know. I may take legal action against them."

"You should. The only way shit like this is gonna stop is if we stop letting them get away with it," argued Michelle.

Denise piped in. "Well, Mitch, you should leave on good terms. I mean, you don't want them giving you a bad reputation in circles."

I sighed. "Well, they would want not to do that and I don't see how they could. I've already informed Steven that I expect a letter from him, sort of an end evaluation, saying that I worked my ass off, despite our disagreement over my promotion and my leaving."

Denise sighed. "Well, I don't want you to go. Steven would be stupid to let you. And if he does, I may not be too far behind. I am not that thrilled about working under Senior Asshole Elias either."

"I hear that..."

"If you do leave, we'll take you out to lunch on Friday," suggested Michelle.

"Yes. And *Your World* will pay," added Denise.

"Oh, you two are terrific. You are the only things I will miss about the place."

"Listen to us, you'd think it was all over," cried Denise. "He's got until Friday. Let's just hope he doesn't allow his ignorance to prevail over his more positive aspects."

"I think I've had too much of an affect on you, Denise. I have a feeling you'll be just fine."

"I'll call you later if I find out anything else," said Michelle.

"Thanks, you two. Bye."

"Bye," they both sang.

⊕

Needless to say, Steven didn't come to his senses. So, when I showed up on Friday, I got my money and his letter, which said he was sorry to see me go; that *Your World* would "not be the same" without me; that I was "an outstanding journalist who will go places"; and that he wished me the best.

Yeah, *right*.

Martin wanted me to sit for an exit interview and fill out an evaluation questionnaire, but I refused. "Why should I?" I bellowed. "You all know how I feel." He informed me, though, that despite my quitting, *Your World* would "do the right thing" by me: in two weeks, I would receive my remaining sick and vacation pay plus two months salary. How nice...

Uh-huh, shut-up money.

Denise, Michelle, and I had a blast at Pizzeria Uno with this really cute Puerto Rican waiter who favored Jon Secada. He was flirting with all of us. Denise is the one who ended up taking home his number. You go, girl.

The office was deserted when we returned. The next day was Yom Kippur and most people left for the weekend at lunch. I was about to leave myself when I remembered that I wanted to get a few copies of the family issue – just for sentiment's sake. That was my last hurrah on the magazine and it was very special for two other reasons.

There were none in the filing copy drawers, so I went up to the ninth-floor storage room. I got a few and, as I was walking back toward the stairs to say good-bye to Denise, I heard grunting sounds. They became louder and louder as I approached a large office where the copy desk people used to sit. It was being revamped for the art staff.

I knew my ears were deceiving me, but as I quietly stepped over the wood panels and cans of paint and slowly turned the corner, peeking in the sunshine-lit empty room, I geeked.

That's right, *geeked*.

There was Elias Whitley, minus his glasses and shirt, bending over with his pale ass in the air, as Phillip Cooper, also shirtless and drenched in sweat, violently banged the shit out of him with his blue-black dick. Both had their pants around their ankles.

"Yeah, fuck me hard, darkie. Yeah, give me that big black cock...," Elias laughed, jerking off with his right hand and slapping Phillip on his thigh and butt cheek with his left hand so hard it made me flinch.

With his right hand around Elias's waist, almost lifting him off the ground, and his left practically tearing out his hair, Phillip picked up the pace. "Oh yeah, white boy, oh yeah, I'm gonna cum..."

"Oh yes, cum in me, darkie, cum in me..."

*That* I did not need to watch.

After I was out of hearing distance, I ran to the bathroom. I knew I was going to be sick. This nightmarish scene certainly explained a lot:

Like Elias's comment regarding my attending the NABJ convention in '91: "Hmmmm ... I bet a lot of *big* prospects will be there..." Uh-huh. Don't we mean big *cock*spects?

Like his shocking the staff when we did an issue on censorship. He, the Jesse Helms fanatic, had no problem with the work of Robert Mapplethorpe. "I know a lot of it offends many people, but I like it. It does something for me." Uh-huh. The objectification of Black men *does something for you*.

Like the few times I found him standing outside the library, which is across from my cubicle, reading a magazine. He'd duck into the bathroom when he saw me coming. Why? He was checking out the view — or, rather, Raheim, who was either standing up or sitting in my chair, wearing little (a bodysuit) or practically nothing (a see-through jumper). Uh-huh, Elias got an eyeful and then a *hand*ful when he went into the john.

Like his "warming up" to Phillip and taking him "under his wing."

What a news bulletin: the heir to Rush Limbaugh's throne is a chocoholic.

But had I heard Elias right? Did he call Phillip *darkie?*

And Phillip ... isn't he "straight"? Is this what he and Elias have been doing all along, and why they are so "close"? Is this what he thinks he has to do in order to get in good with the big boys, to be the first darkie to crack the glass ceiling? I heard many stories about us having to give up the goods to secure or procure a job, mostly from B.D., who says the arts world is notorious for this "casting couch" system. This is one of the reasons why he formed his own company. He got tired of directors and producers (almost all of them white) making passes at him. As he said: "Sorry, I'll flirt and I'll even massage your ego, but I ain't suckin' or fuckin' my way to the top."

Phillip obviously doesn't share his philosophy. He is willing to pay the Price of the Ticket.

I was coming out of the stall (I just coughed a lot and didn't have the nerve to stick my finger down my throat) when who should enter the bathroom but Phillip. He wasn't expecting to see me or anyone else: his clothes were ruffled and rumpled, and he looked at me like a deer caught in headlights. But he tried to stump me.

"Hi, Mitch, how are you?" That was the first time in months he'd even said hello. Uh-huh, guilt.

"Hey," I mumbled, splashing cold water on my face.

He headed for a urinal and pissed. "Ya know, I've been meaning to talk to you."

I wiped my face with a paper towel. "Oh really? About what?"

He shook it and zipped up. "Well, I know you leaving today. I wanted to thank you for bringing me here and wish you luck."

Was he really saying that? I watched him wash his hands. "Well ... thank you."

"It's too bad, though. You really paved the way for me. But at least I know what happened to you won't happen to me."

What? How arrogant can this guy be? "I'm sorry?"

He turned off the water and reached for a towel. "Listen, you are a fabulous journalist, you really are. But you know we gotta go along to get along if we want to get ahead."

Uh-huh ... And *your* idea of "going along" is to kiss – or, in this case, fuck – the new S.E.'s ass? To let him degrade you and treat you like a Big Black Buck? I wanted to say these things – but didn't.

I just picked up the magazines, opened the door, turned, and grinned. "No, thanks. I'm not into volunteer slavery. I'd rather keep my soul."

While it was pouring rain and rather cold on that first Friday in October, Babyface kept his appointment to help me figure out whether I had a discrimination case against *Your World.*

After we chatted briefly, he sat on the sofa, unbuttoned and rolled up his sleeves, loosened his tie, and put on his sexy silver-framed reading glasses to analyze my employment file, which included every memo or note written by or about me during my three years at the company, as well as my evaluations. He was silent the whole time, just making notes on a yellow pad. I filled up his coffee cup twice during that half hour.

When he was done, he squeezed his forehead, took off his glasses, and stretched. "Well, one thing is for sure."

I got up from the folding chair and took a seat next to him. "What's that?"

"You were a damn good employee," he exclaimed, placing his hot hand on my exposed thigh. I was wearing Raheim's gray "janet" t-shirt and a pair of black shorts.

"Tell me something I don't know," I chuckled nervously.

"Well," he began, removing his hand and allowing me to breathe easy, "it is documented that you are, quote, 'emotional and excitable,' and, quote, 'very sensitive.' They can easily point to statements like that and say that's why you weren't promoted. Not management material. And a jury of white folks will probably agree."

I sighed. "What about the pay discrepancy?"

With the help of a not-too-bright clerk in accounting, Michelle was able to get a copy of Elias's salary history. I had a feeling that that might tell me something I expected all along. From the time he started, he was making $3,000 more than I — even though we had the same position with the same duties and he had only a bachelor's degree. That gap never closed after two years. So much for equal pay for equal work, and being paid what you're worth...

"It certainly was wrong and unfair to you," Babyface motioned, "but not necessarily racist."

"Oh, you're really dashing my hopes here, Counselor..."

"I'm sorry. But you do have the awards and citations, and a spotless record. And you did train that guy, so if his record doesn't show he was senior-editor material, then you might have a case."

"And that's a big might, isn't it?"

"Yeah. But, at least you filed a complaint with the EEOC. That's a start and it shows you mean business. Most of us don't even bother to do that."

That's also what the caseworker told me. Because the racism is very subtle (no one, for the most part, says, "Nigger, we ain't giving you no job," or, "We're not giving you no damn promotion 'cause you're the wrong color"), it is hard to prove. Folks may know they have been wronged, but they figure that, after twelve years of Reagan and Bush, no one – not even those organizations founded to help in such matters – will believe them.

Babyface gave me a list of lawyers that specialize in discrimination cases if I wanted to test my luck. I offered him some succotash. We ate at the dining room table and returned to the sofa, both of us sitting sideways, facing each other.

"So, have you two picked out the wedding wardrobe yet?" I asked.

"No. But I've already told B.D. that he cannot wear a veil."

"You're kidding ... he really wants to do that?"

"He's always dreamed of having a traditional ceremony. But I want it to be really Africentric. You know, like jumping the broom."

"I'd expect something like that from you."

"Uh-huh." He sipped his tea. "So, how are you holding up?"

I knew what he was referring to. "I'm OK. Lovesick and lonely, but OK."

"So, you love him?"

"Yeah."

"You want to talk about it?"

I did.

As I talked, he got into what I was saying – and into me. I didn't say anything when his right arm went along the couch or when his left hand found my thigh again. He also got The Look, so I knew it was just a matter of time before he aimed for and made contact with my lips.

The kiss was long and luscious. When I opened my eyes, my arms were around his neck and his strong hands were exploring my legs and buttocks.

"Babyface, no ... we can't do this."

He nibbled on my neck. "Why?"

I pulled away. "Why? *Why?* First of all, you are one of my best friends."

He giggled, going for his again. "Hey, what's a snack between friends?"

I broke away and rose off the sofa. "Second, your soon-to-be-wife is also my best friend. And, third, our mutual best friend, Mr. Daniels, would kill us both if he found out."

He shrugged. "Mitch, it's no big deal."

I stood just outside the kitchen, my hands in the air. "What do you mean 'it's no big deal'? Just a few months ago you were sitting on that very same couch, announcing your engagement, and now you want to fuck me on it?"

He came over to me. "Mitch, just hear me out, OK?"

"What can you say? That what B.D. don't know won't hurt him? That he would understand?"

"B.D. *would* understand."

I sucked my teeth. "Oh yeah? *Why?*"

"Because he knows."

"What?"

He reached for and took hold of my waist (no, I didn't put up a fight). "B.D. knows, Mitch. He knows how much I've wanted you. And he has given me permission."

"*'Given you permission'?* You expect me to believe that?"

"Yes," he said with a straight face.

Babyface had never lied to me; in fact, if you let him tell it, he's never lied in his life. He's always believed in being straight-up about everything. So, why would he lie now? He explained that there are people that he and B.D. want to "be with" before they get married. More like one person each. For B.D., it's Vincent Calloway, a chocolate-drop dancer he's known for five years who is in his troupe. That would surely be a challenge — Vincent is married.

You know who is Babyface's choice.

"Why me?" I asked.

"Because you are one of the most beautiful people I've ever met in my life. And you have one of the juiciest asses I've ever seen." He gave it a feel.

I blushed.

He continued. "Now, if you want me to go, I will. But I want you and I'd love to stay the night. And I know you need someone right now. I'd love to hold you, taste you. I want to make love to you, not fuck you. I want to make you feel good, make you feel better. I've been waiting for some time ... and I think now is as good a time as any."

My mind told me no, but my body said yes. After all that had happened in the past two months, I ached for, as Stephanie Mills would put it, the comfort of a man. As his grip became firm, I started playing with his hairy chest. I stared into those deep baby-light-brown eyes. I grabbed his chin and kissed him.

After the sex, Babyface looked like the cat who had swallowed the canary.

"What?" I asked, running my fingers through his dred-locs. I'd always wanted to do that. He was on his back and I was on top of him. "What are you smiling about?"

"Nothing," he grinned, his hands tapping my buns. "It was good, wasn't it?"

"Excuse me?"

"Don't even play that with me. You liked it."

Yeah, I did. Babyface was a tender lover, but he was also insatiable. And, yes, as B.D. said, he had a dick that wouldn't quit. It — *he* — wore me out.

I didn't want him to know that, though, so I rolled my eyes. "Maybe I did."

"You did."

"How do *you* know?"

"'Cause I was there, that's why. And you were screaming."

"I was not!"

"You were too. And the way you called my name..." His voice became wavery. "Oh, Babyface ... yes, Babyface, yes..."

I hit him on the shoulder. "Stop it!"

He grinded. "Uh-huh, you just can't get enough of my funky stuff, can ya?"

"You are foolish!"

He stole a kiss. I gave him another.

I rested my chin on his chest. "B.D. is lucky to have you."

"Raheim is lucky to have *you.*"

I tensed. "Raheim is not here."

"He'll be back."

"What makes you say that?"

"He'd be stupid to let you go. He realizes that. He's got to get himself together first."

"And how long will that take?"

"Love knows no time, Mitch. But it will be soon, don't you worry. He's going to have his hands full. You are one hungry man. But he will satisfy you."

Silence.

"Babyface?"

"Yes?"

"I love you."

"I love you, too, Baby."

We kissed. He called me Baby ... like Raheim.

"So, are we going to tell B.D.?" I asked.

"B.D. will know that it has happened, believe me; I won't have to say a word. And he won't ask me about it, he'll ask you."

"And what am I supposed to say?"

"Two things: that it was good..."

"Babyface!"

"And, would he like to have a ménage à trois."

We cracked up.

A while later, I started to cry.

Babyface sat up concerned. "What's wrong?"

I wiped my tears. "I'm OK. I'm happy. And sad. Sort of a happy sad."

"Hunh?" he asked, puzzled.

"No, I'm sorry. I'm just glad you're here. I needed this."

He wrapped me in his arms. "I know, Baby, I know."

Pause.

"Babyface?"

"Yes?"

"Thanks."

"Hey, that's what friends are for."

 "So, how was it?"

B.D. and I were having an early Sunday dinner at the Gadabout, a tiny, family-owned and "down-home" restaurant off 125th Street and Fifth Avenue in Harlem. They have some of the best fried chicken and waffles I've ever tasted. I almost choked on mine, though, when B.D. inquired about my friendly frolic with Babyface.

I played it dumb. "What are you talking about?"

"Mitch, please, I may be naive and not that sharp, but one thing I'm not is stupid — and neither are you."

I wiped my mouth with my napkin. "B.D. ... I guess I just don't feel comfortable talking about it."

"Why? It's not like you two did it behind my back."

"Well, we certainly didn't do it in front of you!"

He sat up in his chair and pushed his plate forward. He put his arms on the table. "Mitch, I love Babyface to death. We want to spend the rest of our lives with each other. And when we decided we were going to do that, we knew there were certain things we needed to do."

"Like sleep with those you've always wanted to but haven't yet."

"Yes ... and no. You and Vincent are not one-night fucks, and you know it."

"I know ... I, I guess it ... I mean, how did you two come to this understanding, anyway?"

"We're just very realistic, that's all. We don't want to be together and worry about what we didn't do or experience. Babyface has led a very tame life compared to me, so when we talked about doing this, I knew his list was going to be a page long. But when he said you ... well, that told me not only that he had taste but that I was making the right decision marrying him. I guess you could say we are sowing our wild nuts."

I shook my head. "Your wild *oats,* B.D., sowing your wild oats."

"Oh, yeah, that's it. Must be my Alzheimer's kicking in. Anyway, I know you needed it just as much as he wanted it."

Yeah, I did. I hadn't been sexed since Raheim and I set the sheets afire the night after D.C.'s funeral. Babyface was jood (we did it again that morning and then took a sensuous shower together). But it was even jooder having someone in my bed, feeling the warmth, the hardness, breathing them in, sleeping in their arms and being awakened by a kiss.

B.D. took a bite of his waffle. "I'm sure, though, he wasn't better than Pooquie."

I smiled. Pooquie. While I had thought the name, I hadn't heard or said it out loud in two months. It sounded jood.

B.D. nearly jumped out of his chair. *"He was better than Pooquie?"*

"What? No. I mean, Babyface was Babyface and ... Pooquie..." I loved the way it just came out. So natural. I smiled again.

"Uh-huh..." He nodded his head and made a *tsk, tsk* sound. "You know, it really is a shame."

"What is?"

"That things didn't go right between you two. I guess that's what happens when you play the role."

"Hunh? Play what role?"

"Let me see..." He got that Edith "I'm thinkin'" Bunker look. "Now, I want you to be totally honest, OK?"

"OK..."

"The first time you saw Pooquie, the very first time, what's the first thing that came to mind?"

"The first thing?"

"Yeah."

I thought back to that night at Harry's, Raheim looking so fly. My smile became broader.

"I said to think of it, not relive it!"

"Well, if I had to be perfectly honest, it'd have to be..."

"Sex, right?"

"Right. But that's not a bad thing."

"No, it's not a bad thing. But for you it became *the* thing, defining how you saw him."

"No, it didn't."

"Yes, it did ... think about it."

I did. We couldn't do anything, we couldn't go anywhere without being intimate in some way. Seems we always had a fever for da flavor.

B.D. moved in closer. "Pooquie was your lean, mean sex machine, and, in order to keep that machine pumping, you did the things that you thought would keep him happy and *cuming* back for more."

"Like?"

"May I be frank?"

I was amused. "Yes, you may."

"Being the happy homemaker and wholesome ho."

I gagged. I certainly didn't expect him to say that.

I sighed. "I see..."

"Now, I didn't say that to hurt your feelings, hon."

I played with my fork. "I know, I know."

"Look. Ain't nothin' wrong with wanting to take care of a man in that way. Hell, I do it with Babyface. He loves for me to cook and clean and do all those so-called womanly thangs. But I do it because I want to, *not* because he wants me to and *not* because I think I need to."

I stared at my plate. What he said sounded logical. But was that really the way things were between Raheim and me?

"Come on now, don't be dense like me," snickered B.D. "Raheim is B-boy Supreme, Super MacDaddy, he turns you the fuck out, and what's the one way you can please him? By pampering him, by catering to his every need, by being what most, if not all, of those homies want: a woman with a dick."

A woman ... with a dick.

Now, that one was a little too much for me. After I gulped down a full glass of water, B.D. grabbed my hand.

"Mitch, you are a very special man. You have so much to offer. If Pooquie is smart, he'll come back to you. Whether you'll take him back is another thing. But I know one thing: if you two do get a second chance, ya'll can't be frontin'. He'll have to stop being a boy and you can't be afraid of being a man."

I sat there, pondering all he said. Did I purposely fall into a "feminine" role thinking that that would not threaten Raheim's masculinity, so he'd stick around? Was I surprised about Pooquie being smart, creative, and artistic because I thought B-boys were really only good for one thing? I felt ashamed. And I must have looked it.

"Mitch, baby, I didn't mean to get you upset, please..."

"No, no, I'm not ... I'm just ... I guess I'm just facing the truth."

"I know, it hurts..." He sighed, then grinned. "Despite the fronts you two put up, you were still able to get to know a bit of the real yous – and you both fell for it. That's why he kept coming back. And that's why you kept taking him back."

I just could not believe that I was hearing all of this – and that it was coming out of B.D.'s mouth. "How, just how did you get to be so perceptive?"

"Honey, there are a lot of things I don't know, and even many of the things I do know I often forget about, but when it comes to men? Ha!"

We laughed.

"And speaking of men..." His eyes pointed toward the door. A Black Muslim, the color of a Milky Way and dressed in a black suit and bow tie, strode in. Well over six feet with a straight nose, green eyes, glossy brown lips, and teeth as white and straight as Pooquie's, he smiled and came to our table, holding up a copy of the *Final Call* in his left hand.

"Excuse me, brothers..." The voice was baritone boomin'.

"I'm sorry, but we're not interested," I blurted out. It was a habit. I was used to saying it to them.

"Well, I'll buy a copy of the paper ... but what are you going to give me?" asked B.D., batting those eyelashes down.

I was gasping – but the guy wasn't. "Well," he began, bending down and leaning in closer to B.D., very smug, "what do you have in mind, my brother?"

B.D. grinned. "Give me your phone number and we'll talk."

I then gagged as the gentleman looked around (finding no one, since we were the only folks in the place), went into his inside breast pocket, and pulled out a card.

"Call me." He gave B.D. both the card and the newspaper. "Brother Abdul. Pleased to meet you."

He shook both of our hands. He was a strong one.

"OK, I'll ring you ... *soon.*" B.D. sat up in his chair and went into the pocket of his skin-tight blue jeans to get some change for the paper, but Brother Abdul, who enjoyed the bird's-eye view of B.D.'s packed thighs and butt, protested.

"No, no, no ... you can give it to me later," he winked. "My brothers ... good day."

"Good day," B.D. smiled. All I could do was wave.

After watching his big butt (which couldn't be shielded by the tan trench he wore) bounce out, I snatched the card off of the table. "I don't believe this man."

"What do you mean?"

"I mean he *is* in the Nation of Islam."

"*And?* Chile, he is a man. Besides, contrary to what some might think, we faggots are everywhere. And, some of the stories I've heard about these Muslim men ... wooo! They can drop the dime, you hear me? Just look at all those babies those women be havin'. Hmph, Brother Abdul can certainly covet and convert me!"

Laugh out loud.

"Besides, something told me that something was gonna happen today ... and it all adds up."

"What does?"

"Well, I am getting nowhere with Mr. Vincent Calloway. He is what you and Gene would call an Oreo cookie. He'd cheat on Hugo but not with a Black man. I know; he's told me about some of his other Caucasian conquests. And, never mind that I am whiter than Hugo; that child is almost as dark as Vince, going to that tanning salon every week. Anyway, I told Babyface this morning that the only other person I've wanted and haven't done – well, the only person who hasn't done *me* – is a Muslim. That's always been a fantasy, and now it just might come true ... and I want him to do it with the bow tie *on!*"

"*You* are *so* farcical!"

"I know. If Abdul, ahem, cums through, my list of men will be complete ... and speaking of men ... back to Babyface..."

"What about him?"

He sipped. "You still haven't told me about it ... I want to know."

"Why?"

"Because I'm a dizzy, sex-crazed queen who gets off hearing about her fiancé's sexcapades. So, tell me..."

"Well ... where do I start?"

"*I'll* tell you where ... with the dick that won't quit!"

"B.D., *you* are a *mess!*"

"Ha, you know it's true ... right?"

We cracked up.

"He wants us to have a ménage à trois," I said.

He batted his eyelashes again. "Oh really? When?"

 On Columbus Day, I chose not to celebrate the genocide of the Native American. I spent the day being productive: I had two freelance assignments and a major editing project due later in the week. Bad news travels fast: an editor from *Emerge* contacted me a week after I left *Your World* about an opening on their staff. While the editing position would've allowed me to write, relocating to Virginia was not the move (especially since I don't have a car and I can't drive). Besides, I wanted to breathe after *Your World,* really get a feel for what was out there before committing myself to anything so soon. So I threw out the possibility of becoming a contributor, and the editor liked that idea. My first piece was a simple one – a short feature item on whether dress codes for school kids could help curtail violence.

But I was particularly excited about my gigs with *Rolling Stone* and the *Baldwin Bulletin.* The former was sweet revenge: *RS* is Elias's favorite magazine. He always wanted to write for them but for some reason couldn't get the editors to take him seriously. (I wonder why.) I would love to be a fly on the wall when he opens up the issue with my one-page feature on the growing gospel music industry. I'll also be reviewing the latest by Randy, titled *Don't Say It's Over* (how fitting). I didn't know the first thing about reviewing music, but how hard could it be? Besides, I am so tired of opening magazines and newspapers and reading the work of Caucasians who *think* they can document – and, in essence, define – what Black is. If you want something done right...

The latter job was even more personal: my first time working for a Black gay publication. I contacted Graham and talked with him at length about his magazine's mission and offered myself as both an editor and writer. I knew he was operating on a nonexistent budget; I had no problem not being paid. This was work that had to be done. What spurred this was a conversation I remembered having with Pooquie. We were in bed in our usual position and I was complaining, for the umpteenth time, about the guests on a talk show. The discussion was gay rights, and of the eight people trading ideas and insults, four were homosexual. All were male. All were Caucasian.

I pointed at the screen over Pooquie's head. "Will you look at that? Everytime, *e-ver-y-time* they do anything on gay folks, you never see any of us. And if you do, we're a screaming, silly queen."

Pooquie sighed. "Well, why don'cha stop shootin' off yo' mouth an' go on there."

"Yeah, right, like they want to give a microphone to a Black gay man with a brain?"

"You don' know ... anyway, you always talkin' 'bout it. You don' like wha'cha see, come correc' an' do somethin'..."

Come correct and do somethin'. That is what I kept hearing when I finally stopped crying over our picture in the *Baldwin Bulletin* and read the publication. I was impressed. Graham didn't have a full-time copy editor, so I volunteered for the job. My name would appear on the masthead of the next issue, which would hit newsstands in December. Along with joining a group called the Brotherhood, it's a small step in making the politics I espouse more than just talk.

I was going over his memorandum to readers when my apartment doorbell rang. At first I didn't notice it, because no one ever has to ring it; you can't get to my door without buzzing me from outside. I knew it had to be only one person – Mr. Valdez, the super. He'd said he would drop by around seven-thirty to fix the dripping pipe under my kitchen sink. It was a holiday, but he said he had other things to take care of in the building. It was going on eight. I opened the door without asking who it was.

*"Mitch-hull!"* I couldn't believe it. It was Junior. He was dressed down in a black, three-quarter-length leather coat and cap (turned backwards), dark brown jeans, and black boots. I was so surprised to see him that it didn't click that he could've gotten to my doorstep only one way.

As Junior took off my neck, hugging me as if he hadn't seen me in years, Raheim appeared from behind the landing that led to the top floor of the brownstone. He had on the same outfit. His hands were behind his back. His facial expression was blank.

I rose off of my right knee as Junior held my hand. I was shaking. I was afraid to look at Raheim. I did – but avoided his eyes. "Hi..."

"Hey...," he mumbled, also not looking directly at me.

"Can we come in?" asked Junior, tugging on me.

I looked at him and then Raheim. "Yes ... yes, you can."

"Yay!" applauded Junior, pulling me into the apartment.

As he took off his coat, he told me how much he loved school and his homeroom teacher. ("Her name is Misses Scott and she so preety. She looks like Claire Huckle, Hucks-ta-bull...") As I watched Junior, I could feel Raheim's eyes on me. I was nervous.

"Li'l Brotha Man, take our coats in tha bedroom an' watch TV, a'right?" ordered Raheim.

"Aw, Daddy, I wanna talk to Mitch-hull."

"You can lata, a'right? I wanna talk ta him firs'."

Junior turned to me. "I'll talk to you later, Mitch-hull."

I rubbed his little head, which was close to clean. "OK."

With that, Junior walked away from me, took his father's coat and hat, and proceeded to the bedroom.

"Don' be draggin' them coats," Raheim called out. "An' close tha do'."

"OK."

We were alone, face-to-face, in the exact same spots we were in during the fight. It was so quiet in the room that I could hear Junior's little footsteps in the back. Finally, after trying so hard to make sure our eyes didn't meet, they did. And they locked.

I was paralyzed. He was looking right through me. I couldn't even blink.

He smiled; it made me tingle all over. "You look *jood,* Baby." The words just flowed like music.

I blushed — happy that he said something, happy that he said that, even happier that I could move something on my body. I had on a white "Black Expo" t-shirt and the Spandex he didn't like — or did he? I realized at that moment it was the first time I'd worn them since that day in the Vill.

I accepted his compliment. "Thank you ... you do, too." And he did. The light brown turtleneck and gold hoops in both ears made him glow.

"Thanks," he mumbled.

I'm sure he didn't send Junior out of the room just to say I looked jood. "It" — meaning the fight — was on both of our minds. I decided to cut to the chase. "So ... I guess you think that just because Junior is here, I won't curse your ass out."

He tensed up. He sighed. He put his hands in his pockets and looked up over my head. "Well ... go 'head."

I walked toward him. We were now inches apart. A part of me wanted to hit him ... an eye for an eye. Should I scream on him? I didn't want to do either of those things. Just being so close to him after so long ... His smell ... Mmmmm...

There was only one thing I wanted.

"Hold me," I said, moving forward and into him. I rested my hands and forehead on his chest. I closed my eyes. He slowly and cautiously took his hands out of his pockets, and gently wrapped his arms around my waist.

*Breathe again, breathe again...*

I took him in. Long, deep breaths. I licked my lips. I got chills. I started trembling. He stopped it by holding me tighter. He rested his chin on the top of my head.

We stood like that for ... it seemed like an eternity. No words were spoken. None were needed.

Finally...

"Little Bit?"

I didn't hear him the first time — he had whispered it and I was so into him.

"Little Bit?"

I opened my eyes. "Yes?"

"You wanna sit down?"

I looked up into his eyes and nodded yes.

He released me. He took my right hand with his left and led the way. Slow, easy steps. Almost slow-motion.

He sat in the middle of the sofa. I sat on his left. I placed my head on his shoulder and my right leg over his thigh. I closed my eyes. We snuggled. We still held hands. We breathed together. We sat like that for ... I don't know. Again, it seemed like an eternity.

Until he said...

"Little Bit?"

"Yes?"

He squeezed my hand tighter. "I ... I love you."

My eyes popped opened. Did he say...? No man had ever said it to me ... first. No man had ever said it to me ... that way.

I felt a rush. I smiled like I'd never smiled before. I squeezed his hand tighter. "I love you, too, Pooquie."

I could feel him smile.

⊕

I didn't know I was asleep until I woke up. All I heard was Pooquie's steady breathing and light snore, and the TV set in the bedroom.

Junior.

I squinted to see the clock on the stereo: 10:25.

"Pooquie?"

"Hmmmm, yeah...," he mumbled, half-awake.

"It's after ten. Shouldn't you be taking Junior home?"

"Nah ... he can stay wit us."

He can stay with *us?*

God knows I wanted Raheim to stay and that I was glad he wanted to stay. But were we ready for that? Then it occurred to me: Raheim probably brought Junior for that sole purpose, sort of a security blanket. For the both of us.

I nodded off again. He tapped me at 11:15.

"Little Bit?"

"Yes?"

"Le's go ta bed."

"OK."

We kissed.

It was soft. It was wet. It was light. It was sweet. It was *jood.*

He led us to the bedroom. We were still holding hands.

He opened the door. We stepped in and found Junior at the foot of the bed, snoring away. He let go of my hand – damn! Junior fought as Raheim picked him up and put him on the right side of the bed.

Raheim kicked off his boots and socks. I turned off the TV. Raheim set the clock on the night table. I turned off the light. We got in bed, Raheim placing me in the middle.

"Little Bit?" he asked, so low I could barely hear him.

"Yes?"

"Happy annivers'ry."

It hadn't even dawned on me. I smiled. "Happy anniversary, Pooquie."

Smack.

"G'nite, Baby."

"Good night, Pooquie."

I placed my left arm around Junior.

Raheim rested his left arm on my torso, his warm hand on my thigh, and the weight of his body on me.

I went to sleep with a smile on my face ... and my men beside me.

"And you *believed* him?"

"Yes, I believed him, Gene. Why shouldn't I?"

"Why *should* you?"

"Because I saw it in his eyes ... and I love *him.*"

"Yes, Mitch, I know you do. You've said it every day for the past few weeks."

"Well, I am sorry to have bothered you."

"Don't be sorry, just be cautious. Even if he *does,* what's *I* got to do with it?"

"Everything!"

"Uh-huh. And do I have to quote that infamous Stylistics song, 'Break Up to Make Up'?"

"No, you don't."

"Maybe I do, 'cause that's all you two seem to do. Hello, does someone want to change this record? It's still skipping."

"Gene..."

"Look, I just want you to keep a level head about this. You have to be careful who you give your heart to, because..."

"...it's the only thing you own, yes, I know, Gene."

"And since we're on the topic of hearts, I guess I may as well tell you, before B.D. does..."

"Tell me what?"

Pause.

"Uh, Carl ... and I..."

"Gene ... no!"

"Yes, and don't you dare say *that* word!"

"Gene, you should be happy."

"Don't I *sound* happy?"

"No."

"Well ... I am. I just want to be sure, that's all. Carl ... he is, as you and Homeboy would say, a *jood* man. And I guess I feel jood about him.

He has been there for me like no other. We're just going to see what happens."

"So, you're going steady?"

"I guess you could say that. We are exclusively seeing each other."

"Oh, I think I hear wedding bells."

"*You* hear *nothing.*"

"Oh, Gene, just let go ... have a good time ... be in *l.*"

"Don't even try it. I just don't want to get hurt again. And I don't want to see you hurt again, either."

"Gene, I know what I want and Pooquie is it."

"But does *he* want *you?*"

"I'm sure he does. But I'll find out for sure tonight. He's coming back over."

"Well, we'll see. Just don't get too excited yet. You two have a lot to talk about."

"I know, but when all of that is said and done, it won't change the way I feel. I love that man, and I know he loves me."

"Yeah, well, he's gonna have to prove it."

He did.

At eight o'clock, Pooquie showed up at my door with a dozen red roses.

After I gave him a hot kiss, put eleven of the flowers in a vase filled with water, and wrapped the remaining one in foil and stuck it in the freezer, we sat down to his favorite dinner: smothered pork chops, collard greens, black-eyed peas over white rice, and "hot-water bread." We just exchanged flirtatious glances during the meal.

I didn't wash the dirty dishes; I put them in soaking water. They could wait 'til tomorrow. We had bizness to tend to.

I sat on the right side of the sofa. After he plopped a tape in the cassette deck, he lounged across it, his back on my thighs, his head on one armrest, and his bare feet hanging over the other.

Tony, Toni, Toné ... "Anniversary."

Smack. Smack. *Serious* smack.

He thanked me for the "dope suppa." He switched gears quickly, saying how sad he was that Michael Jordan's father had been killed and that Jordan had retired from basketball. "But it ain't ova yet, cuz he's gonna come back," he predicted. He recapped his rather regular day on the job. I asked why he'd indirectly quit his other job at Simply Dope. "I ain't wanna face you an' Gene," he said. I explained that, if he really wanted to draw, he should beg their forgiveness and ask for his job back. He said he already had. With Monica and Arthur in his corner (and, no doubt, on his dick), Franklin had given in. He starts the first week in November, but he'll be on probation. One slip and he's out. He pulled out a cover of the cassette case for the recently released Ax-2-Grind single he'd designed. It was just the artist's name and the song title in red, black, and green block letters, in a graffiti-like writing style. Simple but sizzlin'.

"I'm so proud of you, Pooquie."

Smack.

Toni (as in Mz. Braxton) ... "You Mean the World to Me."

Rock had been arrested. He fled the city after killing D.C.; they caught up with him in Detroit. He apparently pled guilty to manslaughter, not murder, claiming that he didn't mean to shoot D.C. – the gun "just went off" and he couldn't stop it from firing. "I wan' that motha-fucka twelve feet unda," said Raheim, fisting his own palm so hard that it scared me. Ms. Carter will be giving him some of the insurance money she'll receive, and he'll be using a portion of it to keep up D.C.'s Jeep, which she wants him to have.

Toni (again) ... "Breathe Again."

I told him how the crew was and about B.D.'s show the Saturday before Thanksgiving. "B.D. in tights? *Day-am,* that shit I gotta see!" he laughed. I did too. There would be a smokin' routine off of the house mix of his girl's song, "If," and I'd be doing John Lennon's "Imagine" (a la Randy), dedicated to all of our friends and relatives who have died of AIDS, as B.D. and Vincent did a duet. Raheim asked me to sing it; he turned off Toni as she was about to breathe, and I did.

"Thanks, Little Bit. I loved that."

Smack. Smack. Smack.

"Anytime, Pooquie. Anytime."

Janet .... "One More Chance."

I gave him the *Reader's Digest* version of why I left *Your World*; he said he was proud of me. "You stood up fuh yo' self, Baby. Ain't a whole lota people who do that. You should sue them motha-fuckas." I am. I'll be seeing a lawyer on Monday.

Vanessa Williams & Brian McKnight ... "Love Is."

I surprised him with the photo from the *Baldwin Bulletin.* "Oh shit! This is phat!" he exclaimed. I put it in a gold frame. His face turned serious as he put it on the coffee table and studied it. He then stared straight ahead.

"Little Bit?"

"Yes?"

"I ... I'm sorry. I neva shoulda hit you."

I started "writing" POOQUIE & LITTLE BIT: IS THIS LOVE OR WHAT? along his head with my right pinky. "You're right, you shouldn't have ... but I forgive you."

"Uh, ya do?"

"Yes, I do ... I have ... I've had time to think about everything ... I couldn't stay angry at you forever."

"I wouldn't blame ya if you did ... I ain't neva gonna do it again, Baby."

"Well, I can forgive you for what happened. But in order for us to move on, I have to know why it happened."

The tip of his left thumb went in his mouth.

"When you called me a ... I don' know, I jus' went crazy."

"But why?"

"Cuz..."

"'Cause what?"

"Cuz I ... I ... I guess I ain't wanna face it."

"Face what?"

"You know."

"No, I *don't* know, Pooquie. I can't read your mind. You have to tell me."

"I jus'..." He sighed heavily and talked with his hands. "See ... when me an' D.C. was young, they useta play this game 'round tha way ... punch a punk..."

"Punch a punk?"

"Yeah. If you was sof', if you ain't had tha right walk, tha right talk an' shit, you got called out."

"A punk?"

"Yeah. And then you got jumped..."

"Punched?"

"Yeah."

"Why did they do it, Pooquie?"

"I don' know ... somethin' ta do."

"Why did *you* do it, Pooquie?"

"Why?"

"Yes, why? You knew it was wrong."

"I knew, I knew, but ... but I had to, Baby."

"No, you didn't."

"Yeah, I did. We had to. You don' undastan'. If you didn't, you was called out an' they bum rush yo' ass."

"So, you beat up on people to prove you were down? To prove you were ... a man?"

"Yeah."

Pause.

"Would you have beaten *me* up?"

He dropped his head. That answered my question.

"Did you also do it so people wouldn't suspect you were...?"

He closed his eyes and nodded yes.

"Well, you're not a punk, Pooquie. Being homosexual doesn't mean you're a punk."

His eyes flickered open. "I ... I know."

"Do you, really?"

"Yeah, yeah, I do but ... but I grew up wit that, Little Bit, ya know?"

Brian McKnight ... "Never Felt This Way."

I looked at the ceiling and closed my eyes. "So ... does this mean that you won't — or can't — love me?"

I sensed his eyes widen. "Wha', wha'cha mean?"

"In the world you come from, loving me means you are a punk, a pussy ... or, more to the point, a faggot. So you can't be with me if that is so ... right?"

He got up from the sofa. He paced in front of the coffee table. He stood in front of me, his hands together. He sighed. He then got down on one knee, folding my hands into his. He looked me in my eyes.

"Little Bit ... I ... I love you. An' I know I'm in love wit you. Believe that, Baby, *believe* that. But ... but..."

A tear fell. He sighed. He then stared at my chin.

"Baby, I wanna love you but ... I don' know how."

I broke from his grasp. I cupped his face, wiping his tears away with my thumbs.

"Pooquie, you *do* know how to love ... I know ... I can feel it."

"But, Baby, I, I ... wha' I feel ... I don' know."

He gulped. He sniffed. He stared at my chest.

"Look at me, Pooquie ... please..."

He did.

I smiled. "Half the battle is already over. You know *how* you feel. Now all you have to do is not be afraid or ashamed of it." I let my hands slide down his face to his chin. "And you can't be afraid or ashamed of who you are."

He continued to cry. I took his left hand and pulled him up with me. I led him to the bedroom.

I sat up in the middle of the bed and motioned for him to come to me. He folded his big body into the space between my legs and put his head against my chest. I gently stroked his head.

"Let it out, Pooquie ... let it out..."

He did.

Hurt.

Pain.

Anguish.

Despair.

Confusion.

Uncertainty.

Doubt.

*Silently.*

And I helped him.

There is a song by the O'Jays called "Cry Together." It came to mind as Pooquie and I did just that for three hours.

It was almost one in the morning when Pooquie decided to also play out that song's bridge. He took my hand and pulled me down to the foot of the bed. We stood and faced each other.

We kissed — *down.*

We necked like we were at a basement party, surrounded by blue lights. He removed my clothes with care — his black Public Enemy t-shirt, my white jeans and Fruit of the Looms, giving me a little bite on my butt. I returned the favor — his blue jeans, denim shirt, and light blue briefs, palming his juicy booty.

We held each other. We kissed — *down* — again.

I melted into him. I took him in.

*Oh, Pooquie...*

We began to explore one another, getting reacquainted. I was hotter than July. I stood on his feet on my tippy toes to kiss his face all over. I bit at his neck like Dracula. He giggled. I licked and sucked his chest and nipples. I tongued his belly button. I was about to go down on one of my favorite spots when he stopped me.

"No, Little Bit ... it's my turn."

He fell to his knees. He stared at it, inspected it as if this was the first time he had ever seen one. He let his fingertips travel from the base to the head. His tongue retraced that route. He rubbed and massaged it — with one hand, then the other, then both.

To say that I became stiff and straight would be an understatement.

And, when he opened his mouth and took me in, I swear, the whole room shook.

*"Ohhhh, Pooquie..."*

"Mmmmm ... Bay-bee..."

I closed my eyes, trying to concentrate, trying to control my breathing, but I couldn't. It came out in heavy spurts. I was having heart palpitations. I felt like the Big Bad Wolf — *huff, puff, blow ... huff, puff, blow ... huff, puff, blow...*

Of course, *he* was really doing the blowing. I grabbed him by the back of his head, holding on for dear life.

*"Oh, yes, Pooquie, suck it!"*

The insides of his mouth were as soft (and wet) as his double-down DSLs (that's dick-suckin' lips, if you've forgotten). And he knew what to do with them. Up and down, 'round and 'round, side to side. He bobbed for my apple. He sopped up all the gravy, leaving none for the biscuits. And the more he bobbed, the more he sopped, the louder I got, screeching like a fire engine.

*"Woooo, woooo, woooo!"*

*"Mmmmm, Bay-bee..."*

I'm not as big as he is, but I've been told I'm pretty big for a guy my size. And he ain't had no problem swallowing it whole. And when he went *all* the way down, I started heckling like Daffy Duck.

*"Ha hoo, ha hoo, ha hoo hoo hoo!"*

He laughed.

He must've known my toes had curled and my knees were about to give: still lapping it up, he turned me and pushed me on the bed with one hand.

And he must've felt me on the verge of exploding: after a few more serious slurps, he released me and just watched it erupt like a volcano — all over my chest, all over my legs, all over the comforter, and on the carpet.

And, after my body stopped twitching, I looked up to find him standing over me, his head cocked to one side, tapping his chin, grinning up a storm.

Still delirious from the experience, I reached for him, giggling. Very proud and pleased, he covered me, unbothered by the stickiness.

"Thanks, Pooquie," I whispered. "That was *so* damn jood."

He kept grinning. We kissed.

I finally knew why a banana was his favorite fruit.

After we chilled for a spell, I went into the bathroom and cleaned myself up. Now I could think about what had happened. I didn't have the chance before – I was in shock. *Deep* shock. Pooquie had never gone downtown on me. In fact, he never so much as *touched* my dick in the four months we were together. I know that there is, of course, a first time for everything, but *day-am!* One thing is for sure: that mouth is a lethal weapon. It was the joodest blow job I ever had. I ain't never cum like that before.

I still had a taste for him and was all too ready to be plugged. But, when I found him in his favorite position in the middle of the bed with the comforter off, I knew what I had to do.

I didn't say a word. I climbed in bed. I parted those cheeks, dropped my head, and started blowing on his love canal. He responded by hissing like a snake and stretching his legs out farther, giving me an even better view and easier access.

I marveled at the size, shape, and splendor of his ass.

It *was* a basketball. Big and bouncy. Hard and hairless. But also smooth and hot. And it was so high that it actually sat on his waist and his back.

Simply beautiful.

Aw, yeah, Mitch. Nip it, Gnaw it, Nibble it.

"Ow, oh, ooooh, Little Bit..."

Let's test its reflexes, shall we? Slap it, flip it, rub it down ... Oh yes! Day-am ... it just shakes like a bowl of Jell-o.

"Ow yeah, Little Bit, spank my ass..."

"Whatever you say..."

Whack!

"Ah yeah..."

*Whack!*

"*Sssss,* oh *yeah!*"

*Whackwhack! Whackwhack! Whackwhack!*

*"Ow, yeahmothafuckayeah..."*

Hmmmm ... more bounce to the ounce. What a boomerang booty!

*Boing!*

"Ya love that, hunh, Pooquie?"

*"Hell* fuckin' yeah, Little Bit ... *ooooh."*

"I thought so."

Time for the tongue. Trail it. Tickle it.

"No, Little Bit, don' fuckin' *teeze* me!"

"OK..."

Taste it. Baste it.

*"Yeah,* Little Bit, dat feels *so* fuckin' jood..."

My lips made contact.

"Oh yeah, Little Bit, *yeah!"*

Kiss it – it kisses me back. I bury my face in him.

"Get *all* da fuck in dere!"

"OK..."

The ass was *too* jood. B.D. was right – Raheim had chocolate pound cakes. Moist, plump, sweet. Black puddin'. And I was enjoying this appetizer.

And I was giving it to him so jood that he started flipping about like a fish out of water, banging his fists on the bed, screaming, "No!" and pleading, "Don'... stop ... don' ... stop ... don'... stop..." He knew he loved it, but every time I got a good lip-lock he fought me. At one point, he was hanging over a corner of the bed, clawing at the carpet trying to get away.

I had enough.

"Where the *fuck* you think you going?" I snarled, slapping his cakes so hard that it startled me. "Keep your ass still!"

He let out a very worried "Oh" and slowly eased back on the bed. He turned and looked at me. His eyes begged: *Have mercy on me.* So I held back so he could change position. He returned to the head of the bed, got on all fours, and poked his butt out and up. Maybe now he'll take it like a man.

He did.

He started throwing it at me – and I was catchin' it.

"Aw yeah, Little Bit, eat me da fuck *out* ... Take dat shit ... oh yeah ... Don' stop, don' stop, *don' stop!"*

The ass was so hot you could fry bacon and eggs on it.

I *had* to have a piece of this. There was already a love glove on the bed. Hmmmm, how did *that* get there? I took it out of its wrapper and had it on like that.

I looked over to the night table. The original Pooquie was sitting in the chair. I hopped out of bed and turned the chair toward the window. I didn't want an audience.

I wasted no time. I got another good lick, took the middle fingers on my right hand, and entered the tunnel. Judging by the loud, long groan he let out, he was ripe and ready.

After thinking of it many, *many* times, the moment was finally here: I'm gonna plug my Pooquie. It was time to light that ass up like a Xmas tree, time to cut the cake. I would find out just how deep his love was.

Yes, turnabout is motha-fuckin' fair play.

I whacked him with my dick.

"Ah ha, Little Bit, whip it, whip dat shit on me..."

"Uh-huh, Pooquie, I got your whip appeal..."

After some more whipping, I rimmed him.

"No, Baby, don' teeze me now, *pleeze*...," he begged, pushing and grinding on it.

"You want me to stick it in, home*boy?*"

"*Yeah,*" he growled.

"I can't hear ya now ... tell me you want it!"

"*I want it, I want it, yeah!*"

And, with one smooth move, I took the Pooquie Plunge – all the way in. Pooquie let out a blood-curdling scream.

"*Ohhhhhhhh!*"

Oh, I love the way you receive me...

He was hot, tight, and wet – just the way I like it. He put up a fight, squealing and squirming. I loved that.

"*Oh, God, no, Little Bit, no, no...*"

"Don't tell me no! You know you want me to get under that hood, so just give it up, turn it loose..."

He did.

I dipped and dove, slipped and slapped. Drum roll, puh-leeze!

"Yeah, Pooquie, give up that new jack booty..."

"Ah yeah, Little Bit, *yeah!*"

"That's right, wiggle it now, just a little bit for Little Bit ... open up and let me the fuck in..."

"Oh shit, yeah, *fuck* me!"

"Oh, yeah, I'll fuck you all right..."

I put pressure on his back so that he fell on his stomach. I bucked my thighs around him, securely planted my hands on his shoulders, and started doin' da butt. That *plop flop, plop flop, plop flop,* never sounded so fuckin' jood.

"*Ahhhh* yeah, here we go, now ... ya like it, hunh, Pooquie?"

"Yeah, Daddy, yeah..."

*Daddy?* Daddy, hunh? I loved that shit.

Loved it so much that I pulled out, causing Pooquie to gag. But then he geeked – letting out a *"Woooo!"* – when I grabbed his ankles, flipped him like a pancake, and threw his legs up. They stayed in a V – as in Victory. And why did I do this?

*I wanted to see his face when he called me "Daddy" and I turned him the fuck out.*

"Ah, yeah, Pooquie, Daddy got something for your ass!"

I plunged back in.

*"Aw shit! Yeah, Little Bit, yeah!"*

"That's right, Pooquie, wave those legs in the air, wave 'em like you *just* don't care!"

Uh-huh, rock steady, baby.

"Aw yeah, *rock dat shit* ... *Rock* me, Daddy..."

Uh-huh, like your back ain't got no bone, hunh, Pooquie?

Pump it, pump it, pump it up ... ah, push it ... Push it jood!

"Ah, work me, Daddy, *work* me..."

"Oh, yeah, Daddy's gonna work ya."

I grabbed him by the waist and jerked him up so that he was sitting on it. He grabbed my neck – with both hands.

*"Oh, no, oh, no!"* he cried.

I snatched his hands away and grabbed his chin, shaking his face. "Now we been through this already, so just chill, Pooquie. Just work it."

Hmmmm, haven't I heard *that* someplace before?

I tongued him *down;* I knew that would get him. He went ballistic. He started looping those hips like a Hula Hoop.

"Oh yeah, Pooquie, work that dick!"

He jumped up and down like a kid on a merry-go-round horse.

"That's right, ride that shit, Pooquie ... saddle it!"

"Aw yeah, Daddy...," he grunted.

"Whatcha call me? What's my name?" I grinned.

*"Daddy!"*

"And ya know that..."

I tackled and pushed him down. I threw his legs back; this time they coiled like a slinky, making contact with the bed. (I thought only I could do that!) I grabbed ahold of his shoulders, he mine.

"Ah yeah, Pooquie, it's time to get busy!"

I mounted him, doing the twist, just jockeying away.

"Uh, do me, Daddy, *do me!*"

Growing bigger and bigger, pushing deeper and deeper.

"Oh *yeah,* Daddy! Fill me da fuck *up!*"

Hey, that's *my* line.

Just a-plowing faster and faster, harder and harder...

Slam, bam, thank you, Sam!

"Uh-huh, and *that's* for making me wait so long!" I snarled.

*"Yeahmothafuckayeah!"* he answered.

We tongue-tapped. He lifted his head so we could smack. I nipped on his hard nipples, never losing my rhythm.

*"Oh, I love dat shit, Daddy, yeah! Freak me..."*

"Gladly...," I laughed.

The bed felt like it was about to give out. We didn't knock the lamp down (it was no longer on the dresser). This time it was the phone. I could hear that signal that lets you know the receiver's off the hook.

I was knockin' most boots, you hear? Namin' it and Claimin' it...

"Uh, whose booty is this?" I demanded.

"Oh, yours, Daddy, yours...," he breathed.

"I can't *hear* you..."

*"Yours, Daddy, yours!"*

"And *don't* you forget it..."

And then, out of nowhere...

*"Oh, Daaaaddy!"* he screamed, groping my ass, hoisting me up, stretching those bowlegs out and down, and forming a straight line. He clinched my dick like a very firm handshake. *"Pleeze, it's too much, I can't, I can't, no, no, no!"*

His mouth was saying one thing; his ass another.

"Pooquie, you know you like the way Daddy fucks ya, 'cause ya keep givin' it to me..."

*"Yeah, I know, I mean, but, I don' know..."*

"You do *too* know, so who you tryin' to fool..."

*"Yeah, but I don' know, I don' know if I can, I..."*

"You can and you *will*. Shit, you know you wanna give it all up to Daddy, now don'cha?"

*"Uh, uh, I guess, I don' know, no, I, oh, oh, yeah!"*

"You better, 'cause I'm takin' it!"

I did.

He started speaking in tongues. And, after being rather cool throughout, I began testifying myself.

"Oh my God, I'm cumin' ... *oh my God, I'm cumin'!"*

And when it was all over...

He roared like the Lion after doing dances with the Wolf.

Yes...

Pooquie & Little Bit...
We cried together...
*and then we made love.*

After the love, we came down in our favorite position.

"Pooquie?"

"Uh-huh."

"How ya doin'?"

"Uh, fine."

"I asked how ya doin', not how you look."

He giggled.

"So, are you OK?"

"*Yeah* ... you sex me so fuckin' jood."

"Yeah?"

He opened his legs – wide. *"Mmmmm-hmmmm..."*

"Well, you made it jood. It's the joodest I ever had ... and I'm gonna have some more" – I poked him in that delicious rump roast – "before you go to work tomorrow."

We giggled.

Pause.

He sighed. "Um ... you my firs'..."

Did I hear him right? I scooted off of him and inched up to the head of the bed. I draped my right leg over his back, my foot resting between his cheeks. I moved in close, sitting up on my left arm. I placed my hand on his neck. "What?"

His head, resting on his folded arms, turned. He looked me in the eye. "You my firs'."

"Your first what?"

He grinned. "You *know*..."

"No, I *don't.*"

He chuckled then frowned. "You know, tha firs' ta ... ta love me like that."

"I am?"

"Uh-huh."

Pause.

"So, you were a virgin?"

He rolled his eyes. "If tha's wha'cha wanna call it..."

"Why me?"

"Hunh?"

"Why was I the first?"

"Cuz..."

"Cuz what?"

"Cuz ... I love you."

"You do?"

"Yeah."

"Why?"

He shrugged. "Cuz ... I don' know... I really can't explain it."

"Hmmmm ... I know the feeling."

"You, you ... you jus' send me swingin' ... fo' real tho'..."

"So I saw ... so I *felt.*"

He laughed.

"You a wild thang, Pooquie ... *my* wild thang ... you so loud..."

He sucked his teeth, blushing. "I am not."

"Yes, you are, and you're a freak."

I sat up. I pinched the booty hard.

He yelped. "Oh..."

I slapped it.

He shrieked. "Ah..."

I rubbed it.

He groaned. "Mmmmm..."

I returned to him, sliding my body under his. Our legs tangled. We embraced.

Smack. Smack. *Serious* smack.

I looked at him, seriously. "Uh, and I'm Daddy, hunh?"

He blushed. I grinned.

"Thanks for trusting me, Pooquie ... and for loving me ... you send *me* swingin' ... I love you, too."

We kissed – *down.*

"And, Pooquie?"

"Yeah?"

"Thanks for a late but great anniversary gift."

He chuckled. "Ha, you welcome, Baby."

We kissed *down,* again.

"Little Bit?"

I tapped his nose with mine. "That's Daddy to you, Mister."

He giggled. "Uh ... ha, Daddy?"

"Yes?"

"I ... I'm sorry ... fuh ev'rythang I said ... all that shit I did ... I ain't mean ta hurt you, Baby."

"I forgive you, Pooquie ... just tell me something..."

"Yeah?"

I gave him a serious stare. "Who's tha man?"

He chuckled. "You, Little Bit."

"And ... who is *yo'* man?"

He smiled. "You, Little Bit."

I stabbed him in his dimple and grinned. "And ya know that."

Smack.

# ABOUT THE AUTHOR

A '93 honors graduate of Columbia University's School of Journalism, James Earl Hardy is a freelance feature writer and music critic whose byline has appeared in the *Washington Post, Newsweek, Entertainment Weekly, YSB, Out,* and other publications. He lives in New York City. *B-Boy Blues* is his first novel.

*Alyson Publications publishes a wide variety of books
with gay and lesbian themes. For a free catalog or
to be placed on our mailing list, please write to:*
Alyson Publications
40 Plympton Street
Boston, MA 02118
*Indicate whether you are interested in
books for gay men, lesbians, or both.*